I0637935

SILVER BELLES

BOOK FOUR
MODERN LEGENDS OF DRAGONS & SHADOWS

TRISTA RICKETTS

Silver Belles © Copyright <<2025>> Trista Ricketts

Copyright notice: All rights reserved under the International and Pan-American Copyright Conventions. No part of this book may be reproduced or transmitted in any form or by any means, electronic or mechanical, including photocopying and recording, or by any information storage and retrieval system, without permission in writing from publisher.

This is a work of fiction. Names, places, characters, and incidents are either the product of the author's imagination or are used fictitiously, and any resemblance to any actual persons, living or dead, organizations, events, or locales is entirely coincidental.

Warning: the unauthorized reproduction or distribution of this copyrighted work is illegal. Criminal copyright infringement, including infringement without monetary gain, is investigated by the FBI and is punishable by up to 5 years in prison and a fine of $250,000.

For more information, email: trista@tristaricketts.com

Contributions:

Editor: Caroline Goldsworthy

Cover Art: White Rose Publishing Service IG: @siennas.coverart

Warning: *Here there be Dragons!*

Join forces with the Dragons and Wielders!

The Modern Legends are all about the ongoing battle for ancient magical creatures working to defeat their enemies while facing the challenges of modern society mixed in with the whims of a few old Gods along the way. If you love these stories and want to see what happens with the rest of the clan, then sign up for my newsletter! You'll be the first to know about the launch of the next books in the series, get sneak peeks at other series coming out, deleted scenes, short stories, and more.

Sign up for my newsletter at: www.tristaricketts.com

Want to send me your feedback? You can do that through my site as well. Just beware, the snark dragon sometimes visits my house so if you snark me, it may just snark back.

Also by

To my loyal readers and fans, without you, this wouldn't be possible.

Thank you, truly, thank you.

For the record, Killian told me *maith coleen* means Good Girl. (Swoon)

And for those of you who thought I did Liam dirty, this one's for you.

Contents

Chapter 1

WHY CAN'T I JUST kill him and be done with it? No one would notice. If they did, they'd thank me. Siobhan leaned back in her chair, arms behind her head, fantasizing about all the ways she could end her pest of a big brother's existence. It was a beautiful day, warm and clear. She wanted to finish up the orc battle she was working on so she and Marco could go for a ride on his motorcycle. She should be wrist deep in video game developing, instead, she was stuck in this conference room listening to her idiotic brother charm the silver wielder, Marissa.

"Costa Rica?" Risa asked excitedly.

"Costa lot to go there," Liam laughed, his lips stretched wide.

"Pakistan?"

"Packed a suitcase."

"Ugh," Siobhan grunted, rolling her eyes.

Killian, Risa's boyfriend, slipped into the room. "What's going on here?" he asked Siobhan, his quiet voice barely above a whisper.

Rolling her eyes again without looking up, Siobhan groaned. "Liam is playing 'Guess where I've been'," using exaggerated air quotes, "With Risa, and his answers are an-*noying*," she finished with an aggravated yell.

Liam flashed a cheeky grin before turning back to Risa.

"Galapagos Islands?"

"Met a giant tortoise there."

Killian spoke from the corner of his mouth, "How long have they been at it now?"

Siobhan sighed dramatically, as if her soul was in pain and propped her booted feet on the conference table. "About thirty minutes? Which is twenty-nine minutes too long if you ask me. She didn't even notice you came in, did she?" Siobhan glanced over at Killian as he sat next to her, then did a double-take. "Holy shit, Ki, what happened to you?"

He grimaced, "Ye make it sound like a right bad thing," he grumbled, staring sternly at the table, refusing to meet her gaze.

"It *is* a bad thing," Risa announced primly, without turning away from Liam. She tossed her long, silvery-blonde hair over her shoulder and lifted her chin defiantly.

Siobhan snorted, intrigued as she glanced from Risa back to Killian. *So, Risa did notice him come in, she's just ignoring him.* She sensed contention between the two, and bet it was related to Killian's appearance. She sighed; Killian was quite possibly the most gorgeous man she knew. And that was saying something considering most of the men she knew were serious contenders for that title. Most people didn't realize how incredibly handsome he was because he usually hid behind his hair.

Killian was a silver wielder, and they all shared a common trait of hazel eyes and fine silver-blond hair so pale it was almost white. The front of his hair had always been long, nearly reaching his shoulders and obscuring most of his face. His gorgeous eyes usually held secrets, and his lips were so full and soft, you just knew he was about to say something deliciously sinful. When you got to see them. He was quiet and reserved. His uncanny ability to blend into a room often meant he went unnoticed unless he wanted to be seen. He frequently startled people when he spoke, spooking them because they didn't know he was there.

Now Killian was staring at the ceiling, a frown curving his lips down into a tight grimace. He clearly did not want to have this conversation with Siobhan. Normally, he was very straightforward. He didn't speak much, but when he did, it was direct and to the point. He didn't hide his feelings, he didn't pull his punches, and he liked people to know where he stood. That was something Siobhan adored about him. He was also stubborn, but so was Siobhan, so she continued to stare at him until he sighed, a disgusted groan.

"I'm really not understanding why it's such a commotion." The lilt of his Irish accent thickened, becoming stronger as his agitation grew.

She squinted, studying him consideringly. "Ki, we've known you for years, yeah? You've always looked like, well... you. So, when you come in here like that," she gestured to him and glanced at his girlfriend again, "I'm guessing Risa doesn't like it?"

He glared at Siobhan, his expression fully visible for the first time since she'd known him.

Risa spoke up, her tone terse and clipped, "Risa's opinion doesn't matter. She wasn't asked. And wasn't told until after."

"Oh dude, you're so screwed," Siobhan chuckled with unrestrained glee.

He settled lower in his chair, cursing in Gaelic under his breath.

Serena, Vaughn, and Bridget all strolled into the conference room, their presence commanding everyone's attention. Bridget was due with her third child in a few short weeks, grumbling about being the size of a small house. Vaughn quickly pulled a chair out for her, and she smiled gratefully. He tenderly kissed her on the top of her head as he gazed lovingly at her.

Siobhan grinned; those two were poster children for soulmates. Thinking of soulmates put her head on a swivel as Marco, her own mate, ambled in. He was a fierce red dragon warrior and head of security operations for Vaughn's companies.

Marco hurried over and kissed her upturned face as he came to sit by her. "Missed you, *carina*," he murmured, stroking her cheek before taking her hand.

She rolled her eyes despite the warmth spreading through her body at his words, "It's been thirty-two minutes."

"Felt like a lifetime," he replied softly, tracing his lips over the back of her hand.

"Ugh," came Liam's exaggerated response. He stared at them in disgust, wrinkling his nose and pretending he was gagging.

Siobhan glared at him. She knew he was glad she was mated to Marco. But it was his job to give her grief as her older brother and only living relative; he took that role seriously.

Marco winked at him.

Siobhan stuck her tongue out.

Risa and Rena laughed, their light tinkling voices filling the room. Just another day at Cloud Warrior Gaming.

Killian turned, his eyes longingly tracing Risa's soft smile. She still refused to look at him, and it made his heart ache. He absently rubbed his chest as he watched her chat with her sister.

"Who's the new guy?" Marco inquired with a laugh.

Killian turned back to the rest of the team to see who Marco was referring to. He frowned, only seeing the normal group. Glancing around in confusion, he realized they were all staring at him. "Ah, for fuck's sake! What utter gobshite!" he grumbled loudly.

Everyone sat back, surprised at this uncharacteristic outburst from him.

"Guys, come on! It's just a bleedin' haircut," he pleaded, his hands spread out, begging them to let it go.

Bridget cleared her throat, Siobhan grinned, and Vaughn bit his lip, trying not to laugh.

Serena, ever the peacemaker, spoke up, "I think it looks nice, Killian. I like seeing your face and smile."

"Thanks, Rena," Killian mumbled.

Liam relented, leaning forward, "Killian, it's just... different. It's not the *you* we know. It's going to take some getting used to. We have to mess with you a bit. Guy code!" he grinned.

Killian couldn't believe the uproar over him making a change to his appearance. He was tired of looking like the other silver wielders. Recently, another man flirted with Risa right in front of him because the guy thought Killian was her brother. So, Killian decided it was time to stop hiding. Unsure where to start, he asked Davis, one of the water dragon twins, who gladly took Killian to his barber. Now, it was closely shaved in the back and brushed loosely over on the top, no longer covering his face. But that wasn't enough change, so he also colored it jet black. As far opposite of his natural tone as he could go.

With the new style, his whole face was visible, whether he wanted it to be or not. He toyed with the lip ring most people didn't know about because it was previously covered by his hair. Blowing out a frustrated breath, he wondered if people suspected he was having a mid-life crisis, thus their overreaction. He wasn't, he didn't think.

It didn't go well when he showed up for a date with Risa and didn't warn her beforehand about the change. Risa already knew about the lip ring; she liked it a lot. She wasn't even upset about the new eyebrow ring. It was the hair. She loved intertwining their long hair, so similar, and playing with it when they were lying in bed together. She loved that they possessed similar powers and shared the silver wielder 'look.' He understood to an extent, but it didn't change who he was, just how he appeared to others. He didn't realize she would be *this* upset about it. So upset, she wasn't speaking to him. *Women*, he shook his head, bewildered. After opening his heart again after decades, his feelings were being tossed out because of a haircut.

He knew they were still studying him; the room was completely silent except for the ticking clock on the wall behind him. Leaning back, he met their gazes with his own steely one. Except for Risa who still wouldn't look at him no matter how hard he stared at her.

When it was clear Killian wasn't going to say anything else, Vaughn shook his head. "Alright, we've finally got a breakthrough. Rena, Risa, does the name Dorothy trigger any memories?"

Both women sat for a moment, furrowing their brows, thinking hard. Rena finally shook her head no, her thin shoulders drooping with disappointment.

Risa's expression suggested it was on the tip of her tongue, but she couldn't quite remember. Frustration burned behind her eyes as she bit her lip and scrunched her eyebrows, trying harder to recall the meaning.

They were working to locate Risa and Rena's missing sister. They needed to find out more about the family and determine why they, along with other children, were targeted in the first place. After months, Liam was finally able to crack into Risa's adoption files, providing even more clues. Her adoptive parents were seemingly normal humans with no clue of her true nature. They were good people who treated her well.

The spell placed on Marissa to hide her true identity was deeply bound, entangled in her magic, and not coming out cleanly. From the first night, whenever they discovered something new, Killian removed more of the spell from her. The spell was being worn down slowly, one layer at a time. But it was hard to detect unless something triggered it, causing it to actively block a memory, such as now, when she tried to remember Dorothy. Only then was he able to lock onto it and remove it.

Killian stood quietly, then moved behind Risa.

"I'm fine," she snapped, still not meeting his eyes.

"I know," Killian sighed sadly, his heart giving a little twinge at her rejection. He held his palms out and closed his eyes. Soft silver waves cascaded over her, and he frowned as he found the piece of the spell blocking her memory. These deeper memories, the ones getting them closer to the truth, were becoming considerably more difficult to break.

Killian hadn't told anyone that part; he didn't want to stop. The last time he pulled a piece, it wiped him out for an hour. He hoped he could cover up the effect of this one. Grimacing slightly as the spell clawed at him, it dug in deeper, straining against his efforts. Finally, he sensed it lifting a bit, but it sank back in, refusing to let go. He blew out a sharp breath then shifted his feet, refocusing, a frown between his eyebrows, lips curved down sharply.

"Killian?" Rena whispered, concern evident in her voice.

Eyes closed; he shook his head quickly. He didn't want her to help, concerned she might get hurt. He felt very protective towards Rena; he taught her to wield properly before they even knew Marissa existed. She was like family to him. He continued to pull and weave a cage around the spell, trying to break its hold. To everyone else, it looked like he was plucking strings and moving invisible blocks. In his mind, the strands were visible in front of him; dark, discordant colors that clashed violently against the soft silver glow that made up Risa's powers.

Finally, he relaxed, sighing happily as the spell snapped and the connection broke free.

Risa gasped, her head jerking back and her eyes flashing silver as she was able to access that part of her memory again.

Killian enjoyed a brief second of triumph before a sharp pain akin to an icepick in his brain slammed him back against the wall. He groaned as the blood drained from his face, all color leeching from his skin, leaving him pale and clammy. An alarming warmth trickled from his nose. Lifting a shaky hand to his lip, he pulled it away to see bright red blood coating his fingertips. "Fuck," he moaned, realizing this wasn't going to end well for him.

The others gasped; Risa whirled to look at him.

He smiled tenderly at her in relief, thinking *finally*, then his knees buckled. His vision went grey, tunneling to a pinprick as his eyes rolled back in his head. A pair of strong arms caught him just before he hit the floor. He hung limply on to consciousness by a thread, fighting back against the spell trying to take him down.

Everyone was on their feet, rushing towards them in concern as Liam supported him, helping him stay upright. "Dude, you don't look so hot, and I'm not talking the haircut, man. You need to sit," Liam insisted, trying to help him into a chair, but Killian shook his head.

Killian focused on the green dragon with his long, wavy, red-gold hair and charming classic good looks. When Liam first met Risa, Killian made it clear he'd already laid claim to her, and Liam should keep his distance. Of course, everyone befriended Liam eventually; the dragon was just so darn likeable, unlike him. People rarely noticed Killian, and he liked it that way. Usually. But since he met Risa, he never wanted her to look away. He groaned, his head feeling like it was stuffed with cotton, and there seemed to be two of the irritating dragon whelp.

The filter that usually kept him quiet was suddenly gone, and words started pouring like a flood. "Liam, you're such a pretty man, as annoying as ye are. And ye are that. Annoyin'. Charmin'. Fecking hell, how do ye get away with that? People still like ye. But tell me, pup, do ye like having long hair? Or maybe everyone thinks you're a wee girl and you're her brother, but ye are her brother, so maybe not." His accent thickened, getting heavier by the word. Liam looked confused, unsure, as he glanced at the others and shook his head, bewildered as the rest of them.

Killan grimaced. He knew he wasn't making sense, but he didn't understand why. "Restroom," he nodded with certainty. "Just need to wash my face," he declared, waving at the blood covering his mouth and chin.

Liam turned to Vaughn, who nodded slightly, his eyes wide. With Marco's help, they assisted Killian to the men's room down the hall.

Chapter 2

VAUGHN TURNED TO RISA, who was standing still, gaze locked on three drops of blood on the floor where Killian was standing. "Risa," he murmured slowly, "what — the hell — was that?"

She jolted at her name and shook her head stiffly, "I... I don't know, I've never seen that happen before. I thought he seemed exhausted after last time, but nothing like this. Is he okay? What's going on?" she asked, terrified, her voice rising in pitch. Now her own tongue loosened, and she began explaining how awfully she'd treated him. It was just hair; it would grow back. She was more upset he hadn't told her, but it was his body. She turned to Siobhan, leaning over the table, pleading, "Please, Shi, can you check on him? I... I don't know if he wants to see me." She bit her lips to stop the violent tremble.

Vaughn turned to the green wielder as well. "Please, Siobhan?" he added his own request, fear plainly etched on his face. Killian was his oldest and dearest friend. He was a good man, and Risa knew Vaughn would never forgive himself if something happened to him.

Siobhan nodded back, "I already planned on it. And if that happened because of why I think it did, I'm going to rip him a new ass."

In the restroom, Killian sat on the counter, back against the mirror, singing an Irish folk song. His rich baritone bounced off the tiles, turning it into a concert hall. He paused, grinning, "The acoustics in here are amazing. I should do this more often." He nodded in certainty and launched back into his song. Liam and Marco stared at him, speechless. In all the years they'd known him, they'd never heard him sing. They rarely even heard him speak. Something was seriously wrong with Killian.

Siobhan barreled in just as he began the last verse, and her jaw dropped. *What the actual hell*, she sent to Marco.

I don't know, we got him in here, he splashed water on his face, then jumped on the counter and started singing. Babe, this man speaks the same number of words in a month that most people do in a day, and he hasn't stopped talking. Now he's... singing. And he's GOOD. Marco's tone was half amusement, half confusion as his jaw hung open.

She sighed, grimacing. This was going to be a challenge.

Liam moved to her side, "I think that spell addled his brain."

She nodded in agreement, suspecting he was right. Unfortunately.

Killian finished his song, then spotted Siobhan and waggled a finger at her playfully. "Oh, shame, shame it is on ye, young lady. This is the boy's room, or the men's room. We're men, so it's a men's room an' you're not a men, a man. Ye don't have a penis. Does she, Marco? I mean, he would be after knowing. But anyway, you're here now, ye naughty thing. Maybe... aye, tell me. Why does Marissa hate me now? I just wanted a change, an' now she won't talk to me. Just because I changed my hair. It's not the rings," he waved at his face, "Those really turn her on. But now ye can see me, is that really so bad?" he sighed and waved his hands drunkenly around his features again. Then he stopped, and his face lit up.

"Did I tell ye I'm getting another tattoo? A tree of life. It's meaningful as my life has grown an' branched out. A tattoo should mean something, don't you think? I'm thinking across my back. But it's Risa's persimmon, I mean, permission I'm needing first. I don't want to go an' make her mad at me again. Maybe she'll forgive me, an' we can have make-up sex. That would be fine, just fine. I love being with her. I've never been with anyone that makes me feel the way she does. I love her, ye know? I've not told her, but I'm so incredibly in love with her." He sighed again, wistfully.

The others stared at him in shocked silence, not knowing what to make of this development.

Killian started singing again. This time it was '*Oh, Danny Boy*'.

Siobhan shook herself and hurried over to him. "Okay, Romeo, let's get you sorted out."

"Nay lass, not Romeo, Killian," he corrected her gently, "Kiiiiiil- lee-an. Me ma named me after a pirate she fancied. A bloody pirate. Can ye imagine? I should have a peg leg an' a parrot. Oh, an eye patch! That would be quite romantic. An' dashing. Risa would like that," he declared, nodding, certain he was correct. "Maybe I should do that. I'll become a pirate an' sail the seven seas. I'll drink rum all day, maybe get a sword an' a wee chimp. Yo, ho, ho, an' a bottle of rum. Mmm, not rum, I much prefer whiskey."

Marco leaned over and nudged Siobhan's shoulder. "Does he have an off switch? Please, hit it if he does, I don't know how much more of this I can take," he begged his mate, ignoring Liam's snort of barely contained mirth.

"Killian," Siobhan snapped sharply.

Killian's babbling halted abruptly as he tried to focus on her. "There's three of ye, girly. Are ye a demon, then? Did ye come to drag me to Hell? Well, you're too damned late. I'm already there. I love her, an' she hates me." Killian's eyes filled with tears, running unchecked down his cheeks.

Suddenly, he stiffened, his body jerking into a rigid posture, and his nose started bleeding again. This time, a steady stream gushed over his chin, dripping into his lap, pattering on his jeans. His eyes rolled up, and he slid off the counter unconscious, crumpling to the floor in a boneless heap.

Siobhan grabbed him, and the other men helped her stretch him out on the ground. "Fuck!" she yelled. She whirled to Liam, barking, "Get Rena, not Risa. Marco, keep Risa out of here, sit on her if you have to. I don't need her hysterical."

Both dragons ran quickly to obey, and she held out her hands over the unconscious man in front of her. "C'mon, Killian! Stay with me, baby. Dammit, Ki, stay with me!" she demanded. She pulsed her magic over him and found the problems, one being a symptom of the other. He was suffering the equivalent of a magical concussion, which caused swelling and pressure in his head. It had caused a vessel to rupture, and he was bleeding into his brain. She had to stop the bleeding first, but it would keep happening unless she reduced the pressure. That's why she needed Rena.

The young woman slid down next to her and copied Siobhan's pose. Without speaking, Rena quickly understood her role and focused on it. The two worked feverishly, and after a few minutes, Killian's color returned, and his breathing evened out. The pair slumped down, sweating with the effort it took to stabilize him.

Killian's eyes slowly blinked open and took in their worried expressions. "Ow. That sucked," he moaned, gagging slightly.

They laughed, relieved, and Rena grabbed some wet paper towels to wipe his face.

Siobhan stroked his hair softly as she smiled tenderly at him. "Ki, I really like your haircut, honey, it's actually pretty damn hot. I love seeing more of that handsome face of yours."

Killian smiled back, "Thanks, Shi." Then he squeezed his eyes shut and groaned, "Gods, I hurt all over."

She huffed out a small laugh, "Yeah, that's going to take some time and rest. Let's get you on the couch in Bridget's office, and after an hour or so, you should be alright. Dammit, Ki, you scared the shit out of me. Don't ever do that again, alright?" She lightly stroked his cheek before leaning down to kiss his forehead.

He swallowed, looking a little green and nauseated, "Thanks again, Shi." He turned to Rena and grabbed her hand. He kissed it, saying, "Thank ye, too, Rena doll."

"Of course, Killian, anything for you. I love you, and don't worry about my sister. She'll come around." Rena smiled with certainty.

Marco and Liam rushed back in, and Siobhan directed them to take Killian to Bridget's office. They laid him down on the couch, and he moaned in gratitude. Much better than an unyielding tile floor.

Killian noticed they were grinning at him. "What?" his tone wary.

They shook their heads and strolled out, Marco whistling an old Irish drinking song.

Killian closed his eyes in the dim office and let himself drift. He'd been abysmally stupid to take on that spell without help. He wouldn't make that mistake twice. Sighing, he knew that he just so desperately wanted to help Risa, he was being stupidly stubborn. He heard the door open again and footsteps approached. Groaning, he growled "Look, either ye tell me what was so damned funny, or go the hell away. I feel like hammered shite right now guys, an' I'm not here for it."

"I brought you some water," came a soft voice. Risa.

He gasped and tried to sit up, but a spike went through his temple, making him collapse with a pained grunt. His breathing labored as a cold sweat broke out across his body.

"No, no, stay down," she insisted hurriedly, worry clear in her trembling voice.

"I'm agreeing with that," he whimpered, feeling as pathetic as he sounded.

She lifted his head enough so he could sip the cool water while she held the glass to his lips.

He sighed in relief. "Thank ye," he murmured, settling back down.

She bit her lip and drew in a shaky breath as he closed his eyes.

A small noise made him open one eye and peek at her. "Soooo... Is that it, then? Are ye speaking to me again or?" He let it hang in the air.

She smiled softly at him with a short, mirthless laugh. "Yes, sweetie, I'm speaking to you. Oh, Killian, I'm so sorry," she rushed out as if she were trying to prevent the sobs threatening to choke her voice. "It was ridiculous of me to get so angry over something as stupid as a haircut. It's your hair, of course, you can do what you like. It was just such a big change, and you usually tell me everything. I loved that our hair was the same, but you know, I actually like the new look. It's very sexy."

He opened both eyes and grinned at her. "How sexy?" he asked, with velvety sin threading into his voice.

Her lips curved, and she leaned forward. "Very, very, sexy," she declared.

He pretended he was thinking, tapping a finger on his lips, "On a scale of one to ten?"

She leaned further and paused with her mouth over his. "Definitely a solid eleven," she whispered before she kissed him tenderly. "Are we okay? Do you forgive me?"

He nodded, "Only if you'll forgive me, too, I should've told ye I was doing it."

"Of course I do." She shuddered then. "Ki, you scared me," she admitted quietly, her eyes filling, glassy with unshed tears. "Why didn't you tell anyone you needed help? You could have been killed!"

He threaded her fingers with his and sighed, embarrassed to admit it, but he always spoke the truth. "Pride, Risa. I wanted to be the only one to help ye. I know how important this is, an', well," he toyed with the ends of her hair, "I wanted to be the one ye could always turn to for help. It was stupid an' I'm sorry for it."

She smiled softly and shook her head, "And there's that honesty I love so much. Ki, I will always come to you. Whether I need help or not, you're the first one I think of in everything." She stroked his cheek and traced his lower lip, smirking as it quivered under her touch.

Killian stared at her hungrily, his eyes twinkling with mischief and his lips curving into a sensual pout, just begging to be kissed.

"Oh, no you don't," she warned, "You need rest, and we are *not* doing that on your boss's couch." She laughed heartily.

He pouted for a few more seconds, then sighed, knowing she was right. He did need some recovery time. "I know," he admitted grudgingly.

She pulled a blanket from the chair and covered him up, then kissed his forehead tenderly.

His eyes were closed, and his breathing evened out before she got to the door.

Risa returned to the conference room and sat shakily, smiling at the anxious faces there. "He's resting, he's alright," she announced, her eyes shining with unshed tears, reassuring those gathered.

Rena took her hands and stroked them softly, smiling, "He'll be okay."

Risa turned to Siobhan, who was leaning back in her chair, staring at the ceiling. "Thank you, Siobhan, and Rena. Thank you both for helping him, I can't tell you how much I appreciate you," she told them, her voice still thick with fear.

Siobhan snorted, "You're welcome, Risa. And as much as I like you, it's a good thing I love him so much, or I would have killed him as soon as I healed him."

Marco choked on a laugh, quickly turning it into an unconvincing cough.

Siobhan glanced at him and winked. Anyone else, she probably would've punched, but being her mate, he got a little slack.

Vaughn cleared his throat, announcing dryly, "Yes, well, I appreciate your restraint in not murdering my staff and best friend. But what — the hell — happened?" Smoke trickled from one nostril, betraying his anxiety. He'd sent Bridget home earlier, once they knew Killian would be alright, not wanting to stress her anymore so close to her due date. She had a soft spot for the wielder and was terribly worried.

Sighing, Siobhan straightened. Vaughn was giving her a look that clearly indicated she needed to be a little more respectful. "He's been pulling the spell out one piece at a time as we find it. I don't know for sure, because I can't see what he sees, but I think the closer we get to core memories that are blocked, the more resistant the spell is. It takes a lot out of him. I suspect when he broke the connection with this piece, it recoiled and slapped him internally. It gave him a concussion, if you want to think of it like that.

Combining that with the bounce of his own power when it snapped," she clapped her hands loudly, "Double whammy."

Marco rubbed his nose thoughtfully, "Huh, so it was a head injury. And that's why he didn't have an off switch?"

Siobhan nodded, "It shut off some internal filter that keeps him so quiet. Once he opened his mouth, he couldn't stop."

Liam let out a short, disbelieving laugh, "You guys should've heard it, you wouldn't have recognized him! He was talking nonstop, rambling about everything. Acoustics, tattoos, Risa. He even thought Siobhan was a demon at one point. And when he wasn't talking, he was singing!"

The others looked surprised. Killian? Singing? And babbling? Liam was right; that wasn't him at all.

Siobhan picked up the narrative, "And then all of a sudden it's like the lights went out, and boom, he just... dropped." She blew out a steady breath, waving her hands around her head. "All that pressure ruptured something. I had to stop the bleeding. Thankfully, Rena was able to help me control it, and we got him stable. He just needs a little rest, then he'll be as good as new."

Risa sucked in a harsh, shaky breath of her own, wincing as it felt like glass shards in her lungs. It was so much worse than she thought. *Poor Killian. He does so much to help us, without asking anything in return, and I was an ass because he cut his hair.*

Liam chuckled, and the others looked at him askance; it wasn't the time for jokes. He glanced up, "Sorry, I was just thinking about something he said. Did you know his mother named him after a pirate?"

Chapter 3

KILLIAN SLOWLY CRACKED OPEN his eyes, taking a moment to remember where he was and why he was there. He scrubbed his hands over his face. He vaguely remembered being in the conference room, working some spell, then waking up on the floor in the bathroom. He detected a slight floral perfume that wasn't Bridget's and wondered who it belonged to. It smelled heavenly. He stood gingerly and tested his balance. So far, so good. He took a step with only a slight wobble. *Deep breath,* he thought, suiting action to words. He took another step and was much steadier.

He smiled in relief, then blinked when the door opened, and a goddess stepped through. He watched warily as the gorgeous woman glided towards him with dainty steps, her long silvery hair swaying across her back. She whispered his name and placed a hand on his cheek before gently kissing him. He studied her, taking in her soft features and delicate lips. He almost knew her name, but it wasn't coming to him.

She frowned. "Killian?" she whispered, searching his eyes.

He blinked, a memory of her in his arms flashed through his mind. He knew her; they'd been intimate. He blinked again at the fear settling over her features.

She turned her head and shouted for Siobhan. The green wielder bolted into the room, skidding to a halt when she saw Killian upright and mobile.

"Hey Shi, what's the fuss about?" he asked, confused.

Marco and Liam hurried in behind her, so he nodded to them as well, "Guys."

They shared expressions of relief. "Ki, man, good to see you up and about," Marco rumbled, sounding genuinely happy to see him. They all turned towards the beautiful woman in front of him and stared at her questioningly.

"Killian?" she called softly.

He turned back to her, smiling as he realized it was her perfume he smelled earlier. "That's me. Has anyone ever told ye that you're stunning? A goddess? Also," he frowned, "Ye remind me of my friend Rena."

She sucked in a sharp breath, "Do you not know who I am?"

He started to smile, then stopped. He slowly nodded, "Aye, I think, I mean, I — feel — like I do. Ye seem familiar. We have met, right?"

Her eyes filled with tears, and Siobhan gasped. The other men's jaws dropped.

Killian could tell by their expressions that it was not the right answer. He faced the woman in front of him again. He raised a hand and ran it through her hair, then traced a finger over her cheek. She closed her eyes and leaned against his palm. He brushed away a tear that raced over her skin and gently caressed her lips with his thumb.

His mind helpfully flashed an image of the two of them on the beach in Florida, and it struck him like lightning. He gathered her closer and kissed her. This was familiar, this was right. She melted into his arms and threw hers around his neck. "Marissa," he breathed.

Risa whispered back, relieved, "Killian."

He kissed her forehead and pulled her tightly to him, loathe to let her go. He glared at Siobhan. "What the hell happened, Shi? How could I have forgotten her?"

The green wielder shook her head in frustration; she didn't understand it either. She held up a hand and arched her eyebrow in question.

A single sharp nod indicated his agreement.

Siobhan placed two fingers on his temple and pulsed a gentle wave of her power through him. She laughed in relief, "It's okay, just a little of that spell rebounding in that thick, stupid skull of yours. It dissolved once you remembered her. That should be the end of it. If your dumbass doesn't try anything so incredibly fucking stupid again!" she ended on an angry note.

He grimaced; he deserved that. He held up three fingers, "Scout's honor!"

The prickly woman glared at him, while simultaneously fighting the curve of her lips, betraying her amusement. "I doubt you were ever a scout."

"I still promise," Killian shrugged with a smirk.

Liam winked, "Aye, ye scurvy dog, and ye better not be lying or she'll make ye walk the plank." They all laughed at his terrible pirate impression, all except Killian.

Killian glanced at him sideways. "Why is he doing that?" he asked nervously.

The others laughed again. "*Amigo mio*, do we have so much to tell you," Marco announced, grinning in a way that increased Killian's anxiety about what happened. "But how about a nice sing-along? Maybe you can give us a few lines of 'Oh Danny Boy' to get us started? You didn't get to finish it earlier."

Killian's cheeks warmed as his face flushed, and he suspected he was turning a bright, unflattering, tomato red. "Oh, gods," he whispered, dread coloring his voice as he swallowed hard. "I was singing?" he croaked.

The answering chuckles and nods went unnoticed as he buried his face in his hands.

Killian sat on the end of Risa's bed, staring at the carpet, twisting his fingers together. She and Rena lived in Davis and Shepard's old condo. The twins kept the condo as an investment after they both moved out. They graciously allowed the sisters to move in after Risa ended up in Dallas, starting over.

Risa had flown back to Miami shortly after arriving to pack up her belongings and bring them back to Texas. Her gallery in Florida was destroyed when the rescue team triggered an explosion in the basement. Dismantling the wards of a dark wielder, holding kidnapped children in secret, took a toll on the building structure. Thanks to some creativity on Vaughn's part, the official determination was a gas leak. The insurance payout helped her settle into her new home nicely without having to rush to find a job. The twins refused to take any payment for rent, so she was saving it and supporting her sister while they searched for their missing sibling.

Killian owned his own house not far from hers, but when he tried to leave the office, his car wouldn't start. It was strange, the car was only a year old, but he was too wiped out to fix it. Risa insisted he come home with her. Now, nerves raced through him, unsure if he'd forgotten anything else and hoping she wasn't still mad at him. He remembered her being angry with him before his meltdown. It seemed they worked things out, but he wasn't one hundred percent. He didn't trust his memory right now. He grimaced at another vague memory; he couldn't stand singing in front of others, and apparently, he'd given quite a show. A shadow moved across his feet, drawing his gaze up.

Risa stood in front of him, fresh from a shower. She was brushing out her long, silvery hair. He was mesmerized. She was so beautiful, kind, and everything he ever dreamed of, that he couldn't believe he forgot her. Even for a second. These last months with her were incredible, the best of his long life. He didn't want to miss a single moment. Even when she was mad at her. His smile faltered; she was studying him intently. *Crap,* he thought, *she's still pissed.* He cleared his throat. "Risa, if you're still — angry — with me... I can go," he offered haltingly, fearing she would agree and send him away.

She twitched, looking both surprised and a little sad. "Go? No, Ki, I'm not angry with you. I'm just trying to figure you out. You're always so straightforward with me about everything. You tell me what's on your mind, I never wonder where I am with you. You're honest, almost to a fault. But today, I learned a lot about you. Like, that you have a beautiful singing voice that you've never shared with any of us. You've made this major change to your appearance and didn't even tell me." She held up a hand, anticipating his apology, "I'm over that, I told you, I like it." She gently touched the eyebrow ring, "This, especially, is sexy as hell." She grinned at him, then it slowly faded. "I'm just confused, I guess. But most importantly, I'm glad you're okay. You scared me today, I thought I lost you." Her breath hitched as she lowered her hand to his shoulder.

He stared into her warm, beautiful eyes, very like his own. "I scared myself, Risa. I don't honestly know what's going on with me. I just..." he sighed heavily and shook his head, "I need so badly to be what ye need an' want. I don't want to lose ye. An' it was weird with the constant comparisons to how much we looked alike. I didn't like the insinuations." He shrugged. "I figured, might as well do something about the way I look. I would never ask ye to change."

Marissa nodded. She'd heard the snide comments about him looking like her brother. It was hurtful because aside from their hair, they looked nothing alike. But their coloring was unusual, so it did draw attention.

"I understand. Thank you for explaining. And you aren't going to lose me. Killian. I... well, I'm not as good at explaining things as you are, and I hope you know... I mean, maybe you don't, but I've got feelings for you that are very strong. I'm not going anywhere, I couldn't," she told him, blushing furiously.

He studied her anxious face and the color rushing over her cheeks. Like a bolt of lightning, it hit him that she was trying to tell him she was in love with him without actually saying it. A soft smile wiped away his sadness. He would let her come to terms with it first. He didn't always have to be the most direct. Truth was, he loved her, too. He loved her fiercely, which is why it scared him so much that he forgot her, even for a moment.

Surging to his feet, he crushed his mouth to hers so hard they should have melted from the heat. He tucked her body firmly against him, leaving no space between them. Her hairbrush hit the floor with a clatter, seconds before her arms wound around his neck and her delicate moan filled his mouth. He reached for the belt on her robe and untied it before slipping his hands inside. She was naked underneath, her skin still warm from her shower. She gasped as he feathered his fingers over her ribs and brushed the underside of her breasts.

He loved her body; it was slender and lithe, graceful like a dancer. Her breasts were small but firm, perfect for her frame. He teased the outer slopes of her smooth skin and felt her nipples harden against his chest. Shoving the robe down her shoulders, he contemplated leaving her trapped in it, but his need to see her won. He let it fall the rest of the way to the floor, leaving her exposed. Stepping back to gaze at her, he showed her his appreciation, as his irises flashed silver. She stared back at him, biting her lower lip and flushing under his scrutiny. He grinned as he tugged his shirt over his head. Her own eyes flashed silver then, taking in his body and the tattoo over his heart.

Marissa stepped closer and laid a kiss on his tattoo, tracing it with her tongue while she worked on the fastening of his pants. Her fumbling fingers finally succeeded, and she let the material drop to the floor while he stepped out of them. She hooked her fingers in the waistband of his boxers, slid them down slowly. His heavy erection now rested against her stomach. A feline curve of mischief spread across her lips as she stroked him up and down, squeezing, making him quiver beneath her touch.

"Risa," he gasped, a strangled sound. He picked her up and tossed her down on the bed. "Bad girl," he growled at her while she grinned at him, unrepentantly.

Killian crawled up the bed towards her like a large cat, hunting its prey. She trembled at the feral heat on his face, showing he wanted to devour her. He stopped at her knees and spread her thighs apart. Slowly, he began to lick and kiss his way up her leg, savoring each touch. He lifted it over his shoulder, nipping at her ankle and working his way lower. Finally licking the tender junction of her thigh, he chuckled as she whimpered, shivering in anticipation. He leaned back on his heels then, smirking at her disappointed moan. Grabbing her waist, he rolled her over on her stomach, before pulling her up on her knees. He bent over her lower back and placed gentle kisses at the base of her spine, making her shudder and shake.

"Killian," she pleaded.

He chuckled low and stroked a hand over the soft curve of her bottom, before delivering a ringing smack, wrenching a hoarse cry from her throat. She shook harder as he laughed, a rich, warm sound that made her thighs quake and tremor. Reaching between those thighs, he stroked a finger over her center and moaned as her bare skin glistened for him. "Mm, so wet already, maybe you're a good girl after all," he praised in a deep voice, absolutely dripping with lust.

He kissed the pale red marks his hand left on her cheek and dragged his lips over her skin until he reached his fingers that were still slowly stroking her. He teasingly flicked his tongue at the drops there and made her gasp and squirm before he drove his tongue into her, stabbing it deep and causing her head to drop to the mattress. "Killian," she called out, wild with passion. He pressed firmly against her swollen bud and began circling it with his thumb. She was panting, digging her fingers into the mattress as he pressed harder, increasing the intensity. He started humming against her, and the vibrations sent shockwaves through her that were her final undoing. She shattered for him, and he continued to lap at her until her legs gave out.

"Killian," came another breathy, pleading moan, her voice reflecting how thoroughly he destroyed her. He slowly climbed up her body, kissing and licking his way, stopping a while at her shoulders. She was quivering again by the time he gently rolled her over and nipped at her throat. "There's my good girl, ye did so well, Risa. An' now, are ye going to keep being a good girl, can ye take more?"

She gasped as she felt him, hard and silky, pressing at her entrance. She angled her hips up, nodding, as he slid into her, fully seating himself. They both sighed in pleasure, and he followed with a low groan of satisfaction, his shoulders shaking. She just felt so right, so perfect. She dug her fingers into his back, crying out as he thrust into her. They moved together in a dance as old as time. Soft gasps and moans in the night, tender skin brushing against hard muscle. Her legs wrapped around his waist as he continued his relentless rhythm.

His muscles bunched and twisted as he continued to thrust into her over and over. Her hands gripped him, stroking over his skin, slick with heat. He loved every bit of it. He put one finger on her chin and tipped her head down, "Risa, look how well ye take me, gods ye feel amazing, so very perfect." He felt her tense, and his rhythm changed, knowing she was close. Her body went taut, and she moaned his name, writhing against him. Before she even caught her breath, she leaned forward and gently bit the ring in the corner of his bottom lip. It drove him wild when she played with it, and tonight was no exception. He captured her mouth with his, while she swallowed his coarse cry of ecstasy as he emptied himself in her.

Chapter 4

"RISA, YOU'RE AMAZING, I hope ye know that," Killian murmured softly to her, holding her close against him. He was gently brushing his fingers up and down her back, reveling in the feel of her soft, silky skin while he ran his nose through her hair.

She gave him a silly smile, "I do when I'm with you."

He kissed her tenderly. He loved this part, just lying there on the bed, breathing each other in, enjoying the afterglow. After a few minutes, she got up to use the bathroom, and he lay there with his arms behind his head, thinking through the day. He didn't remember much about what happened in the restroom, but their friends filled in the gaps for him. Every embarrassing detail. The singing, the babbling, the feeling that Marissa hated him. His heart clenched at the last thought.

He sat up, rubbing his chest, the stinging ache making him wince in pain. His breathing quickened, and he reminded himself of what they had just shared. She didn't hate him, she couldn't. She loved him. Maybe. He thought about the fact that he was withholding his feelings for her because he wanted to hear it from her first. That wasn't him. He was upfront and honest, but not about this. It was different once upon a time. Over seventy years prior, because of *her*. He wasn't even thinking *that* name as he'd sworn it would never cross his lips again. He declared his feelings first then, and she broke his heart.

After that, he changed. He stopped speaking unless he needed to and became an observer instead. He said exactly what he meant and was brutally honest. Sometimes that wasn't very welcome, but he was steadfast and unapologetic. He turned being unnoticed into an art form. Studying magic with Vaughn, he eventually discovered he possessed skills others didn't, but he didn't share them. There was no need. He stayed in the background, friendly enough if approached, but kept to himself. By the time he met Marissa, he was used to being alone. Biting his lip, Killian thought back to when he first met her.

The brown-haired young woman stood in the middle of the room, eyes wide, taking in the large group in the rental beach house. Confused and overwhelmed with everything she had just learned. Killian realized with a start he was drawn to her. Unsure why, as he'd merely introduced himself and knew nothing about her. She was alone in the world, much like he was. Well, technically, she'd just made a bunch of new friends, but he looked deeper into her and sensed that spark of magic. It pulled at him, making him want to discover more. When he realized she was a silver wielder like him, fire shot through his veins, burning like a raging inferno. He yearned for the company of another for the first time since he left Ireland, an aching in the pit of his stomach he'd never felt before. He originally planned to take it slow, let her get accustomed to her magic, learn about their world, then see if she might be interested in getting to know him better.

Those plans were tested when he saw the way she watched him, her desire open and hungry. Her delight in the simplest of magics gave him joy. She was so eager to learn, so grateful for his help. Marissa was sharp, a natural talent and quick-witted. Every second he was with her, increased his intense need to know her better. For the first time in decades, he wanted. He desired. He couldn't resist teasing, taking little tastes of her.

Just when he thought he was going to explode with the want of her, she experienced an overload of her power, brought on by her anger with the dark wielders. She was still so new to her wielding, she didn't know how to channel it properly. He took her out to the ocean and showed her how to release the excess magical flow. She lit up then, like a silver goddess, the aura of power surrounding her like a halo. She was ethereal in her beauty, and he'd never wanted anything more in his life. His want turned into a burning, raging hunger that could only be quenched by taking her.

Always straightforward with his words, he told her right then how he felt, and she responded in kind. They made love the first time there on that beach, fast, hot, and wild with abandon.

Blinking rapidly, Killian snapped out of his memory and smiled. They'd been inseparable ever since. He never wanted to be apart from her. His heart was hers to do with what she wanted. The thought that she could ever hate him made his chest tighten again. He rubbed it absently, wondering how he was going to handle this.

Mind whirling, he was at war with his resolutions, and what he swore to himself decades before. He knew it was ridiculous to hold himself to the promise of a kid who had his heart broken so long ago. His heart settled, and he knew without a doubt he needed to tell her how he felt, let her know he loved her. He didn't want to risk losing her to an outdated vow. His decision made, he glanced up and realized she was watching him anxiously.

Marissa stood frozen in the doorway to the bathroom, her gaze locked on Killian. He was sitting up in bed, rubbing his chest as if it ached. His face was a mask of contradictions. He looked both frightened and resolved. She realized he must be coming to a monumental decision and needed space to figure it out. She waited, watching him and saw the minute his mind was made up. He noticed her then, and they locked eyes. He swallowed heavily; whatever he decided, seemed to shake him to his core. Killian was brave, so whatever scared him must be major. "Marissa," he whispered and held out his hand for her as he moved to the edge of the bed.

She stumbled slowly to him, her steps dragging reluctantly, uneasy about where this was going. A wave of freezing dread surged through her; sure, he was about to say goodbye. Her whole body trembled, and her thoughts fluttered like a caged bird. *He realized this isn't what he wants. I'm too much trouble. My background makes me dangerous. He knows I love him, and he doesn't need that complication.* She wilted a little on the way and finally stopped in front of him, eyes downcast, shaking nervously. "Ki," she whispered, her voice pleading, begging him not to leave.

His own eyes widened at her tone, and he smiled softly, reassuringly. "*Mo stór,*" he pulled her to him and wrapped her against his chest. She gazed up at him, and he smiled again, tenderly. "*Mo chuisle, mo chroí,* do ye not know what ye do for me?"

She shook her head dumbly; she had no idea what he was saying.

He brushed a finger across her lips, continuing. "*Is breá liom tú. Is tú mo ghrá.*" She shook her head again in confusion, and he translated softly, "Marissa. My treasure. My pulse. My heart. I love ye. *You* are my love."

She stared at him, his beautiful, gentle smile, the tenderness in his eyes. The soft moonlight filtering through the curtains softened his features as he spoke to her in a language she didn't understand but figured must be Irish or Gaelic. She loved his accent, but apart from a word here and there, he'd never spoken to her like this before. *What a stupid thing to think about now,* she decided. This amazing man just told her he loved her in two languages, and she was pondering his accent. She saw it then, the quick flash of hurt in his eyes that she hadn't said anything.

His arms started to loosen, and she watched his expression shutting down. She did the only thing she could think of and pressed her lips to his, so tenderly it was like touching clouds. She ran her fingers through his hair and let her eyes go silver. She stroked his face with her other hand, and when he gazed at her with hope, she whispered, "Killian Brennan. You dear, sweet, wonderful man. Oh, thank God you told me. I love you, too. So much."

He shuddered and gasped in relief. A moment of clarity burst through her, and she realized his heart had been broken before. That's what he was so scared of. Not of her, but what she could do to him. She rose to her knees in front of him, kissing him deeply. "Killian," she moaned, "My Killian, I love you so much. I'm glad you finally told me. I wanted to tell you, but didn't want to scare you off by saying it too soon. You are my world, my heart, I love you!"

He stared at her, lips parted, eyes wide, his face full of wonder. "Marissa, I thought maybe ye did, but I was being stubborn and wanted ye to say it first. I made a ridiculous promise to myself when I was a young lad that I was never going to say it first. But I realized ye matter more to me than some stupid, angry kid's vow. I can't breathe sometimes from how much I love ye. I knew from the moment I saw ye; I needed ye with me. I'd been so alone, Marissa. My entire world shifted when ye walked into that room an' my heart told me I didn't want to be alone anymore. Please, Risa, tell me again."

She smiled so hard, she thought her face might crack, "I love you, Killian, you're all I need."

They breathed each other in and out until tendrils of silver slipped around her, wrapping her in ribbons of his magic. "Risa," he whispered as the silver bands sank into her, pulling her even closer to him. Quietly, they crawled under the sheets and lay there, letting the dark, the silence cradle them in the warmth of their emotions. Eventually, they fell asleep in each other's arms.

When the sound of birds chirping woke him, Killian glanced at the clock and grumbled. It was late morning, and he was usually an early riser. He heard the shower running and perked up. Risa must be in there. Thinking about her naked and wet, he decided he liked how big that shower was. He stood and stretched, then padded towards the bathroom.

Without warning, the bedroom door opened, and Serena strolled in, holding up a dress. "Risa," she called in a sing-song voice, "We need to get ready soon!" Killian paused mid-stride, and when she glanced up, she froze. Her eyes widened, and her mouth dropped. Her gaze moved from his head to his feet as she took in the sight of Killian standing there, fully nude. She apparently didn't know he was here.

He wasn't the least bit modest when it came to his body, so he casually stood there and smiled. "Hey Rena, good morning! Risa's in the shower."

She gaped, her mouth opening and closing like a fish. She dropped the dress she was holding and finally squeaked out a horrified, "Killian!"

He nodded and strode towards her, then leaned down to pick up the dress. "This for Risa?" he asked.

She nodded, her face scarlet.

"I'll let her know," he grinned and turned to walk away, giving her a view of his backside. He laid the dress on the rumpled bed, straightening it out. Turning, he saw she was still there. "Anythin' else?" he inquired pleasantly.

Rena gasped and yelped, "Your car! Not here! Sorry!" before she ran from the room, slamming the door behind her.

He chuckled; Rena would definitely be knocking from now on. Stepping eagerly into the bathroom, he heard Risa singing cheerfully in the shower. Smirking, he slipped in silently behind her. He leaned over, then murmured, "Is this a private concert or can anyone join?"

She jumped and squealed, but he caught her, so she didn't slip. "Killian!" she chided, "You scared me!" She glared as she slapped a wet hand on his chest.

"Aye," he laughed, "Well, an' it's been quite a busy morning then."

She studied him questioningly.

"I may have scarred Rena doll for life," he admitted, and shared the story about Rena walking in on him.

Risa howled with laughter, "Oh, poor Rena, bet she knocks from now on."

"My thoughts exactly," he chuckled in agreement.

Once they finished their exceedingly long, steamy shower, she wandered out to see what Rena brought. When she saw it, she gasped, "Oh shit!"

He stared at her in alarm. "What?"

She turned wide eyes on him, "We have to hurry! We can't be late for the wedding!"

He smacked his forehead. Jack and Davis were getting married today. They needed to be there for sure. He grabbed his bag and frantically looked for his car keys before he remembered his car was still at the office. He'd ridden here with Risa, which was why Rena didn't know he was here. "Dammit, my suit is at my house." Just then, there was a timid knock at the door. He grinned and hurried to it, a towel around his waist this time. He opened it and saw Rena there, staring hard at the ceiling.

She glanced at him, let out a strangled squeak and looked up again. She choked out, "Vaughn!" then shoved a garment bag in his hands before she scurried off.

He realized it was his suit. Killian didn't know how the dragon managed it, but he was grateful. He turned to tell Risa, but the words died in his mouth when he saw her shimmy into the gorgeous silver gown. She was the goddess from his dreams, and his heart stumbled before restarting. "My god, Marissa, you're stunning," he whispered reverently.

She smiled softly. "I bet you say that to all the women you love."

He returned her smile and held up the bag, "Good news, I have clothes. Bad news, your sister is *definitely* scarred for life." They both laughed and hurried to finish getting ready.

Chapter 5

THEY ARRIVED ON TIME, thankfully. Killian could feel the heat from Rena's embarrassment, the entire car ride over. The second they parked, she ran off like death himself was on her tail. Risa rolled her eyes, "It's bad enough it happened, but do you have to tease her? How many times did you have to say, 'bare minimum' and 'naked truth'?"

Killian leaned over, kissing her cheek. "Absolutely, an' I probably could have said it at least three more times," he confirmed.

She sighed, "Let's go mingle," and smirked as he scrunched up his nose in distaste. They hurried towards the crowd of their friends and family gathered for the event. Killian would usually sit back and watch quietly, but Marissa looped her arm firmly through his, forcing him to interact with the others. It wasn't so bad, really; he did like these people. Mostly.

Jorrie was straightening her dress and glanced up, startled, as Rena scurried over and hid behind her. "What's going on, Re-Re?" she laughed as the young woman covered her face.

"Risa's boyfriend. I walked in and he was naked!" Rena blurted, face flushed a becoming shade of pink.

Jorrie roared with laughter. She craned her neck, searching until she saw Marissa talking to Bridget. Her arm was through that of a devastatingly handsome man, Jorrie didn't know. He was tall, well-built, and his lips were made for kissing. As he laughed, she saw the sun glint off a small ring on his lower lip. Strands of silky black hair brushed another small ring in his silvery eyebrows. Jorrie cleared her throat. "Wait, Risa's got a new boyfriend? I don't know what happened to her and Killian, but, mhmm, sister, he is gorgeous. I wouldn't mind seeing that myself!" she smirked.

At Rena's choked squeak, Jorrie turned to see a wide-eyed look of shock on the young wielder's face. "What now?" Jorrie laughed again.

Rena stared at her, horrified. "That *is* Killian!" she hissed.

Jorrie stopped smiling. She whipped back around and studied the man again, realizing with a start that it was indeed Killian. He just looked completely different. She knew he was good-looking from the little bit she could see of him, but now, he was downright stunning! Her jaw dropped. She did have a thing for the bad boy look.

Her husband, Shepard, a long-haired, tattooed, motorcycle-riding, bad boy in his own right, strolled up. "Who's the fellow with Risa?" he asked.

Jorrie hissed, "It's Killian!"

He gave an amused grunt and rolled his eyes. "Well, I can see why you were drooling now."

She narrowed her eyes and pointed to her swollen stomach. "I'm allowed; you keep doing this to me."

His gaze dropped tenderly on her belly. He leaned over and kissed it, which made her soften as well. "Don't worry, she didn't mean it," he whispered to the little life inside her.

"What's the matter with Rena?" Shepard asked as the young woman hurried away, face still red.

Jorrie grinned. "Seems she forgot to knock on Risa's door this morning and got a full three hundred sixty-degree view of every delicious naked inch of one Killian Brennan. Now she can't bear to look at him at all."

Shepard grinned and shook his head. "Poor thing, she'll get over it." He watched Jorrie as she ogled Killian and sighed, "You're gonna keep drooling, aren't you?"

She laughed, "Probably."

He kissed her cheek, murmuring he was going to check on his brother.

Jorrie nodded absently and watched the two silver wielders circle the group. Many eyes were drawn to the tall, attractive man on Risa's arm. Jorrie smiled, thinking *that girl better lock him down quickly or she's going to have some competition.* From the corner of her eye, she saw a woman with long, silvery hair like Rena and Risa watching Killian with an intense gaze and smirked, *starting with that one.*

In his section of the dressing room, Davis was pacing, shaking his hands at his sides. He checked his watch again and wished for the hundredth time he could have convinced Jack to run off to Vegas. They were already mated, so this was more for Jack and the kids. He softened at the thought. He'd do anything for them. The door opened, and Shepard hurried in, followed by the photographer, Nathan.

Shepard grinned at his brother. "Nice monkey suit, Pond."

"You're jealous because I look better in it than you did in yours, Stream," Davis retorted, the brothers calling each other by their childhood nick-names.

Shepard's eyes filled as he gazed at his identical twin. He straightened Davis' jacket, "You're right, you do look better. I'm so happy for you, little brother." He pulled him in, and they hugged each other tightly.

Davis heard a quiet click. He glanced over at Nathan, who winked at him. "The magazine is going to love that one. The drummer for Still Waters and his twin brother? Whew! I feel like I should be paying you for this."

Davis grinned and shook his hand. "Nathan, good to see you again," he said.

Nathan was a world-renowned photographer they'd met in Miami who set his sights on Jack. Although he was disappointed Jack wasn't single, Nathan tapped him to be a model in an ad he was shooting for a cruise line. Jack had a lot of fun with the shoot, and he was a huge hit. He began receiving other modeling offers as well, but he was so busy since Vaughn made him CEO of Chesapeake, he didn't do many.

Davis' heart began galloping in his chest. Jack was gorgeous, loving, kind, and about to be his husband. He couldn't wait.

"I already got Jack's prep photos, I was going to get some of you, but I see you're a little impatient," Nathan teased.

Shepard yanked Davis' jacket off and undid his tie.

Davis laughed, "Bro, don't choke me."

His brother winked, "Now put it back on."

Davis rolled his eyes and shrugged back into his jacket, then Shepard stepped forward and assisted Davis with his tie. He didn't need to, but he wanted to. Davis smiled and his eyes were shining; Shepard's were too. He leaned forward and put his forehead on his brother's, ignoring the camera clicking away. "Love you, Shep."

"Love you, too, Davis. Now, go marry the hell out of Jack!"

"I'm going to do just that!" Davis whispered.

They heard the music change, and Shepard winked, "That's my cue!" Shepard stepped out to assist Vaughn in escorting Jorrie down the aisle. Bridget was the matron of honor, but she declined to walk because she was due very soon and didn't want to waddle. Her words, but Davis knew better than to repeat them. She was sitting in the front row and would take her place once the rest were there.

It was finally Davis' turn. He walked out and, as planned, met Jack on the path. He immediately lost his breath when he saw Jack standing there. He looked amazing, his baby blue eyes sparkling in merriment. Sunlight glinting off his golden hair, Jack grinned with his perfect white smile, and it was all for him. Davis knew he was the luckiest man in the world.

Jack strolled over and said softly, "Hey, Jack, I mean, hi, I'm Jack."

Davis smiled back. "Hey, yourself, gorgeous, I'm trouble, but you can call me Davis," he answered in the silly greeting they gave each other the day they met years ago.

Jack tilted his head, "You ready to finally make an honest man out of me?"

"I am. I'm ready to marry the hell out of you!" Davis touched his forehead to his mate's.

Jack roared with laughter, "Let's do this!" They joined hands and turned to face their friends and family. If Jack noticed his parents weren't there, he didn't show it. They walked down the aisle together and pledged to love each other forever. When they kissed, the crowd cheered. They picked up their children, took their family photos, then it was time for the party.

The reception was full of laughter, happy tears, and joyful noise. Davis and Jack were dancing, tuned only to each other and blocking out the rest of the world. Gabriel, Bridget's oldest, was home from college and dancing with his little sister Celeste and niece Lily. The girls were screaming in joy as he spun them around. Davis' parents were holding Jonathan, while Jorrie's triplets were running around, blowing bubbles in the air, creating a beautiful effect with their mischief.

Killian was dancing with Risa, holding her close. "Is Rena still avoiding you?" Risa inquired with amusement in her voice.

He gazed lovingly at her and grinned. "Aye, I tried to dance with her, but she squeaked like a wee mouse an' scampered away."

Risa giggled and nudged him to their table, sitting down with a tired sigh.

"Care for a drink?" he offered softly.

She nodded, "Please, yes!"

Killian made his way to the bar and ordered for them both. While he was waiting, he felt a smack on his behind. He whirled in shock, locking eyes with Shepard's wife. He stood there, staring down at Jorrie with his mouth open.

Jorrie reached up and pushed it closed. "Sorry," she shrugged with a non-apologetic grin, "I've been admiring that tight tushy of yours since you got here. Killian, I have to say, I'm here for this new look." She moved in closer. "Mm, the hardware," she purred, tapping his lip piercing. She nodded, "Dance with me." She grabbed his hand and tugged him onto the dance floor.

He stared, still speechless.

She studied him, "You know, Ki, I understand you're the strong, silent type, but say *something*."

He finally laughed, "I've no words." He spun her around gently, then pulled her back.

She leaned into him, "Mm, hot, sexy, and a good dancer. No wonder Risa likes you so much."

He beamed. "Loves me," he corrected.

Jorrie's face relaxed into a sentimental smile, "And you love her, don't you?"

He nodded slowly, trying to figure out where she was going with this.

"Good, keep it that way. I'm happy for you," she raised to her tiptoes and kissed him on the cheek while he stared at her, confusion bunching his eyebrows together. He glanced up, seeing a flash of silvery-blonde hair, hoping it was Risa coming to save him, but she was still sitting at their table. Must've been Circe meandering through the crowd.

Shepard rescued him by pulling Jorrie away, "Sorry, Killian, she's hormonal and has a thing for that look," he gestured at him, grinning.

Killian just nodded; he was a little overwhelmed at the moment. He hurried over to the bar and grabbed the drinks he'd ordered before making his way back to Risa. He could tell she was trying not to laugh, having witnessed the whole thing. Sitting down with a heavy thump, he stared at her, shaking his head. He started to say something, stopped, opened his mouth again, then shook his head. Finally, he laughed, hard, the sound ringing across the room like a gentle wave.

Risa noticed women in the room staring at Killian with lust-filled expressions. She glanced at him; he was completely unaware of the attention he drew. He was always so purposeful at being in the background; he was usually off the radar. Now that he wasn't hiding anymore, others were taking notice. She smirked, *but he loves me!*

After a while, Liam grabbed a microphone from the band to make announcements. "Hi everyone, just a couple of quick things. If you haven't yet, please be sure you sign the guest book with your well wishes for the happy couple." He raised his glass in a toast to Jack and Davis.

"Secondly, not to take away from the happy couple, but Bridget has gone into labor a little early, so Vaughn and Shepard left to get her home and ready to deliver the next round of Drakes!" More applause and cheers. "Which brings me to my last point. Jorrie and Shepard were going to perform a special song for the newlyweds, but since Shepard's indisposed, we'll have a stand-in with Jorrie."

Murmurs of surprise filled the room as Jorrie made her way to the front, eyeing Liam warily.

Grinning ear to ear, Liam continued, "I'm sure you're all wondering who could possibly take Shepard's place alongside our platinum superstar. You'll be pleased to know we've recently discovered some hidden talent amongst our ranks. I'm thrilled to introduce to you, our very own Irish heartthrob, Killian Brennan!" The room echoed with applause as everyone turned to stare.

Killian sat ramrod straight in his chair, shoulders tight, a smile frozen on his face. Risa turned to him, aware he didn't volunteer for this. She knew he hated attention but wouldn't back down from Liam's challenge. Noting the way his hand was white knuckling his drink, she hurriedly leaned forward, breathing into his ear, "You can do this, I have faith in you."

He slowly turned, his jaw clenched, lips thinned, eyes burning. She tried to show him with her gaze that she really did believe in him. He swallowed and threw back the rest of his drink, then stood. More applause and some whistles followed him as he sauntered to the stage without a word. Risa crossed her fingers, praying there would be no bloodshed. She locked eyes with Siobhan across the room as the two women nodded at each other. Both resolved to murder Liam for this stunt.

When Killian reached Liam, he glared at the green dragon with murderous fury. "I *will* kill ye after this is over, ye langer," he whispered through clenched teeth.

Liam grinned cheekily and blew smoke in his face, "Try it, wielder."

Killian nonchalantly placed his hand on Liam's shoulder and sent a pulse of power through him. Liam's eyes widened in shock as he staggered, and Killian smirked, "Happy to, dragon."

Liam backed up a step and studied him, appropriately surprised at the intensity of the surge. Then he grinned, picking up the microphone again. "Okay, folks, Killian is a little shy. I know most of you think he's a functional mute, but the man has some serious chops. Give him some encouragement!" More cheers and applause sounded as he waved at those assembled.

Davis and Jack stood in the middle of the dance floor, smiling excitedly. Killian didn't want to let them down. Locking eyes with Risa, he relaxed a bit as she gave him an encouraging smile and a thumbs up. He glanced at Siobhan and smirked as she pointed at her brother, then drew a finger across her throat in a silent threat. Breathing in slowly, he shook his hands out; he could do this. He would pretend he was alone at home. He shuddered only slightly.

Jorrie glided over and laid a placating hand on his arm. "Killian, if you don't want to, I can sing it by myself. I realize you were set up here," she glared daggers at Liam.

The unrepentant dragon blew her an exaggerated kiss.

She rolled her eyes. "We were going to sing '*Unforgettable*', the duet version. Are you up for that?"

Killian perked up. The song was a favorite of his. "Can we take a moment to run through it together in the back?"

She smiled back and nodded. "Hey everybody, a quick warmup and we'll be right back!" she announced. She grabbed his hand and dragged him back to the kitchen area of the reception hall. "This will have to do; show me what you've got, kid."

"Kid?" He smirked with an arched eyebrow, wondering if she knew he was over twice her age. He took a deep breath and hummed a little, trying to warm up his voice a bit. Opening his mouth, he tried to sing, but nothing came out. He cleared his throat and turned his back on the staff watching in curiosity. He shook his shoulders and tried again; this time, his rich, smooth baritone flowed like warm whiskey from his lips. "Unforgettable, that's what you are. Unforgettable, though near or far. Like a song of love that clings to me —"

"Stop!" Jorrie cried; her mouth hanging open.

He cringed, thinking she hated it and stared at his feet, his face flushing hotly. He heard clapping and turned to find the staff applauding.

Jorrie nodded, fanning herself. "Killian! Holy hell, how did we not know about this before? Where've you been hiding all this time?"

He shrugged, "Not hiding. I've always been around. I just don't like attention. I was happy that way until I met Marissa. She made me realize I was lonely, an' I don't want to be alone anymore."

Her jaw dropped again.

He grinned and closed it for her with a snap, the way she'd done to him on the dance floor.

She snorted, then belted out a rich, bawdy laugh that was so uniquely hers. "You know, I heard that about you. You don't talk much, but when you do, you get straight to the point."

He nodded in agreement.

Jorrie studied him a moment longer, then grabbed his lapels, dragged him down, and kissed him.

He froze. *What the hell?*

She let him go, sighing lustily, "Mm, I was right, pure sin that one." She nodded, "You'll more than do. Now, let's run through this. I need to have you come to the studio with me, Killian!"

They ran through the song together, and the staff cheered their encouragement again, some recording it on their phones. She declared, "You got this," with a wave of her hand, her bright scarlet nails trailing over his shoulder, then strutted back into the reception hall.

Chapter 6

KILLIAN STOOD THERE, ROOTED to the spot another moment. He touched his lips and hoped Shepard never found out Jorrie kissed him. He might go toe to toe with Liam, but he would not care to tangle with Shepard or Davis. Or Jack, for that matter, the man was lethal with just a knife. His head whipped to the side, catching sight of Risa's long swaying hair, except when he looked, she was gone. Surely, she wouldn't have followed him in here. Sighing, he followed after Jorrie.

He stepped cautiously up to his microphone, speaking with more confidence than he felt. His voice cut through the noise in the hall, quickly capturing everyone's attention. "Jack, Davis, I just want ye to know how incredibly loved ye are, by your family, your friends, an' those friends that have become family. I've had the pleasure of working with ye both, an' watching your love blossom these last few years. I'm honored, truly, to stand here tonight with the lovely Jorrie. It gives me immense pleasure to sing with her, this song for ye, my good friends, for your special dance. You're both, in a word, unforgettable."

Risa noticed the astonished expressions on most faces as they listened to Killian. It was quite a lengthy speech compared to his usual two to three-word answers. He also played up the Irish brogue in his voice, and it danced over her skin like electricity.

The opening strains of the music sounded, and Davis took Jack in his arms. Risa only had eyes for Killian as he opened his mouth, and the smoothest, warmest voice she could have imagined came out, singing the iconic words. Her mouth dropped. *Why was he hiding that?* She wiggled in her chair, feeling damp and tight. *Good lord, this man!* He was full of constant surprises. She listened in awe as Jorrie joined him, and their two voices blended so perfectly, it was like the song was written solely for them. She glanced around and beamed with pride as those in attendance were mesmerized. Many were recording it on their phones. Her stomach clenched for a moment; she hoped he would be okay with the attention.

His circle was going to get a lot bigger, whether he wanted it or not. As the song closed, she noticed most people were wiping their eyes, herself included. It was a beautiful tribute to a lovely couple. The newlyweds were already hugging and thanking the singers.

Davis picked Killian up off his feet and swung him around while the wielder laughed and begged Jack to intervene. Jack simply smirked and kissed him instead. A thunderous round of applause swallowed all other sounds, as everyone else rose to their feet. Risa stood as well, eyeing the hungry gazes on other women's faces as they rushed to the small stage. She swallowed back the bitter taste left by the surge of jealousy and hurried outside for some air.

Killian hugged Jack and Davis again, then Jorrie, and tried to make his way back to Risa. Progress was slow, as people swarmed them, offering compliments. Blushing, he tried to give all the credit to Jorrie, but she refused, declaring he carried the song. Quickly, he became flustered and overwhelmed with the attention. He wasn't used to so many people noticing him and having to speak this much. He couldn't disappear with this much focus on him. Now, he needed Risa in the worst way, but didn't see her anywhere. *Maybe she's outside,* he thought. He turned back to the crowd, resigned to listening to them. The sooner he got through them, the sooner he could leave. He hoped.

A flash of her silver blonde hair caught the corner of his eye again. He whirled around, relieved, but she was gone. *Maybe it was Rena?* But it wasn't, as he spotted her across the room speaking with Liam. A strange unease settled into his gut. For some reason he couldn't define, he knew the woman wasn't Risa, but who else could it have been? Circe left earlier to help Bridget, and the only other silver wielder here was another man with short hair. He shrugged it off as a product of his anxiety.

Killian was offered many drinks and phone numbers. He politely declined them all until Siobhan marched over, declaring him off-limits. "Dance with me. Now!" The command was issued in her usual prickly manner, one he appreciated. He gratefully led her to the dance floor, and she leaned towards him.

"First of all," she started, "Great job, you really rose to the challenge."

He nodded his thanks.

"Secondly, my brother's an asshole. I know he set you up like that, and I'm sorry. Did you threaten to kill him?"

He nodded again, a small smirk curving his lips.

"Good," she grinned, "Saves me the trouble. Although I might still do it on principle."

He grunted with amusement, glad he didn't have to voice his thoughts with her. They'd worked together long enough that she knew his nonverbal cues. He spun her around a few times then she was back in his arms.

She giggled as he dipped her. "I love dancing with you!" She gave him a soft smile. "Ki, I know you didn't want to do it, but I'm glad you did. It really meant a lot to Jack and Davis; they were so happy! You're an amazing singer, you know. I'm glad I got to hear something besides Irish ditties."

He frowned, glaring daggers, and her grin grew larger.

"Oh, come on, Ki, lighten up a little. Seriously, though, fantastic job. Now, I'm going to kill Liam. Love you!" She kissed him on the cheek as the song ended and stomped off, murder in her eyes.

Killian stood for a moment, watching her retreating form. He smirked, almost feeling the tiniest bit sorry for Liam. He wandered around but still couldn't locate Risa. Frustrated, he sought out Rena and noticed her back to him, so he easily snuck up behind her. He grabbed her hand, pulling her to the dance floor before she could protest.

Rena's eyes met his, and her face flushed a bright fire-engine red. She leaned back, trying to pull away.

He tugged her closer and quietly begged, "Please, Rena doll, one dance. Let's get this over with so ye can stop being embarrassed an' we can be comfortable with each other again. Please?"

She slowly nodded timidly.

"Rena," he sighed, "I'm sorry about this morning an' teasing ye so. I should've just let it go, but... ye remind me how much I miss my little sister, an' I would've given her a hard time as well. Now, let's work through this. What about it has ye so flustered? Have ye seen a man naked before this morning?"

She smiled shyly, blushing furiously as she nodded.

"Right, dragons? Before, an' after they shift?" he added softly.

She nodded again, faster.

"Alright then, so what's so different about it? Just because I'm not a dragon? I mean, men are men. We all look pretty much the same without our clothes on."

She squeezed her eyes closed and shook her head from side to side rapidly.

He guided her from the dance floor to a quiet corner and sat. He brushed her hair behind her ears like he'd seen her do a thousand times. "Little sister," he started softly, "Rena doll, please, talk to me. I love Marissa, an' I don't want there to be anything awkward between us. We used to be so easy together."

She finally sighed and glanced at him; her cheeks still stained a fetching pink. "Killian, the dragons aren't like you. When they change, they aren't," she gestured helplessly at his midsection.

He tilted his head, confused.

"They aren't, um, and you were. Ugh," she stuttered, covering her face with her hands.

Suddenly, he understood. She was embarrassed because he had an erection that morning, and she had never seen *that* before. When dragons shifted, they were relaxed. "Serena," he called gently, tentatively, "Have ye ever... well, been with a man? Intimately?"

She gasped as her hands dropped, and her eyes flew to his. They flared silver for a moment before she bit her lip and lowered her gaze. She shook her head no, just the slightest amount. If he wasn't watching closely, he might have missed it.

Tilting her chin up, he smiled softly. "Rena doll, it's alright, sweetheart. That's nothing to be ashamed of." He hugged the small woman to him and kissed the top of her head. "Do ye have questions?"

"I was too embarrassed to ask Jorrie too much, and I didn't have anyone I could ask when I was with the Shadows. Do you think Risa…" She trailed off, shuddering at the memories, tucking her face into his neck.

"I know Risa will be happy to answer your questions, love. Thank ye for telling me. Again, I'm sorry for earlier," he murmured, "You're going to be fine. Please, don't be afraid of me, okay? I'm not embarrassed one bit by what happened. I've no shame about my body. It's only regular human anatomy an' nature. What ye saw, it happens to all men when they're with someone they're attracted to. You'll find someone one day ye want to see that way, I promise. And you'll think they're beautiful." He smiled down at her, and she smiled back, nodding.

"Killian," she whispered, "I think you're beautiful." Her eyes went wide, "With your clothes on!"

He laughed quietly and hugged her again before he pulled her to her feet. "Alright, I'm going to put some serious effort into finding your sister, but in the meantime," he escorted her back inside. "Here, dance with Gabriel." He grabbed Bridget's son and put Serena in his arms. Killian knew about Rena's not-so-secret crush on the young man. He also knew Gabe was single as his previous girlfriend moved back to Italy. They were cute together. Gabe appeared dumbstruck by the situation and glanced at Killian in panic. Killian winked and shooed the pair away.

Gabe stared at Rena. Really, truly, looked at her then and smiled softly. He nodded towards the dance floor in inquiry, and she smiled back in shy acceptance. He started to spin her around the room, and soon they were lost in each other.

Killian huffed in satisfaction and glanced around, searching again for Risa. Not seeing her, he pulled out his phone to call her. He caught a glimpse of silver hair running behind him and whirled, but only found a trace of a sickly-sweet perfume. He frowned, unable to locate where the woman had gone.

Risa appeared at Killian's elbow. "That is about the sweetest thing I've ever seen," she murmured, laying her head on his shoulder as she watched her sister and Gabe. Rena's smile was precious, and her head was tilted just so, listening intently to whatever made Gabe's face so animated. His green eyes sparkled as he stared at Rena, a large smile stretching his lips in the biggest puppy-dog grin Risa ever saw.

Killian quickly turned and wrapped his arms around Risa tightly, burying his face in her hair. "Where have ye been?" he breathed, almost crushing her, "I've been searching everywhere, going insane without ye, Risa."

Leaning back, Risa studied him; he did seem inordinately relieved to see her. She smiled ruefully, "I'm sorry, Killian. When that song ended and all those people crowded you, I — well — I got a little jealous and needed some time alone. Those women, licking their lips at you, it wasn't pretty."

He tilted his head, "What women?"

She smirked; he was precious in his obliviousness. "Killian, be honest. How many offered you phone numbers? Dances? Drinks?" she asked quietly.

He contemplated it, running the tip of his tongue over his lip ring in thought, then winced.

"Exactly. I guess..." her smile fell away, "I guess I'm just afraid someone else is going to turn your head."

He gently cupped her cheek and stroked her jaw with his thumb. "My love, *that* is not happening. I've only room in my heart for one, an' that one is the silver goddess in front of me."

"That won't stop them from trying," she huffed, admittedly a little hint of petulance in her tone at war with her pleasure at his words.

Killian rolled his eyes and grunted in frustration. "Fine then, let's make a spectacle," he replied, dragging her to the middle of the dance floor as a faster beat filled the room.

He pulled her roughly into his arms, and they danced. His body pressed against hers so tightly, there was no room for air between them. Killian spun Risa away from him so fast her skirt flared up. He pulled her back just as quickly, and when she slammed into his chest, he slid his hands through her hair as he cupped the back of her head. With a sensual grin, he claimed her mouth fiercely, kissing her deeply, thoroughly, to a chorus of catcalls and whistles. When he finally released her — breathless — she realized he was publicly marking his territory.

She chuckled, "Well, as demonstrations go, I much prefer that to you peeing on me."

He roared with laughter, head thrown back, his deep voice booming as it shivered over her skin. "An' it's glad I am ye approve." He kissed her again, gently this time. "Risa, I love *you* an' only *you*. I don't see anyone else here," he insisted quietly but firmly.

She smiled like a satisfied cat, "Good, because you just broke a lot of hearts."

When the song was over, Killian gestured at Rena, who was sitting with Gabe. "We should talk about Rena an' what happened this morning." He pulled Risa outside to a small bench.

She tilted her head, subconsciously mimicking Killian's habit. "She'll get over it, just stop teasing her."

"Aye, no, I mean... I cornered her earlier when I couldn't find ye an' we talked it out. Risa, the reason she was so embarrassed is because, well... ye know, when guys wake up, sometimes we have an um... erection? This morning, I heard ye in the shower an' I was thinking about ye in there all wet an' slippery an'... Hmm. Never mind that," he blushed and shifted on the seat.

She stared at him knowingly, a feline smile curling her lips again.

"Anyway, let's just say I had one hell of a hard on for ye when she came in an' saw me. All of me, every last inch," he snorted.

Risa grinned wider, delighted in his discomfort. "And my those are a lot of inches."

He frowned, but the edges of his lips fought not to smile, "Not helping. I pointed out that she's seen naked men before when the dragons shift, so she knows it's natural an' nothing to be ashamed of. I told her I wasn't embarrassed, so she didn't need to be either. But it wasn't that, so much as she's never seen a man, um, excited before. Risa, she's never been with anyone that way, so she was ashamed by her reaction to me. She's a... uh... ye should talk to her, she has questions," he finished in a rush.

Marissa stared at him open-mouthed. It made sense. Rena was taken away as a child and held captive for most of her formative years. She only recently hit her adulthood. She probably had 'the talk' with Jorrie, but Risa wasn't sure how much they discussed. It wasn't something one just randomly asked another. She set her jaw. She wished she could kill the Shadow bastard that abused her sister. She was extra grateful now to those who did. She stood quickly, determined to find Rena, take her home, and talk to her.

Killian yanked her back down just as quickly. "For goodness' sakes, don't scare the poor wee thing." He shook his head. "She was embarrassed enough telling me about it. I think she only did it because I've been training her for the past three years, so she knows me. An' I made it clear I love ye an' consider her my little sister."

Marissa's eyes went glassy with unshed tears. "My God, Killian. Just when I think you can't get any more amazing. Thank you," she whispered. She kissed him and stood again, this time slowly, Killian rising with her. "Let's dance some more, then take our little sister home." She turned and paused, "Huh, that's weird. I thought Circe left to help Bridget. I swear I just saw her." She glanced back at Killian, who furrowed his forehead and shrugged.

Chapter 7

K ILLIAN WAS FAIRLY SURE he was going to die of embarrassment. He was sitting at the table having breakfast with Risa and
Rena the morning after the wedding. The two disappeared into Serena's
room to talk the night before, when they got back from the reception.
They talked for a long time, so long in fact, he'd fallen asleep. Now they
were both staring at him intently, and he was decidedly uncomfortable.
Finally, he set down his coffee cup and sighed. "Do I want to know?"
He rubbed his hands over his face, preparing for whatever onslaught was
coming.

Both of them laughed, the sweet tinkling sound not cheering him up
this time. He glared at Risa, as apparently, they'd decided to mess with him.
"So, you're after ganging up on me now?" he grumbled.

Risa giggled, "Sorry, my love, it was hard to resist."

He relaxed, hearing her call him her 'love' made him giddy, warmth
flooding through his body.

Rena spoke up then, "Um, Killian?"

"Yes, Rena doll?" He smiled at her gently.

She giggled too, "I just wanted to say, thank you, for caring about me the way you do. Also, I want to tell you how much I really enjoyed your performance last night. You have a beautiful voice! Why don't you ever sing? I would love to hear it again."

His face closed down as his smile fell flat and his eyes went hard.

Rena sat back, confused. "I... I'm sorry, Killian, I didn't mean..." she whispered.

He shook his head and forced a soft smile as he took her hands. "Rena, sweet sister, it's alright, I know ye didn't mean anything by it. I just don't care to sing in front of other people, bad associations," he told her. He patted her hand and nodded to reassure her he wasn't upset with her. Glancing over, he noticed Risa staring at him thoughtfully. He had a strong suspicion she wasn't letting that go. He smiled brightly, hoping to distract her. "By the way, Vaughn called. He got my car fixed, just a slipped hose. Can ye run me back to it so I can get home an' change clothes? I need to check on Malachi."

Risa narrowed her eyes and nodded slowly. She didn't say much on the drive to the office. It wasn't long, thankfully, since it was Sunday and traffic was light. He never was one to fill silence anyway, so he simply sat and stared out the window. They pulled into the lot, and she stopped next to his car. He gave her a quick smile, mumbling, "Thanks! I'll call ye later!" and hurried out of the vehicle.

"Killian," she called softly, seeing right through him.

He stopped and turned to face her, his stomach in knots, sour with anticipation.

She gazed at him, sadness in her eyes. "What aren't you telling me? We went from excited about being in love to awkward. Why?"

He sighed heavily and closed his eyes, bracing his palms on the roof of the car as he leaned against the open door. "Marissa, I know ye love me, an'

I believe it. But ye don't know all of me. Ye only know what you've seen since we met an' what I've shown ye. Keep in mind, I'm at ninety-nine years of a long life that I lived before I met ye. Not all of it was alone, though. I've been through some challenging times an' seen things, things that shape a man. It's only that we haven't talked about them yet. There are difficult answers, Risa. I'm just feeling some of it today. When you've been alone as long as I have, it's hard to suddenly share everything." He gazed at her, his eyes pleading, willing her to understand.

She nodded slowly, "I guess I can appreciate that. Killian, I do love you, and I want to know these things. Why have you been so alone? Why won't you sing? Why were you scared to tell me you love me? We have to start somewhere. Please don't shut me out. If this is going to work, I can't just love the *you* from the past six months, I need to love *all* of you."

He stared at her, then nodded at the inevitable. He could feel it coating his throat like a thick layer of acidic dread. "Come to my house then?"

Killian opened the front door, clicking his tongue, "C'mere, Malachi! Where are ye wee beastie?" He glanced around but didn't see him anywhere. Rolling his eyes, he thought, *should've gotten a dog*. He heard a sleepy chirp from his bedroom and found Malachi sprawled over his bed, lounging in a patch of sunlight. Malachi blinked his bright blue eyes and licked one paw before stretching and yawning at his housemate. Killian scratched the enormous cat between his ears and received a rumbling purr for his efforts.

Risa strolled in behind him. "That is still the biggest cat I've ever seen in my life. I don't know why you call him *wee*," she announced.

Killian chuckled. Malachi was a Maine Coone, one of the largest breeds of domestic cats in the world. He was the size of a medium dog and took up a lot of space. Hence why Killian bought a king-sized bed, so he would still have room to sleep.

Easing over to the cat, Risa laughed when he rolled on his back and stuck his paws in the air. She reached for his belly, going to give it a good rub, when Killian grabbed her hand. "It's a trap," he warned her.

She grinned and dug her fingers into the floofy belly of the beast. "No, it's not, Malachi wuvs me, don't you wittle baby!" she cooed. The cat mewled and squeezed his eyes at her, purring and making air biscuits with his paws.

Killian shook his head in disgust. "Traitor," he scolded the silly creature.

Risa laughed, the beautiful sound ringing like bells. Just then, the automatic feeder went off in the kitchen, and Malachi sprang from the bed, zooming away before either of them could blink. They both laughed this time, and Killian placed a gentle kiss on her forehead.

"Why don't ye go make yourself comfortable while I change, an' I'll be right back with ye, okay?" he murmured.

She nodded and sat on his bed.

He made a small face, wrinkling his nose. "I didn't mean there; maybe the living room or something?"

"Nope," she shook her head. "I'm perfectly happy right here," she grinned, patting the mattress beside her.

Smirking now, Killian pulled his shirt off slowly, stretching and flexing his arms.

She continued to smile innocently at him.

He unfastened his belt and pulled it through the buckle at a snail's pace. She didn't waver. He unzipped the jeans so slowly, each tooth on the metal zipper clicked loudly in the quiet room. The material bunched in his fingers, and he kept his eyes locked on hers, as the pants rode lower on his hips.

Her smile slowly dropped, her lips parting slightly, and she swallowed heavily.

A dark knowing smile curved one corner of his lips as he slid the jeans the rest of the way down and straightened, now only wearing his boxers.

Her gaze went hungry, running over his chest and arms, following his hand as he rubbed it lazily over his stomach and the well-defined muscles there. She traced her eyes down his lean hips to his strong legs and swallowed again.

Killian slowly moved closer and stood directly in front of her. Her face now level with his navel, her breath stirring the trail of silvery hair that disappeared into his waistband. He lifted her chin with one finger, and she met his eyes. "See something ye like?" he asked teasingly in a low, gravelly voice.

She nodded silently and licked her lips.

He bent down until they were face to face and whispered, "You're a naughty little thing, aren't ye, bad girl?"

She leaned forward and traced her tongue around the small ring on his lip before gently biting his jaw. "You have no idea," she whispered back.

He grabbed the back of her neck and yanked her against his body. He devoured her mouth and dragged her to her feet, pressing firmly against his chest. He came up for air and whispered, "Fuck, Risa!"

She dug her nails into his back, "I wish you would!"

His eyes flashed silver, and he followed up on her request, flinging her clothes off before pulling her down to the floor with him. Her screams of pleasure shattered the air, and he was glad his neighbors couldn't hear, or they might call the police.

They were lying on the floor, panting, when the cat strutted back into the room, heaved a sigh of disgust, and jumped on the bed, grumbling. She laughed, still a little breathless, "I don't know when I've ever felt so judged in my life."

"Aye, Malachi's good at being judgmental. It's a cat thing," he huffed out a wheezing laugh of his own.

She glanced at the large, fluffy beast, "Why Malachi?"

"Well, I saw him when he was but a kitten at a rescue. He reached out to me with his little paw, an' I just knew he needed to live here."

She shook her head, "No, I know how you picked him. I mean, why that name? It's a little... creepy."

He chuckled, "Well, he's a bit bossy an' runs a cult, so I named him after the child in that old movie, 'Children of the Corn'."

She raised her head and stared wide-eyed at the cat grooming his tail on the bed. "I'm never staying the night again," she whispered.

Killian leaned over and kissed her temple, "I was only kidding." He pulled her up and quickly kissed her again. "I'm really getting dressed now an' we'll talk, okay?"

She quickly agreed, searching for her own clothing while he took a shower.

Ten minutes later, they were sitting on the couch, his arm around her shoulders.

She leaned against his chest, tracing a finger over his heart. "Killian?" she inquired softly when it became apparent he wasn't saying anything soon.

He tightened his arm for a second before sucking in a deep breath. "Alright, so you're after knowing more about the history of Killian. Right." He fiddled with a stray thread on the hem of his shirt.

"Tell me more about it all. I thought I knew you, but there's still so much I really don't know, apparently." Her voice was firm but gentle.

He leaned his head back, closed his eyes and began to speak. She knew his parents were both silver wielders, Shannon and Fergus. But he never told her he had a younger sister named Molly, who was also a silver wielder. He talked about his childhood home and what growing up was like.

She listened in fascination to this man who was born long before anything digital, who lived in another country, but the way he described it was almost another world. She could almost see the verdant green landscape of his family home, so enchanting were his words. As he spoke, he relaxed and his accent became thicker, stronger, the way it does when one is homesick. She laughed at his boyhood escapades; she smiled at his childhood dreams and laid a gentle hand on his cheek when he spoke of his sister. "You miss her, don't you? And your parents, too."

He nodded shortly, his eyes going shiny.

"Can you call her? When was the last time you spoke?" Her question was light, but she was beginning to suspect there was more than missing Ireland in his thoughts.

He snorted, "The bratty lass called just last week, she keeps in touch with me. Calls to insult me, makes threats, tells me she misses me an' demands I come home to meet her husband an' child. I've a nephew now. She sent me a picture, cutest thing!" He pulled out his phone and showed her a picture of a baby, about five to six months old. He had silvery-blond hair and the cutest rosiest cheeks she'd ever seen.

"Oh, my goodness, Ki, he's adorable! Why haven't you gone to see him yet?" she gushed.

He shrugged. "Been busy."

"Doing what?" she demanded incredulously.

He glanced at her and smiled softly. "Working. Finding your family."

With a sharp intake of breath, she protested, "Oh Ki, no! Family is so important! You should go see them." She gripped his hands in hers, squeezing gently.

He nodded agreeably, but his expression reflected misery and pain. Her stomach clenched, her earlier suspicion blossoming into full-blown certainty. Something was wrong.

She gently grasped his chin, turning his face towards her, "How long has it been since you saw them?"

He mumbled something unintelligible, and she arched an eyebrow, making it clear he needed to repeat it. He cursed some word she didn't need a translation for, cleared his throat noisily, and grumbled, "Seventy years, give or take."

Risa gasped, "So long?" she shouted.

He gave a quick, miserable nod, wincing as she squeezed his hand hard, a pulse of magic slipping through, amplifying her strength. He pulled it loose, shaking it out.

"Why?" she quietly asked, stroking her fingers along his arm, "Did you have a falling out with them?"

His eyes flew to hers, startled, "No, not at all! I love my family, an' I miss them terribly!" His voice was thick now, emotion choking him.

She gestured for him to go on, as he obviously wasn't going to expand on it without encouragement.

"A moment, I'm needing a drink for this," he grunted as he stood and strode quickly to his kitchen.

She sat there, quietly surprised, as she didn't know Killian to be a big drinker. At least around her, he rarely indulged, and when he did, it was minimal.

He came back with a bottle of whiskey and two glasses, offering her one. She agreed silently, so he poured some for her, then filled his own. He promptly drained it and poured another, quickly draining that one, too.

"Killian?" she murmured, her voice reflecting the worry she was feeling, watching him trying to drown whatever sorrow was haunting him so deeply.

He stared at her, pain etched on his face and poured a third drink. This time, he sat back and held up the glass. Studying it. Contemplating the liquid as if it held the secrets he didn't want to reveal. He sighed and started again, "I didn't leave or stay away because of my family. I did because of my wife."

Risa sat u, gasping. "You're married?" she demanded, anger and betrayal warring with hurt in her heart over this seeming lie by omission. The edges of her world began to fray and unravel.

"Not anymore. I was," he murmured quietly as he shook his head.

She threw herself back on the sofa, leaning away from him. "Until you left her, ran away, hiding until you met me?" she snapped. Accusation colored her voice as she lashed out at his cowardly actions.

"No!" he roared, jumping to his feet, startling her. "She left *me!*" He slammed a fist against his chest and stared at her with tears in his eyes. "She broke my fucking heart, Risa, shattered it to pieces," his voice breaking. He stalked across the room and drained his drink. Glaring at the glass as silver sparks snapped from his hands, his grip tightened before smashing it against the wall with a yell full of fury and pain. He stood there and braced his arms on the fireplace mantel, hanging his head and breathing heavily. Blood dripped slowly, pattering on the stone hearth beneath him.

The shattered glass had sliced through his palm, but he ignored it as he worked to calm his ragged breathing. His shoulders shook visibly with the effort.

Chapter 8

MARISSA WATCHED KILLIAN FALL apart. He seemed so defeated, his mind in shambles. She felt a terrible shame burning through her veins like molten metal. She'd asked him to dredge this up, then jumped to conclusions without giving him a chance to explain. Again, she'd hurt him by her overreaction, like she did about his haircut, only this was much worse. She owed him a significant apology.

She stood and moved determinedly to his side. Gently, she rubbed his back, whispering, "I'm so sorry, Killian. I'm such an idiot, please, forgive me." She stood quietly, waiting for him, just letting him know she was there.

He finally straightened and turned to her, wiping his eyes with his non-injured hand, staring at her like he was lost. He shuddered, "Risa, I... how can ye think that of me? What have I ever done to make ye think I'm that heartless? It was the worst time of my life. I'm not that way. Aye, I'm quiet an' private, but I'm not a monster." His voice was low and sharp, full of disbelief.

"I know. I just... I feel awful that this is so painful for you and that I was jumping to conclusions. It wasn't fair, and I'm incredibly sorry. You're right. I should have known better. I don't think you're a monster at all. It caught me off guard, and I reacted badly. Please... Killian, I was very wrong. Can you forgive me?" She stared deep into his eyes that were filled with pain, holding her breath as she waited for his response.

He made a small soft noise, like he was choking back a sob, before he pulled her tightly to his chest. He rubbed his cheek on top of her head. "Risa, I do forgive ye. I understand how surprising that was. I didn't scare ye, did I?"

She shook her head, "No, Killian, you didn't scare me. Well, maybe a little because I've never seen you this angry before. But I'm not scared of *you*. I'm an ass. I didn't mean to hurt you like that. I mean it, Killian, I don't know what came over me. I should have let you explain first. Sometimes my mouth gets ahead of my brain."

He huffed a small, wry laugh. "Bound to happen eventually. It's why I've been in my self-imposed isolation. I figured if I didn't let anyone in, no one would hurt me ever again. Then I met this beautiful woman in front of me, an' I knew some things were worth risking yourself for." He led her back to the couch, so she sat again. He handed her the discarded glass, and she took a small sip.

"Please, Killian, tell me the rest? I promise, I'll be quiet and listen to all of it. I won't rush to conclusions," she offered quietly.

"Aye, I will. But I'll be right back, need to bandage this," he mumbled before hurrying off.

After he returned, he sat facing her and started his story again. When he was younger, he was selected for an arranged marriage with a woman from the next village over. It was an edict by the Dragon Council to keep their lines strong. She was a silver dragon, and it was meant to tie their two communities together since there were no dragons in his village and no wielders in hers. Out of the available men, she picked him. He was fascinated by her the moment they met. She was beautiful, kind, and claimed she was intrigued by him as well. They'd fallen in love, and soon the marriage wasn't just for duty but for affection. Or so he thought. Back then, he sang at taverns and clubs in the evenings to make extra money. He often wrote his own music, many of them love songs. She always begged him to keep those just for her alone.

After two years of being married, he asked her: Why weren't they mated yet? Why wouldn't she show him her dragon? She responded that he must not love her enough, or it would have happened already. He tried everything he could think of to prove his love to her and to make her realize they were meant to be together. After one particularly long day of traveling, he hurried home early to surprise her with a new song he'd written for her. He made it to the bedroom before he realized she wasn't alone. He found her in bed with another man. Not just any man, his best friend Padric, another wielder.

Risa gasped, covering her mouth with trembling fingers. The levels of cruelty compounding on one another were overwhelming. He lapsed into silence, so she took his hand in hers. A single tear rolled down his cheek, and she gently brushed it away with her thumb. "Killian," she whispered achingly, pain for him clear in her voice.

He shook his head and lifted her glass, taking a long drink but not finishing it the way he had earlier. Gazing at her, his expression was haunted, eyes full of betrayal at the memory. "She was seeing him behind my back for the previous six months. I was pathetic, I cried an' begged her to forgive me."

Surprised by this admission, Risa made a small noise of disbelief.

A small deprecating laugh slipped from his throat, "I was convinced I loved her. She claimed she loved me an' wanted me for her mate, but I didn't love *her* enough. She told me that over an' over 'til I believed it was my fault. I drove her away with my lack of feelings. I told her of the song I wrote for her, describing my love. She laughed; told me it was pathetic. That I should just give up on music, I'd no talent anyway. She wanted nothing further to do with me. She was going to mate Padric, my former friend." He finished the drink then and refilled the glass, handing it to her.

"That bitch!" Risa snapped with venom in her voice as she shook her head in anger.

Killian studied her thoughtfully, as if surprised by her reaction.

"She was totally gaslighting you. Using your emotions against you like a weapon," she explained, her eyes narrowed.

He nodded, "Aye, it took me a much longer time to figure that out, Risa. I was young, blind to the ways of the world. I was only a simple farm boy. She was a dragon. Exotic. Unattainable. The ultimate dream of any wielder, or so I thought." He continued his tale in a faint voice full of shame. The first two years after his wife left him, he drank himself into a stupor. He stopped using his powers. He stopped speaking. He stopped singing. He shut himself away from the world, a shell of a person.

Risa shuddered, biting her lip, "I can't imagine how painful it must have been."

"Then she came back," he announced flatly.

Risa's eyes widened; she shook her head.

Sighing, he explained, "She came back, apologized, begging for forgiveness. She made a terrible mistake. Padric wasn't her real mate, 'twas me all along. She claimed she was confused. I was stupid an' I let her back in, even though my family begged me not to. Even Vaughn warned me. I kept my suspicions, but was convinced I loved her still. In truth, I wanted so badly to have someone in my life, to be wanted by someone. I sobered up an' played the part of the loving husband. Then she started in again. Why wouldn't I tell her I loved her anymore? She couldn't admit it to me unless I told her first, an' we couldn't be mates if I didn't love her enough."

He shook his head. She continued with more demands about him proving himself to her first. A long year of misery later, she told him it was too late, and she shouldn't have come back. He filed for the final dissolution of their marriage, and it was done. After the two years of hell he went through the first time, he wasn't going to let it drag him down a second time. He stayed sober, but she kept appearing wherever he was. Complaining to his family, his few remaining friends, until he couldn't stand seeing her around and left. He fled to America, accepting an offer to work with his good friend, Vaughn Drake.

"I took my time, settling in, finding my new way." He stared blankly at the wall, not really seeing it. "I went back, after a year or so, to see my family. She immediately came 'round, pestering me, making sure I knew what I was missing an' that it was my fault. So, I ran. I left again, an' I haven't been back since."

Risa nodded; so much about him made sense now.

He took her hands in his, idly brushing his thumbs over her palms. "When I returned here, I vowed I wasn't going to let anyone in ever again. I stayed to myself, hiding away every part of me that was vulnerable. I learned to be observant, to watch. I simply lived each day from one to the next. That was my goal. Each day a challenge to make it through. I've been content an' thought I was happy. Until I met a lonely silver wielder who didn't even know who she was," he whispered and locked his haunted eyes with hers.

She smiled gently, "Killian, I know that was hard for you. Thank you for sharing your story with me. I love you, and I know you love me. I would never ask you to prove it because you do. Every time you look at me, no words needed."

He smiled back and brushed her cheek. "I understand. Because ye know what just I figured out? I never loved her. She was right. I loved the idea of her. I loved the idea of being her mate. But what I feel now? I never had anything even close to that for her. She didn't know that, of course, she was just using me. But even if she did, it still wouldn't have worked." He hummed low in his throat, embarrassed. "It's ashamed I am for my stupidity. Letting myself be manipulated like that." He stared deep into her eyes, clearly wanting her to understand.

She gazed at him shyly as she tilted her head, "So... you haven't been with anyone else since you left Ireland?"

He smirked, "I said I hadn't been in any relationships, not that I'd been a saint. I am a man after all. I don't mean to sound crass, but there was no shortage of lasses willing to warm my bed, even knowing it was only for a brief time. I've not accepted all the offers or kept company with many, though, mind ye. It's been a few years since the last. I was quite ready to be inside ye the night ye gave yourself to me," he grinned and studied her expression, slowly tracing her jaw with the pad of his thumb. "Ye cannot tell me ye were pure when we met." He arched an eyebrow at her when she cringed.

She shook her head quickly, her cheeks flushing pink. "No, I wasn't. But I didn't have a lot of boyfriends, so I worry sometimes I'm not — exciting — enough for you. Guys said I was pretty, but when they got to know me, they said I was a nerd or too flighty. I realize now a lot of that was my powers trying to break through the barrier, but nothing more than a few months long. Most of my relationships didn't get to the physical phase. Those that did, well, they left soon after. I wasn't interesting, I guess," she blushed harder at her lack of experience compared to his.

He ran his fingers through her hair and toyed with the ends. "*Mo stor*, you're not a nerd or flighty. You're a highly creative, amazing lover. The things ye do to me are incredible. My love, a silver goddess, an' the sole reason my heart beats anew, making each day better than the last." He glanced up at her, his hazel eyes twinkling.

She smiled softly. "Killian Brennan, that's quite possibly the most romantic thing anyone's ever said to me. I don't know what her name was, but she didn't deserve you."

"Kiera," he whispered.

She tilted her head questioningly.

"A name I swore to never speak again or even think, but there it is. I promised a lot of things when I was younger. I'm letting go of some of them. But one thing I swore, that I don't intend to break, is she will *never* be in my life again."

Risa nodded, she was glad to hear that. Although, if she ever met the bitch, she would sure give her a piece of her mind. *Dragon or not, that trashy ho needs to be taught a lesson.*

Killian chuckled then, a warm sound that wrapped around her like a soft, cozy blanket. "My, my, Marissa. I don't know what's going through that pretty head of yours, but I'd hate to be on the receiving end of it."

She barked a short laugh, a wicked grin spreading across her lips. "You're right!" She tapped his nose and leaned into him, her smile softening. "Killian, I'm going to ask you something, and it's okay if you want to tell me no. I know it's hard for you, and you've already done a lot of hard things today, which I appreciate. But would you consider..." she paused.

He stared at her warily, tensed like an animal backed into a corner.

Taking a deep breath, she continued, "Would you consider singing a song to me? I loved hearing you last night." She finished her request in a near whisper.

Sitting back, he studied her quietly.

She worried her lower lip with her teeth, afraid he might get angry at her request.

"I've realized how stupid I was to stop making music. I do enjoy it. I've even learned recently, others enjoy it as well. I know everything else Kiera told me was a lie, so why should I still believe that one?" He pulled her to her feet and held her close in his arms as he began to dance with her, singing *Unforgettable*.

She sighed and laid her head on his chest. His voice was like velvet and sin, or a comforting fire on a wintry night. It wrapped around her, warming her from head to toe. When the song ended, he cupped the back of her head and tilted her chin up before he softly kissed her. "I will sing for ye any time ye want, my love."

They stood there for a while longer, just holding each other. At Malachi's plaintive meow, she noticed the shadows growing longer and realized they'd been talking for hours. "Wow, it's getting late!" she exclaimed, surprised.

He stared at her, his expression unreadable as he absently scratched the cat's ears. "Stay," he whispered, "Stay with me tonight. Risa, today brought back a lot of bad memories, an' I don't want to be alone with them. Please, don't go." He brushed her hair behind her ear and placed a tender kiss on her temple.

"Of course I'll stay," she nodded, "But you have to feed me!" she added as her stomach rumbled.

"I would be happy to," he laughed, the sound light-hearted once more. He led her to the kitchen and swung her up to sit on the counter while he prepared their meal.

She loved watching him cook. She guessed when you were ninety-nine and lived mostly alone, you learned to do things like that. She was terrible in the kitchen, so was happy to let him do it. The first time she cooked for him, he'd bravely eaten it, but she could tell it was awful, and he was humoring her. After she threw down her fork and declared it a disaster, he grinned, saying, "Thank the gods, let's order a pizza, my treat." She smiled now, laughing at the memory.

He grinned at her; loving the sound of her laugh. like bells ringing, he always claimed. "Ye know, if ye didn't look so much alike, I still would have known Rena was your sister just by the laugh alone."

Laughing again, she nodded. "That reminds me! We never talked about what we discovered on Friday when you broke that most recent spell!"

"Ye mean when I broke myself," he wrinkled his nose as he sighed.

She jumped down and wrapped her arms around him. "Thank you for trying so hard to help with this, but please don't ever do that again."

As they ate, she updated him with what they learned while he was sleeping off his magical concussion. Dorothy was the woman who took Marissa to the adoption agency. She claimed she was a family friend, and the girls' parents were deceased. Risa vaguely remembered the woman from before, so it was possible she was telling the truth. They still couldn't figure out why she didn't put all three girls together or if she was the one who placed the spell. Liam and Marco were tracking her down so they could ask. There was a meeting already scheduled for the next day to discuss what, if anything, the guys found and plan their next steps.

He studied her consideringly, and inquired, "Risa, I know ye don't need a job right now, but have ye given any more thought to accepting Vaughn's offer?"

"It's a sweet offer," she smiled gently, "But I don't want to take on that job just because he feels he owes me. What happened in Miami wasn't his fault."

"Vaughn doesn't hire people for pity," he replied with a shrug, "He offered to help ye financially until ye could get on your feet because ye were displaced by our siege. The job itself he offered because of your talent. Our art director moved to Fiji or something to 'find himself, '" Killian smirked, making air quotes. "I think he accidentally caught Bridget zapping Liam one day an' it freaked him out. But with your artistic eye an' talent, you'd be fantastic. We could use a fresh perspective."

She sat back, contemplating his explanation. Vaughn recently offered her a job as Director of Art and Animation for his gaming company. The salary and benefits were outstanding, and it seemed like something she would enjoy. She hesitated because she wanted to have a job that she merited, not a pity offer. She believed Killian, though. He'd worked for Vaughn at various companies for almost sixty years; he would know. Killian was the Senior Director of Software Development at Cloud Warrior Gaming. He oversaw the group that wrote the code for the games they made. They could work together to an extent. Risa smiled, "In that case, I think I'll take him up on that."

"Just watch out for Marty," he grinned, then shook as laughter trickled out, "He thinks he's God's gift to animators. He's good, but sometimes he comes up with things that just don't work. It's not like we can magic these scenes together."

Her jaw dropped, "Do you..." she trailed off with her eyebrows raised.

He snorted and rolled his eyes, "No, Risa, we actually create them by hand. We take inspiration from our world, but the rest is simply good old-fashioned technology."

Chapter 9

THAT NIGHT, AS THEY lay in his bed, Malachi curled at their feet, Killian stroked her hair and placed kisses along her shoulder. "Marissa," he whispered, "I love ye so much."

She turned to him and smiled, "I love you, too, Killian."

He returned the smile shyly, "This bed feels so empty without ye in it. I know this may seem sudden with us only just admitting how we feel, but... would ye consider living here with me? Or we can find another place if ye don't like my house. Rena can come, too. I've plenty of room for her. I just... want ye here with me an' it would be easier on us going back an' forth to each other's places an' —"

"Shh," she placed a finger over his lips. "I would love to come live here with you and Malachi. As long as he doesn't try to sacrifice my soul to some corn god."

"No guarantees," he murmured as the cat yawned, showing his fangs.

When the alarm went off the next morning, Risa groaned and covered her head with a pillow. A pair of strong arms went around her as Killian whispered in her ear, "Good morning, my silver goddess. If you're going to take that job, ye better get used to waking up early again." He placed a gentle kiss on her sleep-softened lips.

She stretched, murmuring, "I won't mind it if I get to wake up like this."

He smirked and pulled her warm body under his, wedging himself between her thighs. "How about this?" he asked, slipping just inside of her. She gasped, and he covered her mouth with his own, surging forward. They made love gently until they were both shaking.

She sighed against his shoulder, "Especially that," her voice breathy and low.

"Shower?" he asked innocently.

She grinned, "Are we conserving water?"

He laughed, "That's my bad girl." By the time they were both dressed and had coffee, they were running out the door laughing, carefree and light.

Until they reached their cars. Marissa had a flat tire. He gave her his keys and shooed her off, reassuring her he didn't mind changing the tire. He watched the taillights disappearing down the road before he turned to her car, rolling up his sleeves. Crouching down, expecting to find a nail or other object in the tire, he noticed the valve stem was severed, and frowned. *Vandalism? But who would...* He heard a throaty, feminine laugh and caught a glimpse of chestnut brown hair from the corner of his eye. He turned quickly, frowning as his stomach clenched. There was no one there. "What the hell?" he whispered. *Maybe it's time to get a security camera.*

"I don't understand," complained the man with the scraggly brown ponytail, crouching near a woman with long silvery-blonde hair. They watched Killian from behind a bush across the street. "He's right there, and alone. Why can't we just grab him?"

"Patience," she cautioned, "We still need the other ones, ye know that. If we take him now, they'll close ranks an' that will delay us further. Ye don't want to face *her* wrath, do ye?" She smirked knowingly. "Ye know what will happen if ye make her, or me, angry, don't ye?" she cooed and dragged a long nail down his pale cheek.

Flinching away in disgust, he merely nodded and turned to leave.

The silver-haired woman turned back to Killian as he studied the surrounding area, smiling to herself. "Soon, you'll pay soon."

When Killian strolled in late, which never happened, his team appraised him with knowing smiles and began cheering. He spun around in confusion, surely, they weren't congratulating him on changing a tire.

"Way to go, Killer!" one voice called.

He stared at them, certain they'd lost their minds. "What for?" he asked slowly, warily.

"Your debut single, man!" another person shouted.

He glanced around, shaking his head, still confused.

One of them took pity, "Killian, dude, you're going viral! People posted videos of you singing with Jorrie at the wedding. It's blowing up!"

Killian stared in disbelief at the man's phone. As he claimed, videos of Killian and Jorrie singing were on YouTube with captions like, 'Unknown artist dueting with Still Waters' singer' and 'New singer for Still Waters?'. His jaw dropped. He scrolled down and saw one video was already close to two million views. He sat heavily on a table nearby. His skin flushed hot and cold all over at the same time as his stomach churned. He swallowed hard, turning his head stiffly as he took in the concerned faces around him.

"Killian, you okay, man?"

He stared at his employee. *Edgar, worked here two years, married, one son,* he thought, focusing on something more than the panic oozing up his throat. He peeked at the phone again, and his gaze focused on the word 'Unknown'. He sucked in a deep breath, *well, at least I have that.* He handed the phone back and stood. "Okay, alright, ha, ha, back to work ye lunatics!" he laughed in what he hoped was a convincing manner.

Several of the men started singing, badly, off-key and warbly. He laughed again, genuinely this time. "Guys, seriously, knock it off." Shouts of encore followed him to his office, where he dropped heavily into his chair, scrubbing his hands over his face.

He logged into his computer and got to work, hoping the feral call of ogres and goblins would distract him from this new predicament. He was deep in the inner workings of the coding when he detected a sweet scent that soothed his frayed nerves. He glanced up and noted Risa leaning in his doorway, arms crossed under her breasts, smiling. He arched an eyebrow in inquiry.

She waved a folder, trilling in a sing-song voice, "It's official."

He hurried over, kissing her lightly on the cheek. "When do ye start?" he asked excitedly.

Vaughn appeared behind her, grinning, "Killian, I see you've heard the news. Ms. Marissa Thompson has graciously accepted the position of Director of Art and Animation. I'm sure I can count on you to show her around and introduce her to the team?" Killian nodded quickly, and Vaughn smirked. "I'm sure you also remember that we have a strict non-fraternization policy here."

Killian's face fell, and his mouth dropped open.

Vaughn laughed, "I'm kidding, just keep it PG, okay?"

"How's Bridget? An' your little one?" Killian snorted, shaking his head at his friend, amused that he fell for Vaughn's joke.

Vaughn's face lit up with pride, his grin stretching from ear to ear. "She's great! And Connor is wonderful as well! Look!" He showed them pictures of his newborn son. They oohed and aahed appropriately. The baby was adorable with his chubby cheeks and a full head of black hair like his father. Vaughn smiled gently at the picture. "In fact, I'm just here for our meeting today, then I'm going back home to be with them. Give Risa a tour and meet us in the conference room in an hour?" Killian nodded and Vaughn wandered away, still smiling down at the picture of the baby on his phone.

Killian shook his head, studying Risa thoughtfully as she grinned after Vaughn. She turned his world upside down just like Bridget had turned Vaughn's life around. It was a good thing. He grabbed her, kissing her passionately in front of his entire team. He leaned back and grinned at her. She blushed at the public display.

He turned towards his staff, amused, as they were staring at him in curiosity and awe. He understood their confusion. In the span of three days, he'd changed his appearance drastically and was seen on multiple occasions doing things out of character for him. Including making out with a beautiful woman in the middle of the workday.

One came up and poked him in the shoulder, his eyes widened in exaggeration. "Are you really Killer?" he stage-whispered dramatically.

Killian rolled his eyes, "Aye, an' I can still fire your ass if ye don't shut it," he snapped grumpily. The rest of the team snickered.

"Killer?" Risa repeated curiously, fighting back the smile curling her lips.

He groaned, "Some of these guys think they're comedians an' gave me that nickname after one of the ladies in HR was in a panic over a spider in the breakroom. I killed it for her, an' it's stuck with me since."

Siobhan trotted by calling, "Hey K-Star," as she plopped down in a chair and set her coffee on the desk. Another bout of laughter rippled through the team.

Killian pointed at them menacingly, "Don't even *think* about it," he warned them.

"Too late!" one hollered back.

Risa leaned towards Killian, murmuring, "I didn't realize Siobhan worked directly for you. I knew she worked here, but she's your employee?"

He nodded, "She's on my team, that's how we know each other so well." He turned towards the group again. "Alright, everyone, listen up, this is Marissa Thompson, an' as of this morning, she's the new Director of Art and Animation. She'll be treated with more respect than ye show me, understood?"

Thumbs up and nods of agreement followed until, "Do we get to kiss her, too?"

Siobhan slapped the man on the back of the head.

Killian narrowed his eyes, "Not if ye value your life." The others oohed at the threat, and Killian smiled, "But I'll kiss her all I want, because she's my girlfriend. So back off."

Risa laughed, "It's true, but please, call me Risa. I look forward to working with you all!" The calls of welcome followed as he steered her down the hall to the next group.

It went on like that for most of their allotted time, introducing her to the various groups and important personnel. He announced her to her staff, and they hit it off well. Finally, he showed her to her new office, which was conveniently just down the hall from his own. She exclaimed joyfully about the space, enjoying how airy and light it was. She ran her fingers over the desk and the sleek computer set up there. Turning, her eyes landed on the lightbox table set up on one side and squeaked a little in glee. She was really excited now.

She turned towards Killian, where he was leaning against the doorframe, watching her intensely. She gave him a quick, nervous smile, and he smiled back, but in the way a wolf smiles at a lamb.

He slowly straightened and stalked towards her, shutting the door behind him with a decisive snap.

She backed away without realizing it until she came to a jolting stop against the desk behind her. The edge of the cherry wood surface was now digging into her thighs.

He pressed his body firmly against hers and took her face tenderly in his hands. "This place suits ye," he whispered, then laid his lips on hers, kissing her until she was breathless.

She moaned, then pulled back. "Vaughn said keep it PG," she reminded him, slightly dizzy from the desire pulsing from him.

He groaned, a deep, frustrated sound that made her grin.

She leaned forward and licked his lower lip, toying with the little ring there. He loved it when she did that, and she knew it. She felt him go rigid against her hips right before he pulled away from her.

"Not fair!" he complained with a grin.

She grinned back, knowing he was extremely turned on and there wasn't a thing he could do about it.

"Ye evil woman," he laughed, pressing a hand over his groin and wincing. "If I'd known you'd like that ring so much, I'd have gotten more of them sooner. Ye know lass," he murmured, stepping back into her, "There's — *other* — things I can get pierced," he whispered in her ear, letting his accent deepen, dropping his voice. "I hear it can make intimacy, much... more... intense."

Her jaw dropped, and she stared at him as he laughed low, a satisfied chuckle now that he'd evened the score.

He winked and sauntered off to his office. "Conference room in five," he called to her over his shoulder.

Marisa spent most of those five minutes fantasizing about what other piercings Killian meant. She shivered and grabbed her things, hurrying to the conference room. She saw Killian was already there, speaking quietly to Siobhan about a project they were working on. Liam was there, too, leaning over a map with Vaughn. They all glanced up when she came in and greeted her, Killian with heat in his eyes. She murmured hello, hurrying to sit across the table, not trusting herself at the moment.

Rena was next in the room, followed by Marco. Risa chuckled when her sister ran to her.

"Well?" Rena asked breathlessly.

Risa smiled, "It's a done deal!"

Jumping up and down, Rena gave her a hug, squealing, "Congrats, Risa!"

Liam glanced over curiously, an inquiring hum as he studied them.

Vaughn answered his question, announcing with a smile, "Risa accepted my offer to be our new Director of Art and Animation. We're excited to have her on the team!"

Liam groaned in disgust and shook his head.

Risa stared at Liam in surprise; it wasn't the reaction she expected.

"Sorry, Risa, nothing against you," Liam smiled apologetically. "It's just getting really cozy around here. First, Vaughn and Bridget, then Marco and Siobhan, now you and K-Star. Ugh."

Killian sprang to his feet, startling the others. "Do *not* call me that, dragon," he spat out the last word like a curse.

Liam growled as he surged to his feet as well, flames filling his eyes.

Killian's eyes lit up silver, magic snapping along his chest in silver sparks. It was like a small fireworks show exploding around his body. Everyone in the room gasped at the display.

Vaughn stood quickly then. "What the hell, Liam?" he roared, flames in his own eyes. They both sat but continued to glare at each other. "Killian, what has gotten into you?" Vaughn demanded, startled by his friend's uncharacteristic outburst.

Risa studied the others as tension built in the room. If Vaughn was surprised by this behavior, it was worth noting.

Siobhan spoke up, drawling lazily, "It would seem my idiot of a brother has once again inserted his head up his ass and decided to wear it as a hat."

Liam shot her a dirty look, snarling quietly, but Vaughn waved for her to continue.

She leaned back and outlined the stunt Liam pulled at the wedding after Vaughn left to take Bridget home. She congratulated Killian on a job well done and for stepping up, considering Liam put him on the spot. Pulling out her phone, she showed Vaughn how videos of the event were posted online and going viral. In the last few hours, the views had increased by another half million. The comments ranged from marriage proposals to people speculating he was joining Still Waters. Most people wanted to know who he was and where they could hear more of him.

Liam pointed out it was all positive, "See, Ki? They love you. What's the big deal?"

Killian's gaze was thunderous. He slowly stood and gritted through his teeth, "I. Don't. Want. This. I've never wanted this. Get it through your thick skull, ye overgrown lizard!" He slammed his fist on the table. "I've my reasons for staying hidden an' anonymous an' they're *my* reasons. My own personal reasons, an' ye had no right to do that. None." He closed his eyes and rolled his neck, then his shoulders, as silver sparks snapped around his upper body.

His eyes flew open, solid silver, as he yelled, "My life is under a fecking microscope. All morning, I heard it from my team, an' ye think it's going to get any better? Ye manky arsehole, I thought ye were better than that. I meant what I said that night, dragon. But out of respect for Vaughn an' Siobhan, I cannot kill ye yet." He paced behind the table, breathing deep, trying to calm himself. Silver lines arced across his body again, only this time, he couldn't pull them back. A bolt of magic flew from him, scorching the table. "Fuck!" he shouted, then stormed out of the conference room.

They all sat in stunned silence at this uncharacteristic display. Killian was the quiet one, the calm one who didn't yell or shout. Not so today.

Vaughn turned his steely gaze to Liam, who stared open-mouthed at the door. "Liam!" he growled, dragging the name out while smoke billowed from his nostrils.

Risa stood. "Vaughn," she called sweetly as he turned to her, "May I start tomorrow? I have some personal affairs to get in order before I can become an official employee."

Vaughn nodded slowly, confusion bunching his eyebrows together as his frown deepened.

She angrily strode over to Liam and poked him in the chest. "How dare you! Do you have any idea what you've done to him? What he's spent the last seventy years trying to handle? He's right, you're an asshole." Her fist sparking silver, she punched his nose as hard as she could.

Liam yelped and simply stood there. Staring at her in shock, stunned as blood began to drip down his face.

"Listen closely, Liam. I love him. And you better remember from now on, you fuck with him, you fuck with me. And two silver wielders against one dragon? Try me, Liam, just try me," she snapped as she followed after Killian.

Chapter 10

RISA TRACKED KILLIAN DOWN outside by the pond at the back of the complex. He wasn't sure how she knew where to find him, but it was his go-to place when he needed quiet. He sat on a bench, head in his hands, staring at the grass. She sat quietly and placed her palm on his thigh, not saying anything, just letting him know she was there when he was ready.

He finally took her hand in his, but noticed her wince as he squeezed it. He studied her fingers, and his gaze snapped to hers. "Risa, darling, what happened?" he asked in a deceptively calm, low voice as he studied her scraped knuckles and the bruise forming over the tender skin there. His magic thrummed in his veins, ready to end whoever hurt her.

"I may have, um... well... I punched something," she offered meekly.

He narrowed his eyes. "What did ye punch?"

"Liam's nose," she grinned, "Fairly sure I broke it, too."

Staring at her incredulously for a moment, his jaw working side to side, Killian threw back his head and laughed. Hard. The remaining tension and magic drained from him completely as he relaxed. He pulled her to his chest, murmuring, "Gods, I love ye so much." He kissed her temple. They sat there for a few minutes, leaning on each other, and he sighed before asking, "So, how much trouble are we in with Vaughn?"

"Honestly? None, I think," she shook her head.

He snorted in disbelief. "I threatened to kill his godson, made a scene, then ye punched another employee, an' Vaughn's not mad?"

"I asked him if I could start tomorrow before I did it," she smirked. "He already agreed, so technically, I haven't punched a *co-worker* yet. Just a smart-mouthed dragon who had it coming. Besides, Vaughn was really pissed at Liam. Like, smoke billowing, growling, pissed. He was yelling at him when I stormed out."

Killian shook his head, "Ye really are something else, my love. But I guess we better go back in." He glanced behind her. He saw another woman with her same silvery-blonde hair, dancing around, humming in the trees. He was startled at first, then shook his head, realizing it was only Circe. The strange old dragon had a tendency to wander and show up in the weirdest places. He let out a slow breath, relieved there was an explanation for this sighting.

As they made their way towards the conference room, hand in hand, they found Liam leaning against the door frame of Killian's office. He held a bloody cloth to his nose. Killian narrowed his eyes when he caught sight of the dragon.

Liam straightened, holding his hands up in a surrender pose. "Can I see you two in the office, please?" he asked politely.

Killian sighed and nodded, then sat behind his desk, pulling Risa in beside him.

The green dragon stood awkwardly after he closed the door.

Risa glared menacingly.

Liam shuffled his feet around for a moment, then sighed. "Shit, you guys, I'm really sorry. I had no idea this was going to blow up like this. I didn't realize you were staying in the background on purpose, Killian. I thought you were just shy. I guess I haven't been paying attention. I've been doing that a lot lately. I'm sorry again. I want you to know, I didn't mean anything malicious behind it. I was really impressed by your voice, and I knew we needed someone in a pinch. I should have asked you first and not put you on the spot like that. I definitely didn't think it was going to go freaking viral! I promise you that was not my intention, and I don't know what else to say except, I'm sorry." He stared at them with a hopeful look. "Please, forgive me?"

Killian sighed and rubbed a hand over his face. "Liam, I know I've not been the most outgoing or forthcoming about my personal life, but that's what it is, my personal life. I've my reasons as I said, an' I know ye couldn't have anticipated the outcome of it. I get that. Just don't rub it in, fair? And *never* put me on the spot like that again."

Liam nodded quickly, then winced as he tenderly touched his nose.

Killian toyed with his lip ring for a moment, then grinned, "Damn Risa, ye clocked him fine. Do ye forgive him, love?" He turned to her, a tender smile curving his lips now.

She studied Liam before sighing, "Why don't you let Siobhan fix that for you?"

Liam blushed, glancing at his feet as he dragged a toe over the carpet like a child, embarrassed. "Yeah, well, she refused, and Vaughn said she shouldn't do it even if she was willing. Said it's my fault for sticking my nose in other people's business, and I had to wait for it to heal on its own. Sucks, but still faster than a human."

Risa grinned now, "Since Killian forgives you, I forgive you as well. But I meant what I said. Any insult to him, is an insult to me, and you do not want our combined power on your ass, dragon." Her eyes flared silver for a second, and Liam held up his hands.

"Duly noted. Jeez, you guys are scary as fuck when you're riled, you know that?" Liam shook his head.

The two wielders laughed, and Liam joined them. He held out his hand, and Killian shook it. Then he kissed Risa's hand gently where her knuckles were scraped. "C'mon, Siobhan will heal that."

Back in the conference room, Siobhan healed Risa's hand. With a heavy sigh of disgust, she grudgingly healed Liam's broken nose as well, after Risa begged her. His natural dragon healing would've taken care of it eventually, as he mentioned, but something broken took longer to heal than a cut or scratch. Risa didn't want him to be in pain anymore since she and Killian forgave him. Liam thanked her graciously and took his seat, his expression reflective and stoic.

Vaughn rolled his eyes. "Okay, if we're done with the drama, I'd like to get back home to my wife and newborn son?" Smoke still trickled from one nostril, a muscle twitched in his jaw, and flames danced in his eyes. It was clear to everyone that keeping the black dragon from his baby was dangerous for everyone, no matter how close they were. They all nodded, eager to move forward. Satisfied they were sufficiently cowed, Vaughn turned to Marco and inclined his head, indicating he should start.

Marco quickly pulled up images on the large screen at the other end of the room. Flashing onto the thin material were pictures of three little girls. The images were faded and time-worn, but still captured the silvery-blonde hair and cherubic smiles of the sisters. Their arms thrown around each other's shoulders, showing a carefree, happy family not yet torn asunder. A simpler time before their lives became shrouded in mystery, intrigue, and in Serena's case, pain. Rena shivered quietly as she took in her oldest sister's face for the first time in years.

Risa stood and slowly moved towards the screen, as if compelled. Reaching out a trembling hand, her fingers lightly brushed the image of her sister. Tears began streaming like a waterfall down her face, dripping steadily onto the carpet beneath her feet. "Isabella," she whispered thickly. She turned to Killian, and he stood, holding out his arms for her. She ran to him and buried her face against his shoulder. He held her while she sobbed, gut-wrenching heartache pouring from deep within.

Killian's own shoulders shook, so he began crooning an Irish lullaby to her. He glanced over and, seeing Rena crying too, motioned for her to join them. She ran, throwing herself into his embrace. He placed his cheek on her head, continuing to sing softly as he held them both.

Vaughn's face softened, and Siobhan surreptitiously wiped a few tears away. Even Liam swallowed hard and rubbed his hands over his face.

Marco stared at his prickly mate in astonishment, then spoke quietly. "We were able to retrieve these pictures from Dorothy Cedars. She lives in a town in France called Crozon. She confirmed she brought Marissa to the adoption agency in Florida. Apparently she took all three girls to different agencies to separate them. Your parents were targeted by the Shadow Claw, as we suspected. Dorothy was a friend of the family and was afraid the people who were responsible for your parents' deaths would come after you three. So, she split you up. Rena went to a place in Spain, which is where we think Arturo found her. Marissa obviously was adopted in Florida."

"We know what agency Isabella went to, but the trail is cold there. They refuse to speak to anyone who isn't a family member. Risa, Rena, we may need to send you there to see if they'll talk to you," Liam added.

Risa nodded; she would go anywhere for her sister. She went cold all over and stared at Vaughn in dismay. She was starting a new job; she couldn't go now.

Vaughn smiled gently. "Go, Risa. In fact, all of you go. Find Isabella and reunite your family. The work will be here when you get back. You have my plane for as long as you need it."

Rena ran and hugged him, hard, Risa right behind her.

He hugged them both in return, his rumbling dragon purrs a comforting sound. They each kissed him on his cheeks, and he wiped away his tears. Having children of his own made him sentimental. The fierce black dragon was a marshmallow these days. "Okay, that's settled. I'm going home to see my own family." Vaughn sniffled and turned, a silly grin softening the sharp angles of his face.

"Um, sir?" Liam called tentatively.

Vaughn turned back, arching an eyebrow at him.

"Which one of us is going? Marco or me?"

"Both of you are going," Vaughn replied, "Shepard's going to step in and cover for a bit. Apparently, he needs a break from drumming and traveling. Jack's got Chesapeake now, and Davis is helping. I hope. With my luck, the twins will raise all kinds of hell. Fortunately, I'm only a phone call away." He shook his head, grinning ruefully.

Liam's face lit up, a huge smile stretching his mouth, "You got it, boss; I won't let you down." He turned to the sisters, "None of you!"

Risa smiled gratefully at Liam. He might be silly sometimes, but he was loyal and big-hearted. She knew he would work tirelessly on their behalf. He really was a wonderful man, and she enjoyed his friendship. She turned to Marco. "Dorothy's still alive?"

Marco nodded, "She is, and she would very much like to see you."

"Yes, I'd like to visit her if we could. Find out more about our parents, how she's connected, and if she knows about the spell on me and Rena."

Vaughn agreed; he recommended they go there first. He told them to clear their calendars for the next few weeks; they would leave in the morning. "Okay, now I'm really leaving. Good luck!" He hurried out before anyone else could stop him.

Rena slipped her hand into Risa's. "I'm scared," she whispered.

Risa belatedly remembered Serena didn't go on any trips or missions. The only travel experience she had was of being captive, then her rescue. She was still extremely nervous about leaving the safety of her surroundings. "Do you want to stay here, Rena?" she asked gently.

The young wielder nodded and bit her lip, her eyes downcast. It was clear she wasn't ready yet, but felt guilty for admitting it.

Killian murmured, "Rena doll, it's alright then, we understand. This is a big trip. In fact, since you're going to stay, I need a favor. One I don't trust just anyone to do, maybe ye can help me out?"

Rena gazed at him in curiosity, nodding slowly.

"I'm after needing someone to care for Malachi. He gets lonely an' needs someone to feed him an' give him fresh water. He likes scratching right under his chin an' between his ears. Someone also needs to look after my house, bring in mail, water plants, things like that. Can I impose on ye for that?" He knew Rena was hooked as soon as he said Malachai; she loved the enormous cat.

Risa added, "Rena, Killian asked me to move in with him. He invited you as well if you'd like. I'm going to do it, Rena; I want to spend my life with him. Why don't you think about it while we're gone?"

Rena smiled in relief. She hugged them both, "I'm happy for you two! Maybe I can work on packing some of your things and taking them over while you're gone?"

"That would be wonderful," Risa exclaimed gratefully.

Killian studied the young woman. "Ye could use some help with that. Gabriel is home for the summer, why don't ye call him to help ye? I know he'd be happy to do it."

Risa grinned at Killian. He was so obviously trying to set her sister up with Gabe, and she admitted the two were cute together. She didn't know Gabe that well, but knew he was Bridget's son and often came in to help Killian's team when he was home from college. He knew Gabe better, and as protective of Rena as he was, she knew Killian wouldn't suggest this if Gabe would mistreat her.

He quickly texted Gabe letting the young man know the plan as well. He got an enthusiastic reply in return. Killian turned to Risa, "I've some things to wrap up here. Do ye want to pack an' meet me at my house, our house, later?" he smiled.

"Yeah, I'll do that," she answered softly, "And meet you at our house after you get off work. And I'll grab some dinner for us, so you don't have to cook. And you don't have to suffer mine."

He pulled her close, "Maybe you'll let me teach ye," he murmured against her lips.

"I may be a hopeless cause, but I'm willing to learn," she giggled.

Siobhan sighed, "You guys are so cute!" a wistful note in her voice.

Killian stared at her, surprised.

Noticing everyone was looking at her the same way, Siobhan rolled her eyes. "Guys, I don't kick puppies, contrary to popular belief. I'm just happy for you all. Killian's a great guy, and he deserves happiness. Risa, you're a sweet person, and I'm relieved he's got you, okay? Stop staring at me like I'm an alien!" She stomped out, cursing under her breath.

Liam snorted, "And there she is."

They were still discussing their plans when the power went out for the whole building. Calls of surprise and shouts of alarm filtered into the hallways. Muffled curses as people fumbled for doors in the darkened areas, searching for exits and windows. The glow of phone flashlights soon filled the space like a drunken disco as everyone milled about in confusion.

Marco bolted from the conference room with an order for them to stay put while he checked the electrical room. After a few minutes, emergency power kicked in and cheers of relief replaced the concerned murmurs. Marco reappeared with a puzzled expression. "I need to check the cameras," he told Liam quietly, "Someone broke into the riser room and shut down the power, disconnected the emergency backups. Nothing permanent, but strange anyway. Weirdest thing though, I think it was a woman, because I smelled perfume."

Chapter 11

"IT'S WEIRD TO FEEL like I've never been to France, even though I guess I used to live there," Risa gushed excitedly. "Like every good little artist, I've always dreamed of going to Paris and the Louvre, of seeing the countryside. Versailles." She sighed wistfully, "But I'll settle for Crozon."

Killian smiled softly at her enthusiasm. "Well, ye never know where this will take us. Maybe we'll see it after all. How about, if we don't make it to any of those places this trip, I've got plenty of vacation time, I'll take ye." The smile that lit up her face was worth taking her any place she wanted to go.

"What about you? Where would you like to go?" she asked.

He tilted his head, staring at her thoughtfully. He hadn't really thought about it before. He'd seen a lot in his years working for Vaughn, and like Liam, there weren't many places he hadn't been. But no one ever asked him before. He hesitated, then replied, "Well, I've seen most of the world, so I guess the place I'd most like to go is back to Ireland to see my family."

Her lips curled into a sweet curve that filled him with peace as she whispered, "Well, that's also on my bucket list of places to see. Let's do that first."

He kissed her lightly, his heart beating a rapid tattoo in his chest. "You're too good to me," he told her.

"Never," she replied.

Siobhan flopped down next to them and grumbled something about the rough flight. "Pilot must be new," she complained.

Killian stared at Siobhan consideringly, until she squirmed.

"Stop it, Ki," she snapped. "You know I hate it when you do that."

He grinned.

"Really, would you quit?" she said.

He narrowed his eyes.

"No, I'm not!" she groused.

He tilted his head and arched an eyebrow.

"Fine, whatever," she threw up her hands and stomped off.

Risa watched Siobhan's retreating form, then turned back to Killian, dumbfounded. "Okay, I'm missing something here. You didn't say a single word, yet you two just held a whole conversation. How?"

He laughed and shrugged.

"No, don't try to get out of it. How did you do that?" she demanded.

He smiled at her and tilted his head.

"Because it's weird and I want to know…" She stopped, suddenly realizing he was doing it to her now.

Killian rubbed his cheek where Risa whacked him with a travel pillow. He was getting them both a drink from the kitchenette. He glanced at Marco, who was also getting a drink and grinned. "Why are they so violent?" he asked.

The red dragon laughed, "I know! I don't know what it is, but I like it." He shrugged and gazed softly at the prickly woman he'd marked as his mate. The love in his eyes for Siobhan was unmistakable.

"Did ye find anything on those security tapes yesterday? About who cut the power?" Killian asked, worried Marco would mention it was a silver-haired woman. The sightings were getting too frequent to be explained away easily. But he didn't know if anyone else was seeing her.

Marco huffed out a frustrated breath. "No!" he ground through his teeth, "All we saw was a short guy with long brown hair getting close, but no one we know. Not an employee. Then the cameras went out, and we don't know what happened until the power comes back on. I've got a team working on identifying him, but so far, nothing. Best I can tell, just a harmless prank."

Sighing in relief, Killian leaned towards Marco. "Can I ask a... personal question?" he mumbled, somewhat hesitantly.

Marco glanced at him, clearly surprised. That wasn't something Killian ever did, so curiosity spread across his features, widening his eyes as he promptly agreed.

"You're mated to Siobhan, have ye talked about getting married?"

"Yeah," Marco barked out a laugh. "I've asked her three times, but apparently, I don't ask the right way, and it pisses her off. Watch." He turned and called to Siobhan, "Shi, love of my life, reason for my existence, my true mate and one that I couldn't live without, please marry me?"

Siobhan rolled her eyes. "Fuck off," she replied.

Risa stared at her in surprise, and Liam smirked as he shook his head.

Marco shrugged and turned back to Killian, who was struggling not to laugh. "See what I mean? I don't know why she doesn't want to get married. She told Jack I had three months to ask, or she was going to ask me. It's been over six, and she keeps turning me down. I dunno. But she's my mate, and she loves me, and I love her. I don't know what else we need." Marco studied Killian and the thoughtful expression on his face. "Why do you ask?" he nudged his elbow.

Killian replied in a low voice, "I love Risa, an' I've asked her to move in with me. Wielders don't mark their mates the way dragons do, but we do have something similar. If ye could do it over again, would ye have asked Siobhan to marry ye first before marking her?"

The dragon laughed then; understanding now. "*Mi amigo*, I'm sorry. I would say don't do either! It's a trap," he laughed again before he sobered, "But seriously, I would offer both at the same time. Hey, man," Marco clapped him on the shoulder, and his face softened. "It looks good on you. I'm really happy for you, Ki. She's wonderful, and it's nice to see you coming out of your crab shell."

Killian rolled his eyes. "Why does everyone think I needed to be pulled out? I was perfectly happy in my solitude."

Marco snorted incredulously, "Seriously? You were basically a hermit. But I like this new you. I've known you for what, forty years? And I've learned more about you in the last six months than I did in the rest of that time. It's cool."

"Ye wanted to know something, ye could've asked," Killian told him, grinning innocently, knowing he wasn't fooling the dragon. Marco was their best tracker and usually the first person to notice Killian was in a room. Killian befriended the other man because Marco was kind enough to leave him be with his disappearing act, not calling him out when the others didn't see him.

"Yeah," Marco thought about it, "You've always been blunt, but it's more that you didn't want people to notice you and ask. Anyway, you want her, I'd wrap it up and don't be afraid to tell her how you feel. Don't wait too long and run the risk of losing her. I almost did. Remember, it took me almost dying for Siobhan and me to admit it to each other. Liam? Never told Jorrie he loved her until she'd turned to someone else. Of course, he disappeared for almost a year, so that compounded his stupidity, but don't wait. That's my best advice."

Killian nodded his thanks and made his way back to Risa. He passed by Liam, who muttered, "He's right, listen to him." Killian settled into his seat, remembering belatedly that dragons had exceptional hearing, so Liam probably heard the whole conversation. *Good, that lizard needs to know I'm serious about this.* He handed Risa her soda and studied her. "Ten years."

She blinked at him in confusion.

"That's how long Siobhan has worked for me. That's why she an' I can have a conversation like that. She took the time to learn a lot of my cues an' has come to understand how I think more than most people have. So, most of the time I don't have to tell her anything. She figures it out on her own. Like Vaughn."

Risa nodded slowly and studied Siobhan. The feisty woman was at the other end of the cabin, curled up in her seat, reading a book, and looking a little green. "You know if she wasn't firmly mated to Marco now, I might be jealous of that," she admitted. "Why was she so interested in taking the time when no one else was?"

Killian stared at the ceiling for a moment, squirming in his seat, then sighed, "When she first came to work there, she flirted with me. Lightly, in the beginning, more... overly friendly. But when she admitted she was attracted to me, it got awkward. I didn't encourage it, but she was persistent. I finally politely, but firmly, shut her down. She respected that, an' we became friends. I'm the one that introduced her to Marco an' pushed her to go out with him in the first place. Since then, she's one of a handful of people who let me just be me."

She studied him for a moment, then took his hand. "Love you," she whispered.

He smiled and tilted his head.

She chuckled, "Okay, I understood that!"

Once the plane landed, they checked into their hotel and went to dinner, settling in for a delicious meal.

Risa wanted to try one of everything, while Siobhan only picked at her food. Risa patted her on the arm. "You okay?"

"Just tired, a little airsick, I guess," Siobhan responded while Risa nodded in commiseration.

Killian watched Siobhan picking at her food and pushed down a sinking feeling. When the group returned to the lobby of the hotel, he pulled her aside. "Talk," he insisted.

Siobhan snorted, "That's a joke coming from you."

He stared at her, an intense expression and simply raised one eyebrow.

She finally broke eye contact and stared down at her feet as her thin shoulders began to tremble.

"How long?" he asked quietly, gently.

Her gaze flew back to his, and something akin to panic flew across her features. "What do you mean? I don't understand," she stammered.

He gave her a disapproving frown. "Shi, don't play me. I know ye better. How long?"

She sighed, and her voice broke as she finally choked out the words, "Eight, nine weeks maybe."

"Does Marco know?"

She shook her head vehemently.

"Is that why ye won't marry him?"

Her eyes glossed with tears, and she shook her head even harder this time, to the point it almost knocked her off balance.

"Shi, please, honey, talk to me," he pleaded with her, putting a hand on her cheek.

She threw her arms around his neck and sobbed into his shoulder, bawling with every ounce of breath she had as the dam finally broke.

Killian held her tightly, letting her get her emotions out, stroking her hair and humming.

After a few minutes, she was able to suck in a deeper breath and regain her composure. She straightened up and ground the tears from her eyes, then wiped her cheeks. "Okay," she blew out a sharp breath, "Here goes." She squared her shoulders like she was about to enter a boxing ring and lifted her chin in defiance.

"I love Marco with all my heart, he loves me with all his, and we're mated. He's asked me to marry him, but he doesn't really want to. Not that he doesn't want me, he does, I think he's just asking because he thinks it's what I want. I mean, I do want to, very much. But I want him to want it too, not just because he thinks it's some formality that I need. I want him to have pride in calling me his wife. The way he does by calling me his mate. Outside of our kind, that doesn't mean anything to anyone. That's why I keep turning him down. And now this," her eyes watered, and she looked at her stomach, her earlier bravado gone again, slipping away like a whisper on the wind. She gazed back at him, misery etched firmly on every inch of her face.

Siobhan was clearly terrified. "Killian, what do I do?" she whispered.

He smiled gently as he brushed her red-gold hair from her face and kissed her forehead. He pulled her to his chest and squeezed her. "My darlin' girl. Ye go tell him *exactly* what ye told me. Tell him why it's important to ye. An' for god's sake tell him you're pregnant. He needs, no, deserves to know, an' we need to know so we can keep ye extra safe. Shi, I love ye like a sister. I have one, ye know? A younger sister. She got married a few years ago an' now has a son, six months old, cutest little thing ever. I'm so happy for her an' I want to see them so badly. Ye fill that void for me. Rena, too. So please, take some brotherly advice from someone who is smarter than your actual brother. Tell him. Everythin'. Now." He smiled and let her go.

She stared at him, awe on her face. "Ki, I love you so much. You're the older brother I wanted. Is it too late to trade Liam for you?"

He laughed. "Aye, I'm afraid it is. But I love ye too. Now, get your grumpy arse up there an' make him the happiest red dragon on the planet. An' Siobhan, if he hurts ye? I'll kill him."

"Spoken like a true brother," she grinned, "And I'll tell you what I told Liam. If he hurts me, get in line!" She ran off, lighter than before and looking downright happy.

A large smile on his own face, he crossed his fingers that it went well. He turned to make his way to his own room, but stopped when he saw Risa watching him from down the hall. She was clutching a bottle of water tightly, and from the blank look on her face, she'd seen him talking to Siobhan. He couldn't tell what her expression meant and resigned himself to some tough questions. Continuing towards her, he kept his face carefully neutral and ran a hand down her arm as he reached her. "Alright then?" he asked.

She nodded, turning silently back to the room.

He sighed wearily; this didn't bode well. Risa always had something to say.

Chapter 12

RISA PACED AROUND THEIR room restlessly, then finally threw her hands in the air. "Dammit, Killian, say something. I don't know what I saw, and it's making me uncomfortable."

He tilted his head, about to speak, when she put her finger in his face. "Don't do that! Use words!" she snapped.

He grinned, nipping at her finger, then tugged her against his body, locking his lips on hers. She gasped into his mouth as he pressed even harder, the kiss taking on an edge of frustration. Finally, she relaxed in his arms, so he pulled back from her while she caught her breath.

"Marissa, my little unicorn, green with jealousy. You're beautiful when you're angry, but I don't like ye bein' angry with me. If ye ever want to know somethin', anythin', just ask. I don't have any secrets." He rubbed her shoulders and smiled softly.

She smiled back, "Okay, why were you holding Siobhan in your arms and kissing her and having an intense conversation right before you came in here and kissed me brainless?"

He snorted. "Ye aren't brainless, but I'll take the compliment. I kissed ye because of how much I love ye, even when you're bein' a right stubborn arse." He dodged her playful swat, then pulled her to the bed to sit next to him. "I was talking to Siobhan because she's hiding a big secret, an' I could tell. It's eating her up inside, so I wanted to help her. I told ye; I think of her as a little sister. It's true, same with Rena. They help fill the void left by my little Molly girl. I miss her, Risa, so much. Talking about her with ye, really nailed it home for me. I'm the right arse for staying away all this time for my own pride. I miss my family." He sighed, sadness settling deep inside him, dragging his shoulders down with it.

She stroked his cheek then and kissed him tenderly. "We will fix that. I promise you, Killian. Even if we never find my sister, you are going to see yours again."

He held her tightly. "She's pregnant," he muttered.

"Your sister?" she gasped, "Didn't she just have a baby six months ago?"

"No, not her," Killian laughed, "I mean, aye, she did have one, but she's not pregnant. Siobhan is. She thinks eight to nine weeks. An' no, before ye ask, she hasn't told Marco. That's what I was telling her. She needs to tell him an' be honest with him about how she feels." Risa's mouth was hanging open, and he pushed it closed with a small smile.

She stared at him in confusion, then laughed. "Oh my god, I'm getting it now. Your looks and single-word answers. Geez, I hope I don't start talking like that."

"No chance of that, my love," he replied with an arched eyebrow, the corner of his mouth tucked in as he tried not to smile.

She punched him on the shoulder and was about to say something snarky when they heard a roar that shook the paintings on the walls.

"I believe Marco is aware he's going to be a father," Killian grinned. They heard happy, excited shouts all the way down the hall. "An' it's good news to him."

Risa smiled softly and brushed her hand over his cheek. "You really are just the sweetest man."

He smiled devilishly at her, "Oh no, I cannot have ye thinkin' that now, can I? I'm after needin' to fix that impression," he declared, just before he shoved her flat on the bed, covering her body with his own.

At breakfast the next morning, the others were already seated when Marco and Siobhan joined them. Marco strutted in like a peacock, grinning ear to ear. His expression suggesting he'd won the lottery, or some other marvelous prize. Liam glanced at him warily as they sat. "What are you so happy about? Could you have been any louder last night? Jesus, the whole hotel probably knows you were getting laid."

Siobhan kicked her brother under the table.

"*Si*, that wasn't because we were having sex," Marco said, "Well, I mean, we were, but —"

"Marco," Siobhan hissed.

He grinned unrepentantly. "We have an announcement," he said, grabbing her hand. "My darling mate and I are expecting!"

Risa and Killian cheered and clapped as if they were hearing this news for the first time.

Liam simply stared, his lips turning down into a slight frown, "Expecting what?"

Marco squinted at him like he was daft. "*Bambino,* a baby," he explained slowly.

"A baby what?" Liam shook his head, clearly in denial.

Siobhan slammed her hand down on the table, making him jump. "I'm pregnant, you idiot!" she snapped in frustration.

Liam's left eye twitched, his mouth opening and closing a few times before he leapt from his chair, knocking it over. Turning on his heel, he ran right out the front door. They all stared after him in shock.

Marco snorted, then laughed, "You know, I figured he'd take a swing at me or something. That's not what I was expecting. You think he's okay?" He looked worried now.

Siobhan leaned back in her chair, arms crossed, looking surlier than usual.

Killian sighed, "I'll go." He stood and went after Liam.

Outside, Killian didn't have to go far. Liam was sitting on a bench, staring at the ground, intensely studying the dark rocks between his boots. Killian sat, saying nothing. He leaned back, letting the sun warm his face until Liam was ready to talk.

Finally, Liam sighed, "I cannot *believe* my baby sister is pregnant."

Killian nodded. "Oh, I get it. My little sister had a baby six months ago, an' she's been married a few years now. Sucks, doesn't it? Thing is, the guy she married, he's a good guy an' takes care of her. He's good for her, balances out her fiery temper. Calms her when she's acting like a wet cat. Sound familiar?"

Liam nodded miserably and hung his head even lower.

"An' her son is adorable. Look." He showed Liam pictures of his sister and her baby.

Liam sat up and smiled, "Damn, Ki, that is a cute kid. I didn't even know you had a sister. How do you do it? She's younger than you, but she's found everything she wants, and you're still out here... well, I guess you're not exactly single anymore, but you know what I mean. I'm older, by a lot, and she's got a mate, a baby on the way, a happy ending. This, from the girl who wouldn't even admit she had a heart until Marco almost died. Meanwhile, I'm... alone. I'm not that kind of person. I don't like solitude. Bridget calls me a social dragonfly, but the only person kissing me these days is Shepard." He shuddered, "It's just depressing, man."

Killian laughed, "I don't know, Liam, I enjoyed solitude for a long time. It taught me to appreciate what I have now. Honestly, don't try so hard, an' love will find ye when it's right. You'll just be walking along, an' it will smack ye right in the face."

"I hope you're right, Ki," Liam sighed, "Just... when I think about how old Vaughn, Shepard, and Davis were when they found their mates, I don't want to be alone for centuries." He shuddered again as Killian patted his back. "Thanks, by the way, for coming out here. Talking to me. It's kind of surprising. I mean that it was *you*. I didn't think you liked me, or did you just draw the short stick?"

Grunting, Killian rolled his eyes. "Listen, dragon," his tone much more relaxed than the last time he said those same words, smirking at Liam's cheeky grin, "I don't dislike ye. Alright? Ye just get right on my nerves sometimes. But," he sighed, "You're not a bad sort an' I know you've had a shite hand dealt in your life these last few years. Just... try to be less annoyin', aye?"

Liam chuckled and nodded.

Killian stood. He noticed Liam staring at him consideringly. "What now?"

Liam smirked, pointing at the piercings and asked, "Those hurt?"

"Eh, when they first did it, but after, no." Killian grinned, "Gotta tell ye though, this one?" He pointed at the ring on his lip. "Risa loves it, likes to play with it with her tongue. It makes things more intense sometimes. Honestly, the tattoos hurt worse."

"That's right, you said you were getting another one. Can I see what you have?" Liam asked excitedly.

Pulled his shirt aside, Killian showed him the one on his chest, then rolled up his sleeve to show him the one on his arm.

Liam grinned. "Okay, that's just badass. I've been thinking of getting something done. I really like Shepard's, but I don't want something quite that big."

"I'll give ye my guy's name," Killian grinned back.

Nodding, Liam held out his hand as he stood.

Killian snorted, hugging him instead. "Go, congratulate your sister," he whispered.

The dragon saluted cheekily and hurried through the door. Killian was about to follow him when he caught a whiff of a familiar perfume, but couldn't place it. He spun around, confused, as he saw no one who could be the source of the smell. He thought he saw a flash of silvery-blonde hair from the corner of his eye, but when he turned, it was gone. Noticing a small fountain, he tried to shake off the unsettling feeling, reasoning it must have been a reflection off the water. It certainly wouldn't be Circe, not here. He hurried inside, shaking his head, hoping he was just imagining things and the mystery woman hadn't followed them to France.

"He saw you," the brown-haired man hissed, tugging the woman's arm, pulling her back around the corner.

"He was supposed to," she replied, rolling her eyes. "I want to keep him on edge, make him doubt himself, his own eyes. An' I'll thank ye to keep your filthy hands off me," she growled, malice flashing across her face.

Dropping his hand as if he were burned, the man backed away, grumbling. "Why did we have to follow them here? The younger one is still in the US; we can't make a move until they go back. You said so!"

"Aye, I did. Now quit your whining. I need to be sure they find 'Isabella'. Won't they be in for a surprise when they do!" She laughed, a decidedly evil sound, resonating like the peal from a bell with a deep crack running through it.

Inside the hotel, Liam strode purposefully to Siobhan, yanked her from her chair, and held her tightly.

"Liam," she choked out, slapping him on the back, "I'm pregnant, not dying."

He loosened his grip a bit, murmuring, "I wish mom and dad were here to see this. They'd be so happy for you. I'm happy for you. I love you, Siobhan."

She laid her head on his shoulder, sniffling, "Love you, too, Liam. Thank you."

The siblings stood there for a minute holding each other before he finally let her go.

She lightly punched him in the shoulder, "Jerk," she declared with a watery smile.

He brushed away a strand of her red-gold hair that matched his own and kissed her forehead. "Porcupine," he grinned. He turned to Marco and squared his shoulders. Marco held out his hand, but Liam took a page from Killian's book and pulled him in for a hug. "Brother," he told Marco quietly, "You think she's moody now, wait until she goes into labor." He grinned at the red dragon, who suddenly looked several shades paler than before, which was impressive given his perpetually tanned complexion.

Siobhan narrowed her eyes. "What did you say?" she gritted through her teeth.

Both dragons wisely shook their heads, laughing.

Chapter 13

I N THEIR RENTAL VEHICLE, Risa twisted her fingers together nervously, knuckles white with the pressure. Killian took one hand, silently intertwining their fingers before giving it a reassuring squeeze. She smiled gratefully, squeezing his in return.

He leaned closer, whispering, "It's absolutely normal to be nervous. This is a big step in your search. I know it must be exhilaratin' an' frightenin' at the same time. Talk to me."

She took a deep breath and blew it out slowly through pursed lips. "We've been working on this for six months, so you're right. It's just another step. I don't know why this is so different, but I guess it's because we're here. Going to meet someone who actually knew me... my parents..." She smiled softly, "My sister."

He squeezed her hand again, "We're going to find her, Risa, we're going to find Isabella."

The vehicle coasted to an easy stop that still made her stomach lurch, as Liam turned to them, "Alright, kids, we're here."

They stood in the street, staring at the small cottage. Risa's entire body tingled with nervous anticipation, like electricity running through her veins. She took a grateful gulp of the ocean breeze wafting towards them, feeling it cool her skin. She grabbed Killian's hand and grimaced at the fact that hers was clammy and gross. "Sorry," she whispered.

He simply raised their joined hands, kissing her fingers, smiling.

She relaxed a little, knowing he was right by her side, her rock to lean on if her own strength failed her. She took a deep, shaky breath as he pulled her forward to knock on the door. His hand was still raised when it opened, and an older woman of about seventy appeared.

Dorothy was smiling, tears from faded denim-blue eyes running down softly wrinkled cheeks. "Marissa! My darling, it's so good to see you again!"

Inside the small home, they gathered in Dorothy's cozy, warm living room, where she regaled them with stories about the girls growing up not far from here. "I remember you," Risa whispered, her voice raw and choked with emotion. "You watched us when Mom and Dad had to go somewhere. You, ugh, why can't I remember?" she grimaced, her tone laced with frustration now.

Killian quietly stood, placing his hands over her.

"No," Risa yelped, jumping to her feet. "I don't want you to get hurt again," she insisted. "I couldn't stand it if you were injured because of me."

Siobhan spoke up, "I can help him."

"*No!*" everyone shouted.

Startled, Siobhan jumped then sat back, pouting.

Marco leaned over, trying to soothe her ruffled feelings, "Darling, we know you can, but not in your condition."

Liam growled at her in warning as she inhaled to give a blistering reply.

Dorothy stood. "Oh dear, that pesky spell still lingering?"

Silence filled the room as they stared at her.

Smiling apologetically, Dorothy nodded. "I'm afraid that was a rather rush job. I'm so terribly sorry, my dear, but Bill and I were hurrying, and I'm sure it was sloppy. We were scared if we didn't hide your identities, it would make you too easy to find. Let me see what's left of it." She held out her hands over Risa and closed her eyes. Green waves washed over the young woman.

Killian sucked in a deep breath. "You're a green wielder."

Dorothy nodded silently, then frowned. "Oh, my darling girl, I'm so sorry. Yes, I can see the spell fragmented. Some enormously powerful magic removed the top layer, and someone very clever has been removing it piece by piece. Very clever indeed." She opened her eyes and studied Killian. "You are not all that you seem," she nodded in approval. "Very nice work."

He tilted his head at her, narrowing his eyes.

"Yes, darling, I can remove the rest of the spell. Without hurting her or myself. And I will be happy to do so," Dororthy replied and patted him on the cheek.

Risa snorted. They turned to her, and she shook her head. "I just don't understand how he does that."

Everyone laughed at her indignant expression, and Dorothy set about removing the spell.

After twenty minutes, Dorothy dropped her hands, sweating with effort. "Sorry, my love, it's almost gone, just this one last little part that is being stubborn. It seems to be twined up in you somehow. It's something that Bill did, and I don't know how he was able to do it."

Killian spoke up, "Bill, was he a silver wielder by chance?" When she nodded, he smiled. "I thought I recognized the signature. I can help ye." He stood next to her and gestured for her to continue. She lifted her hands and concentrated again. He held his hands near hers and pulsed silver waves towards her green in a way that braided the lights together in a shimmery stream.

It was beautiful, and Dorothy gasped, "That is amazing, it's so clear now. How on earth..." She fell silent as Killian began moving his hands like he'd done in the conference room. Pulling strands and moving blocks. "Young man, that is exquisite. I haven't seen the like before," she whispered to him in awe and reverence. Together they pulled and pushed, twisted, and plucked until Risa shuddered, feeling the last of the spell pull free of her.

The two wielders dropped their hands, and Killian sat next to Risa, running his hands anxiously over her shoulders. "Are ye alright?"

"Better than okay," Risa beamed, "Killian, I can remember everything!"

He smiled, brushing her lips gently with his thumb.

She turned excitedly to Dorothy, "Thank you! And I'm sorry about Bill, he was such a lovely, dear man as well."

The woman's eyes filled with tears, but she smiled. "He was, my dear, and he loved you girls."

Killian stood then and took the woman's hand into his own, before kissing the back of it. "Thank ye for helping her an' ensuring she was safe."

Dorothy studied him and leaned forward. "She's lucky to have found you, dear Killian. Although I'm not sure why anyone would want to put metal in their face. You're still a handsome one, though, aren't you?" She patted his cheek before gliding away towards her kitchen.

He stood there, lips twitching with laughter, then sat quickly, shaking his head.

Dorothy came back with a plate of cookies and a teapot. "Now then, let me tell you everything else." The kind woman told them the story of why they were forced to hide the girls years ago. Their parents were a younger couple. Their father a silver wielder, their mother a silver dragon. They'd grown their family quickly, the girls fairly close in age. Firstborn, Isabella, was a dragon as they suspected, and the younger two, Marissa and Serena, wielders like their father. The family was incredibly happy, with a loving home and the girls were well cared for. Dorothy and her husband, Bill, were friends of the family and always excited to watch the girls, having no children of their own. The girls' parents were often assigned on missions for the Dragon Council. That same Council was now defunct after one of its members was executed as a traitor. Another was a god in disguise who'd since gone back home. Wherever that was.

The traitor, Baltrus, was also the one who ordered the death of Risa's parents. They'd managed to stumble across information showing his true nature, and he silenced them in retaliation. By turning the girls into orphans, he realized he could give them to some of his associates who were experimenting with dark magic. It gave him the idea that small families were ideal targets to take the children and turn their magic dark before they were too grown-up to resist the training.

"The Dark Wielders," Dorothy told them, in a heavy voice, laced with regret.

Marco nodded, "We encountered one not too long ago. That's how we found Risa." He told her the story of Baltrus' son, Cyrus. How he kidnapped Vaughn Drake, and the team rescued him. They met Marissa along the way, and Killian recognized her hidden power. He and Siobhan removed part of the spell that revealed who she really was. It was then they realized she was the target, along with the other two children the dark wielders were hiding.

Dorothy sighed ruefully, her eyes shining with sorrow and happiness, each battling for control of her emotions. "And I'm so glad you did! Darling, I'm thrilled you ended up with a happy childhood despite it all." She picked up her story where they left off. She and Bill received a frantic call from the girls' mother, telling them to hide, shouting to be heard over the screams of her husband in the background before the line went dead. They packed the children up immediately and went on the run. They travelled for months, place to place, country to country, trying to escape.

Risa nodded slowly. "I remember that," she whispered, the pain from those memories clear on her face. "We were so scared. We wanted our parents, but you and Papa Bill were so kind to us, doing everything you could to keep us happy. Then, nothing until the family came to adopt me."

Dorothy nodded slowly. "We realized we couldn't keep running with three small children. Your heritage gave you away. That beautiful silvery hair, I'm glad to see it again, by the way. I hated turning it brown." She glanced at Killian with a questioning arch of her eyebrow.

"Aye, mine is normally that color, I just changed it," he explained.

Dorothy exclaimed in disbelief, "Why would you want to cover up your heritage like that? You should be proud of what you are!"

He pouted while Risa laughed and showed Dorothy a picture of what he looked like before.

Pursing her lips, Dorothy studied him, then smiled. "Okay, Killian, I do like to see your handsome face, but maybe let it go back to its natural color at least. It's so pretty," she sighed.

He threw his hands up in surrender before glaring at Liam and Marco, who were barely containing their amusement. Siobhan had dozed off, or no doubt she would have scolded them.

Dorothy cleared her throat, then described how they made the difficult decision to split the girls up for their safety. Putting a spell on Marissa and Isabella, placing them with agencies in different countries. They tried to keep Serena with them for as long as they could, but they were almost caught, so they gave her away as well. They placed a lighter version of the spell on her because she was so little, they weren't sure what it would do to her. Dorothy smiled gently. "I understand you're reunited with her. Why didn't she come? I would love to see her sweet face."

Marissa sighed and glanced at Killian while biting her lip. This part would be painful.

Liam stepped in and invited Dorothy to go for a walk with him around her garden. He gently told her about Serena's abduction and years-long imprisonment by the Shadow Claw. How they'd abused her power and taken her childhood. He shared the story of her rescue and how, with therapy, and the love of her adoptive family, she was recovering nicely. She was still scared to go too far from home and elected to stay behind because of her fears. Dorothy was beside herself, and those inside could hear her pain as she sobbed in agony. Liam consoled her and held her while she cried. She finally patted his chest and kissed his cheek, thanking him for rescuing Serena and caring for her.

Dorothy hurried in and hugged Risa. "I'm so sorry, my darling, we did what we thought was best."

Risa hugged her back. "Mama Dorothy, you couldn't have known, you did what you thought would give us the best chance of survival, and it worked. Serena is just fine now. She has a huge, loving family looking out for her." Risa scrolled through pictures of Rena on her phone. Dancing at the wedding, making silly faces with her, playing with Jorrie's children, learning to drive, and just being happy.

Dorothy's face softened as she tapped her finger on the picture of the little woman Rena had become and thanked Risa for sharing with her.

Killian cleared his throat. "We still need to know about Isabella," he reminded them.

All eyes turned to Dorothy, and she nodded. "We left her in Ireland. Cork, to be precise. I was able to keep my eyes on her for a while, not being too far, but I'm afraid after she was adopted, I lost track of her. I think that's the best place to start."

Flopping back, dumbfounded, Killian mumbled, "We need to go to Ireland? To Cork?" He glanced at Liam, "I thought the agency was here, in France. Didn't ye say that?" As Liam slowly shook his head no, Killiam realized he had never asked before. He toyed with the silver ring on his lip, a nervous tick no one saw before, as his hair usually hid it.

Risa saw it, recognized what it meant to him. "Ireland, it is!" she declared, "And we'll need to make a side trip while we're there."

His gaze flew to hers, settling heavily as he nodded, grateful she understood.

Outside the cottage, another silver-haired woman watched, eager to know the group's next steps. "Come on, off to Cork with ye," she huffed. "Agh, why is this takin' so fecking long?"

Leaning against a tree in the distance, the brown-haired man grimaced and kept watch, hoping his shield magic kept them hidden well. He glanced towards the gardens, wondering if the owner would notice if he snatched a single flower so he could enchant it. He knew someone who would love it.

Chapter 14

FEOHANAGH. KILLIAN SAW THE sign as he drove towards his hometown. His heart raced, pounding in his chest. A gentle hand on his leg made him glance at Risa. She smiled warmly at him. Siobhan and Liam went to visit their ancestral home. Their grandparents had emigrated to America, so they had no more family here, but they wanted to see where their roots were from. Marco went with the siblings, leaving Killian and Marissa to go see his family. Once in town, Killian gazed around, lost in nostalgia. So much had changed, he didn't recognize it anymore. He laughed mirthlessly in his head, not sure why he expected he would have. On the outskirts of town, he pulled up to his family's home and parked. He sat behind the wheel for a moment. Not moving, just staring.

"This is beautiful, Killian," Risa breathed, "How wonderful to grow up here."

He merely nodded, swallowing heavily, still not moving.

She reached over and turned the car off. "Killian, do you want to do this?"

He turned his head and nodded again, stiffly. His heart jumped to his throat, and he felt vaguely ill. He was excited to see his family, but would they want to see him? Guilt was eating him from the inside out.

"Then let's go see them," she whispered. She hurried around and opened his door, holding out her hand. "You know this is supposed to work the other way around, right?"

He finally laughed and took her hand, stepping out of the car and kissing her softly.

They started towards the door, but footsteps behind them halted their progress. "An' where might ye be heading?" they heard a deep voice call. Marissa whirled around, then nudged Killian, grinning. She recognized the man was obviously his father, which Killian knew from the first word. "Hello, Mr. Brennan, it's so nice to meet you!" she beamed.

His father chuckled, "Well, lass, ye certainly have the advantage of me. Shame, a pretty girl like ye walking here an' I don't have the pleasure of knowing your name or this one with ye?"

Risa nudged Killian again, and he blew out a heavy breath. His back tensed; given they hadn't seen each other in so long, his father hadn't recognized him. Risa cleared her throat and nudged him even harder, this time with a small pulse of magic. He winced at the sting but knew she was trying to help.

Killian took another deep breath, trying to quell the panic lodged in his throat and slowly turned. His father studied him, and he saw the moment the realization hit. Fergus Brennan dropped the rake he was holding, and his eyes filled with tears.

"Killian," he whispered, his hands shaking, "Is that really... my boy?"

"Hi, Pa," he replied softly, smiling.

His father grabbed him then and pulled him to his massive chest, bawling like a baby. "My son!" he cried, "Shannon! Shannon!" he yelled.

A beautiful woman with silvery hair came running around the house. "What's all the…" she came to a jarring halt when she saw her husband crying and holding a strange man. "What happened, Fergus? Is it Molly? What…" She gasped, her hands to her mouth, when Killian turned to her. "My baby!" she cried, dropping to her knees.

Killian hurried to his mother and knelt beside her. "Aye, I'm back, an' I've missed ye so much," he whispered and held her while she cried against his neck, his own tears mingling with hers. His father appeared shortly after, putting his arms around them both, holding tightly as if he were afraid Killian would disappear again.

Marissa moved quietly to the front porch and sat, giving the family some privacy. She wiped her own tears at the touching scene. At some point, Shannon shifted from being embraced by Killian, to wrapping him up in her arms. The way Killian held himself curled into his mother made Risa's chest tight. He'd needed this more than he let on. They sat like that for a long time, and finally she could see they were talking. Just sitting there on the green, lush grass, taking each other in. His mother kept touching his face, his hair, his shoulders, like she couldn't quite believe he was real. Finally, they all looked her way, and she suspected he was telling them about her now.

His mother stood, rushing over and taking Risa's hands. "Darling girl, it's my eternal gratitude ye have for bringing my boy home to me." Shannon's eyes filled with tears again, so Risa hugged her. Shannon hugged her back while they cried together.

Fergus pulled Killian off the ground, and they joined them on the porch. His arm around his boy's shoulders, he glanced at his son. "Women," he muttered, "Always bawling about something," he grumbled while wiping his own eyes.

Killian laughed loudly, and his parents stared at him lovingly, obviously they'd missed that sound. It warmed Risa straight to her core to see how relaxed and genuinely happy he finally seemed.

"Well, come in, come in, this calls for a celebration!" Shannon declared and shooed them all inside.

After Killian and Risa were through the door, Shannon turned to her husband. "Fergus, he's so different!" she whispered, her voice tight with concern.

He nodded, "My heart, he's been gone for so long. He was different when he left because of that she-devil. This one he's got here, I've a feeling about her, she seems to be what his soul needed."

Shannon nodded back and sighed, "I hope that's true."

Marissa studied the charming family home, cooing over the pictures of Killian as a small child. She saw another silver-haired girl, who she imagined was his younger sister, Molly. There were also newer images of Molly with her husband and baby. She noticed some pictures of Killian as a teenager and then as a young man. His face clear, his smile wide, his hair shorter, out of his face, much different from when Marissa first met him. Risa ran her finger over one photo of Killian with his head thrown back, laughing, and her heart thumped hard in her chest as a new revelation hit her. Killian's long hair was part of his defense mechanism; he hid behind it. She knew that. He admitted it. But her eyes burned hot as she realized when he cut it, it meant he no longer felt the need to hide.

There was another photo of him with a gorgeous woman that she imagined was his ex-wife. Her hair was blonde like Risa's, only curly and much shorter. He was beaming, but she was barely smiling, even though it appeared to be a wedding photo. *So, that's Kiera,* she mused. *Stupid bitch.*

"Aye, those were some dark times there," Shannon murmured softly, picking up the picture. "I hate that manky cur she-devil, but he's so handsome in this picture, an' it's the last one I had of him before he left. So, I kept it." Shannon glanced at Risa and grinned. She opened the frame and pulled out the picture, ripping the half with Kiera off and putting just the part with Killian back in. She wadded up the other piece of the photo then tossed it into the fire that was crackling merrily in the hearth. Flames eagerly turned Kiera's image to ash while both women grinned at it.

Killian wandered in just then, carrying a tray of tea and biscuits.

Shannon stared lovingly at him, then frowned and reached up to his forehead. "My baby, what happened to your beautiful hair? It was always so soft an' blond, like a duckling's down."

He rolled his eyes, "Ma," he complained, sounding exactly like a sulky teenager instead of a ninety-nine-year-old man, as his mother ruffled his hair.

Risa smothered a laugh.

"Ma," he leaned back so she would stop touching it. "I had the same haircut for going on seventy years, I just cut it nearly a week ago. I wanted something different."

Shannon narrowed her eyes, putting her hands on her hips, "An' how was I supposed to know? Ye don't visit, ye barely call us. I haven't laid eyes on ye in so long." Her eyes were filling again.

He nodded slowly, "I know, Ma, an' it's sorry I am. It was my stupid arse pride getting in me way."

Risa smiled as he lapsed further into his native brogue. This visit was doing so much for him, she could tell. She felt a hand on her shoulder and glanced at his father. He was smiling at her, it seemed he agreed. She stepped forward, "I have some pictures, Shannon. I can send them to you."

His mother nodded and leaned over to look. She oohed and ahhed at how cute he was. She pursed her lips at pictures of him with his long blond hair covering most of his face. "Aye, I do agree with the shorter cut. I can see your handsome face better. But the color my love," she shook her head, "An' why did ye go an' stab metal through your face? How do ye get through the airport?" she snapped.

Killian laughed then. He grabbed his mother around the waist and danced her around the room, "I love ye, too, Ma. I missed ye, so very much."

She sighed and danced with her son.

Fergus leaned in towards Risa then, "Thank ye, sweet lass, for bringing him home."

Killian's parents insisted they stay for dinner and the night. They called Molly and asked her to come over the next day, not telling her why, wanting it to be a surprise. They talked late into the night, and Risa was in heaven with the home-cooked meal. It was obvious where Killian learned to cook. He laughed, talked, and carried on with his parents, telling them about his life from the time he'd arrived in North America to now. About his work, his house, his cat, his adventures. How he and Marissa met. She watched him in astonishment. He was so alive, and he spoke in an animated way she hadn't heard before.

Shannon noticed, asking Risa, "Darling, why do ye look like ye never have seen him before?"

Risa chuckled. "Sorry, Shannon, it's just that Killian doesn't really talk much. When we first met, he hardly spoke at all. He speaks more now, to me mostly. But still, I've never heard him talk *this* much." She met his eyes across the table, and they burned into hers as he pulled absently at his collar. Almost like he couldn't breathe. She understood he was just realizing it as well, and the emotion it exposed was choking him with its strength.

Shannon laughed, "Our Killian? Oh lord no, a bigger chatterbox there never was growing up. Not a moment of silence from that one. Every thought he had flew from his mouth. But that voice was so sweet. Did ye know he used to sing in the church choir? A regular angel he was."

Risa grinned, "No, I wasn't aware. I only learned last week he could even sing at all."

Shannon gasped, "Killian Niall Brennan! Have ye not been appreciating your gods given talents?"

He stared at the ceiling. "Ma, I think we need to talk."

Nodding slowly, Shannon seemed to understand there was more he hadn't told them yet.

Risa stood. "I'll take care of the dishes while you do that," she offered, wanting to give him some privacy.

Shannon started to protest, but Killian stopped her. "Ma, we need to talk. Besides, that's as close as ye should let Risa to your kitchen if ye value your stomach." He grinned, and Risa flicked his ear as she walked past.

His father stifled a laugh at Killian's pained grumble. "Oh, that fine lady has got your number there, son."

Risa turned the water on in the kitchen to rinse the plates. She could hear the soft murmur of their voices. She heard Shannon crying at one point, and the sound broke her heart. She couldn't imagine not knowing your child was suffering the way he did. Not coming home because of painful associations. Being alone for so long because he felt he didn't deserve better. She rubbed her chest briefly before picking up another plate. If she and Killian ever had children, she would hold them tight and make sure they were always happy.

The dish she was wiping slipped from her hand, but she caught it before it hit the floor. She stood there, staring at it in surprise, not actually seeing the plate. Children? With Killian? They'd never talked about it. Hell, they hadn't even talked about marriage. He just asked her to move in with him, but with what he'd been through before? *Would he even want to get married again?* She wanted to, but shook her head. *He wouldn't, not after what he's gone through and how much it hurt him to stay away.* Her heart broke a little. She could see it. Her and Killian. Married. Watching their two children, maybe three, playing in the yard. Malachi watching over them in his pretentious way. Their beautiful, silvery-blonde heads shining in the sun. Then she shook her head again. *No sense in dreaming about something that won't happen.* A scalding drop landed on her hand as bitter tears fell.

Killian moved silently to her side, taking the dish from her hand and setting it on the counter before wiping her tears with his thumbs. "*Mo stor*," he murmured, "An' what is it that has made ye so sad?" His voice was low, soothing, and she shivered.

"Just thinking of family." She leaned her head on his chest, and he wrapped her in his arms.

Shannon was preparing a room for Risa; Killian's already set. She'd kept it ready for decades just in case. A mother's hopeful love bloomed eternally. She smiled, patting the floral bedspread in Molly's old room. She liked Risa; she was a good girl. Hurrying back to the kitchen, she found Killian pinning Risa back against the counter, kissing her deeply. His fingers were threaded through her hair, and there wasn't an inch of space between them. She cleared her throat, a little surprised but also relieved to see this much emotion and passion from her son after what he shared earlier. He was a grown man after all. He still jumped back like a guilty teenager caught necking in his parents' station wagon. "Well, I was going to put ye in separate rooms, but I can see there's no point in that now. Ye keep that up an' I'll have more grandchildren in no time. Killian, your old room is ready for ye. Risa, ye can use Molly's room or stay with him. Your choice."

Killian grinned, "She's staying in my room, Ma. I need her with me." He turned towards Risa and stroked her cheek, "*Is tú mo ghrá*."

Shannon gasped softly and clutched her heart before she quietly left to tell Fergus what she'd seen. The expression on Killian's face when he announced he loved Risa was the happiest she'd ever seen her son.

Killian stroked Risa's other cheek, noticing his mother hurrying away, smiling. He knew telling Risa he loved her in front of Shannon Brennan was as good as declaring his intentions. No doubt she was dreaming of more silvery-haired grandbabies now. He grinned. "Want to go scandalize my parents some more?"

She smiled back softly. "Only if you promise to talk dirty to me with that accent of yours, it makes me hot. Mmm." She nipped at his lip and shivered as he ran his tongue along her neck and whispered to her in Gaelic all the things he wanted to do to her.

Chapter 15

RISA WOKE TO SUNLIGHT filtering through the curtains and a warm body wrapped around hers. The owner of that warm body was currently kissing his way down her stomach. *"Maidin mhaith,"* Killian whispered to her.

She grinned as she stretched, "Is that Gaelic for I'm insatiable?"

He laughed and lay his head on her hip. "No, it means good morning. But I am insatiable when it comes to ye. I can't get enough." He ran his nose over her ribs and murmured, "Your soft skin, your sweet taste, those indecent moans ye make when I'm inside ye."

"Killian, this is your parents' house, and it was hard enough keeping quiet last night," her protest was weak and half-hearted as she squirmed.

"Well, an' fine it is, I hadn't an idea ye were such a prude, my love. I dinna expect that from ye," he grinned and moved to lie beside her, facing her with a sinful pout on his lips. He crossed his arms over his stomach, keeping his hands tucked in, pretending he didn't hear her disappointed moan.

He was laying on the accent thick because he knew what it did to her. Risa curled herself against him before she smacked his chest, glaring at him. "Killian Brennan, you stop that right now," she seethed in mock fury.

He laughed, pure joy in his voice. He rolled on his back and pulled her over on his lap. "Let me at least look at ye then. The sunlight on your hair, the way it makes your eyes dance like the fae folk in the foothills. How it caresses your skin like a silken gown, an' the breeze whispers of your beauty on the wind."

Her mouth dropped. "Killian," she gasped. He gazed at her with such devotion she trembled as she leaned down to kiss him.

He watched as she rose over him and settled down on the hard length that was pressing against her. He wasn't lying. The sunlight, dappled by the curtains, flitted over her skin like butterflies and made her hair sparkle like so many diamonds. Her flushed lips and the tips of her breasts were rosy in the soft light. She truly looked like a faerie princess before him. His heart pounded as she rose and fell, her body arching gracefully, her stomach taut as she quivered around him.

He surged up and latched his mouth around one of her nipples and pressed it to the roof of his mouth. She bit her lip, trying to keep from crying out. He suckled hard, then moved to the other side. Her hips became frantic as she was close to reaching her peak. He reached between them and applied pressure to the small bud there, sending her crashing over the edge and flooding him with her heat. He fastened his mouth to hers and swallowed her cries.

She started to go limp above him, so he lay her down and wrapped her legs around him as he continued to thrust into her. A soft, slight whimper came from his lips as she clamped tightly around him, the velvety feel of her skin on his undid him. His breathing became ragged, as she arched her back, letting him go even deeper. He cried out then, filling her with his release. He groaned into her mouth, and a pulse of his magic flowed with it. The wave left her gasping and wrenched another strangled moan from them both. They lay there, spent, trying to catch their breath, wrapped up in each other tightly. "Marissa, I love ye so much. So very much," he whispered.

She nuzzled his neck. "I love you, too, Killian, more than anything else. You are my everything."

He shuddered as her words touched him deep inside. The warmth that seeped into his very core left him reeling, dizzy and giddy with exquisite joy. The sensation was so overwhelming, he almost asked her to marry him and be his for eternity. The words were on the tip of his tongue, but he held back. He didn't know why, because he wanted Marissa to be his with every breath in his body. Needed her. He tensed, opening his mouth again, then closed it. *Kiera*, his brain helpfully supplied. He stilled, thinking: *why am I still letting her affect my life? It's been decades, and I didn't love her. Not like my Marissa.* His brain and heart were at war. Neither wanted to be hurt again. Both argued Risa either would or wouldn't.

She seemed to sense the turmoil in him and studied his face with a slight frown, concern filling her eyes.

He closed his own, slowing his breathing, trying to recenter.

She wrapped herself even more tightly around him. "Killian," she murmured, "Please tell me what you're thinking about that has you tied up in knots."

His mouth opened, and one word fell out, "Kiera." He immediately bit his tongue, his stomach lurching with dread. It wasn't what a woman you just made love to wanted to hear. That you were thinking about your ex-wife. She lay still like a stone for a moment before he felt her pull away from him. Not just physically, but emotionally as well. He watched her eyes squeeze tight as she tried not to cry. *Gods, I'm an idiot of the highest degree!* "Risa, no, please, my heart, that's not what it sounded like," he begged, his voice frantic as he cupped her cheek.

She whipped her head side to side rapidly. "Killian," she gasped, her eyes flying open, blazing into his very soul with their pain, "You don't say things you don't mean, and you don't waste words. You were thinking about another woman after you just told me you loved me. How did you mean it then?" Now there was anger as well as hurt in her eyes and voice. She shoved him away and rolled over, curling in on herself.

He growled and pulled her back, but she fought him. He grabbed her wrists and pulled them over her head, turning her body under his. He leaned down closer to her. "Damn it all, Risa, listen to me!" He put his cheek on hers and shook his head side to side. "Gods, I'm so fucking sorry. It really didn't come out right. I'm an idiot, I know. But my darling, my love, please, just hear me. Please, let me explain before ye take your heart away from me. I can't live without ye, Marissa. Please," he begged her.

Her face softened a bit, and she nodded slightly, indicating she would listen. Her lip trembled and she pulled it in to stop it.

He shuddered, then sucked in a deep breath that felt like molten glass in his throat. "Marissa, she did cross my mind, but not in a good way. I swear it. My heart is at war right now. I want ye more than I want air to breathe, more than anything that keeps my spirit. All I need in this world is your smile, to know that you're mine."

She tried to pull her wrists away, but he wouldn't let go.

His eyes flashed silver, and she stilled. "*Mo stor,*" he whispered, "I was thinking about *you*. I was about to ask ye to marry me."

She gasped and her entire body froze, disbelief and shivers coursing through her.

"The words were on the tip of my tongue, then Kiera flashed through my head. I swore I was never going to let anyone get that close to me again. But ye did. Ye got under my defenses, an' you're closer than anyone ever has been. Gods, I love ye so much, my heart, my soul. I can't, I can't live without ye. Please, Marissa, forgive me. I was thinking about how wonderful an' true ye are. An' that I'm absolutely done letting her rule my life, my happiness."

This time, when she tried to pull her hands back, he let go. She gently cupped his cheeks and stared deep into his eyes, her own swimming with emotions he dared not define. "Are you asking me?" her voice trembled.

His gaze searched hers. He blinked once. Twice.

"Are you asking me, Killian Brennan?" she repeated with a soft, tender curve of her lips this time.

He nodded slowly, his chest tightening as hope bloomed in his chest, expanding his lungs with joy. "I am. Marissa, please, will ye honor me an' bless me with your love by becoming my wife? Will ye marry me an' spend the rest of your life by my side?" He held his breath, terrified of her answer.

She huffed out a quick laugh and pulled him down to her. "Killian, nothing would make me happier than to stand by your side for the rest of our lives. Yes, I will marry you."

His breath whooshed out a second before his lips found hers in a gentle caress. "Thank god," he whispered, "I promise to spend the rest of my life making ye happy."

She smiled, "You already are."

"Well, about time it is ye sleepy heads. Thought I'd have to shield my eyes to rouse ye out of that room," Shannon teased them as they finally made their way to the living room. "Come on then, breakfast is in the kitchen."

"Mother," Killian called, stopping her in her tracks. She turned, and Fergus glanced up from his cup at the seriousness of his tone. "I was after asking ye a favor," he grinned.

She squinted at him suspiciously but nodded. Killian leaned over and whispered his request in her ear. She gave a tiny, strangled squeak and ran off.

When she returned, she was carrying a small wooden box with a Celtic knot carved on the lid, much like the tattoo he had on his chest. He took it from his mother with reverence and turned to Marissa. "No woman should ever be proposed to without a ring, *mo stor*, so," he dropped to one knee and opened the box, revealing a gorgeous diamond ring, woven into a band of silver so fine it was almost white. "Marissa Thompson, please will ye be my wife, my heart, my love, an' join the Brennan family as my bonded partner for the rest of our lives."

Marissa's heart stuttered and almost stopped. He wasn't just asking her to marry him this time. He was asking her to bind herself to him as a wielder as well. Their equivalent to how the dragons marked their mates. Her throat became tight and hot. For him to take this extra step meant more than anything else, more than a wedding vow. She nodded, not trusting her voice and held out her hand.

He slid the ring on her finger, his eyes flashing silver. Hers did as well. Suddenly, a stream of pure magic burst from each of them then wrapped around them both. It looped about like a beautiful silver ribbon on a present before tying itself into a knot and sinking back into their skin. The very air around them seemed to tingle and sparkle, before a large wave blew outward from where they stood, embracing each other tightly.

Shannon gasped, then burst into tears. Fergus held her close, patting her shoulder, "There, there, *mo ghra*."

Risa glanced around at the fading silvery glow. "What was that?" she asked, stunned.

"The binding glow, although I've never seen it quite like that," Killian told her slowly, awe in his voice. He turned to his mother, "I thought there was a ritual needed."

She smiled, her eyes damp, "Usually yes, my dear boy, but sometimes, when the love is just that strong, it happens. The two of ye..." she sniffled, and with her voice full of tears continued, "Ye recognized each other as soulmates, an' it happened on its own. It's rare, but oh, my Killian, I'm so happy for ye!" She hugged them both then and kissed Risa again. "Welcome to the family, daughter."

Risa sank into Shannon's embrace, clearly overwhelmed by the moment.

Killian's phone vibrated with a text from Siobhan. *Wondering if you're alive. Can we come meet your family?* He asked his parents if they minded a little more company, and with their enthusiastic approval, he invited the others. He was excited to share the news. After he sent his friends the address, they finally sat down to eat, not even minding the food was cold.

An amused, derisive chuckle hummed from the brown-haired man's throat. "Well, that's something. You didn't see that coming, did you? You thought they were looking for poor, missing Isabella, but they came here instead. And now he's engaged to her? Oh, this is fantastic. Guess sister dearest wasn't so important after all." His gloating words died in his throat as the woman he was taunting turned to him with an icy stare and bared her fangs.

"If you're after knowing what's best for ye, I imagine you'll shut yer mouth before I shut it permanently." Her silver hair flung about her shoulders as she whirled back to face the house, staring through the window, she watched as Shannon Brennan embraced her future daughter-in-law. "Bitch," she grumbled under her breath, "Ignoring your sister while she's out in the world alone. I'll make ye regret this."

The man crouching behind her shivered at the venom in her tone, feeling sorry for those inside who had no idea what was coming.

About half an hour later, the others showed up, and Killian introduced his friends to his family.

"Siobhan, Liam, good strong names! Wherein are your people from then?" Fergus asked.

"Kilmaekedar," Liam answered, wincing slightly as he mangled the pronunciation. "Our grandparents hailed from there, and we were visiting the old town." They spoke a little longer about what they saw before Shannon inquired about their parents. Liam hugged Siobhan close and quietly described how their parents died some years before at the hands of the Shadow Claw.

Shannon pulled them to her in a tight hug. "Ye poor dears! An' here you are on my doorstep, your hearts missing them an' such good friends to my Killian. You've always got a home here now, ye ken? You're part of this family now. Another son an' daughter for me." She smiled at them.

Siobhan stared at the woman calling her daughter and threw her arms around her, sobbing, apologizing, trying to explain why she had no control over her emotions lately.

Shannon's eyes flew wide, then softened. She took the young woman into the kitchen and made her a soothing cup of tea while they talked.

Marco's face was a mix of emotions, not quite knowing where he fit in. His dark features and bronze tan definitely wouldn't let him pass for Irish. Fergus clapped him on the back. "Aye, Marco, ye were included in that, son. You're an honorary Irishman now," he laughed.

"*Gracias*, Papa Brennan," Marco grinned in relief, making Fergus chuckle.

Chapter 16

THE DOOR BANGED OPEN as a fireball of a woman stalked in, a baby on her hip, followed by a red-haired man hurrying after her with an apologetic grin. "Ma!" she called, "We're here, what's the all-fired hurry? An' who the hell are all these people?" She kissed her father on the cheek. "Pa, here's Aidan, do ye mind?" She handed him the chubby baby, and his face lit up. The woman glanced at all of them in turn, her gaze passing right over Killian. He stood there grinning, not saying anything. They were all staring at her, waiting for her to notice.

Fergus cooed at the baby, pretending he didn't notice either.

Shannon hurried in, and Molly threw out her arms, hugging her mother. "Well, dear, I'm surprised you're this quiet. I'd figured ye for a lot more noise about this," Shannon declared, amusement and surprise coloring her tone.

Molly stared at her in confusion, her eyebrows raising to her hairline. "What kind of noise should I be making 'round a room full of strangers?" she demanded, her hands planting on her hips.

Shannon narrowed her eyes dangerously. "Molly Brennan O'Malley. How dare ye speak about your brother that way!"

Molly stepped back, alarmed. "My brother? But Killian's..." she trailed off and whipped around, studying the faces once more. Finally, she saw him. Standing at the back of the room, hands in his pockets, smiling innocently. Her jaw dropped, and her eyes locked on him. "Killian Brennan. Ye got some damn nerve," she growled at him.

His grin spread even further. "C'mere, Molly Lolly," he called, opening his arms wide.

She launched herself, jumping into his arms. Wrapping herself around him, bawling for all she was worth, Molly wailed loudly. She hit him so hard, he fell on his back and lay on the floor cackling like a loon. Everyone watched in further shock as she sat up and began hitting him in the chest.

"Ye bleedin'," smack, "Arsehole," smack, "How dare," smack, "Ye stay," smack, "Away," smack, "This," smack, "LONG!" she screamed. Then she started crying again and threw herself down on him, repeating his name over and over as she sobbed.

Killian simply lay there and held her, singing an old lullaby in her ear the way he'd done since she was little.

Liam wrapped an arm around Siobhan as she lay her head on his shoulder. "I used to do that for you," he whispered, "And I'll do it for your little one, too."

"You better," she whispered back and kissed his cheek.

Shannon snorted at her children and shook her head, "That's more of what I expected." Little Aidan blew a raspberry then, and they all laughed, ignoring the siblings lying on the floor.

Molly and Killian sat on the sofa next to each other. Like everyone else, she mourned the loss of his blond hair. She tweaked his facial piercings, asking him what kind of gobshite they were. He rolled his eyes. "Hey, I like them."

She kept putting a hand on his shoulder, his arm, his leg, and back to his face. She shook her head. "Ki, I can't believe you're here," she whispered, her eyes filling again.

He leaned forward, putting his forehead against hers. "I know Molly Lolly. I've missed ye so very much. An' I'm sorry. If it wasn't for Marissa, I probably still wouldn't be here." He glanced around then, his gaze settling on the woman who held his heart. His eyes flashed silver for a brief moment. "Marissa, please, come meet my baby sister. Molly, this is the love of my life, my fiancée, Marissa."

Molly jumped up and hugged Risa tightly. "I love ye already. Ye brought my brother back," she exclaimed through her tears.

Risa hugged the woman back just as tight before joining them on the sofa. She took Killian's hand as he toyed with the ring on her finger.

Molly caught sight of it. "Killian," she gasped in astonishment, "Ye gave her *the* ring?"

He nodded slowly, knowing she would understand the monumental meaning behind it.

She seemed uncertain, wrestling with her thoughts before she quietly asked, "Are ye sure?"

Scrunching his nose, Killian glared at her, "Molly, the ring bound us together already *without* the ritual. I've never been so sure in my life."

Gasping, Molly turned to her parents for confirmation. Shannon nodded tearfully, happily, and Fergus grinned, patting his wife's hand. Molly squealed, then hugged Risa again, "Welcome, sister of mine!" She danced in joy.

Liam leaned over to Marco and whispered, "You have any idea what's going on here?"

The red dragon shook his head slowly, "I think —"

Siobhan rolled her eyes, interrupting. "Stupid dragons, you think because you have a mating bond, that others don't have something similar? Just because you mate wielders, doesn't mean wielders can't mate each other. We have binding rituals that tie our powers together in a ceremony involving a ring of the wielder's own power. Once in a while, when a match is so strong, when two people are fated to be, they can bind even without the ceremony. I think what we are hearing is that Killian and Marissa are soulmates, and the ring bound them when he put it on her finger."

Killian nodded, staring into Risa's eyes, drawn to her like a magnet. "She is, forever my heart." He kissed her gently, and the whole room broke into applause.

Apparently, Shannon was busy while her children were catching up. The whole area knew her beloved son had returned home after a long absence and was newly engaged. Dozens of friends and neighbors started arriving en masse, bringing food, instruments, drink, and an overwhelming sense of family. Soon, there was a large party set up, and people were milling about everywhere.

Lots of folks she didn't know hugged Risa and welcomed her to the family, much to Killian's amusement. She seemed to be enjoying the music and camaraderie that continued into the night, dancing, laughing, and trying new foods. She wasn't even upset when a woman bumped into her, spilling a drink down her back. Killian was irritated, but with so many silver wielders here, it was hard to tell which one it was.

Killian heard a snippet of an all too familiar song coming from somewhere, and his face froze as he realized someone was playing the video of him singing at the wedding. Molly came running over, waving the phone in her hand. "Killian, how stupid am I that I didn't realize that was my own brother? Do ye really know the people in Still Waters?" she hissed, her mouth hanging open in awe.

He simply laughed and rolled his eyes. "Aye, I do. Ye remember my friend, Vaughn? His wife an' Jorrie are best friends. We used to work together before she became a star. Anyhow, the drummer, Shepard, who is also a friend of mine, was supposed to sing that song. But he left the wedding to help Vaughn. See, the wedding was for Shepard's twin brother, who was marrying Jorrie's best friend. I got tricked into it by that giant lizard over there," gesturing at Liam.

"Shut up," she said disbelievingly and punched him on the arm.

Killian glanced over at Siobhan, then back at his sister. He suddenly realized that's why he'd always thought of the prickly woman as a sibling. The two really were just alike. "Shi, come here," he called.

The green wielder strolled over. "Yeah?"

"I'm just letting ye know that Molly an' ye were apparently separated at birth." He nodded seriously, and they both punched him at the same time, one on each shoulder.

The two women smiled at each other and walked away arm in arm, griping about men, brothers in particular. They pulled Risa with them, and she smirked over her shoulder. He held his smile until they were far enough away, then rubbed his shoulders, mouthing a silent ouch.

Liam strolled over. "Brave man," he snorted, trying to cover up a laugh.

Killian grinned. "Aye, but it distracted her, lizard boy."

"Ki," Liam sighed and hung his head, "I really am sorry," he mumbled as he scuffed his toes across the ground as he often did, looking just like a sulky child.

Shaking his head at his goofy friend, Killian chuckled. Even though Liam was an idiot at times, he was still a solid, loyal, good person. "Honestly, it doesn't bother me that much anymore. I've come to realize that my desire to be alone is no longer there, an' I don't care what anyone thinks or says, if I have Marissa."

Liam glanced at him with an aching sadness dulling the mischievous sparkle in his emerald eyes. "I envy you, Killian, I really do," he whispered.

Smiling at the green dragon, Killian threw an arm around his shoulder, "She's out there, Liam. You'll find her."

Shannon wandered over then. "Killian, as happy as I am that you're here an' bringing us this joyous news, ye didn't come all the way to Ireland with your friends just to see us. What's going on?" She studied his face, a knowing frown forcing her full lips, so like his own, into a thin downturned bow.

"Too many ears, Ma, I'll tell ye later tonight after the others go home," he mumbled.

She smiled then, "My boy, always up to something."

A loud hail had Killian turning to the musicians that were providing some lively tunes. They enthusiastically waved him over. He made his way warily to them, and sure enough, they asked him to sing a few songs with them. The crowd started chanting. They wanted to hear more after the video finished circulating.

Molly jumped up and down with glee. She loved hearing her brother sing.

Risa waved in encouragement; she wanted to hear it, too.

He rolled his eyes grudgingly and agreed he would do a few. They started playing a popular folk song as he took the microphone and began to sing. By the second song, he was having fun. Everyone was dancing, many were singing along. He tried to leave after that, but he was dragged back up and coerced into several more songs.

After he claimed he desperately needed a break and a beer, he was able to escape. He found his friends and collapsed into a chair, gratefully accepting the beer Liam held out for him. He used the bottom of his shirt to wipe his face, sweating despite the cooler temperature. He noticed Risa admiring the section of his abdomen on display while his shirt was pulled up. He grinned at her and winked when she blushed at being caught. He was about to spirit her off to a quiet corner when a couple of young ladies scurried over, shyly asking him to dance. He begged off, citing the need to take a break, but shoved Liam in their direction, telling them he was good friends with the band Still Waters and loved to dance. Liam shot him a grateful look as the young women dragged him away.

Siobhan laughed, cheering Liam on as they fawned all over him. Marco smirked but wisely kept quiet when she glared at the women who approached him.

Killian was still sitting with Risa when Molly wandered over and plopped in his lap, looping her arm around his shoulders and kissing his temple. "Dear brother of mine. Ye missed my wedding an' the birth of your nephew, ye right arse."

He leaned against her and kissed her cheek. "I know, an' I'm so sorry, Molly Lolly."

She rolled her eyes. "See, I'm thinking you're owing me. I want ye to sing me a song. The one ye promised for my wedding."

He stilled, then smiled, "Sorry, my love, but I don't have them anymore. I couldn't do it tonight. But I can write ye a new one an' come back soon?"

"I'd a feeling you'd be saying that," she grinned, "Trying to shimmy your way out of it. Always the smooth-talking, slippery one ye were. Ma kept them all an' I have a copy of that one because ye promised me. Ye. Promised. Me. Killian," she poked his chest with each word. Each stab harder than the last. "An' ye weren't there." Sadness filled her eyes now.

"Molly, dear, I made that promise to ye nigh eighty years ago, a lot's changed since then," he reminded her quietly.

She leaned in, her forehead to his, "I know. It took me a long time to forgive ye for leaving, but I know why ye did, an' I understand. But now... now it seems you're owing me a song, my dear brother, an' I'm not forgetting it."

He sighed; she was right. He did owe her. "Fine, fine, but only because you're a right pain in me arse, ye narkey hole," he muttered.

She threw her head back and laughed gleefully, kicking her feet in victory.

He smiled at Risa, "An' I'm guessing I'll be back in a bit. Hope ye like it."

As he stood, Siobhan leaned over with a loud whisper to Risa, "You know, I've always thought Killian was extremely good-looking under all that hair and that accent. But girl, he's getting more Irish by the minute and holy shit, I've never wanted a bite out of a leprechaun so bad in my life! I bet he's magically delicious!"

Marco's eyes closed. A pained expression crossed his face as if he tasted something terrible.

Risa snickered, "Oh, that he is Shi, that he is." She winked at Killian as he jogged away laughing.

"Disgusting," hissed the silver-haired woman. She'd purposefully spilled a drink down Marissa's back, which she admitted was petty, but her rage at seeing the middle sister so happy made her stomach roil. "Out there acting like a bitch in heat while she should be looking for poor, lost Isabella. Wretched dog."

Behind her, the brown-hair man rolled his eyes, wisely keeping quiet so he didn't raise her ire any further. He didn't want her malicious attention directed at him. Then again... "What if we take the other woman? The redhead? We could lead them to where they'll miraculously find Isabella, and we can move forward with the plan that way?"

Her eyes dancing with flame, and fangs dropping, she spun to face him, snarling. Then she paused. "Hmm, not a bad plan. But how do I get those dragons away? That other woman is the dark one's mate, an' I'd not care to tangle with a red dragon." She considered darkly, her gaze thunderous and bordering on insanity. "I'll need to create a distraction." She eyed a table at the back of the party. "I know how. Be ready," she grinned, an oily, evil sneer that made the man feel even sorrier for the unsuspecting dragons.

Killian took a deep, steadying breath. The song was simple, one the cobbled together band could easily handle. He wasn't sure if he could. He hadn't sung this song in decades, and he only ever sang it to his sister. Closing his eyes, he imagined her, standing there in her wedding gown, smiling at her husband, Brendon. Their parents were watching with tears in their eyes next to a big gaping hole where he should've been. He could do this; he had to. He owed it to his Molly.

He picked up the microphone. "Years ago, I wrote a song." Cheers resounded. "Ah, pipe down ya saps," he grinned. "I wrote this song for my baby sister, for her wedding day. An' then like an absolute langer, I wasn't there for her." He gave an apologetic glance to Molly, standing in front of him with her husband by her side.

"This was supposed to be the song for their first dance. Apparently, the pestering wench," more laughter, "She's not gone an' forgotten about it. So family, friends, an' anyone else who snuck in for the beer, please stand back an' let my sister Molly, an' her husband Brendon have this dance, for their wedding. I love ye, Molly Lolly." He toasted her with his beer and nodded to the band. They started playing, and he took a deep breath, then began to sing. Molly smiled dreamily as Brendon took her in his arms, and they danced.

Risa's breath caught in her throat; the song was beautiful. She couldn't understand most of it because it wasn't all in English, but you didn't need to know the words to realize it was a musical interpretation of true love. Her heart warmed in her chest as she watched the way Molly sank into her husband's eyes. Brendon obviously adored her as well; his expression was one of utter devotion.

Turning back to watch Killian, Risa fell in love with him all over again. She put her finger on the ring he'd given her and thought of him, how much she loved him, how necessary he was to her now. How fortunate she was to have the love of a man like him. His eyes flew to hers, startled, and he placed his hand over his heart. She glanced down at the ring, then back at him. *No way.* She did it again. He grinned and winked at her. "Holy shit," she whispered.

Chapter 17

KILLIAN WAS LOST IN the music, singing Molly's song, when a hard pulse of emotion washed through his body. His eyes flew wide, and he immediately knew it came from Risa. She was holding her ring and thinking of her love for him. Her mouth dropped when she realized he felt it. She did it again just to be sure, and he winked to let her know he got the message. It would seem she wasn't aware of how truly special her ring was. It floored him to feel the depth of her love for him. To have it confirmed in a way he'd never experienced before. He wrapped up the song and congratulated his sister. She and her husband both thanked him, tears in their eyes.

He turned towards Risa, who was still staring at him, moved by the song. Glancing out over the crowd, Killian realized he wanted to make his engagement public, to share his joy. He waved her up, planning to announce it, when he saw a silvery-blonde head bobbing through the back of those gathered near the buffet set up. Narrowing his eyes, he peered deeply into the throng of friends and neighbors, trying to catch sight of the person with the silver hair. It wasn't uncommon here, but this particular woman looked familiar somehow. This was happening too often to be a coincidence.

He forgot about the mystery woman when he caught sight of Risa as she maneuvered her way up to him through the crowd. Smiling softly, he took her hand and called out to those assembled, "Everyone, a moment if I may. As many of ye already know, my Ma, the lovely Shannon Brennan, spread news of my engagement faster than a wildfire."

Shannon shook a finger at him playfully.

"I'd like to take a moment to introduce ye all to my lovely bride-to-be. Marissa Thompson, the woman that made the earth shift for me, the one who stole my heart, an' refuses to let it go. gave me back my voice. She's my everything, an' I'm so glad she's here with me, by my side, part of the Brennan family."

He dipped her low to cheers and applause. They both jolted in surprise as panicked screams replaced the happy sounds from the back of the crowd. Flames flickered from one of the tables where various food offerings were placed. The cheerful crackle and dance of the blaze roared in stark contrast to the fear of those standing nearby when the flames soared high in the air. Shouts of caution and reassurance came as someone grabbed a hose and began spraying down the burning table. Within moments, the fire was extinguished, and nervous chatter filled the air. The speculation was that someone either dropped a lit cigarette or a spark from a nearby grill caught something flammable on the table. Fortunately, no injuries let the party continue soon afterwards.

It was extremely late by the time the last of the partygoers finally left, and the cleanup of the fire was completed. Marco and Liam were conspiring about something in the corner, and Siobhan was asleep on the couch.

Killian wandered over to the dragons, asking if they were still discussing the mysterious fire. Marco had mentioned earlier that the fire was started by magic, most likely a dragon, but he and Liam were nowhere near it. They closed ranks quickly around Siobhan, knowing Risa was safe with Killian. He wanted to mention the woman he thought he was seeing, but the smirks on his friend's faces hinted there was something else on their minds.

Marco grinned, "Wasn't us this time, you did this on your own." He turned his phone around, revealing videos of Killian singing from earlier that night on social media. Captions ranged from 'Texas heartthrob shows up in Ireland' to 'Mysterious singer identified — his ties to Still Waters'.

Rolling his eyes, Killian declared, "I canna' believe how me singing a few folk songs is so fascinatin'."

"Well, believe it, there's a lot of women after your Lucky Charms!" Liam chuckled.

Killian narrowed his gaze then flicked the dragon between the eyes, adding a push of his power with it. "Feckin' overgrown lizard."

Liam's head thumped back into the wall. At first, he glared at Killian, then laughed loudly. The sound startled Siobhan, and she grumbled about her stupid brother before going back to sleep.

Shannon marched up behind the men, snatching Liam and Killian both by the ear, dragging them into the dining room and scolding them for their behavior in her house.

"Ma!" Killian groaned, "For Christ's sake, woman, I'm almost a hundred. I'll ask ye not to treat me like a bleedin' child anymore."

She gasped, "Killian Brennan! I'll not have ye taking the Lord's name in vain in my household. An' ye *will* be respectful of the others in this house." She turned her wrathful attention to Liam now. "An' ye disturbing your sister so in her condition! Shame on ye, young man!"

Killian began making faces at Liam behind Shannon's back, crossing his eyes, and thumbing his nose.

Liam wisely nodded, keeping quiet. He was used to an Irish-tempered mother, but his lips were quirking, trying not to laugh at Killian.

Shannon's gaze narrowed in suspicion.

Marco made the mistake of cackling at them both, thinking he was safe.

Shannon whirled and glared at him, so he quickly mimed zipping his lips and batted his eyelashes in his best innocent expression. She nodded, satisfied, and gestured for them all to sit.

Risa joined them with a pot of tea as she bit her lip, trying not to laugh at the hangdog expressions on all the men's faces after being scolded like children. She loved Shannon Brennan. The woman was a pure force of nature.

Shannon pointed at Killian, "Now, boy, speak."

He quickly filled her in on the back story, the rescue of Serena, the kidnapping of Vaughn and how he met Risa. Their work uncovering the sisters' history and breaking the spell. Now they were tracking down the missing sister, Isabella. They were going to Cork next, to speak to the people at the adoption agency. Risa had insisted they take some time to stop here first so Killian could see his family.

Shannon nodded along in understanding, then took Risa's hands, "Sweet girl, it was so thoughtful of ye to put aside your own plans to bring him home to us."

Risa shook her head, smiling gently. "He needed this, too. I'll find my sister, but he's been away longer than she has. His need was greater."

"Dear Marissa," Shannon patted her cheek, "I'm so grateful you're part of our family now. I know you'll take such good care of him. I won't have to worry so much. We just love ye so much already. He *better* take good care of ye!" She turned an icy, but motherly, glare on Killian, who put up his hands.

"Ma, I will, Marissa is my world, an' I couldn't live without her. I will take good care of her, you've my word as your son an' her bonded partner," he promised with alacrity.

Shannon relaxed. "An' there better be some invitations to the wedding? I've a mind to twist the ear of that friend of yours, Vaughn. Married, babies, not a word from him?" she huffed, shaking her head.

Killian tried in vain to hide his grin, "I wouldn't dare forget that."

She smiled and patted his hand. "Good boy." She turned back to Risa. "Now, your sister, ye last heard she was in Cork but haven't been able to find her trail?" They nodded. "An' ye say she's a silver dragon named Isabella?" More nodding. Shannon's expression turned thoughtful before she stood, saying, "You'll be excusing me a moment, I'll be right back."

Killian glanced at his friends and lifted his palms; he wasn't sure what she was doing.

After about ten minutes, Shannon hurried back in, a bright smile on her face. Her excitement was almost palpable. "Well, an' that was time well spent. I think the fates were guiding ye here." She took Risa's hands in hers. "Risa, I've a friend in Ballymore. She runs a boarding school for young women, an' I remembered her telling me about a young woman that works for her. I confirmed with Ciarra just now, her name is Isabella, an' she's a silver dragon. She's from Cork. I've a good feeling she's your sister; she's about the right age. I'll give ye the address. Ciarra's expecting ye tomorrow."

Risa struggled to take a breath, her chest tight, her ears ringing. Shannon knew where they could likely find her sister. Muffled sounds surrounded her, everyone speaking at once, but none of the words reached her. Killian touched her arm, and everything shot back into focus.

"Risa," he repeatedly softly, "Are ye alright, my love?"

First, she nodded, then shook her head, and a gasping sob burst from her lips, "Killian, Isabella, she's..." Risa dissolved into tears, unable to speak further.

"Shhh," he held her to his chest. "Ma," he whispered, his voice thick with emotion. He blinked at her, unable to put into words what he wanted to say.

Shannon smiled softly, misty-eyed; she knew.

Killian lifted Marissa into his arms and carried her to his room. He trusted the others to get the information they needed and settle in for the night. Right now, he needed to care for Risa. He shoved the door closed behind him and gently laid her on the bed before settling next to her. He gathered her close and sang softly to her, soothing her as she let out her emotions. His mother was an absolute saint, saving them so much time.

He thought about fate and the fact that it was Risa who insisted they come here first for him to see his family. She put her own needs on the back burner for him. Because of that, he was able to retrieve the ring he made long ago with his wielding magic, thinking one day to give it to the woman who held his heart. He knew now it was always meant for Risa. It fit her perfectly and immediately bound her to him. Now they would find her sister so much quicker than they would have any other way.

He held her until she fell asleep, then he gently slipped off her shoes and most of her clothing so she would rest comfortably. He was restless, so he quietly made his way out front. He noticed Siobhan was gone, replaced by Liam, and assumed Marco took her to Molly's old room. Killian moved outside where it was still close and warm, so he took his shirt off, enjoying the light breeze rolling through. He leaned against the rail and breathed in deeply of the night air. It was so different from Texas. He filled his lungs again, greedily savoring the feel and let it out slowly.

"So, not enough to put extra holes in your face, ye need drawings on the rest of ye, too?" came a quiet lilting voice.

He turned, finding his mother on the cushioned bench on the porch. She was glaring at his tattoos. "Ma," he sighed.

She patted the seat next to her, and he sat happily with her. She pulled him over and wrapped her arms around him, whispering, "Ye might be closing in on a century, Killian, but you'll always be my baby. My first-born." She poked his chest and teased him a little more before she admitted she actually liked the tattoos. She sighed, "Oh my baby, it's a fine, handsome man you've turned into. I'm proud of ye. So very proud of ye."

He sat up and stared at her, eyes wide, mouth open.

"Flies," she whispered, pushing his mouth closed.

His lips twitched before he laughed heartily, the deep booming sound echoing through the night.

"Killian," she patted his face. "I so love to hear ye laugh. It's such a beautiful sound to my heart. I've always been proud of ye for knowing your own heart an' mind. I'm sorry it took ye away from us, but I understand ye needed to find yourself. And to find Marissa. She's so lovely, Killian. I'm truly happy for ye."

"Momma," he murmured, "thank ye. Thank ye for loving an' supporting me all these years. And thank ye for understanding. I missed ye greatly an' I love ye so very much."

She started to cry, her lips trembling as she covered them with even shakier fingers, "Oh, now that's done it. Ye always dream your babies will say such a thing."

He pulled her to him this time. He might be closing in on a century, but he was never too old to need his mother's approval.

"All right, my love," she sighed, "To bed with ye. You've a long day tomorrow." She patted his head, then kissed his cheek.

Grinning, he kissed her back. "I won't stay gone so long this time, I promise."

"I know," she whispered.

He slid into bed with Risa and slipped his arms around her gently. He put his face against her hair, breathing her in. He sighed, drifting off, peaceful, settled in his heart.

In the morning, they woke, still wrapped around each other. "Did ye sleep well, *mo stor*?" he whispered.

She smirked, "Well, not at first, but when I woke and found you there, I slept much better after that. Killian," she hesitated.

He nuzzled her neck as he kissed his way up to her jaw. "Aye, my silver goddess?" he grinned against the soft skin of her throat.

She squealed, giggled, and whispered, "Are we going to go today to find my sister?"

Lifting his head, he met her gaze. "Of course. We're going to Ballymore, meeting Ciarra an' hopefully Isabella. Darling, I can't promise it will be today we find her, but it will be soon."

She lowered her eyes, worrying her bottom lip with her teeth.

"What's wrong?" he asked, concern warming his voice.

"I just... hate to take you away from your family after you've only just reunited with them."

He laughed, relief flooding through him, "Risa, my family will be here. They weren't lost. We can come back. We need to find Isabella; she's the one that needs us the most. I can never thank ye enough for putting aside your own quest to do this for me."

She smiled, "I would do anything for you."

He let a wolfish grin cross his lips, "Anything?" he smirked, then leaned down to whisper some suggestive ideas in her ear.

"Killian," she gasped, "You kiss your mother with that mouth?"

Wiggling his eyebrows, he replied, "Ye want me to show ye?" then pulled the blanket over them and proceeded to kiss all over her face.

She giggled and shrieked, trying to squirm away from him.

He finally managed to capture the wriggling armful of woman and secured her underneath him. "Ye naughty thing, trying to escape me. I've a mind to spank ye."

She paused, "Really?" She seemed intrigued by the idea.

He grinned. "Later, I smell bacon an' if we don't get there before Liam, we're going hungry today. Besides, we need to get to Ballymore." He stretched out over her, kissing her hard, rubbing his body seductively against hers. Jumping out of bed, Killian slipped some pants on, winking before strutting out of the room.

"So not fair," she groaned.

Chapter 18

"FIFTEEN MINUTES?" RISA demanded incredulously. "That's it? Fifteen minutes to get to Ballymore."

Killian shrugged, "Give or take."

She shook her head. She'd been so worried their day was off to a horrible start when the car wouldn't start that morning. She huffed about their bad luck lately. Killian's car at home, her flat tire, now this. Fortunately, Liam had it running in no time. A loose hose was quickly repaired, and now they were on their way. Killian's soothing voice cut into her reverie.

"Ye forget my love, if you're thinking about driving across Texas, compared to the whole of Ireland, well, it's a lot different."

Liam leaned forward, grinning. "You know, I read Ireland can fit in Texas around ten times. Mind blowing, huh?"

Killian glanced at the dragon in the mirror and flung a jolt of silver magic over his shoulder. The bolt smacked Liam right between the eyes. Chuckling at the cursing coming from behind him, Killian shook his head. "I know ye think Texas is basically its own country but show some respect ye feckin' lizard. Ye may wear a ten-gallon hat, but it's not that hard to blow your two-pint mind."

As the others laughed, Liam narrowed his eyes, "I was just trying to show I was learning about the country. Rude."

Relenting, Killian smiled at the dragon and nodded. He gave them more of the rich history of Ireland as he drove.

Marco, Liam, and Siobhan sat in the back, entranced. They were all fascinated by having their own tour guide and were eager to learn more. Liam asked questions rapid fire, and Killian's smile grew wider at their enthusiasm. He continued to educate his friends about his home country. It was obvious how much he loved it, and they agreed, it was a beautiful place. Before they knew it, they pulled into the parking lot. Before them was the Catholic girls' school where Shannon's friend Ciarra was headmistress.

Risa slowly exited the car and took a deep, calming breath. She wiped her damp palms on her dress. She'd wanted to look nice for this meeting, but now she worried she was trying too hard.

"Stop it," Killian softly chided her.

She glanced at him sheepishly. She knew he was telling her to stop overthinking it. "It's hard," she admitted.

He brushed his thumb over her ring and sent a wave of calm and affection through it.

She inhaled sharply. "How did you do that?"

He lifted her hand and kissed her fingers, then the ring. When he did, it felt like he kissed her in the most intimate place, and she gasped again.

With a devilish grin, he leaned in, whispering in her ear, "The ring is made from my direct power infusing the silver of the band, an' the diamond is pure magic from my heart. It's bound your power to mine an' mine to yours. Like the dragons have their mating bond, this is our version. That's why it was so important for me to give ye this specific ring. Did ye not know that's what it was?"

She shook her head, overwhelmed again by the deep love he held for her.

"I'm sorry, Risa," he told her softly, "You've adapted so well; I forget there're things in our lore ye may not know. If ye ever need me, or want to feel me by your side, just touch the ring an' think of me. It connects us." He touched it again and thought about how much he loved her.

She sighed, the warm feeling caressing over her skin like a gentle embrace. Touching the ring, she sent the emotion back and could tell when he felt it. "That is so cool," she exclaimed, grinning. Then she gasped, staring over his shoulder.

Whirling, Killian pulled her behind him and stared wildly. The dragons also went on high alert, Siobhan firmly between them.

"Sorry," Risa grimaced, "I thought I saw a woman with hair exactly like mine. I thought it might be Isabella, but wishful thinking, I'm sure."

Laughing, Killian relaxed. "Ready?" He took her hands.

She nodded, feeling more confident now. "Let's do this."

"Finally, right where we want them!" the silver-haired woman grinned, running her fingers through her long hair, shaking it behind her before twirling it up in a bun. "Now for the next steps. I need to hurry an' get in there." She gave an evil chuckle as she brushed out her outfit.

The man constantly by her side, eyed her warily. "Are you sure? Is this the right time to reveal yourself?"

Scoffing, she waved him off, "It's the perfect time, ye worry about your own self. You'll see, I have them right where I want them. Now shove off, I need to get in there to make sure they meet 'Isabella' an' fall in love with her."

They sat in the headmistress's office, waiting for Ciarra to join them. According to her assistant, she would be with them shortly. Risa's knee was bouncing, and she was clenching then unclenching her hands. Liam excused himself to find a restroom.

A few minutes later, the door opened, and Ciarra flew in. She was like a whirlwind the way she swept into the room. "Well, little Killian Brennan as I live and breathe!" The woman squealed like a little girl and pinched his cheek. He stared at her in alarm as she breezed around the desk. Marco and Siobhan were trying to stifle their laughter. Risa was speechless. "Young man, I haven't seen you since you were knee high to a grasshopper! About time you came home, your poor mother worried sick about you, she was."

Killian sat there, his mouth opening and closing. Nothing came out.

Marco leaned towards Siobhan, "That's more like the Killian we know."

Siobhan snorted, trying to control her amusement, then giggled as Killian glared at them.

Clearing his throat, Killian turned back to Ciarra, "Forgive me, ma'am, I know you've been friends with my mother for a long time, so I appreciate ye making time for us today."

The boisterous woman bounced in her chair, waving her fingers excitedly. "When I heard that our sweet Isabella possibly had a sister looking for her, I just knew I needed to help." She studied Marissa, and her hands fluttered like startled pigeons, flapping above the desk. "My dear, you *must* be related! You look so much like her!"

Risa's heart stumbled. Her sister *was* here! She could feel it.

Liam wandered down the hall searching for his way back from the restroom. The nice assistant gave him directions to a restroom he could use, but he got turned around on the return trip. He swept around a sharp corner and smacked into someone coming the other way.

"Oof!" she grunted and fell to the floor, landing squarely on her bottom.

Liam stared in shock. "Oh my god, I am so sorry!" he blurted, watching the beautiful blonde woman who was now sitting on the floor trying to recover her senses. Her hair was the color of spun gold and wrapped neatly in a tidy, no-nonsense bun. A whiff of cinnamon and smoke caused his nostrils to flare. Her hazel eyes met his, and the earth shifted. He braced a hand on the wall to steady himself. After staring at her for another moment, he leaned down and held out his hand to pull her to her feet. "Please, let me help you."

Although she still looked dazed, she took his hand, and he felt a slight tingle as he assisted her up. He tensed, and his heart pounded erratically like a war drum. A low rumble threatened in his chest, but he swallowed it down; he didn't want to alarm her.

"Thank ye, I..." she trailed off as she gained her feet, then really looked at him. He was quite possibly the most handsome man she'd ever seen in her life. And he was smiling at her. Her breath hitched as the world spun sideways for a moment before righting itself. "Sorry! For running into ye. I wasn't watching where I was going. I do that a lot. Unfortunately. An' I certainly wasn't expecting to run into such a handsome man. I mean, any man in here. After all, it's a girl's school an' there are no men here. You're not a teacher, I don't think... an' I'm rambling, aren't I?" Her face flushed, and she was sure it was an unbecoming shade of crimson.

He grinned at her and held his fingers barely apart. "Little bit."

She smiled back at him, shyly.

"So, you think I'm handsome?" he widened the dazzling smile that marked him as pure trouble as he tucked a lock of his long red-gold hair behind his ear.

"I said that, aye? Right out loud. Yep, wait to go, Izzy, make the pretty man think you're barking." She stared at him, her face getting redder, if such a thing were possible.

"Izzy, is it?" he laughed, "Well, Izzy, the pretty man doesn't think you're barking, but he thinks you should know his name is Liam, and he's very sorry for knocking you over."

"Liam," Izzy said, trying out the name. It suited him. "Liam of the Irish name, but the American accent. You're not from around here."

Liam smiled again, gently this time. "No ma'am. I'm here with some friends. We're meeting with the headmistress, but I was looking for a restroom. Which I found. Got a little turned around on the way back."

"Alright then, meeting with Ciarra. Well, I'm heading there myself; she called me to her office. I can take ye if you'd like to walk with me." She wished she wasn't feeling so suddenly shy. Her heart was pounding, and her hands were clammy.

Nodding, Liam replied softly, "I'd like that, Izzy." Suddenly, the blood drained from his face, leeching it of its sun-kissed color, leaving the smattering of freckles over his nose standing out in stark contrast. "Izzy, oh shit." He stared at her now like she was a phantom.

She checked over her shoulder to make sure there was no one else there before she studied him in alarm, "Liam, are ye alright?"

Liam reached out and gently touched her arm, as if he were testing to see if she was real. His eyes widened further, and he shook his head rapidly, his hair whipping around his jaw. "Fuck," he whispered.

Her nose scrunched up in distaste. "Well, that's certainly not appropriate language here, Mr. Liam. This is a proper school, I'll have ye know," her tone teetering on the edge of haughty.

"No, no, no, sorry! You just caught me off guard. Izzy," he breathed, "You incredibly gorgeous woman. Please, tell me Izzy is short for Isabella."

She nodded slowly, eyeing him warily. She was fairly sure it was actually the pretty man who was barking now.

Liam was practically bouncing on his toes. He quickly took her hands in his own large, warm grasp. "Do you know why Ciarra called you to her office?"

She stared down at their joined hands. Barking or not, his touch thrilled her to the very center of her being. She glanced back up into his stunning face and shook her head. "Not completely, only that there was someone she needed me to meet. Is that who ye are then?" she asked hopefully.

He shook his head, then nodded, biting his lip.

She laughed, "Well, which is it, Mr. Potty Mouth?"

He smacked his forehead. "Sorry, Isabella! I'm not the person you need to meet, although I am elated that I met you, but I'm with the person you... not *with* but I came with..." He blew out an exasperated breath. "Ugh, come on, which way? Hurry!" he urged her.

Her mouth dropped open in surprise. He wasn't making much sense, but she could sense this was important. She pointed, and he yanked her against his hard body, kissing her forehead before dragging her by the hand towards the office. He was practically running, his long legs churning up the distance. She was nearly sprinting to keep up. "Liam!" she squealed.

He glanced back at her over his shoulder and laughed. His emerald-green eyes sparkled at her with joy and a hint of trouble. "Trust me, Isabella, it's worth it," he called merrily in a sing-song tone.

She grinned, thinking, *What the hell, why not? If he's trouble, I'm here for it,* and ran after him.

Just before they reached the office door, he slowed and came to a halt. He turned, still grinning at her. She smiled back at him uncertainly now, and he held up a finger over his lips. He eased the door open and poked his head in. When the people inside turned to look at him, he made a grand gesture, announcing, "Look... who I found," before ushering Izzy in ahead of him.

Chapter 19

IZZY WAS CONFUSED BY the dramatic production of Liam's introduction. *Who are all these people in Ciarra's office? And why are they all staring at me? Why is that woman crying? She looks familiar.* Suddenly, Izzy's head started to ache fiercely. Her vision wavered, and she grabbed her temple as the pounding was joined by intense nausea.

An incredibly stunning man with short black hair approached her, his voice muffled, nearly drowned out by the drumming in her skull. She barely heard him saying, "Isabella, there's a spell on ye, I can help if ye let me, please."

She stared at him. Glancing over his shoulder, she saw another gorgeous man of Latin descent, next a beautiful woman who resembled Liam. *What the hell? Is there a model convention in town?* The woman with the same red-gold hair as Liam smiled at her and gestured for her to sit. She'd do anything right now to make the pain go away. It was getting worse by the nanosecond. "Please, help her," she heard the silver-haired woman beg tearfully.

"Her spell hasn't been broken yet," the black-haired man murmured, his Irish accent soothing with its familiar lilt. He gently placed his hands on her temples and nodded at the other women to stand behind him. "I'll not have any of ye taking a hit if this blasts back the way Risa's did." He smiled at her, "Easy now, lass, we'll have ye feeling better in no time." His deep, soft voice calmed her nerves, but she still whimpered as the pain intensified.

"Killian?" the silver-haired woman sobbed, tears in her eyes.

Izzy watched in equal parts awe and trepidation as the gorgeous man, who was apparently named Killian, swirled his hands like he was weaving or playing a harp. She could almost see the silver waves coming from him. It was beautiful. Suddenly, there was intense pressure in her head, and then it was gone like the snap of the fingers. She gasped and leapt to her feet. "What did ye do to me?" she shouted in fear. She could feel things, remember things she hadn't before. Her parents dying, being on the run with Dorothy and Bill. Going to the agency. She remembered now she had two sisters. Serena and... "Marissa?" she gasped, her lips trembling as she stared at the silver-haired woman in front of her. Her body was wrapped in silvery warm light, and her head lolled back a second before she passed out.

Liam caught her as she fell, the woman barely weighing anything in his arms despite her tall frame and full curves. He stared at her in reverence as waves of magic washed over her, smoothing out her skin, changing her hair to the same silvery color as Risa's, and making her appear younger before fading away.

"Oh, my dear Izzy!" Ciarra was shouting, "Quick over here, put her here," she called to Liam. She was pointing frantically at a chaise in the corner.

He hurried over, laying her down with her head on his lap. He stroked her hair and wiped her forehead with the cool cloth someone handed him.

Siobhan watched her brother with a soft smile on her face. "Poor thing, for all his moping about being alone, his life just changed, and he doesn't even know it yet," she whispered extra quietly into Killian's ear.

Killian glanced at her in surprise, then studied the two dragons and smiled gently in return, making a motion around them like he was drawing their silhouettes.

Siobhan nodded and winked before moving next to Marco and leaning her head on his shoulder.

Risa sat on the floor next to her sister, holding her hand. Killian quietly slid behind her, reassuring her that Izzy was okay. She just needed a little reset after the big shock of the spell removal. Even now, the woman was stirring and waking up.

Izzy was incredibly sure she was dreaming. She was lying in the strong arms of a very delightful-smelling man, and that shouldn't be. She could smell fresh grass, apples, and a hint of smoke. She opened her eyes and saw the concerned face of the pretty man from the hallway. There was a small trickle of smoke coming from one nostril. *Yeah, definitely dreaming, there's no way that gorgeous man is a dragon, too.* She sighed, *oh well, it's my dream, I can do what I want.* She reached up and pulled that amazing-looking mouth down to her own, kissing him thoroughly. He seemed shocked at first, but warmed to it and kissed her back. *Wow, dream man has really soft, delicious lips, I was right, pure trouble this one.* His kiss turned hungrier, and it sent a burst of heat straight through her.

Liam's brain short-circuited. Isabella woke up and started kissing him. He knew he should stop her, but her touch sent sparks to his very core. Before he knew it, he was kissing her back. He heard a throat clear and jerked away. He looked up to see Killian grinning at him. Risa stared in shock. Marco and Siobhan were smothering their laughter against each other. "Uh, she kissed me," he exclaimed weakly, pulling her closer to him defensively. Despite the awkwardness of the situation, he wasn't ready to let her go yet.

Risa narrowed her eyes. "You didn't have to kiss her back," she hissed.

His jaw dropped, "That would be rude! Besides, I'm a man. She's a stunning woman!"

"But she —" Risa started.

"She," Isabella interrupted, "Is right here, realizing she is *not* dreaming an' is in fact quite awake. To top it all off, she is now also super embarrassed."

Izzy slowly sat up, and Liam's arms let go of her, quite reluctantly, which made her blush harder. She'd no business kissing a stranger like that. What he must think of her! She tried to cover her embarrassment by smoothing her hair before noticing that it was no longer up in her usual bun but down around her face. Her heart began to pound as she realized it was also now a silvery-blonde, not the darker, goldish hue it was before. *No, not before. After.* The spell made it a normal human color. This was her natural color. And that meant... Her gaze flew to meet the eyes of Marissa, her younger sister, missing for so long. She launched herself from the chaise and threw herself at: "Marissa," she sobbed, "I thought I'd never see ye again."

Marissa held her sister tight and cried against her neck. "Isabella, I'm so glad we found you. God, I've missed you!" Anything else she said was muffled by the years of heartache catching up with them both, encompassing the enormity of loss they didn't know they were missing until now.

The others withdrew to the opposite side of the room to allow the women their reunion. Siobhan wasn't the only one wiping her eyes. Ciarra whispered to Killian, "Thank you, young man, you've done a good thing here." She patted him on the shoulder and sighed. "I'm guessing you'll be taking her with you now, I should start looking for another art teacher."

Killian smiled, *art teacher*? She was definitely family. He turned to his fiancée, his chest warming with how much he loved that word. He saw all the worry and strain that she'd worn for the past week melting away, and it relieved his own worry as well. Izzy turned to say something to Ciarra as she moved past, and Killian's stomach clenched as if he'd been sucker punched. For a moment, as he watched Izzy's profile, he swore she looked just like the woman he'd been catching glimpses of, following them.

He shook his head, it couldn't be; they'd just found Izzy, and she was under the spell. He'd only seen that other woman from a distance and the corner of his eye. She never seemed to be facing him, so he couldn't say with any certainty if the features were a match. Rubbing his brow, he decided he was only tired and paranoid. Izzy couldn't be the mystery woman; she seemed genuinely happy to find her sister; she would have said something before now otherwise. He moved silently to Risa's side and kissed her temple. "Sorry to interrupt, I just couldn't help it. Ye look so happy," he told her as he quietly studied Izzy.

Risa smiled at him tenderly. She turned to her sister, "Isabella, this is my fiancé, Killian. He's the one who realized who I was and has been helping rid me of the spell. Our friends," she waved at the others, "Have been helping us find you."

Izzy nodded hard and hugged Killian, nearly choking him with her dragon strength. "Thank ye, ye darling man. I'm forever in your debt!" Then she gasped, "Serena! We have to find her, too!"

"We already have," Liam quickly reassured her as he eased up behind Killian, "We found her first, about four years ago, and she's been part of our family back in the United States ever since."

Izzy slowly moved to stand in front of him, running her fingers through his hair and stroking his cheek, searching his eyes for something. "Ye... you're a dragon, too?" she finally whispered.

He nodded, seeming to be struck mute.

"Ye found my baby sister?" she asked, breathing out the words as faintly as a ghost's sigh.

He swallowed hard, one small nod again.

"Then I'm in debt to ye as well, dream man." Izzy leaned in and kissed him again, gently, lightly this time. Just the tiniest brush of her lips across his.

Liam grinned when she pulled back, finally finding his voice, "Oh, I'm not a dream, and it was a group effort. I can't take all the credit."

She smiled, "Modest, too."

Siobhan snorted and groaned in disbelief.

Izzy glanced at her, confusion wrinkling her brow.

"My brother is anything but modest," Siobhan declared.

Laughing then, Izzy replied, "Of course, you're his sister. That explains why he understands the importance of a family bond. An' why ye look so much alike. How wonderful that ye have each other," she smiled sweetly at the pair.

Siobhan's gaze softened. "Yeah, as siblings go, I did get a good one."

Liam smiled back fondly and tapped her nose. "I knew you loved me; can I get that in writing?"

She stuck her tongue out at him before snapping, "I'd still trade you for Killian," as everyone laughed.

Izzy turned to Marco, holding out a hand. "I don't believe we've met?"

He took her hand and kissed the back of it. "Lovely to make your acquaintance, I'm Marco. A pleasure to meet another sister of the sky." He rolled his Rs as he grinned at her cheekily.

"Okay, loverboy," grumbled Siobhan.

"This gorgeous, prickly creature is my mate and the mother of my child," he said softly, placing a loving hand over Siobhan's stomach and rubbing his nose on her cheek, rumbling his happy dragon sounds.

Izzy smiled at the pair, "Congratulations, how wonderful for ye both!" She turned back to Risa, "I'm so happy right now, I don't know what to do with myself!"

Risa chuckled, "I understand the feeling, but I have an idea. Rena is anxiously awaiting word back home. Would you like to talk to her?"

Izzy's eyes filled with tears. "I would love that more than anything!"

Killian stepped forward then, "How about we go somewhere a little more private where ye can catch up. The rest of us can get some lunch together?" *An' I can figure out if I'm paranoid or there's something there.* They all agreed quickly. Risa and Killian rode with her sister. Liam drove the rest of the group back to Killian's parents' house, where Shannon and Fergus greeted Izzy by promptly welcoming her to the family.

A quick, hurried phone call, "Contact is made. The reunion happened. But there was a complication. That damn green dragon caught me before I was ready. Having to improvise. Stand by."

Click.

A heavy sigh slipped between the brown-haired man's lips as he stared at the silent phone. Nothing about this plan had gone correctly so far, so why hope it would now? She was furious when he failed to capture the green wielder the night before while she set the diversion fire. But the two male dragons surrounded the woman so quickly, there was no way he could have reached her without alerting them to his presence. She got over it quickly when she realized their target was back on track the next day. She had him sabotage the rental car so she could get to Ballymore ahead of them. For all their planning, a simple quirk of timing kept Izzy from being presented how they wanted, and she was going off script. Again. He sighed again and groaned. This was getting worse by the minute, and he was sure he would be blamed.

Chapter 20

IZZY WATCHED THE LARGE family interacting with each other. She realized, with her heart full, that she was part of this family now, too. She smiled, feeling at peace for the first time in a long time. She wasn't unhappy with her current life; she just knew deep down there was more for her. Like something was missing, unfulfilled. She was a dragon, which was pretty special, but there was a relentless tingle in the back of her mind. A gnawing certainty that her story wasn't done yet. Now, she knew why. She mourned the years she lost with her family, but was grateful her sisters didn't give up hope. She thought about Rena, what she suffered. Seeing her sweet face all grown up, hearing her little laugh, like bells in the air, helped immensely. She couldn't wait to see her in person again.

Wandering around the cozy home, she picked up a picture of Killian in an ornate frame, puzzled. It was only half of a photo, the other half torn off. She sucked in a breath when she realized it was part of a wedding photo. She frowned and set it down quickly. She felt a warm body beside her and turned to see the handsome dragon Liam standing close.

He smiled shyly and offered her a glass of wine. "Hey, thought you could use something to drink."

She returned the smile just as shyly. He was absolutely gorgeous, and she was still acutely aware of her lingering mortification for making a fool out of herself. First falling on her ass, then rambling in front of him, and finally kissing him like a common hooker. He probably thought she was some sort of mentally addled hussy. "Thanks!" she blurted belatedly after realizing he was still standing there holding out the glass. She took it and gratefully sipped the crisp white wine. He was smiling at her still. Probably amused now at her staggering stupidity.

"How are you holding up?" he asked, his tone sincere. He really seemed concerned for her.

She stared at him over the rim of the glass. She figured he was probably wondering why she kissed him and hoping she wouldn't try again. His shoulders drooped as she continued to stare, not saying anything. He gave her a small self-deprecating smile and a sad shrug before he turned to go.

"Wait," she called, quickly grabbing his arm. She stared at her hand, wrapped around his bicep. His skin was warm and soft, and her hand tingled where she touched him.

He glanced back at her; one eyebrow arched as a wave of his hair curled around the sharp angle of his jaw.

"Do ye feel that?" she whispered in fascination.

"Your... hand on my arm?" he asked, tilting his head, an uncertain smile reflecting his confusion.

She snatched her hand back like it had been scalded. "Sorry, um, never mind, but I mean, don't go. I'm just a little... overwhelmed. I wanted to thank ye. For the wine," she nodded, saluting him with the glass.

He studied her, his expression now blank. "You already did."

She winced. "Well, thanks again, it's really good wine." She took another sip of the cool liquid that was doing nothing to smother the flames of humiliation coursing through her.

He turned to face her, and the corners of his full lips twitched in amusement. "Am I making you nervous?" His tone was light as he slipped his hands in his pockets and stepped closer.

She nodded slowly. "Aye," she whispered, "I guess so. I feel like I've been nothing but barking around ye an' I don't want ye to have that impression of me." He stepped even closer, and she could feel the heat from his body radiating on her skin. *He is absolutely, undeniably, all dragon*, she thought. She'd never met a male dragon before, this was uncharted territory.

"You care what I think about you?" his voice deepened and held a hint of a purr that teased over her skin like a caress.

He was grinning at her in a knowing way that made her flush head to toe. She nodded then cursed herself internally for admitting it.

His mouth moved down towards hers as he closed the distance between them, stopping a scant inch from her lips. "Isabella, I think you are the most beautiful woman I've ever seen, and I'm really glad we found you. I don't think you're barking, as you so eloquently put it. I think you're doing remarkably well considering the turmoil we've introduced into your life."

He gently pulled back from her, and she felt the loss of his warmth keenly. Her breathing quickened, and she licked her lips. His eyes were drawn there, and she prayed he would kiss her again.

"You can if you want to," he whispered in a seductive drawl.

Her stomach tightened, and she sucked in a sharp breath. *Did he just give me permission to...*

"Liam!" they both heard, snapped in a disapproving tone. Risa stood there, arms crossed, eyes narrowed. "If you're done trying to seduce my sister, we have plans to make."

He chuckled then, a rumbly sound that made Izzy tingle all over. "I don't mind," she heard herself say, then stared horrified as his eyes locked on hers. He gave her a devilish grin and winked before he ambled to the dining room with the others. Izzy grabbed Risa's arm. "Please," she hissed, "Tell me that gorgeous, impossibility of a man is single. He *is* a dragon, isn't he?"

Risa laughed at her sister's confused and eager expression. "Yes, Liam is a dragon, and single. He's quite the flirt, but he is super protective of his sister, kind of a joker sometimes, and loyal to a fault. He'd do anything for his family. He's been through some rough times that I'll let him tell you about." She sighed, "He's actually pretty darn wonderful."

"But what kind of dragon is he? He's not silver like us," Izzy wondered out loud.

Risa smiled, "No, he's green and Marco's red."

Izzy's eyes followed Liam's form as he plucked a small piece of fruit from his sister's plate, dodging the jolt of magic she shot at him, laughing. She nodded absently, "I wonder what shade of green his wings are."

The family was spread around the table, engaged in lively conversation as they ate dinner. Shannon was in absolute heaven, her family getting bigger by the minute. She obviously loved Killian's friends and made sure they knew it, adopting all of them on the spot. Absently putting her hand on his shoulder, Killian watched her eyes get misty as he covered it with his own.

"Killian, you've done so well for yourself, you're happy. It's all a mother wants for her children." Shannon smiled at her son, her eyes shining and hugged him tightly. The tears spilled over when he hugged her back, just as hard.

"So, the Shadows had Serena until ye rescued her, an' they were going to take Marissa, too? But why? What did we do?" Izzy inquired, pursing her lips in confusion.

Liam cleared his throat, "Not sure, that's what we're trying to figure out. The Shadows had Rena, but Risa was being tracked by a different type of wielder. One without a color. She kidnapped our friend earlier this year in some weird revenge plot," he added quietly.

Izzy pondered that for a minute. "Dark wielders," she nodded.

The team glanced at each other in concern. Killian motioned at Liam. They knew the reach was wide, but they needed to know what insight Izzy could give them.

She noticed the shared glance, offering, "Our parents called them dark wielders. Those who abuse their powers, their magic gets dark, evil-like, so... dark wielders. They're nasty. That's who was trying to take me an' my sisters when we were little. Does that mean they're after us again?" She massaged her forehead like a headache was settling in.

Liam rubbed her shoulder. "Are you okay?" he murmured.

Waggling her hand, Izzy gave him a tentative smile. "Aye. At least, I think so," she said slowly, "Just trying to reconcile my memories with what I was taught by my adoptive parents, who were wielders, an' my dragon mentor, Evie. Some of it is conflicting, an' I'm a little overwhelmed."

Liam stood and whipped out his phone while trying to stroll away casually, no doubt to call Vaughn with this development, but not wanting to alarm anyone else.

"Alright," Killian clapped his hands, "We need to get back to the States quickly so we can get ye reunited an' figure out what's going on. If these dark wielders are the ones who killed your parents, then ye could all be in danger still."

Risa nodded, her face going hard. "I just found my sisters; they aren't taking them away again." She noticed Izzy looked troubled, "Izzy? What's wrong?"

Her sister smiled sadly, "I can't go with ye just yet. I never got a passport because of the confusion with my birth an' adoption records."

Liam stood behind Isabella and laughed. "Oh, darlin', that's not a problem at all. We've got you," he drawled. His stomach tightened when she blushed and fidgeted in her chair a bit before whirling back to her sister. It gave him a small burst of warm satisfaction to know she wasn't immune to his charms.

Calling Vaughn once more, Liam paced away as he explained Isabella's lack of a passport. As expected, Vaughn assured him it would be taken care of, just get home ASAP. Liam updated the others and sat at the table again. Feeling eyes on him, he realized Isabella was quietly watching him. He winked, and she flushed again as she quickly glanced away. She was absolutely breathtaking and adorable with her seeming shyness. She was different from Jorrie in almost every way.

His heart thumped hard in a jolt of pain. *Nope, not going there.* That one still hurt. Not quite as much as it used to, but the ache was there. His stupid heart wouldn't let her go, and he was still sitting on the sidelines. Alone. He rubbed his chest absently, grimacing at the memory.

He noticed Siobhan staring at him with a calculating expression. He was about to ask, then decided he was too tired to care. He was tired of the emotional rollercoaster, and her sharp barbs wouldn't help.

Since it was getting late, they decided to call it a night. They were flying out in the morning and needed rest. Isabella was going to her place for the evening so she could pack and not impose on Killian's family. Risa voiced concerns about her being alone, worried about her safety. Killian nodded; he didn't like it either. Isabella tried to protest, insisting it was a one-bedroom apartment, she'd be fine and didn't have enough space for others.

Killian cleared his throat, "Liam will go with ye. He can sleep on your sofa, he's great in a fight an' will protect ye if needed. Besides, he's either sleeping on the sofa here or there. Might as well be useful."

Liam glared at Killian for a moment until the wielder squinted at him, staring hard. He realized then what Killian was doing and flashed him a quick smile in thanks. He turned casually towards Isabella, "I don't mind. Like he said, one sofa is as good as another." He tried to keep his voice level, trying not to betray the nerves waging a war inside of him as he waited on pins and needles for her answer.

Isabella gave him a shy smile. "I guess, if ye don't mind."

Risa opened her mouth, about to protest, and Killian plopped a hand over it. She tried to bite his hand, so he picked her up, threw her over his shoulder, and smacked her firmly on her bottom. "Aye, sure an' the lass is tired, taking her to bed. Night all, see ye in the morn'. Love ye, Ma, Pa!" he called as he hurried to his room. They heard Risa squeal a second before his door shut.

Shannon stared after her son in shock. Fergus patted her on the arm, "Darling, it's a grown man he is now. Leave him be." He pulled her up and dragged her off to their own room, chuckling.

Marco leered at Siobhan, bouncing his eyebrows suggestively.

She snorted, "Don't you dare, Baby Daddy!"

He rolled his eyes. "Don't call me that!" he groaned, "Unless you want me to start calling you Von-Von again." He plumed smoke at her.

Siobhan stood and nodded at Liam and Isabella. "See y'all in the morning," she called as she strolled to the other bedroom, Marco hot on her heels, a rumble in his chest.

Liam turned to Isabella. "Ready to go?" he asked her quietly.

Izzy nodded and swallowed heavily. He handed her purse over, and she pulled out her keys, gripping them tightly. Her palms were sweaty, and she didn't want to drop them. "Ye don't have to..." she started.

He stepped close, wrapping his hands around her wrists. "But I want to. Risa is worried, we all are. I want to help, Isabella. Please, let me make sure you're safe."

She shivered, the sound of her name on his lips like a magic spell. It felt like fingers dragging up her spine softly. "Ye can call me Izzy," she murmured, her voice thin and breathy.

"Do you want me to? Isabella is such a beautiful name," he asked, his voice dropping lower, quietly caressing her skin.

She wrangled back the sudden urge to close the distance and kiss him, barely holding herself back. It was a simple question, but the weight of it was overwhelming. She shook her head, "Isabella is fine," she whispered back.

He smiled and turned her to the door.

Chapter 21

I ZZY LIVED CLOSE TO Ballymore, so it was only a twenty-minute trip. The entire journey occurred in total silence. She didn't even turn on the radio. When they arrived, Liam jumped out of the car first, advising her to stay put as he studied the area. She sucked in a surprised breath; he looked like a soldier scouting for enemies. Every line of his body was taught and tense. She watched him as he sniffed the air and scanned the dark. It was a side of the man she didn't expect. Different from his outgoing and fun personality from earlier, he was now intense, lethal, and hard. Certainty coursed through her that he'd seen things she couldn't imagine.

He finally nodded and opened her door, holding his hand out to assist her from the vehicle.

She didn't need it, but appreciated the gesture. Gone was the warrior exterior, and in its place, the friendly, charming man she'd met. She studied him with interest. "What was that?" she asked him, waving a hand over his frame.

He tilted his head and stared at her silently.

Izzy clarified, "That whole 'thing' ye just did. Like ye were scouting for an enemy. Ye turned it on an' off like a light switch." She snapped her fingers to demonstrate.

He shrugged, rumbling, "Because that's what I was doing. I was checking to be sure it was safe before you got out." He plucked her keys from her hand. "I'm going to do it again before you go inside your place. Now, which one?" He nodded at her building, scanning the doors.

"Ye don't need to clear my home, it's perfectly safe," she laughed.

Izzy was pressed against her car, pinned between the door and a wall of hard muscle before she could blink. Liam's face was a mask of serious, deadly calm, the tips of his fangs peeking from his lips. His talons gripped her shoulders. "You don't know that. I will *not* let anything happen to you. I'm sorry, Isabella, but you don't know what we're dealing with here. These people have and *will* kill again. They kidnap children and abuse them. They snatch magic users and torture them. They torment and tear apart families. They will not touch you. *I won't let them*," he growled through his teeth.

She swallowed hard. She was right, he'd seen terrible things, and he was scared for her. Nodding slowly, she gently stroked his cheek. "Alright, Liam, I'm sorry. You're right, I didn't realize. I would appreciate it very much if ye would make sure it's safe."

He backed up suddenly, shame etched across his handsome face. "I'm sorry, I didn't mean to scare you."

She studied him, shaking her head slowly. "It's okay, ye did scare me a little, but I think I needed to be scared. I honestly wasn't taking this seriously, an' I should be. Let's get inside. I don't like being this exposed." She glanced around at the once-friendly trees and worried about what might be lurking behind them.

He gently took her arm and pulled her to him as he closed her car door. "I'm sorry you have to worry about this after just finding your sisters, Isabella," he whispered, a soft soothing rumble in his chest.

She snuggled into him, she couldn't believe how soft and warm he was, considering how muscular he seemed. She sighed in contentment, comforted by the vibration of his purr.

Watching from behind a warding, the brown-haired man shook his head as he watched Liam and Isabella embracing. This was not going as planned at all. This was a new wrinkle they didn't anticipate. He thought about saying something, interrupting, but knew she would not take kindly to his opinions or appreciate his interference.

Pulling out his phone, he studied an image. A smiling face, beaming in joy, staring into the camera with clear affection for the photo taker. He stroked one finger over the screen, reminding himself why he was here.

Five minutes had passed since Izzy leaned into Liam's arms. Headlights washed over them, where they stood in the parking lot. Liam chuckled softly, "Isabella?"

She smiled. "Hm?" she murmured dreamily, enjoying his soothing rumble as her ear pressed to his chest, listening to his heart beating steadily.

"As lovely as this night is, I thought you wanted to go inside?" He laughed at her shocked expression.

"Aye, sorry, twelve-B," she sputtered.

He escorted her to the door, still laughing as he unlocked it and motioned for her to wait outside. Creeping in, he swept the apartment in that same lethal manner. He came back shortly, announcing it was clear.

She entered her own home warily and closed the door, locking it firmly before she turned to face him. Now she was acutely aware of how alone she was in her space with an extremely handsome dragon facing her.

He stood in her living room, one hip cocked out, his thumbs in his belt loops, grinning at her. She smiled back nervously.

Liam held his arms open. "Hey, wanna pick up where we left off?"

She launched herself back into him, sighing happily as he wrapped her tightly against him. He put his cheek on her silvery hair, and she heard him rumble again, a happy noise. This time, she rumbled back, and he seemed startled. She laughed, tilting her head, smirking at him. "You're not the only dragon here, ye know."

His sultry smile faded as he stared into her eyes. He brushed his fingers across her cheek and slowly lowered his mouth to hers, kissing her tentatively and softly.

She was too stunned at first to respond. When he started to pull away, her desire kicked into overdrive, and she yanked him back with a growl, kissing him hungrily.

Liam moaned; *this is an abysmally bad idea*. He was taking advantage of her when she was overwhelmed, and that's not who he was. He needed to stop. She was so warm and delicious, though, he couldn't. Finally, he wrenched his lips from hers, jerking back, gasping. "I'm sorry!" he said quickly, his chest heaving. "I shouldn't have done that." He watched her face close down, eyes filled with hurt, before she turned and escaped to her room, shutting the door firmly. He smacked himself on the forehead. *Why am I always such an idiot?*

He heard her sniffle and knew she was crying. The sound cracked his heart into smaller pieces. He trudged to her door and leaned heavily on it, his palm rasping against the rough grain of the wood. He closed his eyes, wincing as she tried to hide her tears. "Isabella," he called to her softly, knowing she could hear him. "Please, Isabella, I'm sorry. I kind of suck at words sometimes, but let me try to explain." He didn't hear a response, so he opened the door quietly.

She was lying on her bed, her face buried in a pillow. She heard him apologizing, but she was too embarrassed to respond. She just met this man and had thrown herself at him like a common street walker not once, but twice today. No wonder he pushed her away. The door opened, and a few seconds later, the bed dipped as he sat down next to her.

"Isabella," he whispered, stroking her hair, "I'm sorry. I didn't mean to hurt you. I'm not rejecting you. I meant I shouldn't have done that because you've been through so much today already, and the last thing you need is me mucking up your feelings and emotions. I shouldn't have taken advantage of you like that, and I'm sorry. I truly am. You're such a beautiful woman; I was attracted to you the moment I saw you, before I even knew who you were. Believe me, I want you in ways I shouldn't. But I'll leave you alone. Your place is safe; I'll head back to Killian's."

She sat up then and glared at him, anger flaring in her eyes. "An' I don't get a say in it? Ye want me, but you'll decide if ye have me? Besides, I drove ye here, how will ye get back?"

He laughed ruefully, "Darlin', I'm a dragon, remember? How else do you think I'd get back?" He pulled his shirt off and unfurled his wings.

Their emerald-green scales winking in the lamplight, the lighter clover colors swirling through the webbing mesmerized her.

Her jaw dropped. His wings were the most beautiful thing she'd ever seen. They shimmered as he fluttered them, reminding her of the rolling green hills around the area. She rose to her knees and reached over his shoulder, stroking them, fascinated by their beauty.

He stilled and closed his eyes as she ran her hands over the scales. A loud, rumbling purr rose from his chest as she continued her exploration. His teeth clenched, his hands fisted, as if he were trying ridiculously hard to hold still. Finally, he grabbed her wrists, pulling her hands away. "Isabella," he gasped, his chest heaving as he shuddered.

She snatched her hands back, eyes wide. "Oh god, Liam, I'm sorry, did I hurt ye?" She covered her mouth, feeling terrible. He opened his eyes, and they were shockingly bright blue although they'd been green before. She stared into their depths and lost herself in them.

He blinked a few times, and they flickered back to green. "Isabella," he breathed her name hard, "Are you trying to kill me, woman?"

She blinked at him now, confused. "What? I don't..." she asked, her voice trembling.

He gazed at her, an expression of disbelief widening his eyes and parting his lips. "Isabella, do you... I mean, do you not know how *intimate* that is? To touch a dragon's wings? It's a very — *erotic* — thing." His voice dropped to a husky, strained whisper, "Has no one ever touched your wings before, sweetheart?"

Her hands flew to her mouth again, and she shook her head frantically. *Oh, dear lord above,* she thought, mortified. *I was just stroking that man like nobody's business.* "Liam, I'm so sorry, I didn't know." She flushed the darkest shade of red she possibly could and felt the embarrassment crashing over her like a tidal wave.

He laughed, a choked sound before clearing his throat. "It's okay, like you said, you didn't know. But um, now you do. So, if you're around any other guys with, uh, wings, hands off unless you plan to, uh, follow through." He straightened, wincing a little.

She noticed him standing awkwardly, a rather large bulge in his jeans telling the story of his discomfort. Her body went hot and slick all over, tingling in all the right places. *He said erotic, intimate.* Apparently, he was very turned on right now. Her mind helpfully reminded her of what he said when he first sat down. *He's attracted to you.* She grinned; poor Liam was about to learn what she thought of that. "Follow through?" she repeated in a sultry purr as she stood in front of him. She linked her arms around his neck and pulled him down to her mouth, kissing him with barely restrained fervor.

He tried to pull away, moaning, "Isabella, it's okay! You didn't know. I'm not asking you to —"

She stopped him by kissing him again. Leaning back, she chuckled, "Oh, Liam, I know you're not asking. My pretty man, I'm offering. I want to." She latched her teeth to his lower lip and stroked the arches of his wings firmly. His whole frame went rigid, then he yanked her body to his. His mouth was hot and wild on hers. She moaned and reveled in the feel of his hands all over her body now. She stepped away from him and held up a hand. She pulled her blouse off and stood there in her bra, shaking out her hair before unfurling her own wings.

Liam was dumbstruck. Gobsmacked. Overcome. The gorgeous creature in front of him said she wanted him, then flared out her own wings. They were the most beautiful wings he'd ever laid eyes on. He stared in awe as they sparkled like diamonds and opals. He felt the blood leave his upper body and rush to his cock, making it harder than he ever imagined possible. It was throbbing, aching, and straining in his jeans.

She took his hands and put them on her shoulders. "Touch them, Liam, I want to feel what ye were feeling," she whispered.

He nearly choked on his own breath and stared at her, unsure if he should. She squeezed the back of his hands in encouragement. He gently reached over and stroked the arch of one of her wings. It felt like velvet. He'd never touched a woman's wings before. Dragons usually didn't date other dragons. It happened, but they were usually more attracted to wielders. It was probably an ego thing.

Right now, as Liam watched her head fall back while she gasped in ecstasy, he didn't care about pride one bit. He would lie on his back and give her his neck willingly. He touched the other wing, and she arched her spine, her breasts brushing against his chest. He reached one hand behind her and unclasped her bra, then slid it slowly down her shoulders. He pulled her close, quite sure this was nearly heaven.

She inhaled sharply as she felt her nipples harden against his chest. Just those two light strokes of her wings, and she'd felt more pleasure than ever before. She was breathing heavily, as she refocused on his beautiful face. She was not done with him by a long shot. She realized if she didn't tell him to stop now, they were going to end up in this bed together, him deep inside of her. She wanted that more than anything she'd ever desired in her life. She breathed to him, "Again."

His eyes full of wonder at the sensation, he stroked both wings at the same time, and she moaned, panting at the sensation. He began to run his hands over them, and he kissed her again, swallowing her sounds greedily. They were both purring now, and she started stroking his wings as well.

Izzy was becoming overwhelmed, never imagining anything could ever feel this pleasurable. His hands were strong and sure, but soft on her body. The sensations were intense and erotic as he'd said. She felt pressure building inside her, and suddenly she went over that edge, crying out. She stared at him in shock. She couldn't believe she orgasmed just from him touching her wings and kissing her! He was staring at her in awe again. Apparently, he hadn't known that was a possibility either. She gripped his wings in her hands and wrapped herself around him, crushing her mouth to his. Pressing tightly to him, she ground her hips against his hard length, begging for more. His body spasmed, and he groaned hard. Izzy realized she'd just inadvertently returned the favor.

He let out a shaky laugh as he adjusted his jeans and cleared his throat. "Well, that's embarrassing. I haven't done that since I was a teenager."

She flushed, "I'm sorry, I really wanted to be with ye, I didn't mean to..."

He tilted his head and smirked at her, "Oh, Isabella, have I got news for you."

Chapter 22

IZZY LAY ON HER bed, feeling cool air brush across her skin. Her stomach quivered as she thought of the pleasure he'd given her. She was disappointed they weren't able to go further, but she grinned in the knowledge she was able to get him that hot. He'd stepped into her bathroom to clean up. She did feel kind of bad about that part; it wouldn't be very comfortable to be all wet and sticky like that.

She heard a low, masculine laugh as he stepped back into her room. "What's that smile for?" he asked.

Her eyes flew wide when she realized he was completely naked and not the least bit shy about it. She took in the sight of his body. He was hard and muscular, sculpted like a statue. Her mouth watered at the sight of his abs, then her attention was drawn lower, focusing on his thighs. Or more accurately, between them. He was fully erect and hard again. Her eyes flew to his, wide with surprise.

He rumbled and laughed louder, "Isabella, dragons have rapid healing, which you knew. But I bet you didn't know it comes in handy when a man wants a woman as much as I want you right now." He stalked across the room like the dangerous beast he was. A trickle of smoke from his nose, flames showing in his eyes, he crawled onto her bed and sat on his knees between her legs. He grabbed one of her ankles and pulled her closer to him, keeping his fingers wrapped around her like a shackle as he gently kissed the top of her foot.

She stared at him disbelievingly; he was stunningly beautiful.

He stroked his long length with his other hand, drawing her eyes to it. "Isabella," he whispered, his voice raspy with an intense need, "Is this what you want?"

She nodded rapidly, "God, yes, more than anything."

His talons flicked out, and he ripped her skirt from her body, followed shortly by her panties before she could squirm away. He gently lowered her leg, chuckling low in his throat.

"Liam!" she squealed. *Okay, that was so unexpectedly hot!* He grinned at her, completely wild and feral, flames swirling in his eyes. She saw his fangs drop down, and it made her own gums ache. She gulped in air as he used those razor-sharp points to graze her inner thigh. Her head fell back, and she moaned, clenching her sheets.

He nuzzled her thighs, forcing her to spread them more and settled himself between them. He blew a heated breath over her center and gently licked up the middle, spreading her with his tongue.

She cried out and shook her head side to side. She felt a fang scrape across her again and almost lost herself to him. She trembled and bucked as he began to lick and suckle her deeply. Her whole body was on fire, and she felt like she was going to burst. He gently pushed one finger, then two inside of her, unerringly and miraculously finding that deep secret spot. He flicked his fingers, and she felt the dam was about to break. She thrashed, her hips straining. Unable to help herself.

He clamped his forearm across her waist to hold her down and growled at her, demanding she be still.

Her eyes flew open, and she felt flames in them. *Did he just growl at me?* She growled back then, and his eyes locked on hers, their flames matching in intensity. She hissed at him, her fangs shining in the lamplight. He grinned evilly, winked at her, then stabbed his tongue deep. She roared her release.

Liam almost lost control of himself again. Her roar was more erotic than anything he'd ever experienced. Her growling back at him made him throb and ache. He licked and swallowed her, taking in every bit of her pleasure that he could. When she finally lay quivering, completely undone, he crawled up her body, nipping at her along the way. He suckled on her breasts and nicked one with a fang before licking away the small drop of blood there. She sat up suddenly and latched her fangs to his throat. She snarled at him, and he growled in response, every primal instinct in him urging him to bite her back, but he resisted. The leash he kept himself on taut and straining. He chuffed, a small soothing sound to rein her back in.

She let go, her expression reflecting her own surprise at her reaction. He smiled at her, not minding in the least.

He retracted his fangs, then gently pulled one of her legs up. He bent it around his waist, positioning himself at her entrance. He prayed she would let him take her fully now, his body quivering in anticipation. He breathed her name as the question and watched her face anxiously.

"Please, Liam," Isabella called softly, desire brimming in her eyes, conveying how much she wanted him in return. He braced his hands on each side of her as the tip of his aching length pressed against her. He almost wept in joy at the sensation as the head of his cock moved inside her walls and paused, overcome with how incredible she felt. She whimpered and raised her hips slightly, asking for more. He pushed further, locking his eyes on hers, watching with satisfaction as her lashes fluttered while he continued his slow slide. Filling and stretching her, it was glorious. He pushed deeper into her than he thought possible, the slick heat of her clenched around him, stroking him, urging him on. He hadn't known it could be this primal, this intense. She ground her hips up to him, wanting more.

He obliged her and began to move, gliding in and out while her shoulders shook, and her thighs clenched. He began stroking her leg, where he held it wrapped around him. She lifted the other leg, locking her ankles around his waist, letting him angle even deeper. He groaned then and dropped his head. "Fuck Isabella, you're killing me." He expected she would frown at his language, but her response shocked him.

"Then fuck me harder, Liam," she moaned.

He stilled, then grinned at her, the bad word coming from her prim lips sending a wave of heat surging through him. "As you wish, my dear." His wings unfurled again, and he picked her up, flying her to the wall above them before wrapping her legs back around his waist. He held her there in shock. "Hold on," he warned her. Then he used his wings to drive into her, pounding in harder and harder against the wall.

She cried out and screamed his name as she shattered again. He kept going, not letting her catch her breath between one wave of pleasure and the next. He worried at first that he was hurting her, then remembered she was a dragon and was giving back as good as she got. He snarled but didn't slow as her talons dug into his back, and a deep, satisfied rumble emanated from her chest. Her fangs were fully extended, and smoke billowed from them both. Finally, his wings faltered, their rhythm becoming jagged. She surged forward, scraping her fangs over his throat, and he roared his release. Liam swore lava was in his veins as he spasmed and filled her, the heat and intensity almost unbearable.

He slowly lowered them back down, collapsing on his back with her sprawled over his chest. His chest was heaving in and out, breathing as if he'd run a marathon. His wings were crumpled beneath him, but he barely noticed.

Izzy was struggling to catch her breath. She'd never felt more alive and used at the same time. She never wanted to move from this spot. Hearing Liam get so lost in her and the primal way he took her was the most intense encounter of her life. This man was fire, and she was ready to be burned.

She blew her hair out of her mouth and grinned at him. She was about to compliment him or weep with gratitude, she wasn't sure which, when a frantic banging came from her door.

She scrambled for a robe, then ran to open it. It was her neighbor, a terrified look on her face beneath the gobs of night cream covering her skin. "My dear, are ye alright? I heard the most terrible growling an' roaring!"

Izzy shook her head, biting her lip to keep from laughing. "I'm fine, Clara, I didn't hear a thing, fast asleep as I was. Do ye think it was someone's television? Or maybe there's a wild animal on the loose then?" She glanced over her neighbor's shoulder, pretending to scan the parking lot. She heard Liam's low chuckles in her room. She stifled her own laugh; there was a wild animal on the loose, but it wasn't outside.

Clara studied her and nodded slowly, "Alright, dear, I'm glad you're safe, ye keep these doors locked. If I hear it again, I'll ring the police."

Nodding back, Izzy replied, "Good plan, thank ye, 'night, Clara." She shut the door and leaned against it. *Holy hell, who knew?* She thought to herself. Liam was all shades of delicious and talented. She'd never had so many orgasms in one setting. Ever. She ran her hands down her body, feeling flushed all over. Then she remembered biting his throat, and her face heated. The feel of his pulse thrumming on her tongue, the spicy taste of his skin, the way he'd growled but with pleasure instead of pain. She grew even warmer.

"I can feel you blushing all the way in here. Come tell me what's got you so flustered," he called, his masculine rumble making her quiver.

She slowly eased into the room. He was sitting up against her headboard, arms behind his head, grinning at her. The lamp shone on his beautiful, shoulder-length, red-gold hair. His tan skin was tight and perfect, his green eyes that matched his wings were twinkling with mischief. She started towards him, and he held up a finger.

"Lose the robe," he purred.

She untied it and let it slowly slide off her shoulders an inch at a time. She watched him swallow hard and stiffen. He wasn't kidding; dragons did have a fast recovery. This was going to be a long night. She grinned and climbed into the bed with him.

He pulled her body over his and held her against him, her head resting on his chest, where she felt so right. "Isabella," he purred, "That was incredible, amazing." He breathed deeply and sighed in contentment.

She nodded, "I've never... I mean it was... wow," she finished lamely. She glanced up at him, and he smiled tenderly down at her. "I didn't know it could be like that," she whispered.

He studied her face, then grinned and kissed her nose. "I knew I was a fantastic lover, of course, but I didn't know you were such a wild cat yourself." Her mouth dropped open, and he laughed hard. "Isabella, I'm teasing. I've never been with another dragon either. I didn't know it could be so... intense."

She relaxed back against him; it was certainly the right word. He was also right about him being a fantastic lover. She was going to like being in Texas, she thought. She slowly tensed as an intrusive thought entered her mind.

Risa said he was single, but it was complicated; there was baggage there. What if Risa was wrong? For that matter, what if he wasn't interested in more? After all, she'd already given in to him the day they met; what else was there? She gazed up at him then, concern filling her eyes, and pinching her lips.

"What's the matter?" he whispered to her softly.

She squirmed a bit, "Liam, I don't want ye to get the wrong idea of me. This was —very — out of character. I'm not the kind of woman who jumps into bed the moment she meets a man."

He put a finger over her lips. "I know. It's okay. Isabella, there's something between us. Something at work here, drawing us together. I've never been so pulled to someone so hard the way I have been with you. I certainly haven't done anything like this before either."

She nodded. She definitely felt pulled to him for reasons she didn't understand, yet. She hoped it wasn't just because he was the first male dragon she'd met, but as the specimen went, he was certainly a good example. She hesitated again, and he put a finger under her chin, tilting her face up.

"What else is bothering you, sweetheart? I don't want you to be uncomfortable with this." Concern filled his emerald eyes.

She smiled at the endearment. He was charming, which let the intrusive thoughts win, and she blurted, "I'm just wondering about your life back in Texas. Do ye have someone waiting there for ye? A girlfriend, a lover, a wife?"

He frowned at her as his hand fell to his side. "Isabella, good lord, is that what you take me for? Someone who could come here and just hop into bed with another woman when there's someone waiting at home? Is that really what you think of me?" His arm, which was wrapped around her tightly before, slipped away. His voice shook, an edge of disbelief coloring it as he asked, "Is that why you slept with me? Because you think I'm that shallow?"

He was angry, she could see she'd hurt him. Her stomach sank to her toes, leaving only a hollow, sick feeling behind. Her face burned again, but this time for a different reason. She didn't mean it the way it sounded. "Liam, no! I... I was just wondering what will happen to me when we get to your home. I didn't mean it like that. Will I see ye again?" She pleaded with him to understand.

He closed his eyes, clenching his teeth before his expression went blank. With a flat tone, devoid of any emotion, he answered, "I doubt it, Isabella. Apparently, I'm really fucking good at screwing shit up and being the fallback choice for everyone. Do you mind if I use your shower?" He stood and strode angrily to the bathroom without waiting for an answer.

She stared after him in shock. Apparently, she'd struck a nerve and hurt him deeply. A tear scorched her skin as it raced down her cheek. *Maybe it's better this way; I shouldn't get too attached to a man I might not see again once we get to Texas.*

Liam stood under the running water and banged his forehead lightly on the tile. *How could I be so stupid?* He took a chance with someone and was promptly slapped down. Of course, she thought he was some sort of cad. She was very inexperienced, and he let his lust rule, taking advantage of her. They'd just met! True, she asked him to be with her, but she didn't know what she was getting into. Well, he didn't either, honestly. But something he couldn't define was drawing him to her, like a magnet. He thought about Killian's words, that love would just walk into his life when he least expected it. He certainly walked right into Isabella. Maybe he was letting his heartache and loneliness get to him. All he really knew was his desire for her was off the charts, and he thought she wanted him with the same intensity.

But now he knew, she thought he was the kind of man to sleep with her, then abandon her. His shoulders slumped. *Why not? That's what I did to Jorrie, and I lost her. It wasn't in one night, but why not just speed up the process this time? Might as well avoid the heartache before it begins. Besides, she should be focused on reuniting with her sisters, her family. She won't have time for me anyway. I can live up to everyone's expectations, prove them right.*

He shut off the water then toweled himself dry. He pulled his pants on but left them unfastened. They were about to come right back off anyway. Squaring his shoulders, he took a deep breath and walked with his head high back to her room. Quietly, he gathered the rest of his things. She was sitting on the edge of the bed, back in her robe, watching him with an unreadable expression. He nodded at her and turned to leave.

"Ye don't have to go," she whispered.

"I think I should, I've done enough here," he kept his voice flat and level.

"Where are ye going?"

"Killian's," he mumbled over his shoulder before he hurried out the door. He shuffled into the parking lot and gazed around. It was deserted, and there was enough room. He shucked his pants and gathered his clothes in his hand. He let the change take over and shifted into his dragon form. He spread his wings and, with a sad chuffing sound, he took off into the night.

Chapter 23

LIAM HAD JUST FLOWN outside of the town limits, gliding easily on the warm currents, when something slammed into him from behind. Caught off guard, he flapped wildly trying to regain control as pain shot through his tail. He tumbled in the sky and had barely righted himself when a silver beast hovered in front of him, wings beating a furious tattoo. It was growling and snarling, fury wafting from every scale as fire flickered at its snout. He growled back as the smaller dragon swiped a wicked claw at him before it lunged at his throat. He was so startled, his wings stopped beating, and he dropped. Which, fortunately, saved him from being bitten again. He'd never actually been attacked by another dragon in the air before, and despite Marco's intensive training, he froze.

Coward, he heard in his head, her anger making the word echo and tremble like an earthquake.

Isabella? You bit me! he thought back, shocked.

Is this what ye do, Liam? Ye run away? Ye could have just talked to me. I may be new to a lot of this, but I'm not an idiot. Ye love someone else; I could see it all over your face earlier. But ye came to my bed anyway. So, forgive me for being concerned. Could I have asked that better? Sure. But seriously?

Once ye have me, ye just run off when the conversation gets too tough? Fuck that, Liam! She growled and snapped at him again.

He was stunned. She was not only one hundred percent correct, but she was glorious in her dragon form. He gazed at the magnificent creature in front of him and simply stared in silent awe of her.

She snarled. *Focus, ye idiot!*

Laughter burst from him with a gurgling, wheezy sound as he quickly flew past her. The draft of his passing spun her around midair while he circled.

She was so startled, her wings fluttered for a moment while she got her bearings. Then her anger caught back up, and he felt it spiking over the mental link like a scorching wave.

Oh, ye want to play games? she growled.

He laughed again. *Oh, honey, yes, I do! Catch me if you can, slowpoke!* He blew a small flame at her before flying away rapidly.

She chuffed before launching herself after him. They twisted and turned, circling and diving.

He flipped over in a somersault, flying right back at her. She was so caught off guard, she didn't react. He dove under her at the last second, a game of chicken in the air. *Slowpoke,* he called again, laughing.

She snorted in disgust, then gleefully gave chase. Soon, her anger was gone, and she was having fun. She showed him the amazing currents in a valley nearby where she liked to fly. He did loop-de-loops and taught her how to do it, too. They chased a few sheep, chuckling together when the lazy things didn't run. Finally, they both landed on a hill and shifted back to human form.

He'd barely steadied his feet on the ground when she launched herself at him. Ending up on his back in the grass, he roared in laughter. He gazed up at her as she straddled his thighs. Her hair was wild, her eyes were shining, and her chest was heaving. She crushed her mouth to his and bit his lower lip before shoving her tongue in his mouth. The silken feel of her bare skin brushing tantalizingly over his, wrenched a rumble from his chest. She sat up, ethereal in the moonlight, making him catch his breath as he was struck by her beauty all over again. She leaned back down and nipped his neck, the tiniest little bit of fang drawing blood this time. He snarled and lifted her up so she could slide down on him, inch by slow inch. He was roaring again as she began to move, riding him into oblivion. He surged up and captured her breast in his mouth while she continued to rock, both of them panting and moaning. His wings came out of their own accord, and hers flared in response. They began to stroke each other's wings and drove themselves to the peak before they fell from the summit and tumbled down the other side. Their roars shattered the night with pleasure.

Liam dropped back to the ground, gasping, and pulled her down with him. They lay there in the grass, under the night sky, full of stars and breathed each other in. He laughed suddenly, and she stared at him curiously as she raked her fingers through his hair where it spread in the grass. "Now I see why dragons don't date other dragons. We'll kill each other if we keep this up." He chuckled and stroked her back, trailing his fingers up and down her spine. He was still breathing hard. "It's a risk I'm willing to take, though," he murmured seriously.

She sat up again and stared at him, her chest rising and falling rapidly. "Are ye, pretty man?" she asked him breathlessly.

He nodded, determination on his face. "I am. For *you*, Isabella, I am," he whispered.

"Ye better be." She hesitated then groaned, her cheeks flushing, "Liam, I'm sorry earlier if it seemed I was implying anything about your character. I was just worried about myself, an' I said it wrong. Very wrong. I wasn't trying to insinuate you're the kind of man who would have a one-night stand with someone while there's another waiting at home. I think ye said it earlier, ye aren't so good with words. I'm not great at them myself," she admitted, the blush spreading fetchingly across her throat. "I let the inside thoughts get outside."

He smiled softly and shook his head. "No, Isabella, it's okay. I understand why you were concerned. But you were right earlier. I was in love with someone else some years back. I thought she was the one." He sighed, "But I was stupid and didn't tell her how I actually felt about her. I left for a long time. I didn't tell her where I was going or when I would be back. I was gone for almost a year. She moved on without me." He blew out a sharp, heavy breath. "As much as it hurts to admit it, she was right to do so and certainly deserved better. She's happier now." He looked miserable.

"What were ye doing for so long?" she asked him slowly. Her expression suggested she hated reminding him of this sadness.

His own expression hardened, and he gazed directly at her, flames in his eyes. "I was hunting down and killing the Shadows responsible for the murder of my parents and countless other dragons and wielders. They were the Shadow King's death squad." He squeezed his eyes closed briefly before whispering, "They were probably the ones who killed your parents, too."

She shivered at the look on his face. "I knew it." At his curious glance, she continued, "You've seen terrible things, things I can't imagine." She stared at him, the set of her mouth determined and grim. "Liam, were ye there? At the battle of the Shadows?" she asked quietly.

He nodded slowly and in a low, gravelly voice, answered, "Yes, and I did my share of killing then, too. I've killed a lot of bad men." He looked uncomfortable, his gaze troubled. "Does that bother you?" He could tell she was giving it serious thought before she shook her head emphatically no.

"There's no justice where magic is involved unless we take it ourselves. If ye avenged my family while avenging your own, then I say, all the better. And thank ye, Liam. I hope they suffered."

He shuddered in relief, glad she understood. "I should have called; I should have told her. She was there when I learned my family was killed; she would have understood. But because I'm an idiot, I didn't, and I lost her. She was comforted by another man, and now Jorrie and Shepard are married and have three kids with another on the way." He felt his eyes sting a bit. It was one thing to think about it, but for some reason, it hurt worse saying it out loud.

Isabella looked thoughtful, "Jorrie an' Shepard? Why do those names... wait, Liam! The love of your life, are ye telling me ye used to date the singer of Still Waters?"

He banged his head against the grass. "Yeah, and for the record, she and Shepard are some of my best friends."

She smiled, "You're still friends with both of them?"

"I helped them move into their house and took care of her while she was pregnant so he could set up their recording deals when the band was first starting. I'm the one who told Jorrie about dragons in the first place. Her best friend, Bridget, is married to my Godfather and boss. Bridget's brother is married to Shepard's twin brother, Davis. They're always having me over for dinner. Their kids call me Uncle Liam."

"Liam, that's so sweet, he must trust ye a lot to still be friends," she said, her voice filled with awe and amusement.

Liam laughed, "Well, I care about them both, and they're good together. They deserve the happiness they have in each other. He's a really good guy. Also, considering Shepard has over one hundred and fifty years on me, and could bite my head off, I think he's secure in that relationship." He grinned bashfully.

She glanced at him questioningly.

"Shepard's a dragon, too. A blue one. And Jorrie's a blue wielder. Their triplets are all blue dragons. Just a big happy blue family."

She stared at him open-mouthed, unable to formulate a response.

"Yeah, I know, it's a lot," he said with a rueful laugh. He mused, "The funny thing is that Shepard and I were fighting over her to some extent when we went on the mission to hunt down the last of the Shadows, but we didn't know at the time that Rena was being held. No one knew. That bastard kidnapped Jorrie, and when we went to save her, we found Serena as well."

She searched his face, "An' ye saved her."

He hummed noncommittally, shrugging as he pulled her tightly against his side and kissed her temple. "She told me she knew I was coming for her one day."

"An' ye did," she whispered, kissing him gently. "Thank ye, Liam, for saving my baby sister."

He rumbled in his chest and rubbed his cheek on hers, "Don't thank me, Isabella, I did what anyone would do."

She shook her head, "No, not everyone would have barged into a Shadow lair an' saved a young woman he didn't know at the risk of his own life. You're a hero in my eyes."

He smiled, basking in her adoration. He never wanted that look to leave her face. It was tender, appreciative, and full of everything he was missing. "Well, I will accept your thanks and move forward. Rena is a wonderful young lady, Isabella. But it took her a long time to get comfortable around people." He sighed and shook his head.

"She's still innocent in her ways, almost like a child," he continued, "For the longest time, she would only speak to me, Jorrie, or Shepard. She's also good friends with Killian because he taught her how to use her wielding properly, and she adores him. He's so gentle with her. She's come out of her shell quite a bit lately, but she's still timid sometimes. She's even got a crush on a boy in our circle. She wanted to come so badly on this trip to see you herself, Isabella. I swear she did. She was so torn about it, but she was too scared. She doesn't like to travel."

Isabella's eyes filled with tears. "Then I thank ye again for ending that menace."

"My pleasure, little lady," he drawled, then yawned.

She laughed, "Ye poor thing. I guess we should get some sleep. Come on, it's not far to my place."

He stood, grinning, "I have a better idea, as long as you promise not to bite me again."

Izzy woke up the next morning with the sun beating down on her scales. She felt a heavy pressure on her back and saw Liam's tail lying across her, just behind her wings. Huffing out a laugh, she turned the other way to see him on his back, paws in the air, head upside down. She shook with muffled laughter, making him twitch. She eased out from under his tail and stretched before shifting into human form.

Liam was right, sleeping in dragon form was always the best. He told her he did it every chance he could, and sleeping here, curled up with him, was invigorating. She felt she could run a marathon today. She eased up to his chin and tickled it.

He chuffed a little, smoke puffing from his snout.

She kissed him on his nose, and one large eye opened.

Rolling over, he stretched hard like she had. He grinned at her with his large maw of dragon fangs, the sight of which would terrify most people, but she giggled at the small clump of grass stuck to one of the spikes on his head.

She circled around, appreciating him in the daylight. His scales were stunningly gorgeous, shining like precious gemstones in the soft morning sun. "Liam," she exclaimed breathlessly. "You're beautiful!" He chuffed happily and pranced around on his paws a bit, then blew a few smoke rings around her. She laughed. He was adorable in this form. She liked the fact that he was silly, not taking himself too seriously, even though she knew he could if needed. He dropped his head and nudged her shoulder, gesturing for her to shift too. Grinning in excitement, she backed up, then shimmered into dragon form.

He sat back on his haunches, studying her. She knew her scales gleamed like the surface of a mirror, the sunlight sparkling and reflecting like so many diamonds. She definitely challenged him in the shiny scales department. He was taller than her, longer too, built more for fighting than her lithe form. But she wasn't without her own weapons. He admired her dagger-like talons as she preened one and chuffed at her with pleasure. When she tilted her head at him, he lowered his and lifted his tail like a cat about to pounce, waggling his rear end before doing just that. He knocked her on her back, laughing, then licked her face before quickly flying away.

She growled and lifted off as well, chasing after him. *That wasn't nice,* she called to his retreating form.

Yeah, well, maybe I'm not feeling nice, he cackled.

He flew into a low cloud, and she lost sight of him for a moment. *Liam?* She called, wondering where he went. Suddenly, she heard the flap of wings, and he bit her tail. She roared, but he barrel-rolled out of the way before she could bite him back. They chased each other a little while longer before finally gliding down to her building's parking lot. They quickly shifted and dressed before running inside, slamming the door.

Immediately, they fell into each other and worked off their excess energy in a way that ended in some of her furniture being knocked over.

Liam groaned, stretched out on Isabella's living room floor, staring at the ceiling. He felt thoroughly sated for a change, and he loved it. It was exhilarating being with someone who could match his energy without getting hurt. He didn't have to hold back.

She lifted her head and grinned at him. "Aye, we might kill each other," she declared breathlessly.

"And I'm going to enjoy every second of it. If it kills me, I'll die a happy dragon," he drawled.

She leaned over and kissed his cheek. "Shower, the others are probably waiting on us."

He waved her on, needing a few more minutes on the floor. He heard the water running, and after he caught his breath, finally got up to check his phone. A few texts from the others asking where they were, indeed, awaited him, so he texted back they were getting dressed and would be on their way soon. The immediate reply that the others would pick them up on their way to the airport sent him hurrying to join Isabella in the shower. He grinned as he heard her rumble in happiness when he slipped behind her. *Oh yeah, I could get used to this,* he thought as he dragged his fangs over her neck, forcing a growl from her throat.

"Pack up, we're heading back to the United States," came her quick snapping directive over the phone.

Sighing wearily, the brown-haired man murmured acknowledgement and began flinging items into his bag. He knew better than to warn her she was getting too close and involved; she wouldn't listen. Dragons might like to sleep on grass, but it wasn't his idea of a good rest. At least he could catch a nap on the plane. He stretched and pulled up the picture on his phone, reminding himself once again why he was doing this.

Chapter 24

THE FLIGHT WAS A long one, so Liam slouched down in his seat, trying to get some sleep. With the time difference, when they got home, it wouldn't be late enough for bed, and he needed the rest. Marco and Killian sat next to him, but he ignored them. At least he tried. He could feel their stares like a nagging itch on his skin. Finally, he opened one eye with a disgusted sigh and found them grinning at him. "What?" he grumped.

Marco's smile stretched even wider. "Liam, why so tired, *hermano*? Was Izzy's sofa... uncomfortable?"

Shrugging, Liam yawned before mumbling, "I dunno, didn't sleep there."

Killian snorted, and Marco laughed incredulously. "Oh? So where did you sleep then, *piquito amigo verde*?"

Liam rolled his eyes, "On a hillside, about ten miles from her place, *amigo rojo*."

Marco leaned back with a puzzled expression while Killian snorted again, his shoulders shaking with suppressed mirth.

"Not that it's any of your business, but we went on a night flight, then slept in our dragon forms outside. She's a dragon, too, remember?" Liam grunted at them.

Killian cleared his throat, "An' that's all ye did last night wee lizard? Just go for a flight an' sleep? Because it's certain I am, I detected a shine on ye both this morning."

"I liked you better when you were quiet," Liam snapped.

The silver wielder laughed so hard, the women, who were sitting at the other end, glanced over in surprise.

Liam waved and smiled, sighing as they went back to their own discussions.

Marco cleared his throat. "Well, answer the man."

"Okay, that's not all we did," Liam sighed.

The red dragon grunted in triumph. "Told ya," he stage-whispered to Killian, poking him in the shoulder.

Killian whispered back, "I didn't disagree, ye feckin' langer."

Liam glared at his friends. "Jerks," he declared them both with a decisive nod.

Marco rolled his eyes. "*Dios mio, hermano. Por favor,* you were mooning after her all day yesterday. We all knew it was a matter of time. Killian just thought you might give her at least a day."

Liam grinned at them, "Hey, I was planning to leave her alone completely, but she started touching my wings."

Marco and Killian both sat back then, nodding appreciatively. They knew what that meant.

"She didn't know why it was a big deal until I told her. I was going to leave, but then she... well, she asked me to touch her wings," Liam whispered.

"Dude," Marco's eyes went wide, staring at Liam with a hint of hero worship.

Killian simply tilted his head and stared, a knowing smirk on his lips.

Liam grinned. "It was amazing, like nothing I've ever experienced before. We were at each other all night after that. I gotta tell you, being with another dragon, phew, intense," he shook his head.

Marco clapped him on the shoulder and whispered, "You're my hero."

At the other end of the plane, the women were discussing the same thing. "Spill!" Risa demanded, eyeing her sister.

"What?" Izzy glanced innocently at her.

"You slept with him, didn't you?" Risa laughed, steepling her fingers in undisguised glee.

Siobhan put her fingers in her ears, "Lalalala, I do not need to hear about my brother's sexual escapades."

They all laughed. Izzy smiled, then relented, "Well, we had a bit of a misunderstanding."

Siobhan snorted, "Liam's good at that! Wait! I don't want to hear this. Forget I said anything."

Izzy laughed again, "He apologized, he was trying to be a gentleman in his adorably inept way. It was really sweet, an' he offered to go back to Killian's house. When I asked him how, he said he would fly an' pulled out his —"

Siobhan coughed.

"Wings," finished Izzy drily.

Risa giggled.

Squirming like she was uncomfortable, Izzy hesitated, then mumbled, "I didn't expect that. I just thought they were the most beautiful wings I'd ever seen. I've only ever seen silver wings."

Siobhan sighed, "I'll give him that, Liam does have the most gorgeous wings *I've* ever seen. The jerk. And I'll deny it if anyone asks, but he is freaking adorable in his dragon form. The absolute cutest. God, he has this little dance he does, prancing around on his paws. Ugh, it's just too precious. He looks so sweet and cuddly, but he's actually pretty ferocious and a damn good fighter. Again, anyone tells him I said that, and I don't know you." She pointed at each of them in turn, fighting back a grin.

Izzy giggled, "Like I said, I didn't know an' I, well, I started petting them."

"You what?" Siobhan whispered, her jaw dropping.

Flushing scarlet, Izzy shrugged, the embarrassment of her ignorance heating her face uncomfortably.

Risa looked confused, "I don't get it, what's the big deal?"

Siobhan snickered and turned to Risa, lowering her voice, "When a dragon is in human form and they have their wings out, they're super extra sensitive. It's an erogenous area. They find it *very* erotic to have them stroked." She glanced over at Marco and smiled wistfully.

Risa snorted into her drink, choking back her laughter.

Izzy smiled, "Aye, an' he let me rub all over them without saying anything an' then he jumped back an' said he needed to leave. Let's just say something came up."

Siobhan groaned, and Risa giggled again.

"Well, I didn't know," Izzy hissed, her face flushed even more, "I felt terrible, like I'd hurt him."

"Oh, he was hurting all right," Siobhan muttered.

Izzy stared at her bemused, as Siobhan kept getting back into the conversation despite her denial of wanting to hear it. "So, he explained that to me an' just seeing how it, ah, affected him, I um, well I spread my own wings an' asked him to touch mine."

"You dirty hooker, I love it!" Siobhan grinned, waggling her eyebrows.

Coughing on the sip of soda she'd just taken, Izzy wheezed while Risa slapped her on the back, giggling.

Leaning forward, giving up all pretense of disinterest, Siobhan continued, "So, after you got all grabby with my brother, what he got grabby back and wham bam?"

"Well, not as quick as all that," Izzy sputtered, "Anyway, as the night went on, we discovered why dragons don't usually date other dragons. It was intense."

Siobhan's mouth dropped. "Okay, this feels weird to say, but go, Liam!" She cringed, "Eww, never saying that again."

Izzy smiled, "We damn near killed each other. Then I almost did when he left."

"Whoa, back up, he left?" Siobhan demanded, narrowing her eyes.

She nodded, staring at her fingers as she twisted them. "It was my fault, I said something very insulting. It hurt him pretty badly. I didn't mean the way it sounded, an' I felt horrible. He left after that. Turned dragon an' flew right off."

"That idiot, that's what he does," Siobhan mumbled as she ground her teeth together.

"Aye, he mentioned that, when I chased him down an' called him a coward," Izzy offered with a smug smile.

Siobhan appraised the silver dragon approvingly, leaning forward with her elbows on her knees, "Do tell!"

She told them how she'd flown after him and almost knocked him out of the sky, bit his tail, and yelled at him. She also told them about flying around trying to catch him.

Siobhan high-fived her, then laughed, "Yeah, Liam was always the tag champion. Marco's faster, but Liam is great at evasive maneuvers."

Izzy nodded in agreement as she'd seen it first-hand. She told them how they'd talked it out, and he told her about Jorrie.

Siobhan sat back in silence. She scrunched her eyebrows, frowning, with a contemplative expression.

Risa leaned forward, "Shi, what's that look?"

She glanced at the other two, "Well, it's just I'm surprised he told you this soon. It really messed him up badly. He was absolutely head over heels for Jorrie, and when she left him, it destroyed him. He's been in a bad place since."

"Poor Liam," Risa gasped, "He's such a sweetheart. I wondered at how close they all were."

Siobhan nodded. "They danced around each other for a while at first. But there was this silver dragon who gave this long speech about prophecy, circles, and indicated the two of them were fated to be together. So, they began dating, and we were all sure they were going to end up married or something. It was intense. But then Liam left for a while on his mission for vengeance for our family. He didn't handle it well, and he broke her heart. She started dating Shepard, and then they fell in love, and the rest is history. Liam never fully got over it. He's always loved her, and it's made it hard for him to move on.

"Just in the last year, he seemed to be doing better, but I've been worried about him. He's all I've got left of our family, and he's always taken care of me. Ever since I was a baby. He was already an adult and moved out on his own long before I was born. Our dad... wasn't the most loving or involved. He and Liam didn't see eye to eye on most things. But Liam was thrilled to have a baby sister and came back home to help out anyway. How many grown men would do that? He has such a big heart and so much love to give, but not much luck in having it returned. Now, he just seems so alone and down, not his usual cheerfully irritating self. He's been more of a reckless idiot lately. I'm his sister, it's my job to mess with him, but I've hated seeing him like this." She wiped away a tear. "Anyway, he seemed excited at the prospect of this mission. I guess it was a chance to get out of his head a bit, which is why Vaughn assigned him."

Risa nodded and squeezed her hand while Izzy rubbed her shoulder.

Siobhan gazed at Liam with a fond smile as the other guys laughed and teased him. She clearly loved her brother dearly and wanted him to be happy. She sharpened her gaze on Izzy. "I'm glad to see him smiling again, but please, be careful with him. He's more fragile than he seems. If he told you about Jorrie," she shook her head, "That's something he keeps close to his heart, doesn't talk about it. You must have flipped some switch in him to open up about it so quickly. Don't hurt him, Izzy. Please, take care of my brother."

Izzy nodded and took Siobhan's hand, squeezing it gently. "I saw that in him. I promise, I don't want to hurt him, but I do want to see where this might go. When we met, well, it was like a string was pulling us together. I honestly felt the earth stop for a moment. I don't know if it's because he knocked me on my arse or if there's more, but I need to know."

Grinning, Siobhan told her, "Well, if he runs away, you chase him down and bite his tail again!"

"Deal!" Izzy laughed as they hugged each other.

Another hour into the flight, Izzy sat next to Liam. He was asleep, his hands clasped loosely over his stomach. She could see his shirt was riding up a bit, flashing the sprinkle of red-gold hair trailing into his jeans. She smiled, remembering how she traced that trail just this morning. She leaned against his warm chest, and he sighed happily. Listening to his rumbly purr, she fell asleep against him. A short while later, she woke to him tracing her lower lip with his thumb. She lifted her eyes to his, and he smiled gently. Standing, she stretched, arms over her head, then shrieked as he pulled her to his lap and kissed her. The others chuckled while she smiled at his silly expression.

"Hey there, little lady, you wouldn't be heading to my neck of the woods, would ya?" he drawled in a ridiculous parody of his Texan accent.

She giggled, "Why, sir, I would!"

He smiled, tugging a lock of hair on his forehead. "Ma'am, I'd be much obliged if you wouldn't mind this gentleman calling on you once you settle in."

"I've no idea what that means," she smirked, "But you're no gentleman, sir."

He grinned, kissed her, then purred in her ear, "And you like it!"

Siobhan called out playfully, "Get a room!"

"Had one, you made us leave it to get on the plane," he snapped back at his sister.

After the laughter died down, Liam described life in Dallas. How it was nothing like the TV shows depicted. Not many people had oil wells or rode horses to work. He told her about Vaughn and his companies, how he worked for the black dragon doing different jobs, assignments all over the world. She nodded; it sounded exciting. He also told her that he had a house but usually stayed with Vaughn.

"Now that Bridget has delivered their newest baby, I'll be staying at my house more to give them space. Maybe you can come visit me there?" He smiled shyly, hopefully.

Softly, she traced his jaw with one finger, then whispered, "I'd like that. A lot."

"So would I," he replied just as quietly.

"Where am I staying for now?"

Liam looked startled; apparently, they hadn't thought that far ahead. He leaned around his seat, calling out, "Hey Ki, didn't you say Risa was moving in with you?"

Killian nodded.

"What about Rena?" Liam asked.

A shrug.

"You don't know?"

A head shake.

"But you asked her, right?"

Another nod.

Liam sat back, pinching his lower lip between his thumb and pointer finger.

Izzy stared at her sister's fiancé. "He doesn't talk much, does he?"

Chuckling, Liam rolled his eyes, "That's a whole story for another day. Short answer, no, not really, but he's getting better. Risa helps him with that a lot."

"I bet." Izzy smiled softly at her sister; she was really happy for her.

He took her hand, "Well, I guess we can figure it out when we land, but it depends on Rena. She's staying in a condo right now that has two bedrooms. If she stays, maybe you can stay with her. If she moves in with Killian and Risa, maybe you could stay with me for a while until we figure out where we go from here?"

She smiled, "Makes sense." Her smile faltered, "I don't know about staying with Rena. I want to see her an' reunite my family, but I don't know if she wants to live with a stranger."

He leaned forward, "I don't think that will be a problem. She's so excited to see you. When we first brought Risa home, the two were inseparable. Well, three; Risa just learned she was a wielder, so Killian was with her non-stop as well, teaching her."

The plane began its descent, and she stared out the window. As views of Dallas came into sight, her jaw dropped. It was bigger than she imagined. She remembered Killian telling her how vast it was, but until you saw it in person, you just couldn't imagine. The city stretched as far as she could see in every direction. She turned a stunned gaze to Liam. "Ye live *here*?"

"Home sweet home," he happily replied.

She glanced back outside, then at him again, "How do ye find anything?"

He chuckled and held up his phone. "GPS."

She shook her head. She imagined the air smelled terrible out there. Everyone being so close, not a lot of green. She kept her opinions to herself. She wasn't sure she wanted to stay here, and she had a feeling that would hurt Liam almost as much as her sisters.

The plane taxied to its private hangar, where they wearily exited to find a large group waiting for them. Izzy shook with nervousness, her palms sweating and her stomach churning. The people watched her with interest and smiles, so she straightened her shoulders and tried to relax. She'd barely stepped two feet from the plane when she heard her name and turned to see a silvery missile hurtling towards her. The beautiful girl who ran from the crowd was crying. Serena.

Izzy's eyes filled with tears of her own, seeing the young woman her baby sister had become in their years apart. She enveloped Serena in her arms and held her while they both sobbed. The years of not knowing, of missing each other's milestones, of not celebrating or supporting each other hit them all, and the mountain of sorrow dropped them to the floor. Soon, a third pair of arms surrounded them, and Izzy knew it was Marissa. Finally, the three were reunited at last. After over fifteen years, they were whole again.

Liam made his way through everyone to Vaughn. He nodded and expressed his thanks to his godfather for working so quickly to take care of Isabella's return.

Vaughn gently placed his hands on Liam's shoulders, studying him before pulling him close. "Finally. You look well," he said, relief in his voice.

"I wasn't aware I looked unwell before. Did you think I was ill?" Liam gazed at Vaughn in askance.

Smiling fondly and tousling Liam's hair like a child, Vaughn told him, "Not sick, Liam, just not whole. I've been worried about you. You've been so unsettled, not centered. You look like you've realigned yourself and have a better outlook on the world. I'm happy, the trip did you some good."

Liam nodded slowly in understanding and glanced at Isabella, a soft smile curving his lips.

Vaughn followed his line of sight and grinned. The silver dragon was stunning, just like her sisters. Killian had already filled Vaughn in on the budding romance between the two. Liam's hands would be full if he were going to date a dragon, but Vaughn knew Liam was up for the challenge. It was just what he needed. He clapped Liam's shoulder with a chuckle, "Good luck with that, son, I'm cheering for you."

Liam turned back and gazed at Vaughn, startled. The black dragon just smiled.

Chapter 25

KILLIAN APPEARED AT THEIR side, and Vaughn studied him, too. "Killian, I was just telling Liam how well he looked after the trip, and now here you are in front of me, a whole new man yourself!"

The wielder tilted his head and stared at Vaughn warily. "No, I changed that before I went," he said slowly, pointing at his hair, then he smirked, "Are ye growing forgetful in your old age then?"

Vaughn shook his head and laughed, "Not your appearance, Ki, your demeanor. You look relaxed for the first time in... decades."

Killian grinned, then laughed loudly.

Vaughn smiled as his eyes went shiny. He hugged Killian tightly, whispering, "That's what I mean. It's so good to see you outside of yourself, my friend."

Killian hugged Vaughn back then turned and gestured at Risa, waving her over. "She took me to see my family, Vaughn. I saw my Molly girl, was able to sing her the wedding song I wrote for her, an' my parents are proud of me. Most importantly," he said as Risa came to his side, "This incredible woman has honored me by agreeing to be my wife." He held up her hand for Vaughn to see the ring.

Vaughn's eyes flew to Killian's. Outside of Risa, he was the only other person who knew why this was so monumental. The tears that threatened earlier now rolled freely down his cheeks, and he hugged Killian so hard the wielder had to slap him on the back so he could breathe. Vaughn laughed, "Sorry, sorry! Ki, you know I love you, I'm so happy for you." He turned to Risa, "I'm happy for both of you. Thank you, darling woman. Thank you for being so good to him. I love you, too." He hugged her tightly and missed the shocked look on her face at being enveloped by such a large, overwhelming man, especially since he was now her boss.

Killian smirked, hearing the shriek that echoed through the hangar as Rena learned the news, turning to see her jumping up and down behind him. He laughed, "Aye, Rena doll, I missed ye too!" He hugged the tiny woman, and she kissed him hard on the cheek. He swung her around as she shrieked in delight. "Now ye really will be my little sister, lass."

Izzy put her fingers to her lips, watching how easy Killian was with Rena. It was obvious she adored him, and she couldn't be happier for her sisters. As Killian put Rena down, Liam tapped her shoulder, and she turned to him with an even bigger grin.

Rena jumped into his arms, hugging him around the neck before she kissed his cheek. "Liam! I missed you as well! I had to play cards with Ivan while you were gone. He cheats!" she laughed.

Liam grinned at her, "Re-Re, I *told* you he did. You should have stuck to Go Fish!"

Izzy sighed happily. *Okay, that was the cutest thing ever.* She felt a heavy gaze upon her and turned to face one of the most stunning men she'd ever laid eyes on. His jet-black hair waved softly around his jaw, and gorgeous blue eyes studied her closely. The others called him Vaughn and showed deference to him, so she knew this was *the* Vaughn Drake she'd heard so much about. The man who could work miracles. She could see why people submitted to him; power practically radiated from his tall frame. It was a little intimidating. He beckoned her over, and she slowly made her way to him. He smiled warmly, and she felt her lips curving in return. It was irresistible.

"Hello Isabella, we're so happy you're here. We've been looking for you for a while now. It's a relief to know you're safe and that we're able to reunite your family," he said softly.

She glanced at her sisters happily, then turned her eyes back to Vaughn, taking in his genuine smile.

"I want you to feel welcome here because you're family. So, anything you need, just let one of us know, it will be taken care of. That's how we are, we take care of our own." Vaughn put his hands in his pockets and tilted his chin towards Liam.

Liam handed her the documents Vaughn prepared, a passport and visa for her stay. She gazed at them, stunned. She felt her eyes filling again and burst into tears, completely overwhelmed. Liam pulled her close, and she took a deep breath. She was with her own kind now. Maybe she could stay here after all.

Vaughn smiled at his growing family, then found Marco and Siobhan on the edges of the group. They were holding hands and smiling softly. He waved them over. "I understand more congratulations are in order?"

Siobhan shook her head, but Marco couldn't contain his excitement, exclaiming, "We're pregnant!"

Siobhan elbowed him in the ribs.

After a pained grunt, he laughed, "Sorry, *she's* pregnant, I'm going to be a father!"

Izzy wandered around Vaughn's home underneath a skyscraper in down-town Dallas. It was one of the most amazing things she'd ever seen. It was also full of people. They were celebrating her and her sisters being reunited, as well as Siobhan and Marco's announcement. Everyone here was either a dragon or a wielder.

Well, everyone except Jack, who she learned was the husband of Davis, who was Shepard's twin brother, who was Jorrie's husband. She thought she had it all correct in her head now. Jack was the only straight human there, but they treated him the same as the others. He joked with her that he wasn't even a straight human. He was devastatingly handsome and charming, and she already adored him. He and his husband were leaving in the morning to go on their honeymoon.

She loved seeing how easy-going and caring they all were with each other. It really was a huge family. She noticed Killian sitting in a corner by himself, watching everyone. She made her way to him, and he glanced at her, seeming startled.

"Um, hi?" Killian said cautiously to her.

She studied him, "Why are ye surprised to see me?" she asked.

Killian smirked, "I've made being unnoticed a bit of an art form. When I've had enough of people, I find a quiet wall an' blend in with my magic. Usually, people don't see me unless I want them to. When I do move or speak, they've all but forgotten I was there, an' it startles them. But ye saw me right away. I wondered how."

Izzy nodded. Risa told her that he was straightforward and blunt; she was right. Still, she was a little surprised he answered her so directly. "I tend to look beyond things," she told him. "I don't know if it's magic, but I have this ability to look deeper. I guess I saw below your shield."

His expression thoughtful, Killian slowly nodded as well. "I don't mind. It's not that I don't want to talk to anyone, just sometimes I get a little overwhelmed around a lot of people, so I hang back an' re-center."

"I get that, makes perfect sense," Izzy reassured him. "Do ye mind if I hang back with ye here for a bit?"

He smiled and shook his head, gesturing to the seat next to him, "Mi wall, su wall."

She laughed and lightly smacked his arm before joining him on the bench.

Risa later found them there, just sitting quietly. "Oh no, not you, too!" she moaned.

"No, just saw him sitting by his lonesome an' it seemed like a good idea," Izzy laughed.

Risa smiled and joined them. She put her head on Killian's shoulder. "Yeah, he does that. Sometimes I lose him in a crowd. My little hermit crab." She yawned.

Killian smiled tenderly at Risa, then stood. "An' it seems it's time to get my princess back to her castle. Izzy, are ye all set for tonight?"

She nodded, "Rena said she would love to have me stay with her for now at the condo."

He smiled tenderly, "I'm so glad." He glanced back at Risa, his face taking on an expression of reverence and devotion. "Come, *mo stor*, I'll take ye home." He laid a soft kiss on her lips and trailed behind her while she said her goodbyes.

Izzy sighed wistfully; she hoped one day to have a love like that.

Rena wandered over to her then, "Izzy, I'm really tired too. Do you mind if we go home?"

She smiled at her baby sister. She was also ready to go. This had been a long and overwhelming day. She stood, then realized she had no idea how they were going to get there. She wasn't sure if Rena drove or not.

Liam appeared at her elbow, "Ladies, I'll be happy to drive you to the condo, it's on my way home. If you don't mind giving me a few minutes? I want to grab some things from my room here to take to my house." They both nodded in agreement.

Rena excused herself; she wanted to go say goodbye to the baby one more time. Izzy smiled, watching her silver-blonde head bob through the crowd to where Vaughn's wife, Bridget, was holding a tiny baby boy.

"Hi!" came a friendly, bubbly voice.

Izzy turned and found herself staring at a mass of blonde curls on a petite woman who was studying her with a huge grin. Izzy smiled back, "Hi there, I'm Isabella, well, I go by Izzy. I didn't realize we hadn't met."

The woman nodded, "Yeah, sorry, Shepard and I got here a little late, the triple threat was not being cooperative."

Izzy felt her smile freeze in place. She knew who this was. "Jorrie," she breathed, taking in the beautiful woman who Liam loved once upon a time.

The woman tilted her head in curiosity.

"Sorry, I recognized the name Shepard, an' Liam told me ye were his wife. Just put two an' two together. I'm actually a huge fan of your music," Izzy offered meekly.

Jorrie nodded and grinned. "Liam, huh?"

"Aye."

"A good man, Liam," Jorrie smiled softly, "He's one of my best friends, you know."

Izzy's eyes narrowed as she gave a curt nod.

Jorrie narrowed her eyes as well, "I see you do know."

Izzy squared her shoulders and smirked. "Yes, I know. An' I think it's wonderful that Liam is such a good friend to ye, considering."

Jorrie glared at the silver dragon. "Considering what?"

Stepping closer, Izzy growled, "Considering you're about to warn me away from him, an' I have no intention of doing so. He's had his heart broken enough by ye, Jorrie. He made mistakes, but he had a noble cause. Do ye know the same people that killed his parents, likely killed mine, an' were the reason I've been missing my sisters all these years? It's time he found someone who can care for him the way he needs. You've clearly moved on; let him do the same. He said he told ye he can't be your fallback anymore, so why can't ye leave him be? Stop hurting him, an' stay out of it."

Jorrie gritted her teeth, "Look, I don't disagree, but you need to know —"

Izzy snorted, "I know. We had a misunderstanding in Ireland, an' he left. He ran away."

"That's what he does," Jorrie nodded in exasperation.

Izzy grinned at her and leaned down, whispering in her ear so low, no one else could hear. "The difference is, I chased him down an' bit his tail. He almost fell out of the sky; he was so surprised. Liam doesn't believe he's loveable, that he deserves to be cared for. He needs someone willing to fight for him, until he knows he's worth it."

Jorrie stared at her in shock for a minute, then she laughed loudly. "Izzy, I like you, you're exactly what he needs. I'm glad you're here." She pulled the dragon into a hug.

Izzy was stunned but hugged her back.

"I mean it," Jorrie whispered to her, "You're just what he needs. Please, Izzy, help him and heal that sweet heart of his. It's too good to be left broken. I want him to be happy; he deserves it."

Leaning back, Izzy studied her. "Ye still love him," she whispered incredulously.

Jorrie nodded and patted her on the shoulder. "But not in the way I love Shepard. I will always have a place in my heart for Liam; he was the first man I truly loved, and we both made mistakes. I care deeply about him, but that's it. He doesn't know, not really, and I'd like to keep it that way. I *love* Shepard. He's my entire world, my soulmate, and that kind of love can't be denied. I hope Liam finds that one day, maybe it will be you."

Izzy understood the difference and agreed this was something Liam didn't need to know. She hugged Jorrie again, whispering, "I'll try."

Liam was heading back to Isabella, but stopped before he got there. Rena, hot on his heels, ran into his back when he halted suddenly, giggling as she almost fell. He steadied her absent-mindedly as he studied the scene in front of him. He couldn't believe what he was seeing. Jorrie was face to face with Isabella. *Shit*, he thought. Jorrie was obviously sizing the woman up, and they looked like they were squaring off.

He watched their verbal sparring match and then stared in confusion as they hugged each other, laughing. Apparently, they were friends now. He shook his head. *Women*.

Shepard snuck up behind him and wrapped his arms around him, picking him up and shaking him. "Liam!" he shouted, "My darling, I've missed you!" He dipped Liam over his arm and kissed him hard. Liam shoved at Shepard until he let him stand, and they both cackled like lunatics.

The women watched them, Jorrie rolling her eyes, Isabella shocked.

Jorrie looped her arm through Isabella's and pulled her over to introduce her. "Izzy, the handsome idiot making out with Liam is my husband, Shepard. Shepard, this is Izzy, the woman who Liam would much rather kiss than you!"

Shepard grinned and shook Isabella's hand. "I don't blame him, she's much prettier than me! Still, I can't resist his soft lips!" He grabbed Liam's face and acted like he was going to kiss him again.

Liam growled at Shepard as he tackled him. They both ended up on the floor, Liam sitting on Shepard's back this time. "I won this round, old man!"

Shepard cackled. "Jorrie, help me! Your friend is beating me up."

"Only if you stop kissing him!" she snapped.

"Okay, okay," Shepard held up his hands in surrender, "I'll stop kissing luscious Liam and only kiss you, my dear, my beautiful wife and reason for my existence."

Liam nodded, "Much better."

Risa and Killian came over to say goodnight to her sisters so they could finally leave. Liam had just helped Shepard to his feet when the blue dragon saw Killian.

"You! Irish!" he shouted at Killian, "You kissed my wife? And had the nerve to sing at my brother's wedding in my place?" He growled at Killian, who stared at him impassively.

"Technically, she kissed me, an' I only sang because some fecking lizard set me up." He glared at Liam, who grinned back unabashedly.

Shepard sighed in disappointment, "I know. You're no fun, Ki. How can I tease you if you won't get riled up?"

Killian shrugged and smirked at him. "Talent? Besides, Jack and Davis love me more now."

Roaring with laughter, Shepard grabbed Killian, kissing him soundly. Isabella stared in surprise at the crazy people around her. She glanced at Risa to see her sister was rolling her eyes as if this kind of thing happened frequently.

"Aye, I agree with Marco, ye need to shave. Jack's definitely the better kisser," Killian replied casually.

Jack crowed in victory, and Davis patted his brother's shoulder in conciliation.

Shepard threw up his hands in defeat and sighed heavily in disgust, "All this love to give and only my wife wants to kiss me."

Isabella shook her head; they obviously had some inside joke she wasn't privy to.

Shepard turned to Isabella. "I'm sorry, you probably think we're all a bit bonkers, don't you?"

She smiled, "The thought crossed."

He grinned and advanced towards her as her eyes widened. He grabbed her and hugged her instead. "Welcome to the family. And don't worry, I'm not going to kiss you." He whispered in her ear, "Yet." He leaned back and winked.

Chapter 26

I N THE CAR, IZZY stared out the window, enjoying the view of the city around her. Liam told her they were going to another city just north of Dallas called Plano. She nodded absently, and when he exited the massive highway, she turned to him. "Where are we?"

"Plano," he told her.

She shook her head, confused, "But we didn't leave the city?"

He laughed, "Yeah, the cities all run one right up next to each other here. We've been through Richardson already as well."

She gaped at him, feeling a little overwhelmed, but Liam stayed quiet, letting her take it all in, which she appreciated. They pulled into a spot in front of a beautiful building, which he announced was their destination. She got out of the car and gazed around in awe; the area was beautiful and well-maintained.

Liam woke Rena up as she'd fallen asleep in the backseat, but she was really tired and stumbled a bit. Handing Izzy the keys, he lifted the small woman in his arms, carrying her up to the second floor as if she weighed nothing. He nodded at the door, and Izzy unlocked it. After pointing out the light switches to her, he carried Rena through the home until he reached her room. He set her down on her bed and pulled her shoes off before he tucked her in and kissed her temple like a small child.

Izzy smiled, it was so sweet and brotherly. He then walked her through the condo, showing her around and making sure she was familiar with everything. He took her to what used to be Risa's room. She gazed around in awe. The room was bigger than her whole apartment back in Ireland. She was drowning in sensation and emotion, once again unsure if she could stay here. She hurried to the restroom, needing to splash icy water on her face.

Huffing out an angry breath, the brown-haired man hurriedly sent a text message since she wasn't answering her phone.

You were right there. Why didn't you grab them then?

He stared in fury at the screen before three small dots indicated a reply was forthcoming.

Vaughn was there, too many others. Can't take them all on alone. Need to separate them.

Snorting, he ground his teeth in frustration, she was right, but it still chafed. A soft ping indicated another message.

Don't fuck this up! You know what's at stake.

A picture was attached to this final message. He studied it with a dry mouth and aching heart. Once again, she was right.

Liam noticed Isabella seemed unsettled. He imagined she was having some serious culture shock on top of being reunited with her sisters and meeting so many new people. She was surely feeling on edge right now, but he couldn't stay. Not here. When she came out of the bathroom, her face damp and cheeks flushed, he moved closer and ran his hands down her arms. "I'm going to head home now. Are you okay? You need anything?" he asked.

She smiled and shook her head. "I'm alright. Just a lot in my head right now. I can't think of anything I would need between now an' tomorrow morning."

He wanted to ask about the conversation with Jorrie, but didn't want to push. He would let her tell him if she wanted. Kissing her on the cheek, he turned to leave.

"Goodnight, Liam," she called to him.

"Goodnight, Isabella," he replied softly.

Izzy stared at the front door as it closed behind him. She was alone now. Rena was there but was fast asleep. Izzy rubbed her clammy, damp hands on her pants and glanced around at the unfamiliar space. She felt tight in her own skin. Before she could process it, she ran to the door and down the stairs. "Liam!" she yelled as she burst into the lot. He was almost to his car, but heard her and turned, his expression alarmed. She ran across the pavement to him, as he hurried back to her. She threw herself in his arms, sobbing, begging. "Don't go, Liam, please don't go. I don't want to be alone. Will ye stay? Please?"

"Shh," he soothed, stroking her hair and holding her tightly. "Of course I'll stay. Whatever you need, Isabella." His words filled her with warmth and reassurance.

She buried her face in his neck and breathed him in as his rumble calmed her further. He smelled like a warm summer day, fresh grass, and apples. It was soothing and somehow reminded her of Ireland.

He pulled back from her a bit and studied her, brushing her hair behind her ear. "Let me grab my bag from my car, and I'll be right up, okay? Go back inside, and I'll join you shortly."

She nodded and smiled, relief plain on her face. She jogged back to the building, aware he watched her until she was safely inside.

Liam turned and slowly trudged to his car. He opened the trunk and halfheartedly grabbed the bag of clothes he'd packed at Vaughn's place. Closing it, he leaned against the vehicle for a minute before sighing and scrubbing his hands down his face. *What am I doing here? I can't do this. I shouldn't have agreed.* He sighed again. *I told her anything, and she asked for this. She needs me.* His lips curved slightly at the pleasant thought of being needed, then fell as he studied the building again.

He hurried inside and tossed his bag on the floor before he locked up for the night. He found her sitting on the bed, knees to her chest and her arms wrapped around them. She was resting her chin on her knees and glanced up, unease in her eyes.

"Isabella?" he called softly as he sat, "What's wrong?"

She laughed humorlessly, "It's too much. It's everything, all of it. I don't want to be here, but I don't want to leave. I don't know if I can do this, just pick up my life an' start over. I'm just... really overwhelmed."

He nodded, that's what he suspected. He pulled her over and kissed her temple. "Are you tired? Do you want to try to go to sleep, and we can work through some of it tomorrow?" She made a small affirmative noise, and he smiled gently, "Okay, why don't you go get ready? I'm going to turn off the lights out there, and I'll be right back."

When Liam came back in, he was carrying a mug that he offered her. With amusement, he noted she changed into a pair of shorts and a tank with an angry unicorn emblazoned on the front. The caption, 'Try Me!' was so in character it made him smirk. Then he took in her cautious gaze and quietly gestured with the cup. "I brought you some chamomile tea. Rena drinks it sometimes when she's having trouble sleeping. I thought maybe you might like some?"

She stared at him, saying nothing.

His smile faltered. He started to set it down, "I'm sorry, I should have asked, I just don't think sometimes."

"Thank ye!" she blurted quickly and reached for it. "It's sweet. I love it." She took a sip and smiled. The warm, fragrant steam curled around her cheeks. "Sorry, Liam, it was a very thoughtful thing to do, an' it surprised me. Not because ye can't be thoughtful, just I wasn't expecting it. No one's taken care of me in a long time. Not that I'm expecting ye to keep taking care of me, just that... Ugh," she stammered. "Sorry, I'm babbling again."

He grinned, "It's okay, I do that, too. How about this, we can just babble at each other with no apologies needed in the future. Deal?"

She laughed lightly and nodded, drinking more tea.

"Right," he sighed, slapping his hands on his thighs. "I'm gonna," he pointed at the bathroom door.

"And I'm gonna," she pointed at the cup.

He huffed out a small laugh and went to the bathroom, shutting the door softly. He stood, statue-like, for a moment, and glanced around. His chest tightened a bit as he took in the space. He did not want to do this. Blowing out a harsh breath, he thought, *it's one night. I can sleep here, just sleep, one night. Tomorrow, I'll ask her to come stay with me instead.* She'd want to know why of course so he'd tell her. Or not. Maybe he'd think of something else because he didn't want to make her feel bad. He washed his face and brushed his teeth, then stripped down to his boxers. He didn't really have pajamas, so this would have to do.

Isabella had turned down the sheets and turned on the bedside lamp when Liam came back in. He didn't miss the way her eyes were drawn immediately to his sculpted chest and muscular arms, a soft smile curving her lips. His body started getting tight and needy, so he turned away. He didn't want her to think that was the only reason he was here. She crawled in and pulled the blanket over herself, watching him intently as he hesitantly climbed in next to her. She turned the lamp off, and the room was now blessedly dark.

He lay next to her, on his back. Stiff as a board, not settling in like one usually does after getting into bed.

"Liam?" she whispered.

He turned his head towards her. "Hmm?"

"Is something wrong? Ye kind of seem like you'd rather be anywhere but here," her voice full of concern.

Feeling even lower that he was making her doubt him this way, his stomach churned as he sighed. "No, not anywhere. I'm not comfortable being here, but it's nothing to do with you. C'mere," he pulled her close to his chest. As he wrapped her up, some of the tension left him when she snuggled in with a satisfied purr. "That's better."

She yawned, then whispered, "If not me, then what?"

"It doesn't matter," he kissed her forehead. "I'm here for you. Sleep, Isabella."

She yawned again.

He chuckled and stroked her hair as he began to rumble softly in his chest.

She relaxed, falling asleep quickly in the comfort of his arms.

He wasn't so lucky and lay there a long time, staring into the darkness. Finally, he slept for a short while, but not well.

Liam woke early in the gray light of morning feeling stiff and achy. He gazed at Isabella, who was still asleep, so he eased out of the bed and stretched. Slipping on his pants, he made his way to the kitchen. It seemed Rena was still asleep as well. He started some coffee and stood there, hands on the counter, blearily watching it drip into the pot. So focused was he on the stream of reviving caffeine, he jumped when arms went around his waist.

"Sorry!" Isabella cried, "I didn't realize ye didn't hear me."

He turned and smiled as best as he could.

She studied his drawn face and frowned, "Ye didn't sleep well last night, did ye?"

He slowly shook his head no, his hair brushing his jaw as it swung messily around his face.

"Liam," Isabella chided softly, "What's wrong? Ye said it's not me, so why are ye so unhappy here? It's this place. Ye know it well, but ye don't like it."

He stared at her. She was entirely too smart for her own good. He sighed, his shoulders sagging with the weight of her words. "Bingo."

She gave him a sad, knowing smile. "Why? I know ye don't want to talk about it. But if I'm going to come stay with ye while I'm here, I think I deserve to know the reason."

He barked out a short laugh. "Well, that was nicely done. I can't argue with that."

She grinned at him and crossed her arms before waving a hand in a 'go ahead' gesture.

He poured two cups of coffee and handed her one. "There's cream and sugar in..." he trailed off, watching her sip it black, without letting it cool off. He stared, lips parted, eyes wide.

"What?" she asked nervously, glancing over her shoulder.

He smiled again; this time it was genuine. "It's just refreshing to see a woman who knows how to appreciate a good cup of coffee." He took a large sip of his, too. The heat helped him wake up, and he knew the caffeine would at least get him home. She was still watching him expectantly, so he led her to the table.

"Okay, so you might think it's stupid, but please don't judge me too harshly. This condo: it's owned by Shepard and Davis. They used to live here back when they were both single. When Jorrie and I, well, when she moved on from me, Shepard lived here, and they started their relationship here. When they became mates, she moved in with him here."

Isabella nodded then, understanding blooming in her eyes. "So, my room, that's Shepard an' Jorrie's old space. An' it's painful for ye, knowing the woman ye love was with someone else in there."

He groaned, but firmly corrected, "Loved, not love."

"Liam, be honest with me," she studied him, "Ye still love her. It's not the same, but ye still care. Ye can lie to yourself, but don't lie to me." She stood, murmuring she was going to take a shower.

Liam's mind flashed a reminder of Jorrie doing the same thing, being upset with him, walking to the shower. He'd followed her and they'd made love. It had been their last time; she'd gone into Shepard's arms in that very room that same night. The cup he was holding shattered in his grasp. "Don't!" he growled.

Isabella stared at him in surprise.

"Please, don't," he begged as a tear rolled down his cheek.

She walked back, quietly reassuring him, "Liam, I was just going to take a shower."

He shook his head, his breathing getting faster, "Please don't," he repeated, an edge of desperation in his voice.

Isabella squatted next to him. "Liam, come with me while I get dressed an' then we can go to your place, okay? I can take a shower there." Her voice was calm, soothing, reasonable.

His eyes locked onto hers, her soft hazel gaze understanding and caring. He relaxed and blew out pent-up breath. "I'm sorry," he told her, hanging his head in shame now. "I don't know what came over me, I'm an idiot. I can't tell you why I do this, why I get like this."

She laughed, "Nope, we made a deal, we don't have to apologize to each other for this."

He stared at her in surprise, then shook his head. "Well, still an idiot. Go ahead and take your shower. But then, get dressed, and we're leaving this place. I'll clean this up."

She smiled before kissing him gently. She stood and pulled him to his feet, then wrapped her arms around him. "It's going to be okay, Liam."

He hugged her back, relieved to find he believed her. She left the kitchen, smiling over her shoulder, making his heart thunder in his chest. He heard the water running and took a deep, shuddering breath. He was *not* going in there.

Chapter 27

AFTER CLEANING UP THE broken cup, Liam was tidying the rest of the room when Rena wandered in. She was rubbing her eyes, stumbling a bit, seeming half asleep still. Smirking at her tousled appearance, Liam chuckled. "Hey, squirt!" he called.

"Liam!" she squealed, eyes brightening as she ran over and hugged him. "Did you stay the night?"

He nodded, "Yeah, Isabella was feeling a little overwhelmed and didn't want to be alone. It was a big shock for her; she'd had a long day. So, I stayed to keep her company."

Rena smiled softly at him. "I'm surprised," she murmured.

He turned his head to her questioningly.

"Well, you don't like being here because Jorrie and Shepard lived here, so that was nice of you to stay. You must really like my sister," she replied matter-of-factly.

Liam stared at Rena, his mouth slightly open.

She stared back at him, a small knowing curve to her lips.

"You're pretty perceptive. When did you get so grown up?" he asked softly.

She smirked, "While you were all busy treating me like a child."

He studied her closely, a stunned expression on his face that soon turned apologetic.

"I'm not mad," she reassured him. "I know when I first came here, I was basically a child, and everyone was tiptoeing around me. But it's been years, and I've come a long way since then. I'm a grown woman now. I'd like people to treat me that way."

Liam sat heavily. "Okay, wow. Serena, I apologize for my part in it. I'm happy to change that and make sure others do as well. Since you are indeed an adult now, how about we take your sister out tonight and show her the town? We can hit up a nightclub or something. We'll go dancing and I'll buy you a drink."

Rena's face was now wreathed in an enormous smile, as she jumped up and down, "I'd love that!"

He smiled then, fully comfortable for the first time since he walked in the door. "It would be a delight to take two beautiful women out on the town."

"Can we make it three? Will you ask Risa? I guess Killian would want to come too, then, but that's okay. I want to thank him for his offer to move in with them, but he treats me like a kid, too. Not in a bad way, but I want to live on my own for a while. Try being a grown-up."

Pulling out his phone, he nodded, "Tell you what, I'll come back and get you around seven, we'll go to dinner and then hit the town. Sound good?"

"Yes!" she cheered and leaned forward, kissing him on the cheek. "I can't wait! I need to figure out what to wear. Oh my gosh, this is going to be so much fun. Liam, you are the absolute best, and I'm so happy you're dating my sister!" She spun around in a circle and hugged him, squealing, before she planted another soft kiss on him.

He flushed a little; that was a grown woman kissing him. Not the scared, cold, filthy, little girl who had once wrapped her tiny thin arms around his neck and clung to him, shivering in the dark in a foreign country. She wasn't the young girl who had a huge crush on him while learning how to be a normal teenager. He studied her in this new light and saw she was indeed a beautiful grown woman. This was going to take some getting used to.

She ran off then, singing, her long silvery hair swaying behind her.

"Tonight's the night." The cruel smile accompanying her words sent shivers down his back. The brown-haired man stared at the woman in front of him with unease and fear.

She threaded her fingers through her long, silvery locks and absently brushed them out. "They'll be together an' only that dumb, green buffoon will be with them. I'll take care of him while ye stun the others. Then we'll have all of them." She grinned, envisioning her future triumph. She turned to him, "I cannot wait to see their faces when they realize the extent of this betrayal. It will be so delicious."

"Are you sure it's just them? We just need the three. What if others show up? Do you have a backup plan?" he grunted, tired of the delays, just wanting this to be over.

"It doesn't matter; we have to move tonight. *She* called us back to the headquarters; we have to move now. I'm not going back empty-handed. You've seen what happens to those who displease her," she snapped before standing. "I must go, I'm needing to be seen a few more times. I'll let ye know once the location has been decided. Be ready. I don't need to remind ye what happens if ye aren't." The threat hung heavy in the air over him.

Nodding, he murmured, "I'll be ready."

Izzy wandered around Liam's house, amazed at the space. *This is all his, and he barely lives here?* She remembered him saying he traveled a lot, doing different jobs for Vaughn. He was on the phone with Killian, discussing some plans for the evening, so she continued her exploration of his kitchen. After he hung up, he found her there and grabbed a soda from his fridge. She was shocked at how well stocked this room was. For a single man who wasn't home much, this space was a dream.

He noticed her trying to be subtle in checking out his kitchen, but she wasn't doing too well. He smiled, "Go ahead and ask, I know you're dying to."

She laughed, "That obvious? Alright, what is the story with this kitchen? I mean, it's a gourmet dream!"

He shrugged and leaned against the counter, sipping his soda.

"What is that? That shrug," she grinned.

He glanced over, a smirk twisting his full lips into an irresistible smile, "I'm sure you'll see it soon, I always get roped into it, but I like to cook. I'm usually the one doing all the cooking when we go on missions, or have meetings, or get-togethers. I don't mind; I really enjoy it. I even went to culinary school."

She slowly moved over to him. "Ye went to culinary school?"

He nodded and saluted her with the can. "Classically trained chef here."

"Ooh, Mr. Chef, what other hidden talents do ye have?" she smirked.

He took another sip, "I'm a good mechanic and I own a few classic cars."
She nodded.

"I do all of my own maintenance around here."

She grinned and waved to keep it coming.

"I'm well paid. I'm extremely good with the stock market and have an impressive, diversified portfolio, so I'm pretty well off, financially."

She blinked and held up a finger. "Did not see that one coming."

He laughed then and straightened from the counter, finishing off his soda before tossing the can into the recycle bin across the room. "I'm pretty good at basketball."

She took the last step towards him, then reached for his belt and pulled him up against her, "I believe it, you're pretty good with your hands." She grinned, "Hey Liam, I must have missed it, where's your bedroom?"

Killian hung up the phone, tapping it absently against his chin. He stared at nothing for a while before Risa came up behind him, brushing her hair.

"Who was that?"

He glanced over his shoulder, smiling. "Liam," he answered slowly, the surprise in his voice coming through clearly.

"Liam?" she asked incredulously, "What did he want?"

Killian chuckled; his reaction was much the same. "He talked with Rena this morning."

"Oh, stayed the night, did he?" She raised her eyebrows suggestively.

Killian was quietly thoughtful for a moment before shaking his head, "Not willingly, he hates that place."

Risa gazed at him questioningly.

"Ye know about Jorrie, Shepard, an' Liam, right? The love triangle thing?"

She nodded her understanding.

"Shepard used to live in the condo, remember?"

Suddenly, it clicked, and her mouth made an O shape as she realized the ramifications. She shook her head, clearly wondering what would have motivated him to stay if he felt that strongly against the place.

He understood where her mind was going, so he explained, "Izzy was overwhelmed an' asked him to stay. I'm sure she didn't know either, or she wouldn't have asked. Anyway, Rena talked to Liam this morning an' apparently, she feels that everyone still treats her like a child. She wants to be treated like an adult. So, he offered to take her an' Izzy out to dinner, followed by dancing an' drinks. We're invited."

Risa stared at him. Her mouth twisting, nose scrunching as she digested the news.

He stared at her before tilting his head the way he did when he was waiting for an answer. Finally, he smirked, "Ye know, I'm usually the quiet one."

"Oh, yeah, sorry," she chuckled. "I'd love to go. Are you able to come, too?"

He nodded, "Vaughn gave us the week off."

She smiled, relief clear in her eyes and the set of her shoulders. He knew she was fretting over moving in, and starting a new job, all while reuniting with her sister.

"Rena confirmed she doesn't want to live with us," he added with his characteristic bluntness.

She jerked her head back in surprise. "Why not?" she demanded.

"Adult?" he reminded her softly.

She smirked, "Oh, my lovely man of few words, why don't you come over here and do something else with that mouth?"

He grinned and grabbed her waist, pulling her roughly against him. He lowered his mouth to hers, kissing her in a way he was sure would make the devil blush. He pulled back slightly, and she nibbled on the little silver ring on his lip, playing with it. He shivered and moaned as the gesture made him instantly harden against her. She smiled, and he knew she'd done it just for that reason. "*Maith coleen*," he whispered.

Chapter 28

LIAM GAZED AT THE beautiful woman above him before he groaned and fell back on his elbows. She was in his lap, using her sinful hips to drive him crazy when she suddenly unfurled her wings, using them to rock even harder. It was so intense he was barely able to sit up. When she cried out his name, he arched up to her again, and she wrapped those wings of velvet around them both like a cocoon. With a final thrust as he emptied into her, he fell back, pulling her down with him this time. His breath gusted like a heavy wind, blowing her hair off her shoulders.

He couldn't think of a time when he'd ever released as hard as he just did and suspected he wouldn't be able to move for a week. "Woman, you killed me," he finally informed Isabella, panting and shaking.

She was panting too, collapsed over his chest. Her wings lightly fanning them both, trying to cool them. "Well, ye said it would happen." She laughed as she tried to sit up a bit, but collapsed as her arms trembled, then gave out.

He picked up her arm, let it go and smirked as it dropped down like a lead weight. It hit his chest with a loud smack. "You okay?" he chuckled.

"Nope, dead."

He felt her lips curve into a smile against his skin and laughed again. "Are you sure? Because if you were, you wouldn't feel this." He stroked his hands over both of her wings and brought one to his mouth, kissing and licking along the delicate frame.

She cried out and jolted upright, her walls squeezing him tight as she went over the edge again. She stared at him in shock.

"So, not dead then?" he inquired innocently.

"Holy fuck!" Isabella whispered, still trembling.

He roared in laughter. "Ma'am, watch your language," he said in a prim mimic of her voice. She slapped his chest, and he pulled her down against him. "So violent," he whispered, trembling in mock fear as he traced her spine gently with his fingers.

"Well, ye seem to have that effect on me," she retorted playfully as she rolled over next to him.

Liam chuckled, and Izzy felt his breathing slow. *He's tired, I should let him take a nap if he's taking us out tonight,* she thought. She glanced through the patio doors, noticing something for the first time. "Ye have a pool?" she squealed in excitement.

He nodded sleepily, a murmured agreement from his throat.

She sighed wistfully, disappointment lacing her words, "I wish I'd brought a suit. I love to swim."

"Izz'okay," he mumbled, eyes still closed, a hint of a smirk over his lips, "Neighbors can't see, wards, green dragon," he pointed at himself.

She realized he must have warded his yard so he could swim nude without anyone seeing him. Glancing down, she discovered he'd drifted off. She smiled tenderly as she studied his face. Even relaxed in sleep, there were a few deep lines that spoke of demanding times. She hated that for him.

He was young in dragon years, although he was older than her. He was so beautiful, her breath caught in her throat. She gently pulled the sheet up over him, so he didn't get cold in the breeze from the overhead fan.

Opening the curtain in front of the French doors, she stared out at the sparkling blue water. The pool was enormous. She was absolutely going to take advantage of that. She went to the restroom, then put her hair up before stepping outside and diving in. The water was perfect to combat the heat. It was currently one hundred degrees Fahrenheit outside, and the air was dry. Liam had told her earlier that it was the average temperature for summertime in Texas. She understood why he'd have his own swimming pool in this situation. It had a deep area for diving, a beautiful rock waterfall over a grotto, and a shallow area with a large ledge if one just wanted to lie in the sun.

She swam and dove, spent time cooling off in the grotto, before relaxing on the ledge. She lost track of how long she was out there, but she suddenly noticed a shadow over her. She shaded her eyes and glanced up to see Liam standing there.

He was grinning and seemed much more alert. "Have you been out here the whole time?" he asked her incredulously.

"I guess so?" she shrugged.

He chuckled, shaking his head, "Apparently, I needed that nap, because I was out for about three hours."

"Ye look better," she told him, sincerity in her tone. He truly did look refreshed.

He stretched then, his arms over his head, and she took a moment to admire the slide of muscles as they moved under his tan skin. He was nude like her, and completely unselfconscious about it.

"I feel better," he admitted, rubbing a hand over his abdomen. He noticed she was taking in the view of him. His eyes narrowed and took on a mischievous gleam while his lips curled in a lascivious grin. "Finding something interesting over here?" he added a low purr to his voice that set the herd of butterflies in her stomach into a raging stampede.

She smiled brightly, waggling her hand as she scrunched her nose. "Eh, not really."

He gasped in mock offense and grabbed her from her chair, then threw her over his shoulder.

She screamed and smacked his back but stopped to admire his perfectly sculpted behind. "Hey, I like this view," she admitted.

He chuckled deeply before he launched her into the deep end of the pool.

She came up spluttering as he dove in after her. She spun around then felt him tug on her ankle. She squealed and kicked away.

He swam up behind her and tapped her on the shoulder.

She took a moment to admire the way his hair looked. Slicked back and wet, it was the color of the last rays of the setting sun, a magnificent molten gold that gleamed. She stopped thinking when he crushed his mouth to hers and kissed her fiercely. She kissed him back just as hard. When they surfaced for air, he stared at her intensely. She was trying to decipher the look when he shook it off and started swimming laps.

Confused by his response, she stared after him, her mind tingling. She sensed waves of frustration coming from him and wasn't sure how she knew. He didn't say a word, didn't make a sound, but she knew he was trying to work off some thought or feeling. *But what?* She decided to let him figure it out. Suddenly, she was exhausted.

Earlier, while he was asleep, she called her dragon mentor, Evie. She bluntly asked the older woman why she'd warned her away from dragon males. The woman, who was like a mother to her, apologized profusely, telling her it was for her own protection. She revealed to Izzy that a red dragon was responsible for her being an orphan. Male dragons, especially, couldn't be trusted; they were devious, the woman insisted. She warned Izzy that wielders who weren't silver also couldn't be trusted. They would lead her astray because they were the ones who usually became dark wielders. It was safer to stay in her own color spectrum.

Izzy pondered it for a long while after they hung up. She wasn't sure what to believe. While it was true her parents were killed because of a red dragon, that didn't mean the rest was necessarily true. She hadn't seen any of the other issues she'd been warned about. In fact, it was the opposite. She thought of Siobhan and Marco, a green wielder and a red dragon. From Siobhan's stories, Izzy knew Marco was fierce, a warrior dragon, but he was so kind and easygoing. And Vaughn, a black dragon, was gracious and welcoming. She thought of the shenanigans the blue dragon twins got up to at the welcome party, playing jokes on each other. Then she remembered the love and ease with Rena and Liam. Him, a green dragon, her, a silver wielder. It was obvious he treated her like a little sister and was fiercely protective of her. He rescued her at risk of his own life, knowing nothing other than she needed help. Izzy was beginning to think her mentor was more than a little biased, possibly with some ulterior motive. But that didn't solve the problem here and now with her and Liam.

They'd known each other for three days, and she'd already been through some major emotional drama with him. She wasn't sure if this was something she wanted long-term. Granted, the man had been through a lot, but so had she. She needed to work on her own family and unravel their past. He needed to get into a better headspace. She remembered Siobhan and Jorrie's pleas to be careful with him. Her stomach churned, she felt terrible about it, but they needed some distance between them. She wasn't sure how to go about it without hurting him further when he'd been so kind and helpful to her. She could feel the weight of his stare like a hand on her shoulder. She noticed he was watching her intensely, frowning, a wrinkle between his eyebrows.

He shook his head, rivulets of water streaming down his jaw. "No, don't do that. Please."

"Don't do what, Liam?" she asked lightly, trying to hide behind false bravado and hoping the tremor in her voice wasn't detectible.

He swam over and pulled himself up on the ledge next to her. "Don't pull back from me like that. I know I'm a mess, but I am working on it. It's easier with you. And I'm here for you, too. Please, don't shut me out and give up on me already," he breathed, "Isabella," longing in his tone, "Please."

She was stunned. *It's like he heard what I was thinking.*

"Because I did," he offered quietly, his voice low and husky.

Her face drained of all color as she felt blood rushing to her toes. "How?" she whispered, shock making the single word tremble violently.

He shook his head again, his eyes squeezed tightly shut as if he were in pain. "I don't know. When I kissed you, I could feel your lust for me, and it was overwhelming. I fought back the urge to take you right then and there. I don't want you to feel that's all this is. Just sex. There's more to you and me than just physical attraction. I wasn't having emotional drama by the way; I was trying to distract myself from a very painful erection." He smiled ruefully at her now, embarrassment coloring his cheeks, covering up the adorable smattering of freckles over his nose.

She couldn't help it; she laughed. "I'm sorry, Liam, I don't know what came over me. I've found that some things I was taught weren't true. I just... feel so overwhelmed with everything an' what I feel for ye is... intense. It's scary. I've known ye for three days an' I already feel —" She stopped short of saying she was falling for him. Hard. There was a stronger tingling sensation in her mind as a flood of emotion washed over her.

He took her hand gently in his own and lightly caressed the back of it with his thumb, the tingling increasing. "Isabella," he whispered. *I feel it, too.*

She gasped and tightened her grip on his fingers.

His eyes went wide. *Isabella?* he asked gently.

Solas, she replied shakily, giving her dragon's name.

Cu Faoilr, he offered.

She grinned. *Wait... American Liam of the Irish name. Your American dragon's name is Wolfhound?*

He rolled his eyes, *yeah, well, apparently, he was feeling his Celtic roots,* he grumbled in exasperation at his dragon.

Her smile slowly faded, *Wolfy, what's going on? How can we speak like this in human form?*

He snorted in disgust at the nickname. Then his eyes went wider, and his jaw tightened as he stared at her with something akin to panic on his face. *I — well — I think because... I mean, I'm not sure, but usually this happens between a dragon and their, um. Mate?* The last word was thought with a questioning inflection, his tone unsure and nervous.

Izzy stared at him, stunned. *Mates? After three days? That isn't possible, is it?* She thought back to the day they met. When their eyes locked, she thought the earth shifted. She remembered the tingle when they touched. *Could it be?* She gazed down at her hand in his and squeezed. He squeezed back. She smiled. He smiled back. He leaned in and gently kissed her. She kissed him back happily. Leaning back, she studied his face and could see he was wrestling with the idea as well. But like her, he didn't seem overly distressed by *who* it was so much as how *quick* it was. She could sense he was excited by the prospect of spending more time with her. *Liam, ye know, I don't know much about this, other than it does seem rather sudden. But when we met, I felt, well, I felt like the earth moved. I thought it was because ye knocked me down.*

He gazed unblinkingly into her eyes. *I felt it, too. I thought it was just the sight of a beautiful woman, but now I'm not so sure.* He kissed her hand. "I have an idea, come on."

Izzy stared out the window in awe at the sights around her. They were in a town called Frisco, where a professional sports team was headquartered. He explained they played football, but American football, not what they called soccer here. Blue and silver stars were everywhere she turned. He told her they took the sport very seriously here, and based on the prolific advertising, she believed him. He mumbled about taking her to a game in the fall since Vaughn had season tickets, but his attention was soon turned towards finding a parking spot in a large garage.

Liam was taking her to Siobhan and Marco's apartment, so his sister could give them some insight. He was driving one of his classic cars, a 1967 Corvette, he told her. The car was gorgeous, bright red and curvy. She loved it. The garage was connected to another structure that looked more like an office building than a home. They went up to the sixteenth floor, and Liam banged on one of the doors.

Marco opened it, took one look at Liam's face, and yelled for Siobhan. "*Hermano,*" he snorted, chuckling under his breath, "What did you do this time?"

Siobhan sauntered into the room and came to a halt when she saw her brother. She stared at him in surprise. "Liam?"

"Shi!" Liam ran to her, grabbing her shoulders. "Help me out, please. I need a favor."

She nodded slowly, "Of course. What's up?"

"Auras," he told her.

She scoffed, "Why on earth —"

"Just look!" he demanded.

She shrugged. "Liam, I read you both in Ireland when we met her. I don't think you're going to surprise me." Her eyes darted to Izzy and widened. She took a step back and focused on them together. "Holy shit balls," she whispered and dropped to the couch behind her.

Marco ran to her, gathering her in his arms. "Shi, what is it? What's wrong?"

Siobhan shook her head and laughed. "I'm fine, those two, on the other hand." Liam squinted at her as she smiled and stood. She walked to her brother and took his face in her hands, then kissed him on each cheek, whispering, "Finally."

"No, it's too soon, how could it be?" Liam shook his head frantically.

She laughed again, "Oh, Liam, you know the heart wants what it wants. Sometimes when you find the one, you just know. Because you're both dragons, it just happened sooner. They don't wait for human emotions to catch up."

Izzy waved her hand, "Hi, hello, not clear what's going on here. Fill me in?"

Siobhan grinned at the silver dragon. "Izzy, you little hooker, I told you to be nice to my brother. I didn't say go mate him that quick."

Izzy jolted backwards like she'd been slapped. It was one thing to wonder, another to have it confirmed. "Mate?" she repeated, hoping she'd heard wrong.

Siobhan nodded, "I can read auras, and tell lots of things about people that way. I can also see when two people are suited to be mates or are in the process of it, et cetera. I checked when you were passed out in Ciarra's office because Liam was acting so strangely. Well, stranger than usual. I saw you two were suited for each other and had the potential to be mates.

"But now... your auras are so intertwined it's one color. A really pretty silvery green. It's actually quite beautiful. I think you're fated soulmates." The prickly green wielder burst into tears. "Liam, you jerk, I love you so much!" She threw her arms around him. "I'm so happy for you! You finally found your true love! And of course, it's a dragon because who else would put up with your stupid ass? I love you, Izzy!" she wailed as she let go of Liam and threw herself at the startled silver dragon.

Izzy stared at her in alarm, not sure what to do with the weeping woman. A look Liam shared.

"Hormones," explained Marco as he pulled Siobhan off Izzy and into his own arms. "Hey, did I tell you? It's a boy!"

Liam shook off his stupor and grinned. "Congrats, man! Uh, listen, you have your hands full, and we need to talk, so we're going to head out. Thanks, and sorry for, um, all this," he smirked, waving at his sobbing sister.

Marco rolled his eyes and nodded; he was used to it by now. "By the way, welcome to the mated club. Now you can be as miserable as the rest of us!" He grinned and only flinched slightly when Siobhan punched him in the shoulder before crying that she loved him more than anything.

Outside in the hallway, Liam leaned against the wall, took a deep breath, and let it out slowly in a low whistle. Izzy mirrored his pose and rubbed her hands over her thighs. They glanced at each other and both burst into laughter.

"Hungry?" he asked casually.

"Starved," she replied with a grin.

Chapter 29

LIAM TOOK THEM TO his favorite place to eat. As they entered the restaurant, he smirked when her nostrils flared, picking up multiple delicious spices and scents. Several of the waiters greeted him by name. One came to their table and introduced himself as Jorge. Liam asked after his mother.

"Oh, Señor Liam, she will be pleased you ask. She is well, enjoying time with her stories," he winked, "But this lovely senorita, this vision of beauty, you have brought her here to run away with me, yes?" Jorge kissed the back of Isabella's hand, and she giggled.

"Hands off, Jorge, this one's mine," Liam laughingly told him, as he smiled at Isabella.

Jorge laughed and put a hand over his forehead dramatically, "But, Señor, this will break Mama's heart that you have given yourself to another."

Chuckling, Liam explained to Isabella that Jorge's mother, Carmen, owned the restaurant, and it was a running joke that Carmen was in love with Liam. Well, Liam treated it as a joke, though he had a suspicion she might be.

Jorge took their drink order and rushed off to get it. Isabella glanced around at the colorful decor, bobbing her head in time to the cheerful music. "What kind of place is this?"

He grinned, excited to share this with her. "Mexican, or more accurately, Tex-Mex. It's a blend of authentic Mexican with some Texan influence to appease the more American palate. You, my dear, are going to love it."

She narrowed her eyes and sniffed. "Is it spicy?" she asked excitedly.

He nodded enthusiastically, "And they'll make it spicier if you ask. They love watching us eating hot food without breaking a sweat. It's why I come here so much. The food is good, and they don't push back on adding extra heat for me."

Isabella was excited, explaining that she loved spicy foods, but didn't get much at home. When Jorge came back with their drinks, she enthusiastically ordered several items and asked for extra spice like Liam did.

Jorge raised an eyebrow, "Aha, Liam, I see why the lady has captured your heart!" He grinned and strode to the kitchen.

Liam gently clasped her hand, and lifted it, kissing her fingers. "That's not why," he whispered.

"Oh. So, we're talking about this now?" she stared at him in challenge. The car ride over was mostly silent.

He shrugged nonchalantly. "Isabella, my darling, I know this is kind of sudden."

She snorted, "Kind of?"

"Okay, very sudden," he grinned, "But look, it doesn't mean I'm going to mate mark you right here at the table.

She grimaced, "What if I wanted to mate mark ye instead? Why do ye get to do it?"

He stared at her and shifted in his chair as heat rushed straight to his groin, recalling the way she bit him the first night. "Okay, that was unexpectedly, um, well, you just unlocked a new fantasy for me. I wasn't aware I had a thing for biting. You're lucky we're in public. I'm glad we aren't leaving yet because I need to sit here a minute." He cleared his throat, shifting in his chair again and shaking his head.

She blinked as she realized what he meant. Her lips curled into a devilish grin as she leaned over the table towards him, "Oh, am I, Wolfy? Am I lucky? Ye like the idea of me biting your neck? Running my fangs over your throat? Sinking my teeth into your —" the last word was muffled as he grabbed her and kissed her furiously. The intensity of the kiss threatened to set the room on fire, and more than one group of customers cleared their throats at the display. When he let her go, her eyes were wide.

"Yeah," he drawled, smiling wickedly now, "I guess you could say I do. Anyway, what I meant was just because we are fated, doesn't mean we have to act on it right now. We can take it slow and get to know each other. Date for a while and see where it goes."

She tilted her head at him consideringly.

He could feel the direction of her thoughts, unsure if he should tell her she was projecting. He didn't want her to feel he was invading her privacy, but she was so unguarded in the moment. She thought his words were sensible and not at all what she expected. She was taught that male dragons were pushy and demanding. Her dragon mentor told her they took what they wanted and didn't have feelings. That dragon was so very wrong; she didn't know what to believe anymore, but she believed in Liam. His teeth gritted in anger at how horribly this mentor led his Isabella astray, warring with the relief flooding through him, knowing she trusted him.

"I wouldn't define what we're doing as slow," she finally admitted with a smirk.

He relaxed, smiling before taking her hand and kissing her palm. "No, we haven't gone slow, but we can slow it down if you like. I would like to continue seeing you. See where this goes."

She smiled softly at him. "Liam, I don't want to slow down. We're dragons, we're intense, primal by nature. I think we both know where this is going, ye feel it as much as I do. Don't ye?" Her lower lip quivered nervously, making him want to pull her into his lap and soothe her.

His own expression softened in response, and he nodded. "I do, and I'm looking forward to it. Isabella, for the first time in a long time, I'm excited about opening my heart again, because of you," he whispered, trying to convey to her what this meant to him. She knew the history of how his heart was broken before, yet somehow, she wasn't turned away by any of it.

"Then, I think we just keep getting to know each other and see what happens. If we decide to make it official, we mark each other, fair?"

He leaned over and gently brushed her lips over his. "Fair," he whispered against her lips, making her shiver. Jorge brought their food then and began setting up the plates.

Isabella's eyes widened at the variety of colors and dishes in front of them. It was enough food for a horse. Or a couple of hungry dragons. She grinned at Liam and grabbed a fork. After the first mouthful, she moaned in pleasure.

The sound sent heat shooting through him, and his eyes filled with flames. Liam wasn't sure he was going to make it through the meal. This woman was driving him crazy with need. He leaned back and watched her enjoy the food, pleased she liked it as much as he did. In the back of his mind, a niggling comparison to Jorrie tried to worm its way in, but he quickly shut it down; it wasn't fair to Isabella. She was her own woman and didn't deserve that. He watched as she picked up a taco and bit into it. Her eyes rolled back in pleasure, a deep moan escaping from her, accompanied by a low rumble. Oh yeah, she was a whole lot of woman.

"Liam, where has this been all of my life?" she gushed, adding some hot sauce to her plate.

He laughed, delighted in her joy. "Right here with me, sweet darlin'," he drawled.

She smirked at his tone and grabbed Jorge's hand when he came back. "Oh, my goodness, this is wonderful! We don't have this in Ireland," she told him.

Jorge's eyebrows almost touched his hairline. "You're extremely fast. I don't know how you got back to the table before me. I swear I left the bar first. Here's the margarita you ordered. But, Ireland, my goodness! You're a long way from home, senorita!" He patted her on the shoulder and wandered away.

She glanced at Liam in confusion as she hadn't left the table at all since arriving. He simply shrugged, he didn't know what Jorge meant either.

"I didn't order a margarita," she whispered, confused.

Liam shrugged, "Maybe he confused you with someone else. But you should drink it, they're good here!"

She hesitantly took a sip and grinned, "Aye, that is good."

Liam offered her a bite of his enchiladas, and she gladly accepted with a happy hum. He laughed, "He was right about one thing, you are a long way from home."

She smiled shyly at Liam and shook her head, "No, I think I've just arrived."

Killian leaned against the wall and stretched; he was wandering aimlessly around the house. He wasn't used to being at home during the weekday with nothing to do. Malachi was following him, chirping at him in irritation that he wouldn't be still. Risa was stretched out on the couch, reading a book. He silently padded over and flopped on her legs and stomach, his head resting just under her arms. He scooped his arms under her waist and held her tightly.

"Hey," she chuckled, "What gives?"

He stared up at her with a smirk.

"Aww. Bored my love?" she asked, brushing a strand of hair from his forehead.

He nodded, rubbing his nose gently over her ribs. Killian didn't get bored often; he always had something to do. There was one thing he especially enjoyed, but he hadn't shared it with anyone in decades. He studied her intently and knew it was time. She was his bonded partner, soon to be his wife. He trusted her. He grabbed her hand and pulled her off the couch. Tugging her outside in the backyard, he directed her towards another building behind his house.

He knew she'd seen it through the window, but thought it was an oversized tool shed or something. As he unlocked the door and pulled her into an air-conditioned studio, her jaw dropped. There was a large grand piano sitting at one end. The walls were covered in soundproofing materials and acoustic foams. A professional set-up of recording equipment occupied the other end.

Risa wandered around, running her fingers over the top of the magnificent instrument. She lightly tapped one key, and a beautiful liquid note rang out, perfectly in tune.

Killian stood nearby, watching her nervously, his fingers clenching and straightening at his sides. He'd never let anyone in here before. None of his friends knew this existed.

"Killian, what is this?" she asked, awe in her voice as she took in her surroundings.

He slowly moved to the piano and sat down. After stretching his fingers, he began playing softly.

He started with a classical piece, easily recognizable, and she listened quietly. When he finished, he started a new song, the melody haunting and chilling. He watched her shiver as she recognized it a moment before he started singing. He knew it was one of her favorite songs. Tears filled her eyes as he continued, his voice and the emotion he put into seeming to move her more than the original artist.

The final notes of the song fell on a silent room as he studied her. "This is where I come when things get too much, an' I need to play."

She placed a hand over her heart. "Thank you, it was beautiful," she whispered. "Killian, you never stopped making music, did you? You just stopped sharing it."

He smiled crookedly at her, then stared intensely at his hands, reeling at the enormity of what he'd just revealed. She had to know this was monumental to him as far as secrets went. It was the part of himself he guarded as closely as his heart, which he'd already given to her.

She kissed him gently, then touched her ring, filling them both with thankfulness for what he shared. "Killian," she choked out, her whisper thick with emotion.

He sucked in a sharp breath; she'd responded perfectly. He didn't believe it was possible, but he fell even more in love with her then. Silently, he pulled her down on the bench next to him. "Do ye play?" he asked lightly, to distract from the wave of emotion threatening to engulf them both.

Risa shrugged, "My adoptive parents put me in lessons, and I learned a little bit." She plucked out 'Mary Had a Little Lamb' and laughed, the sound self-deprecating as she shook her head. "That's about all I remember. My talents were more on the painting and drawing side."

He faced her, curious, "Do ye still paint? I've not seen ye do that."

She shook her head sadly. "No, my place in Miami didn't have room, and I was always so busy running the gallery. I do miss it."

He jumped up from the bench and grabbed her hand, pulling her with him.

"Killian," she snapped, her tone exasperated, "You know I would go places with you if you just asked. You don't have to drag me everywhere. Words! Use them!"

He stopped suddenly, and she ran into him with a grunt.

"Dammit," she grumped, "You're like a brick wall!"

He turned and grinned, not in the least apologetic. "It's sorry I am my heart; I'll work on that for ye. My dearest love, will ye please come with me into the house, there's something I'd like to show ye."

She laughed then, "Better." As he began to walk forward more sedately, he heard her mutter, "Freaking adorable."

"That I am," he smirked over his shoulder.

Inside, he took her to an empty room. He smiled at her as she wandered around. "Okay, I'll bite," she shrugged, turning to him with curiosity burning in her eyes.

"It's yours."

She shook her head, not understanding.

He laughed, "Risa, I don't use this room. I was going to let Rena set it up how she wanted, but she wants to stay at the condo an' be an adult, remember?"

She nodded slowly.

"So, it's yours. Set up a studio, make it... I don't know, a craft room, or painting place. Make it a library if ye want. But it's yours. I've my space; ye need your own. Make it whatever your heart desires." He stepped closer, brushing his hand over her cheek.

Her eyes welled with tears, and his own eyes widened in alarm. She waved him off, "Happy tears, happy tears. Killian, you're too good to me."

He considered her words but wanted to be sure. "So... ye, like it?" he asked her, uncertainty in his voice.

She filled the room with her laughter, the sound of light, tinkling bells. "I love it. Look at the light in here! It's perfect! And I can see into the backyard, so I'll be able to watch the birds. Oh, Killian, it's perfect, thank you!" She threw herself into his arms and kissed him.

A sigh of relief slipped from his lips; his worry about her reaction draining from his body. He wanted to do whatever he could to make her happy. He grabbed her hand and was about to pull her again when he stopped. Turning back to her, he cleared his throat. "My dearest love, an' key to mine only heart," he began.

She narrowed her eyes and pointed accusingly at him, "Okay, don't go too far in the other direction. I think I liked you better quiet."

He burst into laughter, grateful for her humor. "Then how about this," he cleared his throat, "Risa, we have some time before we go out to dinner, I'd like to take ye shopping for art supplies."

"Okay, that was much better. And it didn't hurt at all, did it?" she smirked.

He winced and held up his thumb and pointer finger about an inch apart. "It hurt a wee little bit."

"Oh, you poor baby, I'm so sorry." She kissed him gently. "Better now?"

He grinned, "Still hurts." His fingers moved closer together.

She smiled and pulled him down to her again, she kissed him harder than before, and as she pulled back, she licked his lip ring and whispered, "Still hurt?"

He nodded but moved his fingers even closer together, "Aye, it hurts, so bad, it aches," he whispered, his voice going thick with desire.

She slid her hand down the front of his pants, stroking the pulsing length of him. "How about now?"

Gasping, he shuddered before he nodded. "Just the tiniest little bit." His hand was shaking as it dropped.

She slowly unzipped his jeans and eased them down his hips. His eyes were silver, and he stared at her as if he were on fire. "Well, I think I know how to ease your pain," she whispered as she dropped to her knees in front of him. His eyes nearly rolled back as she wrapped her hand around him and gave a long, firm lick up the length of his cock.

"Good girl," he whispered, anchoring his fingers in her hair.

Chapter 30

RISA HAPPILY FILLED A cart with paints, brushes, canvases, and an easel, giddy at the thought of being able to paint again. She tapped a finger to her lips, studying the pencils, trying to decide what weight of lead she wanted, when Killian placed his hands on her hips.

He kissed her neck, whispering in her ear, "Those lips are sinful, I love how ye use them."

She flushed the length of her body, and her stomach quivered thinking of how creative he'd felt after she'd shown him her appreciation earlier. She was never going to look at that section of the floor the same. She turned to him. "Yours aren't so bad either," she whispered back.

He grinned, then smacked her on the butt.

"Hey!" she yelped, as an older couple walked by laughing at them.

The woman sighed and placed her hand on her husband's arm. "Young love, it's so cute," she smiled. He smacked her on the butt, and they both laughed.

Risa watched in awe.

Killian wrapped his arms around her from behind and nuzzled her neck. "That's going to be us someday," he whispered in her ear. "I mean, not for a very long time because ye know, magically slowed aging an' all." She laughed, and he kissed her temple. "I'm going to take this cart up, pay for it an' load it in the car. Ye just keep shopping. Whatever ye need."

She shook her head, "No, Killian, I'll pay for it, here," she dug in her purse for her debit card.

He put his hand on hers to stop her search. "Risa," he admonished softly. "I know ye can, but my dear, I can too. I've no one to spend money on besides the ungrateful cat who takes up half my bed. I've led a simple life an' I'm comfortable, so I would like to do this for ye. Because ye make me happy, an' this makes ye happy."

She smiled and shook her head, "No, *you* make me happy." She kissed him and he winked, striding away with the cart. She sent him a pulse of love and happiness through her ring, and he turned, placing his hand solemnly over his own heart, showing her he felt it. She bit her lip, thinking furiously. It wasn't fair that she could send it to him, but he couldn't do it back. She heard a tinkling laugh and glanced up, seeing a flash of silvery hair disappear around a corner. She frowned, hurrying to the end of the aisle, looking for the woman. It wouldn't be Risa or Izzy; they would've said hello. Eager to possibly meet another silver wielder, she spun and searched but couldn't find them. She slowly made her way back to her original spot and shrugged it off, finishing her shopping and heading to the front, where she met Killian coming back in. "I need a jewelry store," she announced, "I want to get a present for my sisters."

Once they had her supplies loaded, he drove her to a large free-standing store nearby.

He started to get out of the car with her, but she stopped him. "I won't be long; I want to do this on my own if you don't mind."

Killian tried to be patient as he waited. He'd gotten used to her being by his side constantly, but recognized she needed her own space as well. He leaned back and turned on the radio, listening to a local station while tapping along on the steering wheel. About twenty minutes later, he saw a flash of silvery-blonde hair and sat up, thinking it was Risa. He blinked, and the woman was gone. He frowned; *where did she go?* Getting out of the car, he cautiously searched the area. He was sure the woman was walking towards him, and that coloring was very distinctive. His heart began to race, and his gut clenched; what if someone took Risa?

He remembered seeing the phantom woman several times before, blowing it off as Circe or his imagination. Doubt crept in, overriding his excuses. He wondered if he was just going crazy. He started towards the store, anxious to find Risa, his chest tight, magic rising and snapping around him.

The sound of alarms and sirens rent the air as the front door of the store opened, and Risa hurried out along with other customers. Fear stamped on their faces as they escaped whatever catastrophe triggered the alarm inside the jeweler. He stopped, rubbing his chest, his panic subsiding, Risa appeared unharmed.

"I guess I got out of there just in time!" She smiled apologetically as she slowed to a halt and took in the tightness of his jaw while he fought to relax. "They had a fire in their storeroom. Maybe electrical. Sorry if it scared you."

He shook his head, "I just missed ye is all," he replied, kissing the top of her head. "But I'm glad you're okay." He shook his head in disbelief as smoke poured from the open front door and employees milled around the parking lot, wringing their hands. "Strange," he murmured.

She grinned at him. "Well, here I am, but let's go home before this turns into a mad house and we get stuck here."

As they made their way to the car, Killian swore he could smell a familiar perfume but couldn't place it. He scrunched his nose and frowned, thinking he must be having olfactory hallucinations as well as visual ones.

Once in the car, she pulled out a box that contained three identical silver necklaces, each with a trio of diamond hearts linked together for the pendant. One for each of her sisters.

"They're beautiful," he admitted, thinking how perfect it would look with their coloring.

"You think so? I want us to have them as a reminder that we will never forget each other again."

He smiled softly. "Marissa, what a wonderful idea. You're so thoughtful. One of the many, many reasons I love ye."

She smiled back, "Love you, too. Now, take me home and feed me."

He saluted, "Yes, ma'am!" After they carried everything inside and ate a quick lunch, he watched her happily arranging things. She puttered around, moving things this way and that. Checking lighting and making adjustments. Even as busy as she was, she still brought him so much peace. He never thought he'd have this in his life again. He paused, thinking about the word, *again*. He realized he didn't have it before, even when things were good with Kiera, he didn't have the inner peace he claimed now. Not the way Risa gave him. He blew out a ragged breath at the ignorance he once possessed, thinking his infatuation with his ex-wife was true love. He should thank her for treating him so badly, so he was ready to enjoy and appreciate the real thing when he found it. He hurried to his own office and sat down at his computer. With a smug smile, he got to work on a few things he wanted to do for Risa and their future together.

A few hours later, Risa was sitting by the window, sketching. She closed her eyes and smiled, recalling the way the sun glinted on Killian's eyes when they ran silver. They were gorgeous. She sighed, *he* was gorgeous, stunning really, and she still couldn't believe sometimes that he was hers. That he loved her.

"Ye need a big cushion there," his voice filled the room, as if summoned by her thoughts. The rich warmth in his tone sent chills over her body. She opened her eyes to find him leaning in the doorway, one arm propped overhead on the frame, his sleeve hugging his bicep. With the light behind him creating a halo effect, he resembled a sculpture of a god come to life.

She swallowed heavily and closed the notebook before nodding, "Yeah, I agree, I love these windows." She turned her face into the sun, trying to calm her mind and distract herself from drooling over him.

He cleared his throat, "Risa, there's someone here I want ye to meet."

"Like, now?" She stood and gazed at him curiously, waiting to see if he was going to pull her along.

He nodded and held out his hand with an eyebrow raised; a clear question for him.

She smirked and gave him her hand. He was trying. She followed him into the dining room and was surprised to find a kindly seeming older man sitting there with a large briefcase in front of him. He stood when she walked in and held out his hand.

"You must be Marissa," he spoke quietly, a pleased grin curving his lips, soft wrinkles around his eyes and mouth where years of smiling had taken their toll.

She dipped her chin and smiled back, liking him instantly. "Pleased to meet you. I'm Marissa, but feel free to call me Risa."

The man's smile brightened, "A lovely name for an even lovelier woman. I'm Jacob Fitzhugh, but you can call me Jake." She took the seat he offered, and Killian helped her scoot the chair in. Jake took a seat across the table as Killian sat next to her.

"Risa dear, Jake here is the crusty old lawyer who's been looking after my legal affairs for years," Killian explained.

She glanced warily at Killian; did he mean Jake knew about their nature?

Killian winked, "Jake an' I went to college together back in the late seventies."

Jake laughed heartily, "And this impertinent miscreant had the audacity to stop aging while I turned into this."

"Old friend, I wish I could make that different for ye," Killian murmured.

"I know, Killian," Jake nodded, "But I enjoy living vicariously through you. I must say I was surprised when I got the call. I didn't think you'd ever settle down, so intent were you on being a loner."

Killian glanced at Risa and raised her hand to his lips, where he brushed a tender kiss across her knuckles. "Jake, I went to Florida to find a dragon an' came home with a treasure beyond compare."

She absolutely melted when he said things like that. She was still confused, though, about why Jake was here. The attorney must have read it in her expression because he cleared his throat and straightened.

"Okay then, so on to business. Killian here tells me you two are getting married. Congratulations, my dear, he's definitely getting the better end of that deal," Jake told her.

She giggled, and Killian protested weakly, grumbling that Jake was right.

Jake continued, "He also tells me you've moved in here with him. Good. He needs someone besides that cat to keep him company. I swear that beast is plotting to overthrow the world. Damn thing's been eyeing me for nigh on thirty years, I tell you."

She glanced at Killian from the corner of her eye, and he mouthed 'later' to her.

Pulling out some documents, Jake explained to Killian, "I just need your signature here, Killian," he pointed to a couple of lines, marked with little flags. Risa watched him sign, still unsure what was going on. "Okay, little lady, now I just need yours here." He turned the papers and pointed to some different flags.

She crossed her arms, "Not that I suspect anything nefarious, but what exactly am I signing here?"

Jake chuckled heartily, "Classic Killian, closed mouth idiot. It's a wonder she agreed to marry you! Did you even ask, or did you just stick a ring on her finger and make puppy dog eyes at her?"

Killian rolled his eyes and crossed his arms. Jake pointed at him, turning to grin at Risa as if to say, 'See?'.

Risa laughed, the tinkling bell sound causing both men to sigh happily. "He actually did ask, but what he didn't do was explain why you're here and what I'm signing."

"Marissa, I'm sorry," Killian turned her towards him, "Ye know this is hard for me." Jake snorted, and Killian shot him a dirty look. "I love ye with all my heart, an' we are going to be together for a very long time. Ye said earlier ye wanted to pay for something, an' I shouldn't spend my money on ye. But Risa, what's mine is yours. I don't want something to be mine alone. So, I asked Jake here to add ye to the title on the house, the cars, an' my bank accounts. He's a slippery weasel. He can get it done so we don't have to spend hours driving to places an' showing IDs an' getting things notarized."

She held her breath. This was a huge gesture of trust. They weren't even married yet, and he was doing this for her? She glanced down at her ring, reflecting on what it symbolized: forever, with a magical bond to tie it all together.

He watched her eyes fill with tears and was clearly worried he'd done wrong as his expression turned to abject panic.

She kissed him hard, and he kissed her back just as passionately.

Finally, Jake cleared his throat, "Still here, you two. I'd better get an invitation to the wedding after watching that!"

Killian threw his head back and laughed, holding Risa to him closely. "Sure an' ye better be there, old man!"

Risa nodded in agreement, not trusting her voice. She picked up the pen and began signing. "Jake," she inquired in a wavering voice. "I wonder if you could help me with something as well?"

He motioned for her to continue.

"I have a younger sister, and her life has been exceedingly difficult. She's recently become an adult and wants to be independent, but doesn't have any means of her own and unfortunately, due to circumstances, not many marketable skills. I'd like to set up a fund for her to use for her needs."

Jake smiled, "I'd be happy to do that for the young lady. Killian, you send me the information, and I'll draw up the paperwork and bring it back next week."

Killian nodded, murmuring how moved he was by her gesture, and he wanted to help, too. "Jake, once ye set it up, I'd like to transfer into it as well."

Risa protested, "Ki, you don't have to do that."

He smiled at her softly. "I know, but I love Rena, too, an' I want to do this for her."

She smiled back, so Jake chimed in, "Happy to do it. Did you have an amount in mind?"

Killian glanced up at the ceiling, then back at the attorney. "Aye, go ahead an' transfer a half into it. By the way, how's Gracie then?"

Jake's shoulders straightened, and his lips lifted with a bright grin. "She's wonderful! She loves that horse. Thank you again, it's really helped her a lot."

Killian's face softened at the news. Risa turned to Jake for clarity, knowing she was more likely to get her answers there, and he obliged.

"Gracie is my granddaughter. She was hurt in a car accident a few years back. Drunk driver hit my son's car. He's okay, but Gracie suffered a traumatic brain injury and has struggled to walk and speak normally since. She's suffered from depression as well. Killian here read about therapeutic riding and got her a horse and trainer. She's doing wonderfully! She has so much more confidence; barely a limp anymore. She lives for that horse." Tears were in Jake's eyes, and Risa felt her own growing hot and damp.

She gazed at Killian. He was a wonderful man. Something he said niggled in her mind. She turned back to Jake. "He mentioned 'a half', what does that mean?" she inquired.

Jake chuckled, "Half a million, of course."

Chapter 31

KILLIAN WAS BEHIND THE wheel, driving to meet the others for dinner. Risa sat silently in the passenger seat, having spoken no more than one or two words since Jake left. He glanced over and saw her mouth set in a grim line. She was pissed at him. "I'm sorry?" he offered, not really sure why he was apologizing, but it seemed like a good place to start.

She grumbled something that sounded suspiciously like, "Half million," in response.

He sighed harshly, irritation crawling over him until his skin was on fire. He whipped into the next lot, roughly putting the car in park. "Risa, explain to me, am I supposed to be apologizing for having money? Or is it for not telling ye how much I had? Perhaps I was supposed to be getting your blessing for spending money ye didn't even know about." His accent thickened as his anger grew.

She turned to face him, exasperation radiating from her. "You just casually dropped five hundred thousand dollars into an account for my sister and didn't even talk to me about it. That's what."

He glared at her. "Were ye this angry at Jorrie an' Shepard for giving her a place to live for these years? Should they have left her on her own then? Did ye refuse to speak to them for paying for the years of therapy? For feeding her, an' giving her clothes an' family? Are ye also mad at me for teaching her to wield? Oh, an' fine it is that ye can put whatever money ye like an' it's okay, but when I want to help it's not okay because I didn't ask ye first," he snapped, his magic began to crackle on his skin as his fury intensified even more.

"Yes! No!" she shouted, "She's *my* sister!"

He reeled back as if she slapped him, hurt plain on his features. The sparks of his magic sputtered and fell like fireflies dropping around him. His voice went low and flat. "So, it doesn't matter how much I love the lass. It doesn't matter what we mean to each other. Engaged. That I opened my heart an' home to ye. That she'll be my sister-in-law. It doesn't matter that I spent the last four years helping her recover. Teaching her how to wield. Letting the wee dear cry on my shoulder when she thought she was all alone in the world before we even knew ye existed. Letting her know she was loved when she wanted to give up on everything. All that matters is that ye share a mother an' father. It's now that I'm clear what I should be apologizing to ye for Marissa Thompson. Absolutely fucking nothing. I gave myself wholly, entirely, completely to ye an' bound myself for eternity. I didn't realize ye would put conditions on me for it. I'll not be apologizing for your damned pride. I learned that lesson too hard recently, an' I'll not go through it again. Never. Again."

He yanked the car in gear and sped towards the restaurant. He was driving a little too fast, but he didn't care. He flew into the parking lot and shoved the car into park again. His jaw clenched. Chest heaving. Anger once again palpable as he flung himself out of the vehicle, slamming the door without a glance at her.

Risa remained quietly in her seat, staring at her hands. Chagrined. Utterly defeated. All the fight drained from her, leaving her feeling wrung out and limp.

She was stupid, and she knew it.

He was pissed, with every right to be.

Killian wasn't trying to outdo her or flash his money. She knew he genuinely loved her sister and wanted to help. He told Risa earlier he never spent his money, and it meant a lot to him to do that for her. Then she turned around and threw it in his face. All the years he spent helping Rena get through her trauma, she'd acted like they were worthless. An image of Killian and his parents sitting on the grass, crying at their reunion, flashed through her head. She knew how much his pride had cost him at the expense of his family. She witnessed firsthand what it did to them. Now here she was, doing the same.

She noticed Killian standing outside of the car, leaning on the hood, arms crossed, and grinding his teeth. At least he was waiting for her. She slowly got out of the vehicle and made her way around to him. He locked the doors but stayed where he was, a sharp exhale through his lips. She reached up to put her hand on his cheek, but he jerked his head away from her touch. Her eyes went hot with bitter tears, and her teeth dug into her lip. She truly realized the magnitude of the injury she'd caused him then, and her soul nearly cracked in two. Not once had he ever turned away from her before. No matter how frustrated he was, he was always there for her. Until now.

"Go on inside with ye," he gritted through his teeth, "I'll be in shortly."

She opened her mouth to protest, then thought better of it. She nodded; he needed some time to cool down. "Killian... I was wrong and... I'm sorry." She turned and started towards the door. Her steps were halting and dragged along the concrete. *What have I done? He's never been so cold. What does this mean?*

Risa fought the urge to look back at him, knowing it wouldn't be welcome. She also didn't want to see the hard set of his jaw, the cold gleam in his eyes. She fought back the deep, gut-wrenching sob that wanted to rip from her throat. Without realizing it, she twisted the ring on her finger and prayed he still loved her. *What if he doesn't forgive me? I can't lose him.* She stumbled at the thought, her vision blurry from her unshed tears.

Halfway to the building, a hand on her shoulder spun her around, and she was crushed within his arms.

Killian held her against his chest, still breathing heavily and sighing. "*Is breá liom tú,*" he whispered, his voice thick but strained. "Of course I do."

She sobbed once, "I love you, too, Killian." She started to say more, but he hushed her.

"Just let me hold ye, *a ghra*," he murmured.

She stood there in his arms, silent as he held her, rubbing his cheek against her hair.

After a minute, he sighed, "Dammit, Risa, ye stubborn arsed woman. Are ye after challenging Molly an' Siobhan for being the most difficult *coleen* in my life?" There was a ghost of a smile in his voice.

She peeked up at him and whispered, "Not on purpose." She blew out a deep breath, "Thank you, Killian, I do appreciate your generosity for my sister. For all you've already done for her as well. I don't know why I make things more difficult than they have to be. I'm always in my own head too much. I guess I feel like I wasn't there for her, and I'm trying to make up for it. All the things I missed, maybe I'm overcompensating now. I... I shouldn't have taken it out on you."

He smiled softly, truly now. "Risa, ye both mean the world to me, an' I only want to help take care of ye. I'm sorry I got so angry. I apparently still have my own issues when it comes to feeling rejected. I'll try harder, too."

"I'm sorry, my love, I truly am," she sighed, wiping away the last tear. "I wasn't trying to downplay what you've already done or belittle your love for us. I guess I'm so used to taking care of myself, it's hard to accept someone else might want to do it for me."

He shook his head. "Not *for* ye, *with* ye."

She melted against him, kissing him softly.

He angled his head and took the kiss deeper. Finally, he leaned back and studied her closely, tucking a strand of hair behind her ear. "Are we okay now, my heart?"

She nodded gratefully, "Better than okay." Her smile faltered, "Killian, I don't know why I keep snapping to these judgments, I keep messing up with you. I'll work on it, I promise."

He stood and took her hand, giving her a gentle smile. "Risa, never worry, I'll stop loving ye, no matter how angry I may be, never that." At her smile, he nodded towards the restaurant. "Shall we?"

They were strolling hand in hand towards the door when Killian saw movement from the corner of his eye. He turned and noticed a woman staring at him from the other side of the lot. She looked like someone he knew, with the same long silvery-blonde hair as all silver wielders, but she was too tall to be Circe. Briefly, he wondered if it was Rena or Izzy as he noted Liam's car nearby. He blinked, and she disappeared. Frowning, he released Risa's hand and started towards the area.

"Killian?" Risa called, confused.

"Be right there," he replied over his shoulder. He hurried to where he last saw the woman and searched for her. He didn't see her anywhere, but he caught the faintest scent that raised the hair on the back of his neck. It was the same perfume he remembered from before, the one that haunted him even overseas. He frowned again. Something was off, and he felt like someone was watching him, but he couldn't see anyone. His justifications from earlier came back to mind, but he could no longer deny it. Now, he knew someone was taunting him, and it was time for it to end.

He turned back to Risa and found her staring at him from the sidewalk, concerned. He didn't want to alarm her, so he shrugged nonchalantly and started back. He would get Liam to help him search more. Just before he reached Risa, he heard his name and a feminine chuckle in the wind. He whirled, searching again, but no one was there. A cool hand brushed his cheek, making him jump, gazing wildly around. "Show yourself!" he shouted, his eyes flashing silver. He heard the woman laughing again, then like a flash, it was gone. He held up his hands, about to throw a wave of magic, when Risa snatched his arm.

"People," she hissed.

He stared at her, realizing she meant there were others in the lot, and he shouldn't do his magic in front of them. He nodded, then took her arm, quickly escorting her into the restaurant. He paused in the foyer to regroup and calm himself.

"What's going on?" she whispered, concern heavy in her tone.

He glanced around to make sure no one was listening, "Risa, I don't want you to think I'm crazy, but I thought someone was hiding out there, messing with me. I've been seeing this same woman everywhere. I thought it was Circe at first, but it's not."

"I didn't see anyone," she frowned, shaking her head.

He shook it off, "Maybe just my imagination, then. Come on, they're waiting." He pointed to Liam and the others, where they were already seated, waving at them.

"What took you guys so long?" Liam inquired with a cheeky grin and arched eyebrow.

Killian rolled his eyes as they sat. "Just enjoying the night air," he retorted. He greeted Izzy, then leaned back, gazing at Rena. She appeared grown up for the first time ever. Or maybe it was the first time he thought of her that way. He grinned, "Liam, I thought you were bringing Rena, who's this beautiful woman here?" Rena rolled her eyes, but he could see she appreciated the compliment.

Risa laughed, "Okay, Prince Charming, enough sweet talk." She handed each of her sisters a velvet box. "I wanted to give you both a little something to link us together. Showing my love for you and a symbol that we'll never forget each other again." She waited anxiously while they opened their gifts. Her sisters gasped in joy at the beautiful pendants.

Izzy's eyes filled with tears, and she reached across the table to take Risa and Rena's hands as they smiled at each other, a silent pact. Izzy turned to Liam, "Please, help me put it on?" He stood as she lifted her hair and fastened the pendant around her throat. Leaning down, he placed a tender kiss on her neck. Liam then helped Rena with hers as well, while Killian assisted Risa.

Liam sat again, exclaiming, "Well, now I can't tell you all apart!"

The three laughed together, a light tinkling sound like small bells. Many heads turned to stare at the trio of beautiful women accompanied by the two gorgeous men.

Izzy turned to Liam questioningly, "Rena was just telling me ye played a naughty prank on Killian. She wasn't sure he'd want to come out with ye."

Killian grinned, "Oh, please, Liam, do explain to dear Izzy about the videos of me online. I liked 'Irish Heartthrob Spotted Again' the best. I do so love being objectified, ye fecking lizard."

"Come on, man, I thought you were over it," Liam groaned, covering his eyes with one hand.

Killian chuckled, "Aye, I am now, but I'm sure an' the dear lass would like to know how it came to be in the first place."

Liam grumbled under his breath, glaring at Killian, but grudgingly told the story of how he set Killian up to sing at Jack and Davis' wedding. He explained because it was with Jorrie, the videos people uploaded went viral. Then it happened again when he was singing in Ireland. "Which I had nothing to do with!" Liam clarified, pointing a finger at Killian.

Risa shot Liam a dirty look, "Which wouldn't have mattered if you didn't start it in the first place! Which is why I broke your nose!"

He held up his hands placatingly as Izzy burst out laughing.

Killian kissed Risa's temple, "Down wee beastie!"

Izzy grinned at Liam thoughtfully, causing him to fidget in his chair.

Finally having mercy, Killian studied the sisters with a grin. "You're all so beautiful, let me get a picture of the three of ye." They quickly agreed, and he took a picture of them with their arms around each other, their smiles lighting up the room, and the lights twinkling off their hair. They were indeed an amazing sight all together. When he had what he wanted, he put his hand over his heart and sank into his chair. "Too... much... beauty," he gasped. They all giggled again, their musical laughter drawing stares once more.

Liam was staring at them in awe as well. They really were a force when together. He leaned over, asking Killian, "Hey, send me that?"

Killian sent the picture along with a question. *Gabe?* To which Liam quickly replied with a thumbs up. Grinning, Killian forwarded the picture to Gabe with the location of where they were going next.

Gabe's reply, *I am so there. Thanks,* came as quickly as if he were sitting in the room.

Killian nodded at Liam, and the dragon grinned. Their plan in place, they turned to their meals.

After a delicious meal, they stood to leave, and Killian turned towards the door. He saw the mystery woman again, winking before she disappeared, blinking out of sight. He blew out a sharp breath in frustration and groaned. *What the hell is going on? I wonder if Liam can —*

"Huh," muttered Liam, standing at Killian's shoulder, interrupting his thoughts.

Killian arched an eyebrow at him in question.

"I could have sworn I just saw a woman over there who looked a lot like our ladies."

Killian grabbed Liam and shook him lightly. "Ye saw her too?"

"Yeah," the dragon drawled slowly, clearly unsure why Killian was so wound up about it.

"Good," Killian blew out a sharp breath, relieved, "That's good. I saw her outside an' thought I was losing my mind. It feels like I've been seeing her everywhere."

Liam snorted, "I'm sorry to tell you this, my friend, but you're as disappointingly sane as the rest of us."

Killian smacked Liam on the back of the head, then hugged him. "Arsehole," he laughed.

"What is it about me that incites violence in everyone?" Liam grumbled, rubbing the back of his head. He narrowed his eyes at Killian as the wielder drew in a breath to answer, grinning when Liam growled in warning.

Chapter 32

THEY ARRIVED AT THE nightclub, and Risa smirked as Killian wrinkled his nose. The place was remarkably busy, and there were a lot of people inside. She laughed, "Come on, baby, you can do it."

"Only because I love ye," he sighed wearily.

Izzy glanced around, remarking how everywhere she looked, she was surrounded by men and women in boots, jeans, and a sea of cowboy hats. Liam explained it was a country and western dance hall.

Risa was also observing the crowd and admired the effect of the tight jeans on the men. She studied Killian's backside and murmured that his jeans looked just as good, if not better.

He rolled his eyes, shaking his head with a small, pleased smile.

"Ki," she grinned with mischief on her lips and a twinkle in her eyes, "Maybe we should get you a cowboy hat."

He made a rude noise with his lips. "I may like the music, an' I might know the dances, but you're not getting me in one of those."

She kept grinning at him, and his expression changed to one of unease, no longer certain he was correct.

Rena giggled, and they all joined in at his discomfort.

Izzy stared at Liam consideringly.

"I'm game," Liam declared, giving Killian a challenging grin.

Inside the enormous bar, the dance floor alone was larger than their homes. There was a giant bar in the middle of the oval-shaped floor, and smaller bars spread out around the sides. There was also a mechanical bull in one corner and a gift shop in another that happened to be selling cowboy hats.

Risa squealed and pulled Killian inside, despite him dragging his feet as if he were being led to his own execution. She convinced him the black hat was devastating on him.

Liam looked great in one, too, but he opted for a lighter color as Izzy fanned herself dramatically.

They took Rena over to the bar and bought her a drink, cheering as she took her first shot like a champ.

Killian kept checking his phone, then grinned suddenly. He sent a quick text message, then nudged Liam. "Let's head over to our table." He led them to an area where tables crowded alongside the dance floor, and they finally found the one Liam had reserved. Holding out a hand to Risa, Killian's lips curved into a self-satisfied smirk, "Fancy a dance, lass?"

She grinned and took his hand.

Liam held out his hand to Izzy, who started to grasp it, then frowned. "What about Rena?"

"I'd be honored to dance with the gorgeous lady, if she's willing," came a new, deep, masculine voice. They turned as one to see a handsome young cowboy grinning at them. He tipped the brim of his black hat and smiled shyly at Rena, "Ma'am." He held out his arm, which she took without a word and followed him to the dance floor.

Izzy glanced at the others, confused. "Who was that?"

The men laughed, sharing a fist bump, while Risa smiled softly. "That, dear sister, was Gabriel Drake, the young man our baby sister has a huge crush on." She turned back to the men. "You set that up, didn't you?" she pointed accusingly at them both.

Killian grinned, "Guilty! An' not sorry."

Chuckling, Liam turned to Izzy, "Gabe is Bridget's son from her first marriage. His father was killed by the Shadows when he was young. When she married Vaughn, he adopted Gabe as his own. He's a wonderful person, like a little brother to me. I can't think of anyone who would treat her better."

"Gabe hangs out with me when he's on breaks from school," Killian added, "He's in his last semester an' then he's coming to work for me full time. I'll back up what Liam said; he's an amazing young man. Good head on his shoulders, smart, determined, a gentleman. He's had hardships in his life. Losing his father so young, then he almost lost his mother. He was dating a pretty little dragon from Italy, but she ended up going back to her home country. Gabe decided to stay to help his mother after she an' Vaughn started having more children. It broke his heart, an' he's been moping. He's known Rena for years, but they didn't run in the same circles. I reintroduced him to her recently, an' the kid has been tripping over his feet to get her attention since. But she's shy, so I figured a little encouragement wouldn't hurt."

They all stared at him in surprise. Liam poked him in the shoulder, "Are you okay, man? That was a long speech. Do you need to sit down?"

Killian surprised them all further by simply laughing.

Izzy smiled softly. "She's obviously happy with him. Thanks, guys." She leaned over and kissed Liam on the cheek.

"Hey," protested Killian, "It was my idea!"

She laughed and kissed him, too.

Risa smacked him on the butt, "Let's dance, cowboy!" She grabbed Killian's hand and pulled him to the dance floor, where he pressed her body close to his and they spun around in a series of complicated steps.

Izzy's mouth dropped. "Oh, I didn't realize this type of dancing was so fast," she muttered softly, disappointment coloring her tone. Smiling, she watched Killian spin Risa away from his body before pulling her back. They whirled around the floor like they were floating. She sighed; it looked like fun. Gabe was dancing similarly with Rena, who was laughing at something he was telling her. She felt an arm go around her waist, and Liam whispered in her ear, "I'll teach you." She took a nervous step on the floor and let Liam position her hands as he pulled her body against his.

"Okay, the trick is you don't actually pick up your feet much. You mostly slide them. That's why there's sand on the floor," he instructed.

She glanced down, fascinated.

He went on to explain the mechanics of the style, then smiled, "Just follow my lead, you'll have it in no time."

Before she could protest, he was pulling her along. She tripped a few times, but finally, she found the rhythm and was soon having the time of her life. "Liam, I *love* this!" she shouted to him over the music, "Where did ye learn to dance like this?"

"Believe it or not, Shepard taught me at a bar in Australia."

Izzy leaned away, in complete shock, speechless for a moment. "You're right, that's pretty unbelievable." She threw her head back and laughed.

He smirked, "But one hundred percent true. We were looking for the Shadows but weren't making progress. We wanted to blow off some steam, and I found that bar, so we all went and had fun. Shepard taught me and our friend Lorenzo both. He's a good dancer." He grinned at her, then stumbled as he noticed her expression was no longer amused, but sad.

"That's when Jorrie was taken, and you found my sister." She shook her head. "Always comes back to Jorrie, doesn't it," she murmured, knowing he'd hear her.

A slow ballad floated through the speakers, the lights lowered, and he pulled her closer. "Isabella, I'm not going to lie and say it wasn't a big part of my life, because it was. I loved her, but I screwed up. I didn't love her enough, and it was a hard lesson. She's a good friend now, she and Shepard both. It hurt, yeah, but Isabella, it doesn't hurt anymore. *You* did that for me. *You* healed my broken heart, and now I'm ready for the next chapter of my life. A chapter I want to spend with you."

She stared wide-eyed at him. It wasn't fair for him to say such things to her when she was already falling in love with him. He opened the bond between them wider so she could sense what he was feeling. She reeled; he felt the same way? But that meant...

Yes, Isabella, it means I'm falling in love with you, too. And it scares the hell out of me to possibly have my heart broken again. What I feel for you, though, is stronger than anything I've ever felt, and I don't know what to do about it. But I'm willing to try if you are.

She gazed into his eyes as they flickered back and forth between blue and green. She noticed that once before and wondered about it. It seemed to happen when he was experiencing strong emotions. She realized he was waiting for an answer. She pushed her thoughts towards him, confirming she was willing as well.

He put his forehead to hers and shuddered, swamped by the relief that she felt the same. *I know it's fast, but I've heard it said so many times, and now I finally understand it. The heart wants what it wants. Isabella, my heart wants you. I used to wonder why I went through all of that before, if it wasn't meant to be, but now I understand. I had to grow the fuck up. It was so I would appreciate my soulmate for the true gift she was when I found her. Found you. I know I'm not good with words. I really suck at emotions. So, Isabella, I beg you, just be patient with me. Let me know if I'm being stupid, please? Sometimes I really can't tell. If I don't tell you enough that I love you, tell me. And for god's sake, if I try to run away, chase me, bite my tail again and call me an idiot. I love it when you chastise me in that schoolteacher's voice.*

Izzy's throat tightened, and she was grateful for their bond because she didn't trust her physical voice just then. *Liam, I will bite your tail so hard. I love you, too, you idiot.*

His eyes flew to hers, glowing bright blue, seeming lit from within.

She gasped as they swirled like the raging ocean, completely mesmerizing.

Lips trembling, Liam drew in a ragged breath. "Isabella," he whispered before gently placing his lips to her. They kissed tenderly before they realized they had a small audience cheering for them. He grinned against her mouth, and she laughed. "Let's dance, my love." He whirled her around the floor while she squealed in delight.

Killian watched the interaction and smiled softly, happy for the two dragons. They needed each other. He leaned forward to Risa, "I've a feeling Liam an' Izzy just professed their love for one another."

She gasped and spun around to look. She saw them kissing with a crowd cheering them on. She cheered, too. "I guess you and Liam will eventually be brothers." She turned back and caught the rather disturbed expression on his face, causing another bubble of laughter to escape from her lips. The sound filled him with warmth.

He pushed his hat high on his forehead and laughed with her. "Unforeseen consequences. I guess, as overgrown lizards go, he's not a bad sort. Really, Liam is a great guy. He's a wee bit of a langer sometimes, but I've a feeling Izzy can keep him in line."

Risa nodded with a knowing grin, "She bit his tail when she got mad at him once."

He snorted, "I would've liked to have seen that. In fact, I owe the lass a drink!"

She tugged the hat down hard over his face, and he chuckled.

He pulled it back in place, then froze. The blonde woman was staring at him from only a few feet away. This time, despite the long hair, he recognized her. His vision narrowed on her face, and the room turned ice cold, despite the press of sweating bodies around them. His fingertips went numb, and acid rose in the back of his throat.

"Killian?" Risa asked, her voice full of worry.

He glanced down at Risa, then back up, but the woman was gone. "Fuck," he whispered, his voice strangled.

"Killian, what's going on with you? You keep acting like you're seeing a ghost," Risa pleaded.

He nodded slowly and stared at her, his eyes burning. "I think I am. We need to find the others, now. Come on." He grabbed her hand, and she didn't protest this time as he dragged her off the floor.

Liam was sitting at the table with Izzy, teaching her how to shoot tequila, when Risa and Killian reached them. "Oh, that's awful," Izzy groaned, "Give me a good whiskey any day!"

"We can switch to that if you want," Liam chuckled.

As Killian rushed over, breathing hard, Liam leapt to his feet. He took in Killian's panicked expression and surveyed the room, searching for the threat, immediately taking a defensive stance.

"Where's Rena?" Killian demanded. He relaxed only slightly when they saw her at the bar with Gabe.

Suddenly, Liam stiffened, "Ki, isn't that the woman from the restaurant?"

Killian whirled and stared in the direction Liam was pointing. He gripped the dragon's shoulder. His knees trembled weakly, and all the blood drained from his face, leaving him pale and cold. His stomach clenched as he shuddered. "It can't be..." he gasped.

The silvery-haired woman grinned at him, giving a tiny wave of her fingers, then disappeared.

He sat, hard, collapsing into the nearest chair.

"Killian? What's wrong?" Liam squatted next to him. "Killian?" he snapped sharply when the wielder didn't respond, "Do you know that woman? The one with the blonde hair?"

Killian just stared at him. He wasn't sure what he saw anymore. It didn't make sense; nothing made sense.

Liam glanced at Risa, "What's going on? Why is he panicked like this?"

Risa watched Killian, concern etching a furrow between her eyebrows as she shook her head. "I don't know. He's been acting weird since earlier this afternoon. He keeps jumping like he's seeing ghosts, but I haven't seen anyone. Did you?"

Liam nodded thoughtfully, "I saw a blonde woman watching us at the restaurant, then I saw her again just now. I don't recognize her, though. She has similar hair to you three. Are you sure you don't have another sister you forgot about?"

Izzy and Risa stared at each other and shook their heads. Risa waved Rena and Gabe over.

Gabe studied Killian in concern. "Hey, Ki man, you okay?"

Killian shook his head no; he most certainly was not.

Rena confirmed that she wasn't aware of another sibling either. Unless there was a younger one they didn't know about.

Liam shook his head. "No, she was older, she couldn't have been a younger sibling. And she wouldn't be the oldest because Isabella is the dragon." They all murmured their agreement.

Risa's brow furrowed, "Describe her."

Liam started telling her about the woman, and Risa gasped, "Wait, I think I saw her too! At the wedding, and in Ireland. But it couldn't be the same woman, could it? Is she following us?" She turned to Killian, who was staring blankly at the floor. He said nothing, but a single tear rolled down his cheek.

Risa squatted beside him; one hand over her stomach like it was also twisted in knots. "My love," she said softly, "Talk to me. Who was that?"

He lifted his gaze then, blinking as if seeing her for the first time. His expression was full of misery and dejection; he shook his head. "It can't be, why now?" he groaned.

Risa frowned, "Killian, who is she? Now!" Her forceful tone snapped his head back, and he stared into her eyes.

His face closed down again, expression blank, before he mumbled flatly, "It's Kiera."

"I've got him. They'll be coming out soon. When they do, be ready. Stun Killian first; he's the most dangerous. He's wearing a black hat, an' has a blue shirt on. He'll be alone with his little silver wench," Kiera hissed, "I'll handle that green pup, Izzy will be too stunned to lift a claw."

A heavy sigh, "Are you sure this time?" the brown-haired man asked, "Kiera, you know our orders are only to get the three women."

She growled at him and flashed her fangs, "Oh, I'm sure. They don't know just how powerful he is. He's also Vaughn's best friend. That bastard always hated me. Once they're finished with the women, I'll have my reward, too. And Killian will be mine again." She grinned, a truly malicious smile that had her companion shuddering in fear.

Chapter 33

"WHO'S KIERA?" demanded Liam.

Risa waited for Killian to answer, but he didn't respond. She huffed out a worried breath. He might get mad at her, but if this woman was a threat of some kind, they needed to know. She stood; her decision made. "Kiera is Killian's ex-wife."

The others gasped. None of them had known he was married before because he was always so private.

"When was that?" Liam blurted incredulously.

She glanced at Killian, but he was still sitting in stoic silence. "Before he came to the U.S. When he was very young. He said it was an arranged marriage. She was horrible to him. Broke his heart. She's the reason he's so quiet and private about everything. That bitch did a number on him. He's finally been able to move on and be happy, then she has the nerve to show up here playing some sort of mind games with him." She blew out a sharp breath. "I remember he said she's a silver dragon, from a town near his in Ireland. So, she would look like us to an extent, I guess, except with short, curly hair?"

Liam shook his head, "No, this woman had long straight hair, like you all. I noticed she had a dimple on the right side." He pointed next to his mouth.

Izzy made a small noise of discomfort before she pulled out her phone. She scrolled through it a moment before she showed them a picture of her smiling with another woman. One with silvery-blonde hair and a dimple on the right side. "Um, please tell me this isn't who you're seeing?"

Liam studied it and nodded, "Yeah, that's her. Wait, you know Kiera?"

"No. I don't know a Kiera. Are ye sure? This is Killian's ex-wife? An' her name is Kiera?" Izzy leaned back, her eyes wide, her lips thinned, bloodless. Risa was staring at her, confused. "Why would she be here?" Izzy demanded of them all. No one answered. "But are ye sure that's her? Her name is Kiera?" she repeated. When she still received no answer, she shoved the picture in Killian's face.

He blinked at it before he finally nodded slowly, his expression pained and bewildered. "That's Kiera. Her hair's longer. But that's her."

Shaking her head frantically, Izzy blanched, taking a step back. "But... no. That can't be. This is Evie. My mentor. She taught me about being a dragon. An' about other dragons. She's the one who..." she trailed off. "She lied to me," Izzy cried softly, her voice shaking.

The others stared at her in shock. Risa gently took her sister's hand. "There's no way she could have known you would end up around Killian. It has to be a horrible coincidence. Izzy, don't worry about it for now. We should go; we can talk about it somewhere more private." She hugged her sister to reassure her before turning to her fiancé. "Killian, are you okay?"

Killian continued to stare at the floor as if he hadn't heard her.

Rena dropped in front of him. "Killian!" she shouted.

He jumped and focused on her.

"Stop it! Stop it right now! She's your past and not worth it. You can't live in the past! You wouldn't let me drown in my own misery and memories, and I won't let you. Every time I tried to break, you helped me build back stronger. When I had nightmares, you listened and helped me through them. Look at my sister! She loves you and is going to marry you. Look at what you have. Don't let that bitch ruin the best thing that's ever happened to you!" She was almost yelling at him; her plea was so passionate.

Everyone stared at Rena in shock. She only stared at him, with her chest heaving, her eyes flashing silver, and her cheeks flushed in anger.

Killian smiled at her softly. "Rena Doll, you're absolutely right. Thank ye." He stood and pulled Risa towards him slowly. "Risa, I'm sorry. I'm a fecking idiot. Of course, I shouldn't let her bother me. Because I have your love an' nothing could compare to that. It caught me off guard, but it shouldn't matter. Rena is right, you're the best thing that's ever happened to me. Please, forgive me?" He leaned down and kissed her tenderly.

Risa smiled and cupped his face. "Killian, there's nothing to forgive. She's messing with you, and that would tear anyone up. I'm glad you're back with us, though. Now let's figure out what that skank wants and kick her ass back to whatever pit she crawled out of."

He laughed hard and kissed her again. Rena clapped until Killian whirled on her. "Rena!" he barked.

Rena gasped, taking a step back while her hands fluttered at her throat.

Killian pulled Rena to him and lifted her right off her feet, kissing her lightly on the surprised O of her lips. "Ye darling woman. So smart. Thank ye for yelling at me an' knocking some sense into me." He gave her a devastating smile as he set her back down, and she giggled with a dreamy smile of her own.

"You're welcome, Ki. You didn't give up on me, I'm not giving up on you," she replied firmly.

Gabe laughed, "Wow, is that all it takes to get a kiss? You just have to let her yell at you?" He gave her a soft smile, "Will you yell at me, Rena?"

The others laughed quietly as Rena turned to stare at him, shocked. "You... you want to k-kiss me?" she stammered, her eyes wide.

Gabe stepped forward, his own bright green gaze darkening into a smolder. "Very much so, Serena," he replied in a low, husky voice.

Smiling softly at the two younger people, the rest of the group turned away to give them privacy. Risa still saw them out of the corner of her eye. Gabe gently pulled a trembling Rena against him and gently cupped the back of her head before he lowered his lips to hers. He kissed her so tenderly; it made Risa's eyes hot with unshed tears. As first kisses went, it was a perfect one.

Liam finally turned back and saw they were staring into each other's eyes. "Okay, guys, coast is clear, the kids are done making out."

Gabe grinned at Liam as Rena blushed, burying her face in Gabe's shoulder.

"My man," Liam laughed.

Rolling his eyes, Gabe looked very much like his mother just then. Risa chuckled, *good thing Gabe hasn't developed powers like Bridget yet, or Liam would be in trouble.* She knew Liam and Gabe were very close. Liam was the older brother Gabe didn't have when he and his mom were first introduced to the world of dragons and wielders.

Liam clapped, "Okay, so we've established that Killian's crazy ex is back in town and somehow has a connection to Isabella. Killian loves Risa, Gabe likes kissing Rena, and Isabella is not a fan of tequila, but she loves me. What now? Do we still want to leave?" He grinned at them, his cheeky smile indicating he was eager to get into trouble.

Killian shook his head as Izzy laughed, "Now we drink!"

Rena leaned over to Risa, "Please tell me you're driving."

Risa snorted, "Oh, you bet I am!"

Liam, Izzy, and Killian were having a stand-off. Irish whiskey being their weapon of choice. They'd gathered quite a crowd at this point. Each of the three with their own team of cheerleaders. The mountain of shot glasses piled up around them. Liam declared he was starting to see double. Izzy and Killian grinned across the table at each other. Liam stared at the four of them, no, two of them, and tapped out. His team of supporters groaned and divided themselves up between the remaining two.

Izzy leaned across towards Killian, whispering, "Dragon metabolism, wielder."

Killian kept a slight smile on his face and nodded graciously. "I'm aware. I'm sure you've got me, ma'am," he drawled and tapped the brim of his hat.

She grinned, and he held up the next round. She threw it back, and he followed suit. This went on for five more rounds before Izzy swayed a little.

Killian matched her gaze levelly and smirked. He held up a credit card to Risa, "Darling, go ahead an' close out the tab, I think we're done here."

Izzy smiled defiantly and picked up the last shot. She swallowed hard, then set it back down. "Dammit!" she groaned and leaned back laughing.

The crowd cheered as Killian stood, took his shot and hers, then bowed. "Lass, ye might have the accent, but if there's one thing ye never do, it's try an' drink a born Irishman under the table, else you'll find yourself hurtin' in the morn." He broke into a popular drinking song, then to the enthusiasm of their audience.

Izzy glared at him. "Fuckin' Leprechaun," she grumbled and put her head down on the table.

Liam began to laugh so hard he fell out of his chair, while Rena and Risa stared at their sister in shock.

Gabe was trying to help Liam stand, but he pulled Gabe down, hugging him instead.

"Gabriel, did I ever apologize to you for being gone so long before?" Liam asked him, slurring slightly.

Gabe snorted and hauled him up, "Only every time you drink and get sentimental, Liam."

Liam turned to Izzy, who was still face down on the table. "Did you know, when I met Gabe, I took him to school in a Lamborghini? It wasn't mine. It was Drake's, but still. It was really cool. Bridget was pissed."

Gabe rolled his eyes, chuckling.

"And did I tell you he used to have a crush on my sister?" Liam continued.

"Dude," protested Gabe, "I was seventeen! And it was for like a week!"

Rena giggled and slipped her arm through Gabe's. "It's okay, when I first met him, I had a crush on Liam, but I got over that *really* quick."

Gabe joined in her laughter while Liam blushed.

Izzy straightened and glared at Killian, then stood, swaying a bit. She pointed at him and growled. "Fuckin' Leprechaun," she repeated and then burst out laughing, hugging him. "I thought I had ye, I forget sometimes I'm not actually Irish."

Risa groaned. "Okay, maybe it's time we go before I lose the ability to pour you into the car?"

Liam grinned, "Yeah, I want to get Isabella home and —"

Izzy slapped her hand over his mouth, and he kissed her palm.

Gabe laughed, "Rena, I can give you a ride home."

She nodded shyly, and he took her hand.

Risa glared at Killian with narrowed eyes. "This is your fault," she declared as she pointed at Liam and Izzy, who were grinning at each other and making faces, trying to make one another laugh. "Help me get them in the car."

Killian protested, "I didn't do anythin'! They challenged me!" He grumbled, "Feckin' overgrown lizards always thinkin' they're better at everythin'."

She glared harder.

He smirked, pulling off his hat and holding it over his heart. "But I'll still help ye because you're beautiful. Prettier than all the twinkling stars in the velvet of the night sky. More beautiful than the fae lights dancin' amongst the hills."

"Smooth. I'll allow it," she grinned as he bowed, only wobbling slightly before plopping his hat on her head.

They gathered their belongings and headed out to the parking lot. Risa and Izzy hugged Rena before she strolled arm in arm with Gabe towards his car, smiling at each other.

Liam sighed, "I hope he remembers to use protection." The others gaped at him. He snorted, "I'm kidding, he wouldn't move that fast on her."

Killian cleared his throat.

They turned and looked back at the couple who were now kissing passionately by the car.

Liam raised his eyebrows. "Or I could be wrong."

Izzy giggled and pulled Liam towards the car with Killian and Risa following slowly behind.

Killian stopped for a moment and leaned down to kiss her. "Risa, I'm sorry again about that in there, with Kiera. I don't know what she's up to, regardless, it doesn't change that I love ye an' I'm happier than I've ever been."

She smiled tenderly at him. "Good. Now let's go home and work on that fantasy list of yours."

He grinned, "Walk faster." They hurried to catch up to the dragons but came to a jolting halt when they heard Rena screaming as a terrifying roar echoed through the night.

They were all sober now with their hearts in their throats and cold fear coursing through their veins. They ran towards where they last saw Gabe and Rena, following the sounds of her screams. It was attracting attention, so Liam threw up a warding to block it.

Killian reached them first and dropped to where Rena was sprawled across Gabe's still form. He was lying motionless on the ground, covered in blood, his shirt a ripped mess, and his throat shredded. His skin was pale, and his eyes were closed. Killian pulled her off and held her tight against him as he checked for any signs the boy was still breathing. "Liam!" he bellowed, "Get Siobhan here now!"

Liam dropped down beside them and shook his head, "She won't get here in time." He stared at Killian, and his face was grim, determined. He snarled, his fangs dropping in anger, "I am not losing him." He turned to Risa and Izzy, his normally emerald eyes full of flames. "You two, put your hands on my shoulders and push your powers into me. I can heal him, but I need help. I didn't lose Shepard, and I'm not fucking losing him. *Not Gabe!*" he shouted.

The sisters did as he asked, and Liam held his hands over Gabe the way Killian had seen Siobhan do on countless occasions. He clenched his jaw as he watched the green dragon close his eyes. Liam gritted his teeth and focused. Killian saw green waves pulsing down towards Gabe, and they all gasped as the wounds slowly began to close.

Liam's hands trembled, and he groaned. His arms started shaking, and he wailed, "No! No! Gabriel!" His voice crackled with desperation, and tears streamed beneath his lids.

Killian whispered to Rena to hold Gabe's hand as he let her go. He put both of his hands on Liam's and pushed for all he was worth. The power flared between them, and Liam made an odd choking sound before his eyes flew open and flashed silver, then blue. The wounds began closing again, and finally, all that was left was a dark red scar on Gabe's neck. He shuddered and took a deep, wheezing breath.

"Serena," he whispered, his voice raspy.

"I'm here, Gabe, I'm here! Oh god, I thought you were dead," she cried.

Risa gathered Rena in her arms, pulling her back to give Gabe room to breathe.

"That... makes... two of us," Gabe groaned and coughed.

Liam had collapsed back into Izzy's arms. He took a few shaky breaths and gazed up at her. "Gabe?" he croaked.

Izzy gasped. "Liam! Your eyes!"

They all stared at Liam then, noticing his eyes were glowing blue, swirling like the ocean, looking eerily like Shepard or Davis' eyes.

"Shit, not again," Liam whispered, "It took me weeks to get rid of that last time." He waved off their questions and sat up, "Later! Gabe, buddy, are you okay?"

Killian was sitting him up.

"I'm gonna... live... holy hell... hurt," Gabe rasped weakly.

"What the fuck happened?" Killian demanded, his tone flat and deadly.

Rena was sobbing still, but she swallowed and snapped, "It was her! That woman, Kiera. She was here with some man I've never seen before.

He slammed some dark-looking power into Gabe. It paralyzed him, then she appeared, screaming, and slashed Gabe with her claws."

Gabe shook his head slowly. "It was… fast… didn't see her." He took a deep breath and tried to steady himself. "I saw him looking like… throwing something at me… just pain, and the ground." A few more deep breaths. "I heard Rena… screaming… then nothing until… minute ago. Rena, are you okay?"

She threw herself at him, "I'm fine."

He grunted, pain in the sound.

She gasped, "Oh no! Gabe, I'm so sorry!"

He patted her arms, "It's okay. Just a little… tender still." He chuckled softly, then winced. "I've never been ripped open… dragon before. Ow," he grinned at her, and she smiled weakly at him.

Risa stared grimly at them both. "Rena, why don't you and Gabe follow me back to Liam's place? It's the closest, and we can talk there. We need to figure out what the hell is going on."

Liam offered to ride with the younger couple just in case of attack, and they all headed out.

Chapter 34

"YE BLATHERING IDIOT!" Kiera screeched. "Ye got the wrong man!"

"You said he was wearing a black hat, a blue shirt, and was with the silver-haired woman. It was dark, that's what I saw!" he retorted, his voice trembling as he vomited a second time. "You didn't have to hurt the kid; you could have just taken her!"

Stomping back and forth, Kiera shrieked wordlessly. "There wasn't time, her screams got everyone's attention. Ye screwed this up! Now I'll have to clean up your mess. Ye better hope I can get them, or *she* will do worse than I will."

Risa handed Gabe a glass of water, and they all listened as Liam reassured Vaughn that Gabe was alive. A loud roar filled the room from the speaker, then a clatter as Liam dropped his phone. He scrambled to pick it up, but the call was already disconnected. "Um, Vaughn's on his way over," he supplied unnecessarily.

"Not my mom too, please tell me she doesn't know yet," Gabe pleaded, his voice still carrying a trace of raspiness.

Liam shook his head. "I managed to convince him to leave her out of this, for now."

Gabe sighed gratefully, leaning back. "I love my mother, but she would fall apart over this, and she needs to care for Connor and Celeste right now. Besides, I'm alive and that's the most important thing."

Killian was pacing the length of the living room, his brow furrowed. Muttering to himself and waving his hands around like he was conducting an orchestra. Silver sparks flew from him as he gestured, and the others realized he was working some spell. Finally, he turned to Gabe, "I'm sorry, lad, but we need to see what happened. Are ye alright seeing it again?"

Gabe nodded and sat up.

Killian shook his head, "Not what ye saw, what she saw," he pointed at Rena. "Rena Doll, are ye willing?"

She jolted, startled, but leapt to her feet with grim determination and nodded. "Do it!" she commanded, steel in her voice.

Killian smiled at her gently. "Don't worry, sweet one, this won't hurt." He used a similar spell to the one Circe taught him to create a projection of a memory.

They all leaned in as the shimmery image appeared from Rena's perspective. Watching as Gabe smiled tenderly, then turned to open her door for her. Suddenly, a man appeared behind Gabe, and she gasped in fear. The man wasn't overly tall, but was pale and drawn, with dark shadows under his eyes. His dark caramel colored hair was long, reaching just below his shoulders and gathered in a tail at the nape of his neck. He had a pronounced widow's peak and thin pale lips.

He waved his hands, and a dark cloud burst forth, slamming into Gabe as Rena described. Gabe froze, and Rena tried to shake him, begging him to run. They saw the blonde woman run out from between the cars, talons out, with a deep fanged scowl on her face. She shouted at the dark wielder, something about the wrong man. She screamed in wordless rage before slashing Gabe. They watched as Gabe fell to the ground and the wielder and dragon disappeared. Killian held the spell until he saw himself grabbing Rena. He dropped his arms, and the memory faded.

They stared at each other quietly. Risa was making detailed notes about the man's appearance. They all agreed, no one recognized him.

Izzy shook her head in disbelief. "Ye say that's Kiera, but it's definitely Evie. I can't believe she lied to me," she shuddered. Liam moved to pull her into his arms.

A loud thump outside was their only warning. With a crash, Liam's front door flew open as a large man with black and gold wings, blazing crystal blue eyes, and hair like raven's wings barreled in. He grabbed Gabe and yanked him into his arms, enveloping them both in a cloud of smoke and scales. He held the young man tightly and closed his eyes. "You're okay. Thank God. Gabriel," he muttered in relief, a deep rumbling noise emanated from his chest.

"Dad, I'm okay," Gabe mumbled, gripping the dragon gratefully in return.

Vaughn stood back and held Gabe in front of him. He turned the boy's head and studied his neck. He growled deep in his throat, and his wings swished in agitation as smoke continued to billow from him, forcing Liam to open some windows.

Risa shivered at the threat in the sound. She would not want to be Kiera if Vaughn found her first.

Liam tossed a shirt to Vaughn; he'd obviously flown to be here this fast and was only wearing a pair of loose pants that were hanging low on his hips.

Vaughn nodded his thanks and pulled it on.

Izzy blinked now that the absolutely gorgeous man was fully clothed. She glanced at Risa to see if she was drooling too, and noticed her sister was studiously looking elsewhere. She was glad she wasn't the only one salivating at the display of manly deliciousness. Risa told her that Bridget and Jorrie called Vaughn Sex God behind his back. She believed it. She appraised Liam, thinking how talented he'd be at that age. He caught her look and grinned, winking as if he knew what she was thinking. Actually, he probably did.

Liam's expression changed from amused to overwhelmed as Vaughn engulfed him in his arms and held him tightly.

The fierce black dragon shuddered lightly, whispering, "Thank you, Liam, thank you for saving my boy." Vaughn had adopted Gabe formally when he was seventeen, but they were so close anyone outside of the family would believe he'd fathered him. Vaughn placed his forehead on Liam's and held the man's face gently in his hands. "I owe you for his life."

Liam shook his head, "No, he's my little brother, I wasn't going to lose him."

Gabe put his arms around them both, while the women all sniffled at the heartfelt moment.

Vaughn eventually pulled back and studied Liam, laughing. "You know your eyes are blue again."

Liam rolled his ocean blue eyes, tinged with sparks of silver now. "Please, don't bring it up," he grumped.

Risa cleared her throat and began to describe what happened.

Vaughn listened closely before murmuring, "The darkness that's coming."

Killian nodded; he hadn't said a word since Vaughn showed up. He'd been there in Miami and repeated the final words of the dark wielder before Jack killed her. "This is the start of that which is coming," he intoned.

Risa shuddered; she'd been there too.

Vaughn studied Killian consideringly, "So, Kiera's back. That bitch." He shook his head, "Do you know why?"

Izzy stepped forward, "I've a connection to her as well. She was my dragon mentor. She worked with me when I had my first turning an' taught me all I know about dragons. She was going by another name, Evie. There's no way she could have predicted I'd have a future connection with Killian. But what if she knew who I was? Despite the spell hiding me? Is she after me or Killian? Or Gabe, or Rena, or Risa?" She huffed out a frustrated breath.

Killian shook his head; he'd been asking himself that since he'd realized it was her. "Honestly, I don't know. I don't know if she's after me an' Gabe was a case of mistaken identity, or this was an awful coincidence."

Vaughn furrowed his brow, "I don't believe in coincidences, and you said she was shouting about the wrong man. We need to know the end goal here. Do you know where she would go?"

"Everything I thought I knew about her was wrong," Killian shook his head in frustration.

Izzy nodded, "Same, everything she told me... was a lie."

The front door banged open again as Siobhan burst in, followed by a disheveled-looking Marco chasing his mate. She ignored everyone and ran to Gabe, inspecting him as Vaughn had. She put a hand over her lips at the sight of the angry scar and burst into tears, throwing herself into Gabe's arms.

Gabe held her awkwardly and patted her shoulder, staring at Marco, bewildered.

"It's a boy," Marco whispered, shrugging.

Gabe smiled softly and hugged her tighter. "Shi, I'm okay. Thanks to Liam."

She turned to her brother then and threw herself at him. "I'm so proud of you, Liam," she whispered and snuggled against him while he lay his cheek on her head, their red-gold hair blending together in a waterfall of beautiful color.

Izzy sighed as her heart fluttered at the sight.

Siobhan glanced at her and quirked her lips. "You two, have you decided if you're okay with this yet or not?"

Vaughn turned to Liam questioningly.

Liam laughed cheerfully. "Vaughn, I know it's sudden, but Isabella and I are apparently fated mates. She loves me." He smiled softly, "And I love her."

"Oh, thank God," Vaughn barked out a short laugh.

Startled, Liam stared at him open-mouthed.

His godfather smiled at him fondly, "I've been hoping you would find someone to settle you down. I've been worried. You've been reckless, distracted, you just haven't been you."

Liam narrowed his eyes as Gabe nodded in agreement.

Killian laughed, "Aye, you've been more of an arse than normal lately. But since ye met Izzy, you've been almost tolerable."

He showed his middle finger to Killian, then turned to Vaughn. "So, I have your blessing to mate another dragon?"

Izzy growled, and they all turned to her. "I'm not needing your permission to choose him. He is *my* mate, an' ye have no say," she snarled at Vaughn.

The black dragon glared at her, and his fangs dropped down. His talons whipped out as his eyes filled with flames. He stalked to her and towered over the smaller dragon as his growl shook the house. "You think to challenge me, little one?" he snarled.

"If I have to!" she growled back.

Vaughn relaxed and grinned at her. "Then no, I don't have a problem with it. Why would I?"

Izzy, startled by this turn of events, glanced around in confusion.

"You can mark me first," Liam smirked at her, "I'm a progressive type of dragon."

She realized then he'd set her up. She smiled sweetly, then punched him in the nose.

He looked stunned as the first drops of blood fell, and Vaughn burst out laughing, "You're at two out of three sisters, Liam. Rena, you're up next."

Liam snarled at Izzy and grabbed her. He picked her up, threw her over his shoulder, and stormed off towards the back door.

Everyone watched in shock, then studiously ignored the shouts and shrieks as Izzy protested and tried to hit him again. The back door slammed as he carried her outside.

Vaughn shook his head, "I can't wait to see those marks."

Rena's eyes grew wide in her dainty face, "You mean they're going to..." she trailed off.

Risa laughed softly. "It's what adults do, Rena, they fight, then have great make-up sex." She winked at her little sister, who swallowed hard and tried hard not to stare at Gabe.

Siobhan was trying to finish healing his neck, but it was only a few shades lighter instead of completely healed. She shook her head in frustration. "I don't understand. Liam did everything right. By all accounts, this should have killed you."

"Gee, thanks, Shi," Gabe muttered, and Vaughn growled at her.

She rolled her eyes, "Obviously it didn't, but I can't get this to finish healing."

Gabe's eyes lowered, "Maybe it was the dark power he hit me with first. You think some of that is embedded in it, the way it was when Dad was attacked?"

The green wielder dropped her suddenly shaking hands, and her eyes filled with tears. "And Marco," she glanced at the faint scar on her mate's throat. "It's likely Gabe. This could take months to heal, or it may never go away," she whispered.

He took a deep breath and slowly let it out. "Well, if that's the case, it is what it is. I'm alive and that's what matters most. Besides, a cool scar gives me a story to tell." He smiled bravely.

Risa glanced at Killian with tears in her eyes.

Killian swallowed hard and spoke up, "Hey, Gabe, I'm sure you're exhausted. Liam won't mind ye staying here. Rena, why don't ye help Gabe into bed an' make sure he's comfortable. I bet he could use your calming presence to help him sleep."

Rena glanced at Gabe, her face red, but nodded silently. Gabe smiled gently at her as she took his hand and led him away.

Vaughn clapped Killian on the shoulder, "I'm going to ignore the fact that you just encouraged her to sleep with my son." Killian choked, and

Vaughn chuckled. "I'm kidding." He turned to look at the wielder, study-ing the man's youthful countenance, the drastic changes in his appearance, the little silver rings adorning his face and grinned. "Damn old friend, you don't look much different than the day we met."

Killian snorted in amusement, then, realizing Vaughn was having a joke at his expense. "Aye, maybe not, but my heart is certainly in fewer pieces." He pulled Risa to him and held her. He glanced up at the black dragon, who was his oldest friend. "Molly sends her love an' said to get your scaly ass over there soon so your babes can meet hers. An' ye know the whole Brennan clan will arrive for the wedding."

Risa watched the two. She knew they were good friends and loved that they were so close. She understood now why Killian volunteered to hunt down those responsible for kidnapping and torturing Vaughn so many months before. Which is how she came to meet them. She was grateful for their friendship. She smiled at her fiancé before grabbing Siobhan's hand and dragging her off to another room to ask for advice. Risa got the information she needed and wrapped her arms around the woman, smiling so hard her face hurt.

Chapter 35

LIAM CARRIED ISABELLA OUTSIDE and set her down none too gently on his patio. He snarled, "What the actual fuck, woman? Can't you take a joke?" He gingerly touched his nose, checking to see if she'd broken it the way Risa did, cringing at how tender it was.

She growled back, "Progressive dragon? Try caveman arsehole!" She tried to stomp past him, but he grabbed her arm, yanking her back.

"Don't walk away from me, I'm not done with you yet," he hissed.

She bared her fangs, "Too bad, because I'm done with *you!*"

Gasping, he dropped her arm. His face was awash in pain while his chest constricted. He couldn't get in another breath and slapped his hand over his heart as if to stop it from falling apart. Backing away from her, his eyes went glassy with the hot tears that filled them.

She glared at him, then realized what she'd said. "No, Liam, I didn't mean, not like that. Just done with this conversation."

He shook his head vigorously, his hair flying around his face. "But you don't want to be my mate either. Isabella, I love you. I thought... I thought you loved me. Despite how fast this happened, I thought we agreed to give this a chance," his voice broke, then hardened. "You know what? Never mind. Just fucking go then, leave. Leave me the hell alone. My life is fucked up enough as it is, no sense making it worse by dragging this out. You don't have time for my emotional drama? I hope you find what you're looking for, Isabella. At least I'm not the one running away this time." His expression wavered for a second, and he turned his back, listening to her retreating footsteps. Each one driving another crack deep into his very soul.

His gaze settled on the beckoning water of his pool. He stripped his clothes off and dove, trying to let the coolness soothe his burning skin as he entered the water. He'd been an idiot once again. He opened himself up to emotion, fell in love with someone, and although he'd made sure to tell her this time, he'd still managed to screw it up somehow. She didn't want him. He felt like he was dying; it was Jorrie again, but ten times worse. His dragon roared in pain in his head. Once again, rejected by someone he desperately needed to care for him.

He stayed under as long as he could, until his chest tightened again, and he came to the surface gasping. Tears mixed with the salty water of the pool as he silently let the pain flow from him. Finally, he couldn't keep it in, and he roared. Every ounce of heartache and misery echoed through the night. Years of heartache and rejection, loneliness and despair ripped through him. Birds took flight, and small creatures in the underbrush scurried from the predator in their midst. He roared until his throat was weak and his chest was heaving. Hearing a splash, he turned to find Isabella behind him. She'd jumped in, still dressed. He frowned and shook his head. "It's okay, Isabella, really, you don't have to stay. I understand this was too fast, not what you wanted. Maybe it's better that we end it now before we get too deep. I can't go through this again. I can't." He sighed and swam towards the other end of the pool.

Izzy stared after him. *What is wrong with me?* The man was desperately in love with her, and she loved him. He was scared — terrified — of being hurt again, but was brave enough to admit it to her. And she destroyed him, shattered him. She'd only made it to the door earlier before she heard the splash. She turned and watched until he surfaced, his shoulders shaking in his pain. His broken roar destroyed her. She'd never heard anything like it and never wanted to again. Siobhan warned her, he was more fragile than he seemed. Being pushed away by an uncaring father, his parents being murdered, rejected by his first love for another man, then her own careless words after he trusted his heart to her.

Sighing in frustration at herself, she swam after him. He was standing, waist deep in the water, staring at the night sky. She pulled off her sodden clothes and stood behind him. Pressing her bare skin against his back.

He sucked in a shaky breath. "Isabella, please, don't," he shuddered, tears clogging his throat.

"Shh, or I'll bite your tail," she told him softly.

He laughed ruefully, "I don't have a tail in this form."

She smiled against his neck. She stroked a hand down his backside, "Then I'll have to bite something else that's sticking out."

Liam jolted and felt himself immediately get painfully hard at the thought of her mouth on him. He stared at the sky again; he was just a glutton for punishment. Shaking his head, he sighed at the inevitable and braced himself for the knife to twist harder. He turned to her, enjoying the way the soft, salty water made her skin slick and slippery against his own. Her breasts slid up his chest as she reached up to wrap her arms around his neck. "Isabella," he whispered softly. "I can't do this. I won't survive it again,

I'm not strong enough." His dragon whimpered in his mind, desperately wanting her.

"Liam, I can't leave. I won't leave. I love ye, an' you're my mate. You're the one I want. No matter how stupid ye act sometimes," she smiled at him.

He snorted, "Are you sure, Isabella?" His expression turned deadly serious, as stirring of hope wiggled in his chest. "Are you? I mean it, if you aren't sure, we can't take this any further."

She nodded, "My heart only belongs to one man. One dragon. I *want* to be your mate, Liam. I *want* to wear your mark on my skin."

His heart fluttered at her words, disbelief coursing through him. Then it calmed, and one thing stood out to him in stark clarity. He shook his head, "No, Isabella, I want you to mark me. I belong to you."

She stared at him incredulously. "Are we really going to argue over this? Who gets to mark who, but it's about us wanting the other to do it? Is this a polite off? Ye go first? No, ye, I insist? I mean it's just about the most ridiculous thing —"

He crushed his lips to hers to stop the flow of words. When he let her up for air, he murmured, "Babbling."

She laughed softly, "I'm sor —"

He cut her off with another kiss. "Nope, we don't apologize to each other for babbling. Remember our deal? Although we started off with you babbling, maybe this is a good way to cement this bond," he chuckled and brushed a strand of her wet hair behind her ear where it fell like a rope of diamonds, sparkling with droplets of water.

She smiled dreamily, then shook her head. "Who knew, just walking around a corner would change my life so much? Finding my family, moving to a new country, an' finding my dream man, the love of my life an' my soulmate."

He traced his nose across the soft line of her jaw, whispering, "I'm glad you chose that corner that day."

She nodded as he pulled her tighter against his body, his hard length digging into her stomach.

"You know," he drawled, wrapping a fist in her hair and pulling her head back as he licked a scorching line up her throat, "They say make-up sex is the best sex. Care to test that theory?"

She trembled, digging her nails into his back, "I thought you'd never ask. Liam, take me hard, like the dragons we are, an' then we mark each other at the same time, okay?"

He ground himself against her, panting and groaning. "Yes, Isabella, god, I need you soon."

She smiled, "And ye have me, but first, I'm needing to give ye something." She led him to the ledge in the shallow end, pushing him to lie back on one of the lounge chairs.

His smile went nearly feral, ready for her to slide down and take him.

She straddled his legs and began to kiss down his stomach, rubbing his length between her breasts.

His head slammed back on the chair, and he gasped. The feeling of her silky hair trailing down his stomach almost brought him. She lightly scraped her fingernails over his thighs, and he shivered. She placed gentle kisses on his skin, and he throbbed as she licked the small droplets oozing from the tip of him before she slid her warm, wet mouth down the length of his cock. His upper body convulsed at the feel of her velvet tongue wrapping around him while her mouth worked wonders. He began to pant, his thighs flexing. He buried his hands in her damp hair, wondering at the strands that looked like ropes of fire opals in the dark. "Isabella, sweet goddess, you're killing me."

He moaned and rolled his head side to side. She took him deeper into her throat, and he jerked his hips. She must have sensed he was close because she hummed a little, the rumble from deep in her chest. He started cursing, and his breathing was jagged, coming out harshly. She purred and scraped her nails over his thighs again. He roared as he jetted down her throat, and she took all of him, licking every single drop from his skin. He went limp on the chair, and she lay her head in his lap. She kept purring and rumbling in pleasure. He sat up and pulled her to him, crushing his mouth to hers.

Izzy felt his length pulse against her and blessed that quick dragon recovery. He dragged her into his lap, and she positioned herself over him. She broke free of the kiss and gasped his name as she felt the tip of him probing her entrance. Reaching between her thighs, Liam stroked her with his fingers, murmuring in approval about how wet she was for him. He brought those fingers to his mouth, holding her gaze while he licked them clean. She shuddered; that had been unexpectedly erotic.

He growled and pulled her up higher, lying back and positioning her over his mouth.

She gasped in shock as he plowed his tongue between her thighs and suckled her. Quickly, she grabbed the arms of the chair, barely holding herself up while her arms shook with effort. She braced her knees over his shoulders and threw her head back, gasping her pleasure at the night sky. He devoured her, and the heat coming from his mouth was enhancing every sensation tenfold. She felt her thighs quaking and knew she was about to fall apart above him.

Liam stroked her opening with his thumbs and swirled his tongue inside of her. He began to purr the same way she had done to him, and it was all she needed to give her that final push. She spasmed and growled his name as he lapped up every drop he could get. She almost fell back, going boneless above him, but he sat up and caught her. He lowered them both into the water. He sat on the ledge with her legs wrapped around his waist as he slid into her with ease. She writhed in ecstasy when he hissed as she wrapped around him.

Draping her arms around him, she kissed him, tasting herself there and reveling in the feel of his warm, strong hands on her back. She began to move, and soon they were straining to join even deeper than ever before. His wings flared, and he thrust into her as hard as he could, a growl erupting from his throat. She shook her head side to side, "Liam, I can't, I can't," she panted as she came close to shattering again, her own wings flaring then, pushing herself back against him.

He let out a ragged breath, "Isabella, now!" as his thighs quivered again. He growled, and she saw his fangs come out, her own slipping down in response. In unison, they both darted forward and bit each other in the tender valley just above the collarbone, drawing in a drink of their mates' blood as they climaxed together. The two roared so loud, the water in the pool sloshed out of the basin, and car alarms began to wail as if there had been an earthquake.

Liam leaned against the foot of the chair he'd managed to grab and drag behind him. He couldn't sit up anymore and didn't want to drown them both after they'd just had the most amazing moment of their lives. He stared at her mark as it manifested and smiled softly. He had to say, it was definitely unique. Not completely what he'd chosen, but then again, it wasn't what she'd chosen either. It was like their bond combined their choices into one.

He traced her mark, as she sat up to look at him. He brushed her hair behind her ears and stared into her eyes. "God, I love you, Isabella."

"I love ye too, Liam, my Wolfy," she grinned mischievously at him.

He laughed, then his expression became earnest. "Solas. My Shining Light, you brought light and love back into my life. I can never thank you enough for that."

She kissed him gently.

He stretched and murmured, "Should we go inside?"

She shook her head, laying it on his chest, "No, I'm happy here, besides, I think they all left."

"I think you're right," he chuckled, then tilted his head, "Although I have a feeling we've got a houseguest in Gabriel. Possibly Rena, too."

Her eyes widened in surprise. "Ye don't think they'll..." she trailed off, obviously not wanting to think of her baby sister doing anything close to what she'd just done with Liam.

He studied her and grinned. "Nah, Gabe will be too tired, and Rena won't start it. Isabella?" She met his gaze as he sat up and pulled her to his level. "I could probably think of more romantic times and places to do this, probably even not be naked, but," he traced her mark, then whispered, "God, I know it's fast, so fast, but the heart wants what it wants. Please, Isabella, marry me?"

"Where's my ring?" her lips quirked as she obviously tried not to laugh.

His eyes went wide, and he blushed. "I'll take you tomorrow and get you any ring you want. Anything."

She rolled her eyes, "An' if the ring I want is fifty thousand?" Her tone was light and teasing.

"You're worth ten times that," he shrugged, knowing she was playing, but he was deadly serious.

She stared at him incredulously, "Liam, ye would seriously do that?"

"Vaughn pays me well, and I told you I'm good at investing."

She shook her head, and his face dropped. "Oh God, Liam, I didn't mean no I won't marry ye; I was just shaking my head at myself that I'm even surprised... an' I'm babbling again. Liam, I would be honored to marry ye an' be your wife."

He grinned, kissing her. "Any ring," he told her again, then brushed her hair back as she smiled softly. He laid her back, and this time they slowly made love under the night sky, savoring each inch of each other.

Chapter 36

KILLIAN WOKE THE NEXT morning feeling heavy and achy. The night before was entirely too long. True, he'd had a lot to drink, but that wasn't what was weighing on him. It wasn't even Kiera's return. It was his reaction to it. He'd blubbered and shut down like a fool rather than getting past it and appreciating what he had. He shook his head and turned to Risa, but found her side of the bed empty, except for an exceptionally large, judgmental cat.

"Mornin' Malachi," he muttered to the beast. The cat squeezed his eyes and sneezed. Killian sighed and swung his feet over the edge of the bed, stretching as Malachi yodeled at him.

"Aye, I'm going to feed ye, there's no need to sing me the song of your people, it's too early," he grumped at the cat. He stumbled to the kitchen and filled the cat's food dish. There, he stared at the coffee pot, already full of fresh hot coffee. *God bless the woman, she's a goddess, I'm sure of it.* He poured a cup and cursed dragons for their ability to drink it scorching hot, while he had to wait for it to cool. He'd almost decided he didn't need taste buds, so it would be alright to burn them off, when he realized it was noticeably quiet in the house. He hadn't seen Risa. She was always making some noise or puttering about.

Feeling more alert, he set the cup down and started searching for her. He wandered about but couldn't find her anywhere in the house. Becoming concerned, he glanced out back at his music studio. *Surely, she wouldn't have gone out there.* He noticed the spare key was missing from the hook and decided she had to be there. His racing heart wouldn't accept any other answer. Running to the door, he threw it open, the acid in his throat boiling higher with his anxiety. He let out a hard, relieved breath when he saw her sitting on the bench at his piano, picking out a few notes.

She glanced up and smiled. "Good morning, sleepy head."

He strode in with determination and yanked her off the bench, crushing her mouth with his.

She made a happy noise at the kiss, and he finally set her back down. "Mmm, not that I mind, but what's the occasion?" She smiled and tousled his hair, still spiky and rumpled from sleep.

He brushed a finger along her brow and down her cheek. "I missed ye," he whispered. "I woke up an' ye weren't there, I couldn't find ye. I was worried," he admitted, staring at the floor, "With everything going on, I thought something may have happened to ye."

She leaned in, kissing his jaw softly. "I'm sorry. I was restless, and I wanted to have some place to work on something. I needed to capture the essence of you. I feel it most strongly out here."

He gazed at her, puzzled, his head tilted in his questioning way.

She patted his cheek. "My love, I have something for you. Close your eyes and hold out your hands."

He arched an eyebrow but closed his eyes as instructed. He felt her take his hands in hers as she whispered, "Killian, I love you more than I could ever explain. You gave me back my life, my family, my power, and your heart. I feel like I could never give you enough to justify it. You've forgiven me when I've done stupid things, and I feel sometimes I don't deserve you. Shh!" she told him as he started to protest. "You gave me this ring you made, wielded and imbued with your power, and with it, I have a special connection to you. But it only works both ways if you're touching it. That's not fair."

He started to protest again, and she put a finger over his lips. He grinned and kissed it, eyes still closed as he fought the urge to peek.

"So, I think it's only fitting," her voice wavered as she slipped a ring on his finger, "That you have one too."

His eyes flew open, and he stared, blinking slowly at his hand. On his finger was a band of silver strands, engraved with a Celtic knot, matching the one tattooed over his heart. He could feel her power emanating from it. She'd made him a wielder binding ring. He slowly lifted his gaze to hers, tears spilling unchecked down his face. "Yes," he whispered and went to his knees as the surge of power from the ring washed over them both.

Risa fell into Killian's arms as the binding looped them once again. Her mouth dropped in awe; she hadn't realized it would happen again since they were already bonded. She smiled; he was grinning like a child on Christmas morning, and his smile was everything.

"Risa, I cannot tell ye what this means to me. To have ye declare your love for me like this," he whispered softly to her, his voice low and tight.

She knew he was referring to when he'd been denied the return of his love before. She nodded, showing she understood. She kissed him, and he brushed his ring, sending her a wave of love and desire that stole her breath.

He surged to his feet, pulling her with him. His frantic hands yanked off her pajamas, roaming her body. She put her hands in his waistband

and shoved down the material, just as a guttural growl escaped from his throat. He lifted her then and sat her on the keys of the piano, a discordant crash of notes from behind her. She was shocked but lost her ability to think as he placed her ankles on his shoulders, spreading her thighs wide for him. Her head fell back, and her hands flailed for the top of the grand instrument as he kissed his way up her body. His lips roamed over her breasts, making her nipples impossibly hard while he plunged his fingers into her. He flicked his tongue over her skin, humming his delight as her thighs quaked. He withdrew his fingers and leaned further forward, the tip of his length nudging her center. "Fuck Risa, you're so ready for me," he gasped.

"You do that to me, only you, Killian," she panted.

He groaned and set her down on her feet, then spun her around, so she was facing away from him, bent over the keyboard now. He grasped her hips, almost bruising her with his strong hands, and she felt him positioned behind her. "Please, Killian," she begged, wanting him in her badly. He slipped just inside her and then pulled away. She moaned and wiggled, while he laughed, a surprisingly dark and feral sound. She tried to rub her thighs together to ease the aching desire there.

"Oh, ye like that do ye," he whispered, "What do ye want?" He leaned over, and she could feel him hard and throbbing, pressed against her bottom.

She moaned again, "Please, Killian, I need you."

"What do ye need?" he asked again.

"You Killian, oh god, I need you in me now." She almost screamed in desperation. He rubbed himself on her again, and she strained backwards. She writhed in his arms as he tightened his grip on her hips, holding her in place. She began to whimper, ready to beg, until he grabbed a handful of her hair, pulling her head back as he leaned down to her ear.

"How bad do ye want it?" he said softly against her skin.

She finally begged, "Killian, please, take me, hard."

Laughing in victory, he surged forward. Impaling her over the piano, which made another discordant sound as the felt hammers bounced crazily on the strings.

Over and over, he drove himself into her, his grip on her thighs tightening on her slick skin. They were both shouting, straining towards release. She screamed his name as he brought her to the peak and shoved her over multiple times until she lost count. Each cry melded into musical chords with the sounds from the piano. His legs trembled, and he sat heavily on the bench. He turned her before dragging her down onto his lap, straddling him. With shaking arms, he pulled her against his chest.

"Take me, Risa, take me over," he murmured.

She began to circle her hips and rock against him. She stared deep into his eyes as he released a small moan and clenched his jaw. She kept up her frantic pace, and finally his arms banded around her so hard she could barely breathe. With a strangled shout, his release emptied into her. He dropped his head against her shoulder, gasping, the strands of his hair dancing in the hard breaths billowing from her.

After a minute, he lowered them both to the floor, and they lay there, their breathing labored, trying to find enough oxygen to survive. He'd never felt anything more powerful or humbling than the way she'd begged for him. He buried his face in her hair.

She laughed then.

He propped himself on his elbow and stared down at her, startled.

"Killian, we should have that piano gold plated," she giggled.

He shook with laughter, finally agreeing, "Aye, I may need to have it retuned, too." They both chuckled and snuggled back into each other's arms.

They eventually returned to the house, where he pinned her to the sofa. He made love to her again lazily and gently this time. He knew she would have bruises on her thighs where he'd gripped her earlier and felt bad about it.

She tapped him on the nose and told him to stop moping about it.

Replying that he didn't mope, he took her mouth with his, stroking her tongue with his own as he gently thrust into her. He felt her tremble and sigh, her thighs tensing, soft little moans from her throat. She bit his lip, running her tongue over the ring there, and he quietly groaned as he buried his face in her hair, shuddering with his climax.

She kissed his temple tenderly as he brushed her hair from her face. "The best day in my life was the day ye agreed to marry me," he told her softly.

She smiled, "What's the second-best day?"

He grinned, "The day I met ye."

She pretended to think, "And the third?"

"Every day since is tied," he laughed, "You'll not catch me in trouble with that answer."

She sighed softly, "Love you."

He stared into her eyes and touched his ring to hers. "Love ye, too."

The rings warmed, and she felt his love gently pulse through her. His eyes closed as her love did the same. She felt him stirring inside her and gasped. "Again?"

He smirked and thrust once, gently, "I can't resist ye. Plus, I know a handy spell."

Her mouth dropped, "You awful man, here all this time I just thought you had extraordinary stamina." He grinned wickedly, and she returned the smile, "I love it."

He thrust again, then groaned when someone banged on the front door calling his name. "Go away!" he yelled and surged into her again, much harder, causing her to gasp.

"Killian! It's us! We need to talk!" called Vaughn. They could hear Liam cackling.

He rolled his eyes. "Give me ten fecking minutes," he yelled back. He laughed at Risa's shocked face as he began to thrust into her harder.

When Killian finally opened the door, he was clad only in his underwear and glared at the crowd of people who'd interrupted his plans. He turned and stalked away from the door, giving everyone an unobstructed view of his backside, as he stomped into the kitchen. Vaughn smirked as he followed, heading towards the living room.

The whole group from the night before came inside and settled in. Killian casually strolled back into his living room, drinking a cup of coffee. He dropped down and propped his feet on the coffee table. His arms spread across the back of the couch, ignoring the people invading his home, a soft smile on his face. "Risa's in the shower," he murmured.

The others stared at him in open fascination. He was more relaxed and happier than they'd ever seen him. That and the fact that he was practically naked but didn't seem to care.

Izzy rubbed her mating mark and smiled, whispering to Rena there was no harm in admiring what he was showing, the man was extremely well made.

Rena blushed furiously as he winked at her, remembering no doubt the day she'd walked into her sister's room without knocking and gotten an eyeful of him.

Siobhan stage whispered, "It's magically delicious." It was just what the group needed to break them out of their stupor as laughter boomed through the room.

"By the way, dragon lass," Killian drawled at Izzy, "How's your head this mornin'? Not having wee hammers banging away in that pretty skull of yours are ye?"

She flipped him off, "I repeat, Fuckin' Leprechaun."

Siobhan and Vaughn stared at her in shock, and Marco almost fell over laughing. Gabe told the story of the drinking contest, after which Liam became the brunt of the lightweight jokes.

Risa rushed in, her hair wet, hastily straightening her shirt. She stopped when she saw Killian sprawled on the couch, practically naked and being ogled by everyone. Her face turned bright red as there was now no doubt what they'd been doing.

Killian grabbed her hand, "Mo stor," he said softly and pulled her to his lap, kissing her deeply.

Liam applauded drily. "Can we get down to business now?"

Risa giggled and made to move from Killian's lap.

"Not a good idea at the moment, my love," he told her, an exaggerated leer on his face.

Rena blushed again as Risa smacked him on the chest.

Izzy nodded, "I see wielders are just as sex crazed as dragons."

Killian barked out a laugh. "Even more so today after she gave me this." He held up his hand, showing his new ring, and Siobhan squealed.

"You did it!" She high-fived Risa.

"Aye," he nodded, "My dear Marissa has bound me to her again."

Liam cleared his throat, "She's not the only one," he lowered his shirt collar and showed a silver dragon intertwined with a green dragon over his collarbone. Izzy showed hers, the inverse of his. Everyone gasped at the beautiful marks and congratulated them.

Vaughn smiled gently. He turned a speculative eye on Gabe, whose eyes grew wide as his cheeks flamed.

Rena waved her hands. "No, no, we only slept together last night." The room went quiet, and Gabe whispered in her ear. Rena gasped, and she covered her mouth.

Laughing gently as he hugged her, Gabe clarified. "She meant we just slept last night. I was out almost as soon as she got me in bed. I woke up this morning and she'd fallen asleep next to me."

Chuckles followed this explanation.

Vaughn shook his head, locking eyes with Killian, who grinned back at him and nodded. "Kids."

"Alright, an' now that we've confirmed who is sleeping with who," Killian muttered, "Can we please get back to why ye are all invading my home an' ruining my plans for the day?"

Risa blushed at Izzy's knowing grin.

"Hey man, I tried," Liam smirked.

Killian glared at the green dragon, then sighed, "I'm going to take a shower." He let Risa scoot off of his lap. "Ye can talk, an' Risa can catch me up when I get back. I won't be long." Liam started to protest, and Killian grunted, "Oh, fine then ye fecking lizard, I'll just sit here in my underwear an' let them stare at me longer."

Liam snorted, shaking his head in disgust.

Killian stood and ran his hand down his well-defined abs and smiled evilly, not missing the way all the women's eyes followed it, his fitted box-er-briefs leaving nothing else to the imagination. "Of course, now they'll all be thinking about me in the shower, completely naked, water running down my body, the room full of thick, hot steam —"

"Killian!" Risa snapped, and he grinned, unrepentantly.

"Oh no, don't stop him," Siobhan giggled, "I want to hear more!"

Marco squeezed his eyes shut as if in pain. "Siobhan, I love you and I want you to be my wife more than anything. I want our son to grow up and know his parents loved each other so much they needed to be joined in every way possible to be there for him. Please marry me?"

Siobhan glanced over and shrugged, "Okay."

A choked gurgle escaped Marco's throat as he stared at her wide-eyed, "Really?"

"Yes, really," she nodded, smiling softly, "Dummy! I love you, I'm your mate, and I'm carrying our child, of course, I want to marry you. You just needed to ask in the right way."

They were all stunned as a single tear rolled down his face. "*Mi amor.*"

"Marco, I love you ridiculously a lot," she told him as she leaned forward and kissed him gently.

He held her in his arms. "My little cactus lady, I love you a lot, too, even when you drive me *loco.*"

Chapter 37

LIAM SMILED SOFTLY AT his sister and her mate; glad the drama was finally over there. He turned back, about to tell Killian off for the mental image he'd given all of them, but the wielder had slipped away during the distraction. He threw up his hands in frustration, and Vaughn laughed.

Izzy leaned towards Risa, "How do ye ever stay dressed around him?"

"Hey! Seriously? What's with all the love for the Leprechaun here?" Liam protested.

"What?" Izzy smiled and shrugged, "The man is seriously hot. So are Vaughn, Marco, an' even Gabe," she pointed to each in turn, "Doesn't mean I'm wanting to sleep with any of them. I marked ye as my mate, remember?"

Vaughn looked startled, then laughed again, "Well, alright then."

"You think I'm hot?" Gabe was grinning as well.

"In a young wielder way, yes, you'll grow into it," Izzy chuckled.

Gabe's eyes dropped then, and he frowned.

Izzy glanced around in confusion. "Did I say something wrong there?"

Gabe shook his head and sighed, glancing over at Vaughn. "I know Mom thinks I'm going to inherit her wielder powers, but nothing's happened. I don't want her to get her hopes up."

Rena slipped her hand in his. "It will, Gabe, they manifest at different times. Your mom's powers showed up later; mine showed up early. It's different for everyone. Don't push it."

Vaughn cleared his throat, "Okay, so the way I see it, we need to figure out what Kiera is doing here, who her real target is. Also, who is this with her, how does he figure into it, and are there others? Is this a single plot or part of a larger plan?"

The others nodded in quiet agreement.

"Kiera's role is whatever will give her the most benefit or profit. She wouldn't do anything out of loyalty to anyone but herself," Killian offered from behind Liam's shoulder.

Liam jumped, "Seriously dude, how do you do that?"

The wielder simply smiled, he'd obviously snuck up behind Liam just to mess with him.

Izzy studied him, then gasped. "Killian, I know that's one of your powers, but what if Kiera can do it, too? Maybe that's how she was able to hide that guy from us. Um, sorry, I didn't mean to spill your secret."

Liam squinted at his mate, questions on his face.

Killian shrugged, "She may be using her dragon perception filter, but as for the man, he's not silver, he's likely a dark wielder. As far as I know, my ability is unique."

"I concur, old friend," Vaughn nodded.

Liam seemed about to explode. "So, you have the superpower of being annoying? This is getting old, everyone with their secrets and the rest of us being in the dark."

"No," Killian laughed, "I can fade into the background. Go unnoticed. It's like your perception filter, but I've done it for so long, sometimes it's just subconscious that I do it." He shrugged and leaned against a wall, then disappeared.

Liam leapt to his feet, startled. "Where'd he go?"

Killian's voice came from the same spot. "I'm still here, ye just don't see me. Look harder."

Walking to where he'd last seen Killian, Liam waved at a faint shimmer but couldn't quite focus on it. He stepped even closer and put out his hand. He encountered something solid before he reached the wall, and suddenly Killian was visible again. Liam's hand was on his stomach.

Glancing down, then back up, Killian grinned. "Why Liam, I wasn't after knowing ye in that way, but if you're after me lucky charms, you'll have to get in line, lizard boy."

Liam snatched his hand back as if it had been burned, rolling his eyes. "Not cool, you manky Leprechaun. You, Shepard, Davis... you guys can all disappear from everyone. I can only hide my dragon from humans and ward shit." He shook his head.

Gabe spoke up quietly, "And save lives, Liam."

Shame for his complaining had him staring at his feet, before he glanced at Gabe, "And that's the best of them all, little brother," he said softly as he hugged him again, squeezing him tightly.

Izzy spoke up then, "Liam, ye still haven't told us why your eyes are blue since ye healed Gabe. And what did ye mean by you didn't lose Shepard? Is that why your eyes look like his?"

The others gasped at the reminder. In the excitement of saving Gabe, no one thought to question it at the time.

Liam sighed, his shoulders drooping. Of everyone there, only Vaughn knew the honest answer. Last time, he'd hidden from others until they'd gone back to normal. Now, he told them the true story of what happened when in Australia. Shepard was shot by Arturo, almost dying, before the Shadow was killed.

"With his dying breath, he asked me to take care of Jorrie, to let him go. But I couldn't do that. They're mates, they belonged together. I had to save him," Liam muttered.

"Liam," Izzy called softly, taking his hand and squeezing it, "What an amazing thing ye did. That's why I love ye, that heart of gold."

Siobhan hugged her brother and kissed him on the cheek.

Killian frowned, "I thought Shepard killed the Shadow, how did he do that if he was dying?"

Liam looked at Vaughn to see if he could tell the rest. Vaughn nodded and swore everyone to secrecy. Liam then admitted that it was Jorrie who killed the Shadow using her wielding, and that was all he could say about it. He continued, explaining how Lorenzo, who learned the healing spell from Siobhan, pushed it into Liam. He started trying to heal Shepard even though the man was on death's doorstep. Finally, he pulled Shepard back from the brink, but he was still struggling. Jorrie, in desperation, pushed her magic into Liam. She was a blue wielder, but she was made, not born. Her power was a gift from a God of the sea, Mannan Mac Lir, and it was immense. So great was the force and the intent behind it that as it rushed into Shepard, some of it rebounded back into Liam. It turned his eyes blue like a water dragon and gave him temporary control over water. It only lasted a few weeks, but occasionally still flared up when he was highly emotional.

Killian clapped the dragon on the back, "It's not a bad look on ye, brother," the pride in his voice unmistakable.

Startled at the tone, Liam waited for the moment Killian called him some derogatory version of lizard. When it didn't come, he stared at Killian, surprised, but saw only acceptance. He realized with their respective mates, they were indeed brothers. He glanced at Marco, who was mated to his sister, and let out a delighted chuckle. "Man, we are one messed-up version of the Brady Bunch here." Turning to Vaughn, he laughed harder, "And you and Bridget are the mom and Dad, you started it all!" Marco and the others joined in laughing while Vaughn straightened his shoulders, doing his best to look stern before giving in and chuckling with them.

When they finally quieted down, Liam sighed, "Now, can we *please* get back to what we're going to do about Kiera and that dark wielder? I'd like not to be constantly worrying about Gabe or Isabella or any one of you. Even you, Ki."

Killian rolled his eyes at the dragon. He tapped his chin thoughtfully and admitted, "We need to make ourselves available. She seems to know where I am. I've seen her in multiple places now. I think she's following me, possibly even before we left an' while we were gone. I kept seeing flashes of her in various places, but I wrote it off; it didn't click. Since we've been back, it's getting more frequent. Just yesterday, it was outside of the jewelry store, the restaurant parking lot, then again inside when you saw her, Liam."

Risa shared her suspected sightings, and Liam mentioned the restaurant incident with Izzy, where she'd appeared to be in two places at once.

Izzy added, "Then inside the bar, twice ye said. But it's interesting that she didn't show herself to me. I guess because she knew I'd recognize her. If she's aligned with the dark wielders, an' they're after my family, why haven't they grabbed us yet? Killian, I hate to say it, but I think this is personal."

"Well, Killian," Vaughn said, rubbing his chin, "It certainly seems she's after you then. Given how she's shown herself to you more than the others."

Killian stared at Vaughn, his lips set in a grim line and nodded in agreement.

Risa made a disgusted huffing sound. "But *why*? Other than their past, what is it about Killian that she's after? I mean, no offense, my love, because I would totally kill for you, but she's been silent for sixty years. Why now? She can't possibly want you back now just because you're with me."

"You'd kill for me?" Killian grinned, brushing his hand over her cheek.

She smiled and nodded determinedly. "If necessary, yes, I would."

He quietly chuckled, "So vicious. Hopefully, that won't ever be necessary." He tugged playfully on the end of her long hair. He appreciated the sentiment but didn't want her anywhere near Kiera.

"Dad," Gabe called to Vaughn thoughtfully.

The powerful black dragon turned quickly and grinned softly at him. Vaughn always turned into mush when one of his children was around.

Gabe continued, "We know from last time you faced the dark wielder that they were after you, but their plan went crazy because of a personal vendetta." He was indicating the incident six months prior, when Vaughn was kidnapped, and one of the wielders responsible had blamed Vaughn for his father's death. It was undeserved blame, but that didn't stop the man from torturing the dragon. "What if they're after you again, but Kiera is trying to use Killian to hurt you. He helped kill those two last time, and he's a close friend of yours. Maybe she's trying to hurt him as well for revenge."

Vaughn nodded slowly; it made sense. "But they attacked you and Rena, not Killian and Risa."

Liam smacked himself on the forehead. "Because from behind, they would have looked the same. They were both wearing blue shirts and black hats. Rena and Risa have the same hair from behind. And Killian and Risa came in a separate car, but because of the drinking, Isabella and I were going to ride with them, and Rena went with Gabe. Someone who doesn't know them the way we do could easily make that mistake."

Killian moaned, "I took off that hat before we left. Risa was wearing it outside. If Kiera described me from how I was dressed inside..." he shuddered and stared at Gabe with haunted eyes.

Risa's mouth dropped with the realization that it could have been her and Killian. Her eyes narrowed, and silver sparks began to crackle from her skin. Her eyes went silver, and her hair started to shimmer.

Killian scooped her up, carrying her out back, and calling for Liam. The dragon followed him outside, and Killian barked, "Wards!"

Liam immediately threw up a sound shield around the yard.

He set Risa down then, still sparking and trembling. "Let it out, my love."

She nodded, knowing what he meant. She threw her head back and screamed for all she was worth. The sound seemed amplified, and Liam covered his ears.

Killian rubbed her shoulders until all of the pent-up magic siphoned off her, bouncing around the yard. He tracked it and finally threw out a wave of his own power, calling it all together in a small ball. Crushing it between his hands like a wad of paper. When he opened them, the magic was replaced by a small sparkly diamond.

Liam cocked his head to the side and stared, alarmed. "I... I've never seen anyone do that before."

Judging by the expression on Risa's face, she'd never seen that either. She stared at Killian in shock. "What was that? If you can do that, why didn't you do that in Miami?" He shrugged and said nothing. She put her hands on her hips and glared at him. He finally told her that he'd wanted her to know how to do it in case he wasn't around. She nodded slowly; it made sense, but that wasn't all.

Vaughn stepped forward. "That's why, isn't it? They want your ability to manipulate other people's powers."

Killian stared at the ground and shrugged.

"Dammit, Killian, you need to use words. We need to know what's going on here before someone else gets hurt." Risa snapped at him, of all the times for the man to be stubborn and secretive.

His eyes went silver, and sparks flew from him, much like Risa's magic earlier. He began to pace around the yard, shaking his head, muttering.

"Killian?" Risa called.

He turned his back and screamed, a wordless yell full of rage, even louder than her own shout. A stream of silver slammed into a tree, leaving a smoking hole in the trunk. Just as the sound tapered off, he was gone.

Risa stared in shock, her mouth hanging open, her eyes wide with disbelief. She wasn't sure what had just happened. "Killian?" she whispered, glancing around, "Killian," she called louder, "Please, Killian, don't do this." There was no response. Her legs shook, and Izzy caught her as the others came outside to see what was going on. "He... he left," Risa gasped and stared at her sister in horror.

Izzy shook her head no; she pointed to the studio behind them. "He went in there," she said.

Risa stared at her sister, "How do you know?"

"Listen," Izzy smiled softly.

In the quiet that followed, they heard a piano being played quietly. Risa slowly moved to the door and noticed it was partially open. She slipped inside, and the others crowded behind her. Everyone else was surprised to see the studio setup. Like her, they'd thought it was just a storage shed. Killian was slumped on the bench, morosely playing something very slow and sad. He didn't acknowledge anyone who came in. He kept playing until he got to the end of the song. When he reached it, his hands rested limply on the keys.

The room was silent; no one dared speak. Risa walked to him and wedged herself between him and the keys, forcing him to look at her.

Finally, he shuddered, "Marissa, I'm so sorry. I never meant to put ye in harm's way. I hoped no one would ever find out. I thought Vaughn was the only one who knew. I... have the ability to manipulate and change wielding powers. I can affect dragon powers, too. I discovered it about fifty years ago by accident."

Liam studied him thoughtfully, asking, "Is that why you do the..." He waved his hands like he was weaving.

Killian nodded miserably.

"Huh," the dragon replied.

"I could take away your magic or change it completely an' all ye have to say is huh?" Killian shot to his feet, "That's it?"

Liam shrugged, "Yeah, makes sense now."

Killian started towards him, but Risa held him back, snapping, "Why are you mad at him? Because he's not properly impressed? What? You disappeared on me! Because you're being moody again! Ridiculous!"

He gritted his teeth. "Dammit, Marissa, do ye not understand? I could take away your wielding while ye slept. I could render all of ye powerless. What's a dragon that has no magic? Human! Do ye not see what that makes me? I'm a threat to every dragon an' wielder out there. What do ye think would happen if that got out? I'd be number one on everyone's hit list. How do ye think they would hurt me, get close to me? Through the one I love more than life! I would do anything anyone asked of me to keep ye safe. Anything, Marissa." He crushed her to him and sobbed.

Liam put his arms around them both. "No, you wouldn't, because we would kill them first, Killian."

He lifted his head and hugged Liam, the dragon holding him close.

"I've got you, brother, no one is touching you, or her, or any of us again. We're going to take the fight to them before they try. They fucked around, now they're going to find out." Liam growled then, an impressive rumble that threatened the very building they were standing in.

Killian shuddered, and Izzy wrapped her arms around him, too. Everyone came together in a circle around him and held together as a family. Because that's what they were, a family. And they weren't going to let anyone hurt him.

"Well, an' isn't this touching?" came a dry voice, followed by a slow clap. They all turned to face Kiera as she sauntered through the door.

Chapter 38

A LOW RUMBLE FILLED the building as the four dragons in the room all faced her with talons out and fangs down. The wielders moved behind them, pushing Killian to the back. Kiera rolled her eyes, "Oh, Killian, pitiful thing, still whining about nobody loving ye? Still demanding people give ye affection. How tiring." She pretended to yawn and leaned against the door frame as if she hadn't a care in the world.

Killian laughed then, surprising them all. "Oh, Kiera, still pretending ye don't have a heart? Well, I guess ye aren't pretending, are ye? Poor, heartless, little bitch. Spent all this time being cold an' not understanding ye don't have to ask for love. It's freely given. That's why they're here. They love me an' I love them. My family, an' my fiancée, who is also my soulmate, who has already bound herself to me freely with no demands. I've no need of ye."

Kiera's face underwent a myriad of emotions, including shock, hurt, and anger. She bared her fangs, "Ye were never anything an' just because ye have some supposed superpower, it doesn't make ye special. You're still just as useless an' undeserving as ye were seventy years ago. I begged my parents not to shackle me to ye. God, listening to ye whine to me to mate ye, like I would waste such a thing on a pathetic fool." She shook her head, "Fuck ye, Killian."

"No thanks, Kiera," Killian rolled his eyes, "I've been over ye a long time. Marissa appreciates me as I am. Again, I don't need ye."

The sisters moved closer to each other, glaring.

The silver dragon growled then, staring at the three women facing her. All had the same silver hair and wore identical expressions of hate.

"Isabella, stupid twit, despite my warnings, ye still ended up here. At least now I can take all three of ye together," Kiera sneered.

Izzy snorted smoke at her, "Try me bitch, you're not touching my sisters. I'll break your fucking nose." She grinned at Liam's suppressed snort of laughter.

The dragon smiled evilly then and turned to Marissa; she narrowed her eyes on the ring. "Did he tell ye he made that ring for me?" she smirked, "How does it feel to have hand me down junk?"

Risa laughed, "Oh, come on, Dragon Barbie. I know better. He never gave you this ring. I know because it recognized me and bound our powers together. Even if he had put it on your finger, it would have just been a lump of cold metal. So, I'm incredibly happy with it, because I can feel what he feels, and he can feel what I feel. Killian?" she called sweetly.

"Yes, Risa, my darling, love of my life an' reason for my existence?" he kissed her neck.

Kiera glared.

"What am I thinking right now?" Risa practically purred.

He laughed, "First of all, rude, it was an arranged marriage, I didn't pick her. Second, that's not a nice name, my dear, but I'll paraphrase. You're thinking the... ahem... dumb bimbo should've been paying closer attention so she would have seen Siobhan behind her, locking her in a warding so she can't move."

Kiera's face hardened, and she lunged forward. She came to an abrupt halt then as she hit the boundaries of the wards, Siobhan had quietly slipped around her.

The green wielder ambled casually around behind the dragon and shook her head. "Good grief, I thought villains only monologued in movies. That was stupidly easy." She skipped over to Marco and kissed him on the cheek. "What did I miss?"

He smiled and shook his head. "Not much, *mi amor,* only that Killian has an amazing power none of us knew about because the close-mouthed hermit crab doesn't talk about anything. Then he and Liam hugged each other. The usual."

She nodded and glanced at Vaughn, "So, how do we make the bitch talk?"

Vaughn turned to Killian as a mask of anger and hatred warred over his face. He sighed then nodded at the wielder. It was his decision.

Killian stepped out from behind the others, staring at the woman he'd once thought he loved. He stepped close to her and gently cupped her cheek. "Ye could have accepted me the way I was, an' I would've been amazing for ye."

She glared at him and shook her head violently. "No, I couldn't love ye, I can't love anyone. You're right, I don't have a heart!" She spat at him, and he simply blinked away. She spun around, startled, then laughed, "Oh, run away again, Killian, you're so good at that."

Liam lunged forward and punched her in the mouth. Her head snapped back with a sickening crunch, and she spat out a mouth full of blood. Everyone stared at him in awe.

"Normally, I wouldn't hit a woman, but that bitch deserved it. Killian doesn't run away, I'm the one who does that, and my running days are over. You were never worthy of him; you didn't deserve him at all. His is one thousand times your better, and I hope he rips your heart out of your throat," he snarled and continued to rumble warningly in his chest.

Izzy slipped her arm through his and nodded, growling at the other silver dragon.

Kiera laughed then, spitting more blood, "Oh please, where is he then?"

"Right here," Killian said as he reappeared, this time dragging an unconscious dark wielder behind him. "Found this guy, lurking out there ready to strike. I knew she wouldn't show up without him. She won't get her own hands dirty an' there's no way she's going to take on four dragons an' five wielders single-handedly. She talks a big game, but at the heart of things, she's a cowardly manipulator."

Marco laughed, showing his fangs, "So which one of us gets to rip her throat out?" he snapped them together with an audible click that made Kiera flinch. "If you do not wish to dirty your hands, *mi amigo*, I am happy to volunteer." He growled menacingly.

"I kindly thank ye, brother, but we need her to talk first," Killian stared at the slowly wilting form of the dragon he once thought to spend forever with. He shook his head. "How low ye have fallen, Kiera. Working for the dark wielders? Why? What could ye possibly gain from it?"

She turned her gaze away, refusing to answer or even look at him.

Sighing, Killian grasped her jaw and forced her gaze to his, "It was ye who was doing all the tricks, wasn't it? The car trouble, the fire at my parents' house, the power outage at the office. Ye were behind it all." He nodded and glanced at the unconscious man at his feet. "Marco, is that the man from the security footage?"

The red dragon gave an affirmative rumble.

"Ye kept appearing just far enough away so I wouldn't recognize ye, but ye wanted me to suspect Izzy for a time," Killian murmured. The others gasped. "Why, Kiera, what is the point of it all?"

The silver dragon snarled and spat blood at him, "Ye wouldn't understand."

Shaking his head, he stepped away to wipe his neck. "I guess ye don't want to talk to me. Anyone else want to try?"

Rena stepped forward, close to Kiera, "I do!" They all stared at her in shocked silence then. Sweet Rena had silver eyes and sparks snapping from her body. She looked fierce. "I'm tired of you people hurting others and separating families for fun. Killing people and using them how you want. It's not right, and it stops now. You aren't touching my sisters or my brothers ever again! I want you dead for what you did to Gabriel, too."

Kiera laughed cruelly, "Oh, that's hilarious! The little baby wielder thinks she can hurt me! You couldn't even kiss that man without turning into a mouse an' ye think ye can hurt someone?" She lunged then and struck out at Rena with her talons. Rena had foolishly gotten within her reach.

"*NO!*"

A sudden burst of light filled the room, and everyone shielded their eyes as a crackling sound followed. The overhead lights burst, and only the sunlight coming from the doorway showed Kiera convulsing on the ground. Rena was still there, but now there was a man between her and Kiera's prone form.

Gabe was standing with his hands out, eyes glowing, chest heaving. He'd wielded electricity like his mother. Kiera slowly stopped twitching and lay on the ground, gasping like a fish out of water. Lowering his hands shakily, Gabe simply stood there. Staring at her. Dumbfounded.

Vaughn stepped forward and gently pulled him and Rena back, "That answers that question. You definitely inherited your mother's wielding. Good job, son." He nodded to Killian as Rena threw her arms around Gabe.

Killian crouched down over the still dragon and sighed heavily. "Kiera, once again, you've underestimated what people who love each other will do to keep them safe. You've gone an' forgotten about family. Or maybe it is that ye never understood it in the beginning. I'm after making sure you're done hurting those I love." He reached out and placed one hand on her forehead, then closed his eyes. She tried to flinch back, but still had no control over her muscles. He began moving his free hand around like he was winding something around his fist, then yanked them both back hard and fast. She grunted and doubled over as if he'd punched her in the stomach.

He sat back on his heels, staring at her, a small, satisfied smile on his face. "Ye took something valuable from me once, an' it's shame on me that I let ye. Now I've taken something ye valued just as much. Enjoy the rest of your miserable existence." He stood and watched her with disinterest as she uncurled and slowly crawled to her feet.

She pulled herself up by the doorframe, hand over hand. Whispering the word no, over and over until it became a shriek. She tried to shift but couldn't. She tried to send out magic, but there was nothing for her to draw from. Panic crossed her face, and she screamed again, "What did ye do?"

Shaking his head slowly, Killian replied, "I told ye, I took the most important thing in your life. I removed the magic that made ye what ye are. Were. Congratulations, Kiera, you're human."

"Give it back!" she wailed, "I'll tell ye everything, anything! Please, give it back!" Tears streamed down her face in a flood as she begged. Pitiful and broken.

Simply nodding, he uttered one low word. "Speak."

She whimpered, then began to tell her story, "We were to get the three women, the silver ones. The Dark Wielders, they want them, I don't know what they were going to do to them, I swear I don't. They've been taking children, turning them, training them. I don't know why they want them now that they're grown. But when I found they were with ye, I knew they'd want ye too once they found out how powerful ye are, an' with ye being friends with him." She gestured at Vaughn, then stared at Killian with pain in her eyes. "I wanted ye back, Killian, ye were the only one who ever showed me any kindness, even though I didn't deserve it. I thought if I gave ye to them, they'd let me have ye as a reward."

"Who's the leader of the dark ones?" his tone flat, ignoring the last part of her statement.

"I don't know her name," she whispered fervently, her eyes shifting, "I only know ye don't cross her or she'll do horrible things to ye. Like him." She nudged the man at her feet. "He resisted; he paid the price." Her eyes locked on Killian's, "I told ye, now please, give it back," she begged once more.

He smiled then, a wide grin stretching his face from ear to ear. "Oh Kiera, I don't believe ye genuinely care enough to have it back. I'll need ye to prove that ye deserve it, otherwise it would have happened already."

"Killian," she whispered, horrified as she realized he'd turned the tables on her.

Killian turned his back on her and went to Risa with a smile still on his face. He bent and kissed her tenderly, then whispered, "Can we make them leave so we can finish what we were doing earlier?"

She grinned, "Well, we did finish that round, but we can start something else."

His eyes lit up in delight, then alarm as he heard a shriek and snarling behind him. At the wet crunching sound, he turned slowly, concerned by what he would see.

Izzy growled as Kiera screeched and lunged at Killian's back. The former dragon tried to stab Killian with a knife she'd pulled from the dark wielder's boot. Now, Izzy stared down at the dead woman in front of her. She spat out a mouthful of blood and wiped her face on her shaking arm, noticing her talons were covered in blood as well. The blonde woman was missing most of her throat, Izzy having ripped it out with her fangs. She shivered and stared around her in shock. She'd never killed anyone before, and this was a woman whom she'd once looked up to. "I... I..." she stammered. She gagged at the taste of blood and almost fainted.

Liam caught her and held her close, "You did good, Isabella, you saved our brother and sister."

She nervously turned to him and saw he was smiling, not repulsed by what she'd done. He held her close as she shivered. He whispered soothing words and stroked her hair. Risa hugged her as well, "Thank you, sister," she whispered, "Well done."

Chapter 39

THE DARK WIELDER JOLTED awake and scrambled against the wall as Marco doused him with water. The man huffed out a laugh that grew exponentially louder and unhinged when he saw the dead woman in front of him. He glared at her corpse, seemingly unaware that everyone was staring at him menacingly. As suddenly as the laughter started, it came to an unnerving halt. Without removing his eyes from her, he whispered, "Finally got what you deserved." He leaned forward and spat on her, tears in his eyes. "Thank god, thank you, thank you." He began to cry in earnest, a low keening wail.

They all exchanged glances of uncertainty and confusion. Vaughn crouched down, then, "What's your name?"

The tired and haunted looking man stared up at them with hollow eyes, swallowing heavily, "Evan. Evan Carter. That crazy bitch has been holding me and my daughter hostage the last two years. She brought me here to capture the sisters, which was the original order," he indicated Killian with his chin, "but she decided to mess with him first. Please, I didn't want to do it. She had my little girl; she already killed my wife when I tried to resist, and was going to kill Sabrina if I didn't help her. I couldn't let her, not my baby." He shook his head, and sobs overcame him again. "Not my baby," he whispered, his voice full of heartache and regret.

Vaughn glanced at the others. They nodded; they believed him. Kiera was crazy, and his reaction seemed genuine.

Killian crouched down next to Vaughn, "Evan," he said gently, "May I examine your powers? How is it ye have this dark magic in ye?"

Evan nodded frantically, "Please, you can even take it from me, I don't want it! I'd rather be human than have them force me again."

"Take it from ye?" Killian asked, surprised at the urgency in the man's voice.

The man nodded again, "She said you could do that. Change people's powers. It's why she wanted you." When Killian narrowed his eyes, Evan held up his hands, "No, man, no, I don't want to hurt any of you. I just want to get my baby safe and away from this. Take my magic, let me get my daughter, and you'll never see me again. I swear!" His eyes were wide with desperation as he gripped Killian's wrist tightly.

Risa walked over then, laying her hand on Killian's shoulder. "Help him, please?"

Killian put two fingers on the man's forehead and closed his eyes. He sent a gentle wave through him. "His father was a Shadow, an' his mother a green wielder. Huh."

Evan's mouth dropped, "It's true, that's how all of us 'dark wielders' came to be. It's not always... consensual. One parent is Shadow, the other a wielder. Then the dark power manifests as wielding instead of Shadow. I'm sorry, but that's why they wanted the sisters, for breeding. I hate it. I don't want it." He turned to Vaughn, "Please, if he won't, your wife, can she take it away?"

Vaughn studied him, then turned to Killian thoughtfully. "Killian, can you change it?"

Studying the man before him, Killian smiled. He took Evan's hand in his and placed the other on his forehead, then closed his eyes.

Evan's back arched, and he gasped as something resembling an oily black cloud burst out of him, then dissipated. He shivered, then stared in shock. "But... I still have magic."

Risa smiled, "But I bet it's green now, like it should have been. He removed the darkness from it."

Evan smiled tentatively and turned to a plant in the window. He sent a small pulse towards it, and it burst into bloom. He grinned and laughed in joy. He threw himself around Killian and Risa, sobbing and hugging them. "Thank you, oh god, thank you. Please, my little girl?"

Liam walked over, "Do you know where she is?"

He glared at Kiera's body, "She keeps her locked up at the house where we were staying. She should have a key." He leaned over and searched her pockets, finally locating a small brass key that he clutched to his heart like a lifeline. "Sabrina," he whispered.

Vaughn nodded, "Let's go get her," and hurried out with his arm around the man's shoulders.

Everyone else went back inside while Vaughn helped Evan. Marco was taking care of Kiera's remains. Killian pulled Risa aside, "I didn't, ye know."

She shook her head, not understanding what he meant.

"I didn't make that ring for her. I made it after she left me the first time. I still believed then that I would find someone who would love me. So, I made that ring. When she came back, she found it in my belongings, but I never gave it to her. I knew even then she wasn't the right one. I just had a tough time admitting my mistake. After she destroyed my heart again, I gave it to my family to hold an' left. When we were there, I could feel it pulling me an' calling for ye. Risa, I put ye in danger, an' I'm so sorry, my love. I never meant for that to happen."

She smiled softly and cupped his cheek. "Killian, it just means we are double the threat, and people better think twice before they mess with us."

He breathed out slowly and held her tighter, "I hope you're right. I won't forgive myself if something happens to ye because of this."

She shook her head. "Oh, Killian, I won't be able to convince you otherwise, will I?"

He smiled and shook his head as well.

"Okay," she sighed, "Well, I guess we just work extra hard to keep each other safe."

He grinned, "I'll be your bodyguard. I won't let your body out of my sight." He pulled her against his own suggestively and wiggled his eyebrows.

"Remember, once upon a time, when you told me you wanted to wait until I was settled into my new life before we started a relationship?" she laughed.

"I categorically deny I ever said that," he rolled his eyes, "Lies, I say."

She laughed again; the tinkling bell sound rang through the house.

Izzy hurried over then. "Killian, I'm sorry! I didn't think! I just... reacted an' well, I don't know what happened. She was trying to hurt ye." She stared at the floor, twisting her hands and sniffling as she tried to hold back tears. "I couldn't let that happen."

Killian lifted her chin and gently kissed her downturned mouth before using his thumbs to wipe away the tears that fell. He smiled softly as she gazed at him in shock. "Isabella, I'll not have ye ever apologize again for that. I won't! Ye saved me some serious pain an' injury, possibly Risa too. Ye did what needed to be done. I'm only sorry that ye had to take a life, because I know how it can weigh on a heart. I love ye, my sweet sister." She burst into tears, and he wrapped her in his arms. He kissed the top of her head and held her tightly as she let go of the fear and tension that had been building in her. He softly hummed an Irish lullaby he figured she would know, and it seemed to soothe her.

Liam started forward, concerned, but Killian waved him off. He knew Izzy wanted his forgiveness for killing his ex-wife, someone he'd loved once upon a time. He reassured her gently that in his heart, Kiera died long ago. All Izzy did was neutralize a threat to the family.

She smiled at him, relieved. She leaned forward, kissing him again and looked at her sister. "Ye lucky woman, he's a keeper."

He laughed and hugged her once more before giving her back over to Liam, who was vibrating in indignation that Killian was kissing his mate.

Risa sighed, "Why does everyone keep kissing you?"

"I'm irresistible?" he batted his eyelashes innocently.

Siobhan snorted and deadpanned, "Magically delicious."

Vaughn returned with Evan and a small girl of about six years old. She had the hollow-eyed look of a child who's seen far too much. She clung to her father's leg, her thumb slowly making its way to her mouth as she clutched a bedraggled stuffed rabbit close to her chest.

Rena sat on the floor. "Hi Sabrina, my name is Serena, my friends call me Rena. Our names are so similar! Do you have a nickname?" The little girl shook her head shyly. Rena smiled softly, "How about we call you Brina? We can be Brina and Rena!"

The child smiled timidly, and Rena held out her hand, "Your hair is so pretty, can I braid it?" The little girl ran into Rena's arms then and hugged her, nodding. Rena sat quietly, talking to her while she worked on her hair.

Evan smiled at them, tears in his eyes. Vaughn led him gently to the sofa, and Killian resigned himself to not getting his way soon. Risa smothered a laugh at Killian's obvious disappointment, but knew this was important.

Vaughn shared with the team that the former dark wielder was willing to help them locate the other dark wielders. Those who were working to take down everyone who helped end the Shadow reign. The group of dark wielders and those who were loyal to Baltrus were small, but lethal. They were taking children from families they thought wouldn't be missed and raising them to continue their evil legacy. Evan was originally from Michigan and explained it was just him and Sabrina now; he had no other family. His wife's family had been taken too, but he didn't know what happened to them.

They all glanced at the little girl who was chirping away in Rena's lap about her favorite cartoons. Vaughn offered to set them up locally until Evan could get on his feet and figure out where he wanted to go. Rena offered to help him with Sabrina, who was now snuggled sleepily in her arms. Finally, they all agreed that no matter what, they needed to meet with the others to help protect everyone and get the word out.

A meeting was set, and it was time to take their leave. They all filed out with the exception of Liam and Izzy. The dragons held hands and Liam cheerfully spoke up, "Hey Ki, since you two are getting married, and we are too, what do you think about..."

Killian shouted, "*OUT!*"

Izzy laughed, dragging a shocked Liam out the front door.

"That was rude!" Risa huffed.

He turned to her, "You know the lizard was about to ask for a double wedding," he groaned. "Now, I'm done talking about dark wielders. Tomorrow is soon enough. Be a good girl an' run," he smirked, as he stripped off his shirt and ran after her, laughing.

Thank You!

Thank you for reading

Silver Belles

(I hope you enjoyed reading it as much as I loved writing it.)
Love this book? Don't forget to leave a review!

Every review matters, and it matters a *lot!*
Head over to Amazon, Goodreads, or wherever you purchased this book
to leave a review for me.
The Dragons and I thank you endlessly.

Read More

If you're like me, you get invested in characters and want to know what happens after the last page. Head over to my website to subscribe to my newsletter to be the first to know when the next book in the series will be released. Who knows, I may give you a sneak peek at it!

www.tristaricketts.com

Book 1: Lahaina Noon

Book 2: Circles in the Sand

Book 3: The Waters Edge

Book 4: Silver Belles

Book 5: Ashes of Eternity (Coming Nov 2025)